PRAISE FO

"If you have an appetite for werewolves, this book is an all-you-can-eat buffet! Carl has done for werewolves what Romero did for zombies, and he's done it with flair and a sense of gruesome fun."

—Ray Garton, author of *Live Girls* and *Ravenous*

"*Bestial* grabs hard from the first page and doesn't let up. Carl is an accomplished writer, and this is an excellent first novel with an engaging story and well-drawn characters. Can't wait to see what he does next!"

—Nate Kenyon author of *Bloodstone*

"With pithy but smart prose, William Carl paints gruesome scenes of unrelenting savagery. But what really sets this book apart is how it gently and eloquently examines human emotions and relationships—some good, some monstrous, but all deep, compelling, and fascinating. This is the kind of debut novel authors dream of writing."

—Kim Paffenroth, Bram Stoker Award-winning author of *Dying to Live*

"Dread-Destruction-Death… William Carl's *Bestial* delivers these three D's en masse, taking us into a world where survival of the fittest is a gross understatement and fear is the norm. In this page-turning, rocket-paced novel, Carl goes about proving once and for all that monsters *do* exist. And they're ravenous, unrelenting… and could very well live in us all."

—Deborah LeBlanc, author of *Morbid Curiosity* and *Water Witch*

BESTIAL

A Werewolf Novel by

William D. Carl

Permuted Press
The formula has been changed...
Shifted... Altered... *Twisted.*
www.permutedpress.com

This book wouldn't have been possible without the encouragement of my family... Bill and Jackie, Gina and Andrew and Mary Jane Carl. My thanks go out to my beta readers, who helped shape the book, Chesya Burke, Beth Blue, Brandy Huber, and Tracey West. This book is dedicated to Don Smith, for everything.

A **Permuted Press** book
published by arrangement with the author

ISBN-10: 1-934861-04-9
ISBN-13: 978-1-934861-04-2
Library of Congress Control Number: 2008927505

Cover art by Michael Brack.
Edited by D.L. Snell.
Special thanks to Leah Clarke.

PROLOGUE

Before...

Andrei Sokosovich waited in the cell, naked and a little cold. He reached out and swiped his fingers along the side of the Plexiglas wall, tracing a nearly invisible seam, wondering if his family was still being paid their monthly stipend. His captors had promised him financial remuneration last year if he cooperated. In his small village of Kirskania in Siberia, a man's word was golden, but he wasn't sure he could trust these Americans. They seemed to be hurrying, hurrying, hurrying, rushing everywhere they went. They held no true conversations, only shouting matches.

The only man he knew was reliable in the entire building was the Frenchman. At his mother's insistence, Andrei had learned French at an early age. Although he was steadily acquiring a working knowledge of English from listening to the Americans, he was more comfortable utilizing the French language, and he was more comfortable with this old Frenchman, who visited him regularly, taking blood and inquiring about his health. He was probably a doctor of some kind. Weren't they all doctors in America?

Andrei paced the twenty lengths of his prison, leaned against the bulletproof Plexiglas, pressed his face against its coolness. A red-haired woman watched him from the other side, taking notes on a clipboard. He waved at her, and she, as always, ignored the gesture.

When he had first been placed under glass for observation, he had tried to hide his nudity from the people watching him. In Siberia, he'd rarely been naked, even in front of his wife. Freezing temperatures dictated this modesty. Now, dozens of people a week studied him, their eyes cold and controlling. The shame had eventually faded, along with many of the memories of his village, lost in an unknown expanse of time.

How long... how long... how long had he been here?

The floor beneath his bare feet was cold concrete. At one end of the cell was a cot with a mattress, a single thin blanket, and a small, cheap table where he kept his books. The rest of the room was as bare as the man inhabiting it. Other than the one wall made of Plexiglas, the other three consisted of shiny stainless steel. All of it was sanitized.

He must have been imprisoned more than a year, although the true length of time was ungraspable. More than a year since his capture, his hesitant acceptance of the scientists' terms, his tearful farewell to his wife and children. He never did learn how they had found him, which villager had reported his dark secret.

Had they found him based on the rumors in the newspapers, or through the complicity of a neighbor? One day, he would have to ask the Frenchman.

***

Andrei stalked, screamed, felt it happening again. The flash of teeth, eyes golden and wet with emotion.

A single window had been opened directly across from the cell so that he would receive a bit of moonlight from outside.

He padded to the other side of the room, threw his body against the strong Plexiglas.

Howling in rage, he tore at the walls of his prison with deformed hands. He was eager to escape, hungry, and sexually excited.

It would be over soon, some inner voice explained, trying to calm him. Just wait it out. Just wait until morning, when the sunlight would stream through the window. The need to kill would dissipate, and his arousal would wane. The hellish pain would cease for a while.

Somewhere, inside of the beast, he knew this.

He whipped his head at a noise across the room.

In a far corner, a man adjusted a video camera tripod, nodded at him.

***

"Are you really sending Betta money?" Andrei asked. "Tell me that you are, and I will accept your word as truth."

"Yes," said the man on the other side of the Plexiglas, his words a soft, lilting French. "They are being well cared for. You should have no worries."

"Good. Good."

"How do you feel this morning?"

"Like... how goes it, something the cat dragged in? I am tired. I am tired of so much... this prison, those people watching. I am ready to go home."

"You know our agreement."

"Yes." A sigh.

"You signed the papers, giving us authorization over your welfare."

"I did."

"It's for your own good. Don't you realize? For your good, and the good of many, many others like you."

"It does not mean I have to like it."

"We take no pleasure in studying your case."

"Some do. I have seen them smiling, seen their traitorous faces."

"Then you must rise above them."

"Rise above?"

"You are more of a man than most of these weak specimens."

Andrei Sokosovich laughed deep and loud.

***

Pacing the cell. Stepping one through twenty. Turn. Going back the other way. One through twenty.

Waiting for the light to change.

Wilting beneath it.

Rising again, towering, snapping anxiously at the air.

A mournful sound, echoing throughout the cell.

The smell of meat and blood beyond his reach.

Claws and teeth.

3

Death of the man, resurrection of the beast.

PART 1

CHAPTER 1

September 16, 6:59 p.m.

"Good evening, everyone," Rick Morrison yelled. "My name's unimportant, but I'll be your bank robber on this fine evening. I want to see everybody down on the floor! Nobody tries to be a hero, nobody gets hurt."

Christ, he thought, *what a cliché.*

He fired a round from his Glock into the nearest surveillance camera, showering a howling bank teller with shards of glass and plastic. The woman dropped to the floor, her hands covering her head to protect herself from the debris.

Pausing while his associates completed their assigned jobs, Rick grinned beneath the pantyhose that smashed his features into a Halloween grimace. The damn pantyhose were hotter than hell, but quite effective.

Jones scurried around the room, spray-painting the lenses of the thirteen remaining cameras. He laughed in his coarse, horsy manner, pausing for a moment to decorate a bare wall with a smiley face while he made his way to the back.

Rick said, "Hey, Jones. We can do without the artistic flourishes. Just get the job done."

Jones nodded, making his way to the next camera, which hung perpendicular to the tellers' booths in the Cincinnati First National Bank. He passed Jack Browning, who was forcing the tellers to their knees in the far corner behind the tall booths and ascertaining if anyone had pressed a silent alarm. Two of the three women and both of the men were crying, but a middle-aged black woman was glaring at Jack. A wannabe hero always seemed to rise from among the victims of every robbery, and Rick feared he'd have his hands full with this large-framed woman with an afro. Her attitude belied years of discrimination or abuse. She'd been around. Her nametag read, "Chesya."

Behind Rick, Saul Wiseman locked the front doors at 7:00 p.m. exactly, the hour the bank typically closed. He placed a gun against the temple of the elderly, bald security guard, walking him to the corner where the tellers knelt. The veins throbbed blue on the old man's head.

"Not a word, Pops," Saul said in his nasal voice. "I'm itchin' to try out this new revolver. Any excuse will do."

Visibly shaking, the old man handed Saul his nightstick, the only weapon he carried. The robber threw it across the room, striking a desk at the far end of the bank; the guard flinched as if struck.

Rick moved towards the little cluster of people, his eyes resting on Chesya's contemptuous, slightly yellow gaze. Scratching his head with the barrel of his gun, he asked, "Anyone else in here? Officers or vice presidents?"

The defiant teller maintained eye contact, her chin held high. She looked as though she could spit in his face.

Saul, breaking off from the group, said, "Lemme have a look, boss." He ransacked the side offices, and from the last one, he hauled out a fat man wearing glasses. "Found him behind his desk," he said, slapping the man's sweaty face.

"Bring him out here to join the party," Rick said. "We wouldn't wanna neglect anyone."

When the man was positioned on the floor, hands clasped behind his head like the rest of the bank's staff, he began to sob, big, belly-shaking sobs that threatened to unravel into hysteria at any moment.

"Stop your crying," Rick warned, holding his Glock so he observed the man down the sights.

"I… I…can't… I can't."

"Aw, shit," Rick said. He pistol-whipped the back of the man's skull. There was a soft thunk, and the corporate drone dropped face-first to the tiled floor. Three bright drops of blood spattered Rick's hand, and he wiped it on his jeans. He checked the man's pulse and exhaled with relief; the fat man would be fine for now.

"Jones, you get all those cameras? You didn't miss any?"

"Hell, no." The man began to giggle again, aiming at a blonde's pretty head. "I got 'em all, boss."

"Good," Rick said, pulling the suffocating stocking from his head and dropping it on the floor. "Okay, everyone, pay attention. What we have here is your basic, everyday bank robbery. We'll be taking any cash you have in your teller's drawers as well as anything in the safe. If you people do what I tell you to do and nobody gets all courageous or heroic on me, we'll be gone within an hour and you can all go home to your families. We've done this before, so I can tell if someone's going to be a problem." He looked pointedly at Chesya, and damned if she didn't try to stare him down. "Now, did anyone press any alarms? Alert the cops in any way?"

They all shook their heads except Chesya, whose nostrils flared. Rick mused that she'd be extremely pretty beneath that mask of fury. She had deep, brown eyes with perfectly plucked eyebrows, a wide nose and a broad mouth, the lips especially full.

"No?" he asked. "Nobody'd better be lying. If I so much as hear a single police siren, there's gonna be blood all over this nice white floor."

He continued, "Well, I'll need someone to volunteer." Pointing his gun successively at each of the cowering tellers, he chanted, "Eeny, meeny, miny, moe…"

The blonde teller hid her face in her hands, shaking uncontrollably.

Rick grinned, adjusting his count as he said, "Catch a teller by her toe…"

Chesya looked as though she would launch herself at him at any moment. He was making this act of violence into a childish game, and she wasn't about to play with him. Still, he wanted her to be intimidated, and most people reacted to this off-the-cuff casualness with utter horror.

"If she hollers, let her go…" *Yeah, woman, mess with me. I've got the gun. I'm in control here, no matter how much you hate it.* "Eeny… meeny… Miny… moe. Looks like you're it, sweetheart." The gun was pointed at the blonde woman.

Chesya rolled her eyes. *He's picking Gloria? She'll fall to pieces the minute he cusses her.*

Blondie shrieked when he lifted her by the hair and dragged her toward the vault. "Shut up," he warned. "I said shut the fuck up." Profanity was always a good way to keep people frightened, too, and it really seemed to work on the blonde teller. Perhaps too well. Her cries ceased, replaced by a muffled keening behind her pursed lips.

Meanwhile, Saul began emptying out the drawers at the teller's stations, stashing the cash in a couple of white garbage bags. His weird laughter echoed in the tomb-like silence.

"Hefty bags!" he said. "For those tough, tough jobs."

As Rick reached the locked vault, he shoved the woman in front of him. She was thin to the point of emaciation, as though she were a victim of an eating disorder. Hollow cheeks, hollow eyes, probably a hollow mind. Her hands traipsed bird-like along the front of her sweater.

He'd seen her type many times in the past—someone scared enough to follow his orders without challenging anything he demanded, yet coherent enough to do the job. He didn't think she'd try anything stupid and put her co-workers in harm's way.

"Please," she begged. "Please, don't kill me. I've got kids at home."

"Open the vault," he said, "and you'll have nothing to worry about."

He recognized the repository as a Class III Bank Vault from Hamilton. He'd seen them before, marvels of brushed stainless steel with the huge dial of an operating wheel gleaming in the front along a regiment of locks. A tungsten plate surrounded the main lock to prevent anyone from drilling into it. It was a sight to behold, truly a beautiful thing. From his research and years of experience, Rick knew that this model was pre-constructed, modular, and welded together into a nearly inaccessible rectangle of fifteen-inch steel. The door alone was ten inches thick. Nobody could blast into one of these babies. This was why he required a bank employee to assist him in opening the vault.

But this particular teller still shook and cried.

"Get it open," he said.

"I… I'm trying…"

"I suggest you try faster."

Chesya thought, *Sweet Jesus, she's gonna get us all killed.*

Gloria dropped the keys, letting out a small scream. Rick slapped her across the face, not very hard, but it stopped the sound. She seemed to lose her ability to stand.

When he was a child, Rick had owned a toy, a plastic figurine of a deer. When you pressed on the base, the joints would loosen, and the deer would sway, then fall into a heap, only to rise again when you released the button. The way the blonde slumped gracefully to the floor, the way her knees wobbled and buckled beneath her skirt, reminded Rick of this toy.

He had made a mistake choosing her. She was too fragile, too emotional. He'd have to pick someone else, and any deviation from his researched plans pissed him off. He pointed the gun at the blonde's head.

"Wait!" Chesya shouted from the tellers' booths.

Jones swooped down on her with his revolver. "You best shut your mouth!"

Chesya wasn't cowed. "She can't do it. Can't you see? She's on the damn floor, she's so scared. I'll do it for you."

Rick said, "If this is some sort of trick..."

"Then I'm just a stupid bitch who doesn't deserve to live. Listen, you want the money. I wanna go home and take a long, hot bath. I don't wanna die, and I don't want my friends to die. I'll get the vault open, and you can leave us be. How's that sound?"

Cocking his head, Rick admired the woman's audacity. "Okay," he said. "Get over here. Blondie, you get your cute little ass back there with the others."

The skinny woman crawled back on her hands and knees, and Rick felt her humiliation with every timid step she took. It wasn't a good feeling, and he had to force his attention back to the brash teller that had dared to stand up to him.

Chesya grabbed a set of keys off the unconscious manager, holding them up as she stood, so that the robbers could see they were only keys.

"You need both sets to get it open," she explained. "Manager on duty has one set, and I have the other. I'm the head teller."

Rick nodded. She walked to the vault door, her stride confident and a little sassy. When she passed the blonde teller, who was still crawling, she looked down at her.

"Gloria, you get on back now," she said. "We'll get this over with, then me and you will go grab a couple of margaritas at Universal Cafe." Gloria nodded, but her face registered little more than shock. Turning, she continued her creeping until Saul grabbed her by the back of her sweater and tossed her into the corner with the other tellers. An olive-skinned man wrapped his arms around her, and she cried into the shoulder of his suit. The way he held her, Rick wondered if they had some relationship besides co-workers, a little loving on the side.

When Chesya reached him, Rick said, "Get to it. I want that vault open quick as shit."

"Lovely phrase," she drawled, working the big dial.

"Careful, you don't wanna piss me off."

"I imagine it's pretty easy to do."

Rick bristled, wanting to hit her, but she had finished the combination, and he could hear the sound of the big security bar withdrawing from the floor and ceiling. She was already working on the locks, inserting the various keys, when the hair on the back of Rick's neck stood up. Something was wrong.

Glancing around the bank, he saw that Saul had nearly finished emptying the drawers. The garbage bags bulged with the weight of the money. The idiot had even grabbed the rolls of coins, which would only weigh them down in the end. The hostages were still kneeling obediently, his men were still in charge, the manager was still unconscious. Outside the front windows, he could see the sunlight dissipating between the drawn blinds. It would be dark soon, and Jason was waiting outside in the getaway car. Everything seemed fine, so he turned back to the woman and the vault.

She shivered for a second, turned her big eyes to him. "Someone just walked over my grave."

Surprised, he wanted to say that he'd just experienced the same sensation, but he kept quiet. It wouldn't do to show weakness. Any kind of weakness.

As she turned another lock, he asked, "You got a last name, Chesya?"

"Why? You have some sick need to know who you're holding a gun on?"

"I like to know who I'm working with."

She laughed, then said, "Work? You call this work? Ha!"

"You know what I mean."

"Mister, all I gotta do is open this here door for you. That's it. I don't plan on making nice with just any man who's pointing a gun at my head."

"Oh, come on, we can be civil, can't we?"

There was a clank of keys, and a moan. Then the lock's pins fell into position with a click, and the huge stainless steel door eased open about a half inch.

Rick turned to the woman. "Thank you," he said.

"Yeah. Whatever."

"You know, this attitude isn't helping matters, lady. How about you grab those garbage bags and get your fat ass in here with me."

"You got another five or six minutes before the time lock deactivates," she said. "Every night, 7:15 sharp. Didn't you do your homework?"

"This bastard's got a timer on it? I didn't think a Class III would..." He began yanking on the heavy door, but it didn't budge any farther than that half-inch opening. Tugging harder, he realized it was useless.

She nodded. "Yeah, it's a new model. It only opens three times a day. Eight a.m., three p.m., and seven fifteen. Then, you still need the two sets of keys and the combination. If you'd robbed us at, say, 5:00, 'stead of now, you'd only get the cash from the teller drawers up front."

"Jesus... okay, then. Shit! Okay, Chesya, you going to tell me your last name? May as well chat if we aren't getting in there yet."

"Johnson," she answered. "Chesya Johnson. And I'm still not going to be your friend."

"Fine with me."

"Just being neighborly."

And maybe keeping myself alive a little longer, she thought.

In the distance, a car alarm started blaring. Rick cursed, knowing that it would alert the police if it continued to honk. He was beginning to think this was a jinxed heist. Too many things going wrong at the same time.

"You got family, Chesya?"

"No. Just me and myself."

"You aren't gonna do anything stupid, are you?"

She looked at him. "My mother didn't raise any fools. I want to get home in one piece as much as you do. Probably more."

"That's good, then."

She looked him up and down, this man who was forcing her to rob her own workplace, this man who held a gun on her. He wasn't bad looking. Sandy, blond hair, a bit of gray at the temples, high cheekbones. He looked muscular beneath his work shirt and jeans. He'd be someone she'd look at twice on the street, once coming and once going. He was a bit pasty, and she didn't usually date white men, finding them too uptight and business-like in the love department.

She caught herself. Date? The man had a gun pointed at her.

Girl, she thought. *It's been too long since you had a man.*

Cursing herself, she listened to the noise from outside the bank, wondering what was causing it.

It sounded as though a second car alarm had joined the first. Now, Rick knew the cops would come. Probably a gang of kids out on a smash and grab, but they were going to wreck the whole robbery if the police reached them in time. Listening carefully, he thought he could hear a third alarm.

"What's causing all that racket?" Chesya asked, peering around the corner at the lobby.

"It's nothing," he said. "Kids or something."

"Doesn't sound like kids."

There was a soft, welcoming hiss from the vault, and it opened. Grinning, he pulled on the stainless steel door, astonished at how easily it pivoted on the heavy hinges. A light went on inside, and Rick chuckled as he recalled his childhood fascination with whether the refrigerator light stayed on when the door was closed. He had often tried to catch it turning on, but had never been quick enough.

The car alarms on the street seemed to grow even more raucous. Rick knew he had to make this a fast job in order to elude the police.

He prayed that Jason had the getaway car revved up and ready to motor as soon as they rushed out into the street.

"Here," he said, tossing a couple of garbage bags at Chesya. "Take these and fill them with all the cash you can. We're not looking to hit the safety deposit boxes, just the cash. And don't think you can drop a paint bomb in there, or you may not make it home tonight."

"Oh, I'm shaking." She grabbed the bags and entered the vault. Rick followed her.

It was a modular vault, welded tight at the seams. The walls were so thick they deadened most of the sound from the streets, even with the door open. The car alarms were muffled, although they had accumulated in numbers. Dozens of them must have been honking and whistling outside the bank. If he could still hear them within the walls of the vault, he knew they were deafening on the street.

Jones' voice echoed from the lobby. "Hey, Rick… boss… I think you'd better get out here quick."

Chesya thought, *His name's Rick.* She needed to remember that for the inevitable police report.

"What now?" he shouted back.

"Just… get out here."

Rick grabbed the teller by the hand and marched her at gunpoint to the lobby of the bank, leaving the plastic bags on the floor of the vault. When he saw his partner, white as a sheet and leaning against the counter, his gun all but forgotten on the desk beside him, Rick knew something bad was going down.

"What the fuck's wrong with you, Jones? Pick up your gun."

"Boss… I don't… I don't feel so good. My gut… something I… ate…"

Rick scanned the area. The blond teller and one of the male employees writhed on the floor, as though in great pain. They moaned, faces twisted in agony, and the other two tellers scooted away from the sick ones, afraid they'd be shot if they stood up. On the other side of the counter, Jack Browning and Saul Wiseman were doubled over at the middle, clutching their stomachs. Browning vomited, a thick brown, liquid that splattered on the immaculate marble floor. He dropped his revolver, and it landed… plop… in his sick at his feet.

A male teller shouted, "We need to get away from them! Something's wrong."

Chesya and the other female teller, Mary, hurried over to the blonde's side. "Gloria?" Chesya asked. "What is it, honey?"

Jones took a step towards the hostages, then fell to his knees so hard that Rick heard the snap of breaking bone. Dropping into a fetal position, the man began to convulse, as though in the throes of an epileptic fit.

"Jesus, Saul…"

Rick realized that the sound of the car alarms outside had grown thunderous, constant.

Mary placed a hand behind Gloria's neck, then pulled away as if she'd been bitten. Chesya heard Gloria's head hit the floor.

"Gloria, honey, answer me. What's wrong?" Chesya asked.

Mary said, "Chesya, something… I felt… under her skin… like insects…" Mary suddenly scratched behind her own neck.

Gloria turned to face Chesya, exposing the trickle of bile that ran down from the corners of her mouth. When she opened her eyes, they seemed to reflect the meager light from the sunset, gleaming like a mirror, like a cat's eyeshine. The pupils were a rich golden color.

"Hurts… hurts…" she repeated in a low voice that didn't resemble the church-choir soprano Chesya had often heard humming at the cubicle next to her own. Now she sounded animalistic, growling, feral.

And so very full of pain.

Rick glanced at the front of the bank to see Jason at the front entrance. The teenaged getaway driver screamed and motioned wildly. He pulled on the handles, but the doors were locked.

"Get back in the car," Rick shouted, heading for the door. "We need you to wait in the damn car!"

The boy continued to yank on the doors, as if he could will them to unlock. As he got closer, Rick saw the terror in Jason's green eyes, sheer, undiluted fear. In the distance, metal crunched against metal, glass shattered. Cars were slamming into each other. The alarms pulsed over everything.

And something else… something that was almost human…

Jason glanced over his shoulder as Rick reached the door. He was still shouting at the boy to get his ass back in the getaway car.

"Jason, if you don't get…."

Something dark and hairy rushed from Jason's left. It pulled him away from the windows and out of sight.

Rick jumped back from the glass, wondering what had snatched the kid away. It had happened so fast. All he had was the lingering impression of hair and teeth and violence.

That was why the car alarms were going crazy all over the city street. Some kind of animal was loose.

And it had just carried off the getaway driver.

Everywhere he looked, automobiles had wrecked into lampposts and the sides of buildings, some piled on top of others like weird modern sculptures. A motorcycle was turned on its side, the back wheel still spinning. A fire had started in the corner grocery store across the street, smoke pluming out of its shattered front windows. No bodies inhabited the wrecks.

As Rick watched, people ran through the streets, waving their arms, screaming for help. A child, no more than seven or eight, hurried along the sidewalk across the street, only to be grabbed and dragged into the shadows by a beast lurking in the alley. It moved so fast, Rick only had a quick idea of yellowed teeth, fangs and spit. Another lumbering creature leapt from behind an overturned car, pulling a woman into the obscured, topsy-turvy confines of the back seat. Her screams stopped abruptly.

"Oh my God…" Chesya said behind him.

Turning, Rick hurried back to the others, hastening away from the chaos overtaking the darkening street outside. The streetlamps flickered at his back, better illuminating the city.

The sun had almost set, and the animals, whatever they were, grew bolder, emerging from the shadows into the spotty glow of the lamps, which their eyes refracted, flashes of gold in the crisp, autumn night.

"Hey, robber guy… !" Chesya called.

He stepped over the still-quivering bodies of Browning and Wiseman. They were clutching at their throats, tearing the skin away to expose crimson tubes and muscle. Jack opened his eyes as Rick passed, revealing tainted, urine-colored irises.

When Rick reached Chesya and Gloria, he saw that the blonde teller was no longer shaking so badly. In fact, if it weren't for the spooky eyes and the hair sprouting on the woman's face, she would have appeared almost calm.

Chesya said, "I was holding her, and that's when I felt the stubble. It just… pushed its way through her skin, like she was growing fur."

"I felt it too," Mary exclaimed. "It started beneath her skin, like movement, like her bones were shifting." She scratched again, as if feeling something in her own skin, burrowing, growing.

"What the fuck is going on?" the male teller shouted, looking down at a fellow employee who had also ceased to quiver. "John, buddy, what is it?"

John was sprouting tufts of hair all over his body. His lips pulled back in a grimace, exposing elongated, sharp teeth.

"Hey, buddy… John? Talk to me, man."

John launched at the teller's throat, sinking fangs deep into the flesh and cartilage. He bit, shook his head, and pulled off a large chunk from the man's neck. The teller fell to the floor, reaching for the severed carotid artery as his blood spurted a gruesome pop-art pattern on the walls. He screamed. Rick and Chesya did too, moving backwards, watching as the beast-man chewed the flesh in his mouth and swallowed. His teeth shifted, moved.

When his face began to elongate into a snout, the half-man, half-creature shrieked like a terrified dog in pain. There was nothing human in it. Nothing.

Jones lurched awkwardly on all fours, like some newborn wild animal, and he shoved his face towards the darkness outside the glass front doors. Something was happening with his ears.

Wiseman turned himself from his side to a four-legged position similar to Jones'. His long fingernails click-clacked against the floor, and when he opened his mouth, he exposed shifting dental work, teeth that grew longer and pushed others out of their way, teeth expanding into odd angles, positions impossible for a human mouth.

That thing is not Saul Wiseman, Rick had to tell himself.

When Jack Browning began to tear his own face off of his skull, the bones broke and reassembled, like tectonic plates.

All this violence occurred in about ten seconds. Rick had stepped back farther into the bank, trying to comprehend what was happening.

"Rick!" Chesya screamed, and he spun to see Gloria trying to stand, backing the brunette teller into the corner. Chesya was a few feet away, closer to him. They united and retreated towards the depths of the bank.

Gloria's body hair continued to grow at a visible, time-lapse photography rate, and her face had become pointed, almost like a rat's snout. She rent her clothes, tore them from her body, revealing withered breasts covered with fur. Her shoulders and arms were muscular, filled with veins. Her lips had chameleoned to black.

"You've got a gun, Rick," Chesya said. "Use the damn thing."

Amidst the chaos, he had forgotten the Glock, held tightly in his right hand, his knuckles turning white with the effort.

The Gloria-thing took a step towards the woman who was cowering in the corner, tearing at her own skin as though scratching out splinters.

Rick raised his gun.

Chesya shifted towards him.

And the beast that had been Gloria moved fast like a jaguar, grabbing the woman from the corner, tearing a deep handhold into her chest cavity and dragging her behind the teller's counter.

Rick didn't have time to aim, but he fired two shots at her shadow.

Light came in from the street, and Rick and Chesya turned to see Saul Jones and Jack Browning stalking them, still caught in some deranged metamorphosis. Headlights beamed brightly from behind them, from outside the bank, and their features were enshrouded, a reddish aura around their fur-covered bodies.

Headlights... light into the bank... a car's heading this way, Chesya realized. *Right this way!*

"Get down!" she shouted, as the lights grew brighter.

She pulled Rick behind the marble teller's counter. Tripping backwards, Rick caught a glimpse of a police car, a huge Crown Victoria, as it rammed through the front doors of the bank, shattering glass and smashing metal. He thought he saw a hunchbacked shape behind the driver, clawing, clutching, a vague sense of eyes and teeth and fury.

The car rammed into Jones' body, smashing his bones, pinning him against its wide grille. When it slammed into the teller's counter, coming to an abrupt stop, it sliced Jones in two from the legs down. His face and torso hit the hood, his arms reaching for the spider-webbed windshield. Money flew into the air and dropped lazily, like leaves in the fall.

Rick and Chesya stood from their hiding place to look at the obscene accident. The driver was being pulled through a hole in the metal grille that caged off the back seat of the Crown Vic, pulled by some hulking shadow with yellow teeth. The driver screamed, pleaded, but soon his feet disappeared into the darkness, and the chewing noises began.

Worse, Jones was still alive. He pulled his legless, hairy torso towards the windshield, intestines and other purple organs smearing scarlet streaks across the hood of the vehicle. When he reached the cracked window, he began to slam his gargantuan fists into it. The web seemed to grow larger beneath his pounding.

Rick knew he should be moving, running away from the creatures, but he stood still, nearly hypnotized by the mayhem around him. "What the fuck is happening? What the fuck?"

Chesya pulled at his jacket. "Uh... Rick..."

She motioned towards the teller's counter; Browning and Wiseman were slinking around the corner, turning their protracted snouts each way and sniffing. The palms of their hands had grown black pads, and the gold in their eyes flashed.

"Come on," Chesya said, grabbing Rick's arm and pulling him to the back of the bank. "I have an idea."

"What the fuck..."

"Snap out of it, man. Get in the vault. Make a run for the vault."

She slapped him hard across the face, stinging her own hand, and he stared at her a moment.

The thing that had once been Gloria emerged from the darkness of the corner, blood and gore dripping from her newly formed fangs.

Rick screamed, and they dashed for the vault.

"Go, go, go!" Chesya yelled.

There were growls and footfalls behind them, but Rick couldn't look back. He knew if he got a good visualization of what was chasing them, he would stop dead in his tracks. He couldn't bear to see what they were. Not yet. Not in their entirety.

When they reached the vault, they both spun around and grabbed the door, swinging it shut behind them. A hand—Rick didn't know whose it was—reached in, wriggling its fingers before they were caught in the steel trap of the door. The closing mechanism had been activated, and with four pops, each of the fingers snapped off and dropped to the steel floor, each one sporting black-tipped claws, sharp and deadly.

Rick heard the howling, the shrieks of pain from the opposite side of the door as it shut.

Then, with a hiss and a deep clank that stunk of finality, the vault closed, and Rick couldn't hear anything from the outside. The lack of sound was sudden and ominous.

When the light went out, just as he had always expected when he was a child and stationed at his refrigerator, Rick began screaming...

... and screaming...

... and screaming...

CHAPTER 2

September 16, 8:00 p.m.

Christian peered through the hole in the window. He had been dream-
ing about eating a steak dinner, with mashed potatoes and gravy and
apple pie for dessert, when a noise from outside the warehouse awak-
ened him.

His body was thin, lithe, still that of a gangly teenage boy, even
though he was nearing the age of eighteen. Smoothing back his long,
shabby brown hair, he crept closer to the window, peering into the
night with his ice-blue gaze. Lines that had been prematurely etched
into the skin around his eyes crinkled with the effort.

He'd been living in the warehouse for the last two months, ever
since his father had held him down while his buddies raped him.
Situated by the river in downtown Cincinnati, the building was three
stories of empty, unused space, thick with dust and spider webs.
Christian thought it was probably some rich guy's tax shelter.

He slept in the delivery elevator, which was permanently parked on
the ground floor. The doors still closed when he pulled on the leather
strap, though they protested with creaks and groans. It locked from the
inside, and he felt relatively safe there.

Rats and spiders shared his space, sometimes biting him, but usually just ignoring him as though he was an unwanted but necessary
distraction, just another messy roommate. He used half a burnt mattress for a bed and kept a small transistor radio probably constructed in

the late seventies; it served as his only real companion when he needed to hear another human voice.

In the daytime, he begged for money on the streets and at night he turned tricks when things got tough. Sometimes, he went without food for a few days, but he always managed to land on his feet. No matter how arduous life on the streets could get, it was still better than remaining at home, prey for his father and his drinking pals. He would never go back there.

Lately, he had been giving a certain elderly gentleman blowjobs for twenty-five bucks, a shower, and a home-cooked dinner. Afterwards, he stayed overnight, sleeping in the old man's luxurious bed. For the past two months, they had met three or four times a week.

On the other nights, the boy slept in his elevator womb, bundled against the night in flea-infested blankets.

What the hell were those noises? Christian wondered, looking out the window at the parking lot, which was painted blue from the light of the full moon. *Some kind of animal growling? A dog?*

This past week, the old man had divulged his name, Jean Cowell, and had invited Christian to move into his penthouse on Fourth Street. He worked as a geneticist for a company called Bio-Gen, and he conducted some egghead experiments that Christian would have found fascinating in his previous life. Jean's apartment was a great place, beautifully decorated, and the old codger was kind enough to him, but Christian didn't want to be tied down. He only had a few months to go until he was eighteen. Then he would legally find a job and a decent place to live. He didn't want to hurt the old man either. After all, it was twenty-five bucks for very little work, even if he didn't enjoy it, even if he'd had to tell the john he was a year older than he actually was. The dinners and showers didn't hurt, either.

Christian wasn't gay. He'd had a girlfriend before he dropped out of school, and he often thought about her when he was on his knees in front of Jean. He'd been forced to leave her behind with the rest of his life. In some ways, he hoped she found someone else, someone who could make her happy and not drag her through their shitty lives. At other times, he resented her normalcy, her problems seldom rising above what to wear to football games.

Something moved on the other side of the window: a man running for the warehouse. He was thin, with a beard, and he wore pajama bottoms and nothing else. He was screaming for help, waving his hands.

At first, Christian thought the man had seen him and was running towards him, but then he realized the man was fleeing from something. He kept glancing over his shoulder as he sprinted across the parking lot into the streetlights. He wasn't wearing shoes; his feet were bleeding.

Keeping himself deep within the shadows, Christian peered through the jagged hole in the window. Something large and low to the ground loped behind the man, gaining on him with each stride.

Then, the streetlights went out, as well as the electricity in all the apartments surrounding the warehouse. The shape behind the man instantly blended into the darkness, camouflaged by the sudden absence of light.

"Somebody help me!" the man shrieked.

Christian opened his mouth to call the man into the warehouse where it was safe. Instead, he remained silent, unsure if the man would be just another abuser. *What if he's just being chased by the cops?* he thought. *What if I call out and whatever's chasing him goes after me instead?* His selfishness gave him a pain in his chest, an alert as to how much he had changed.

He watched in horror as the man was overtaken by his mysterious pursuer. In the pale moonlight, some twenty yards away, Christian couldn't make out any details, but he saw flashes of fur and teeth, golden specks of eye-flash. The man's screams abruptly ceased. Christian could see the front part of him, his head and outstretched arms, but something was crouched on his shoulders and back, something huge...

... and hungry. Christian listened as the creature devoured the man. He was glad the lights had gone out.

Two hundred yards away, on the other side of a chain-link fence that surrounded a parking lot, more dark hulks ran in the road. A car sped past on the street, racing at a good thirty miles over the speed limit, and it looked as if the dark shapes ran abreast of the vehicle. Christian squinted, rubbed his eyes, trying to determine whether his mind was playing tricks.

Suddenly, something reared up, just on the other side of the window, a giant, animal shape, blocking out the moonlight. It sniffed the air, then snapped its head towards the boy. It roared, almost like a bear, exposing crooked, two-inch teeth, its eyes glowing molten gold in the dark.

Christian cringed, cursed, and retreated to the delivery elevator on the opposite side of the warehouse. He could lock himself inside if he could only reach it before the animal got to him.

Behind him, the window shattered and something heavy landed inside the room with a thump. It roared, deep and guttural. And then it chased after him.

He was nearly to the elevator when another thing leapt through the window, shattering the remaining glass. The two immense shapes bounded after him, leaping five yards at a time.

When he reached the delivery elevator, Christian grasped the leather strap and pulled down with his entire body. The rust in the pulleys moaned, and he pulled harder, feeling the doors emerge from the ceiling and floor, the space between them growing smaller.

One of the monsters arrived at the elevator and tried to pull the doors apart, sticking its toothy muzzle into the space between them. It gnashed its teeth wildly, rolling its eyes, trying to obtain some leverage.

Christian leaned back and kicked its snapping muzzle as hard as he could while maintaining his grip on the leather strap. He screamed incoherently, kicked again and again until the beast yelped and pulled its snout away from the space.

The doors shut with a clanging sound, and Christian flipped the lever that locked them together. He pulled down the interior metal grate and locked this as well. It was feeble and wouldn't stop anything that big for very long, but it offered him a bit more comfort.

He spun around within his ten-by-ten-foot cell. The walls had never seemed so close, the ceiling so low. He reached out for the steel walls, feeling the strength of the metal beneath his fingers. The solid steel brought his heart rate back under control, and he started to breathe easier after his mad dash to safety. These walls were thick. They would hold against any assault.

As he sat on the floor, listening to the beasts struggle and claw futilely at the metal door of the elevator car, he clutched his transistor radio to his chest. He moved across the floor, shoving his butt backwards with his legs until the wall was solidly behind him. He switched on the radio, praying for the comfort of another human's voice—talk radio, a song, anything to reassure him.

Vaguely, he wondered if Jean was all right, if any of the beasts had attacked him. The concern surprised him. The old geezer was nothing but a meal ticket.

He couldn't find anything on the radio, couldn't find a signal from any of the local stations.

"What the hell is going on?" he asked.

He was answered by static.

And by the roar of the beasts outside.

CHAPTER 3

September 16... 8:10 p.m.

The sound of the vault doors locking nearly drove Rick Morrison around the bend and into the bughouse. The conclusiveness of the clanking latches, the vague feeling that the big dial on the outside was turning with a multitude of tiny, crustaceous clicks, the clanking of the huge bolts as the vault was sealed... it seemed like the end of everything. The world, and whatever was taking place in it, was gone, replaced by a twelve-by-fifteen-foot room.

Chesya was shouting at him, "Rick, man, stop it! Stop your screaming!"

He couldn't, even though he fought against them. There were... things... out there killing people. They'd attempted to slaughter him, but he had fought, had found his way into the vault. No, he'd been *led* to the vault... by this woman who seemed so calm and so strong. The woman with the big eyes...

And it was dark... so very dark in here.

"The lights!" he shouted, and he felt the black woman next to him, taking his hand. "I can't see anything."

"Get a hold of yourself," she said. "We're safe here."

"Are you sure?"

"We're gonna be all right. Nothing can get through that door. Nothing."

27

Chesya grasped his hand even tighter within her own. She could feel the tremors in his body as he screamed again, clutching urgently at her fingers.

"Oh Jesus. Oh shit."

"It's just the lights. They're on a timer. It's okay."

"Can't see anything. The air's going to go. Is there enough air for us? Are we going to suffocate in this fucking tomb?"

"Rick, listen to me. The lights are on a timer. Hold on a second, and I'll find the override switch."

"You won't let go of me?" He clutched her hand so hard she thought he might break it, crush the bones into dust. He wanted to stop the quivering in his voice, wanted to stop being such a pussy, but the endorphins flooding his brain overrode his pretensions.

"No, I won't," she answered. "But I'm going to be moving. Follow me where I go. There's a switch on the wall somewhere right over here."

Chesya eased along the side of the vault, fumbling with her free hand and wondering if she could somehow use the bank robber's terror to her advantage.

"It's just along here somewhere," she said.

"Hurry up. Damn it! What about the air?"

"There's a ventilator, like an air pump. It keeps it cool in here. Nothing to worry about."

She felt the nub of the switch beneath her fingers, and she flicked it towards the ceiling. Instantly, florescent bulbs blinked on with a burst of static buzzing. The flickering created a strobe effect, and Rick dropped Chesya's hand as soon as they flashed for the last time. Humming softly, the lights cast a greenish hue to the stifling atmosphere.

"That's better," he said. "I don't think I could've handled the dark right now. I really don't think I could."

"Well, we're safe for the moment… lights or no lights."

His breathing slowed, and she grabbed his head and pivoted his face to hers. The rage was gone from her eyes, replaced by fear and something that surreptitiously resembled concern. There was a true stability within her, and her gaze seemed to ground him, to bring him back to the real world.

"What?" he asked.

"Rick, are you with me? You stopped the screaming, but are you here? With me?" She spoke slowly, methodically.

In her college years, she'd had a roommate who'd taken LSD, and Chesya had been forced to sit with the girl one night, speaking to her gently, coaxing her out of the bad place she'd discovered under the influence of the drug. She felt as though she were doing the same thing with Rick, talking him down off a bad trip.

Only this time there was no drug sculpting the monsters in his mind. She had to remember that the monsters were right outside the vault. Real monsters, with real teeth. Knowing she would need someone cogent and alert by her side, she pushed the terrifying images from her mind and helped Rick regain his senses.

"I... I think so," he finally answered.

"Where are we?"

"We're in the bank vault. You... dragged me in here."

"Do you remember anything that happened?"

He nodded. "Those things attacked us. They were all over the place."

"What else?"

He looked at her. "And our friends... turned, changed into something else. You're going to think I'm crazy. Hell, I think I'm crazy for even considering it, but I think they were turning into werewolves."

As she looked around the tight, claustrophobic room, she thought, *Werewolves? But that's crazy, isn't it?*

"What about getting out of here?" he asked. "Do we have to wait until someone comes and sets us free?"

She shook her head. "No, it's on a timer, remember? It'll unlock from the outside at 8:30 or so. We can use the emergency lever to release the other locks, but I'm afraid we're stuck here until morning."

"I'm not very good at small, tight places." Rick eyed the cream-colored metal walls of the vault, a soothing shade, probably chosen by some poor slob in a cubicle somewhere. Smaller safety deposit boxes, each with their own set of locks, lined one side. At the back of the vault was a rectangular door.

"You'll just have to live with it," Chesya said, sitting down on the floor and leaning against the door at the back. "We're in here for the night. And, honestly, I can't think of a safer place right now. That door is ten inches of steel. The walls of the vault are more than a foot thick. I doubt anything can get in here. Especially those animals."

"Werewolves."

"Whatever. They looked more like bears to me. You think a bunch of bears maybe got loose... no, that wouldn't explain why Gloria and the others started changing. Don't werewolves have to be scratched or bitten before they turn from people into monsters? That's how it always worked in the old movies."

"Maybe the movies lied."

"And only most of the people changed. You didn't turn into one of those things, and neither did I. Everybody else out there did. Why not us?"

"I don't know." He had a thought, a dark, malignant thought that seared itself into his mind. "Hey, what if someone hits a power line out there and the electricity goes off? That door going to open if there's no electricity?"

"It's got a back-up battery that'll work for a couple days. I think I read once that it can last seventy-two hours. We'll get out of here just fine."

He said, "Okay. That's good."

"If they really are werewolves," she continued, "why are there so many of them? And what was going on with Gloria and Roger and all your partners in crime? How come they were affected?"

"Well, they didn't get scratched. Not that I saw."

"No. But they still changed."

"It looked like they had stomach cramps when it all started. You remember Jones said that he wasn't feeling so good? You think... no, it's too crazy."

"What? There isn't much I wouldn't believe right now."

"You don't think it was some kind of disease, do you? Like, they caught some weird werewolf virus?"

"You're right. That's crazy."

"No, listen." He was getting excited about his theory, moving his big hands in the air, gesticulating wildly. At least he wasn't obsessing over the enclosed space of the vault. Small favors were welcome right now. "Think about it. They all got sick and started changing into those animals. Some of us didn't. We could be immune to this werewolf disease, kind of like those people who never catch measles."

"I don't know," Chesya said. "I still don't think they're werewolves. They didn't really look much like wolves."

"No, they didn't. They were mixed-up versions of all kinds of animals... like you said, big and bulky like bears."

"But they moved like cats..."

"Snouts like a dog or a wolf, and the ears were definitely wolf-like."

She shivered. "Their eyes, too. So weird. I used to have a cat that ran away from me. She had eyeshine like they had."

"They were fast as shit, though. Never seen anything move that fast."

They stopped talking for a moment, glancing at each other. The hum of the lights and the nearly undetectable whir of the air ventilator were comforting. Rick's heartbeat slowed down for the first time since the aborted robbery had begun. It seemed like a long time to have that much adrenaline coursing through his system.

"You rob a lot of banks?" Chesya asked.

Rick leaned back against the wall, feeling its coolness through his Oxford shirt. Slowly, he lowered himself to the floor until he was sitting, looking across the pre-fab room at this woman who had saved his skin.

"Why you wanna know?"

"Just being neighborly. We're going to be in here a while, and it could get our minds off what's outside. So, have you?"

He just grinned and waved a finger at her.

"Well then," she continued. "Why do you do it?"

"Why do you work here?" he asked.

She shrugged. "For the money, the benefits."

"Same with robbing a bank. It's all about the money, Chesya. You knock over a decent sized bank, you got enough to live on for a good year or two. All for one night of work and a couple of days of planning. If that's not a great benefit, I don't know what is."

"What if you get caught?"

"Then, I'll go to jail. The risks come with the territory. Just like you take a risk being a teller here. There's always a chance some sonofabitch like me might come along and stick up the place."

"That's a pretty fatalistic way of looking at things."

"Well, I'm just that kind of a guy. I never saw the glass as half full. I always just wanted to refill it to the top."

"But if you had a steady job, you'd get the money without the danger."

"Yeah, but that isn't for me," he said with a hint of a grin. "I kind of like the danger, living on the edge. I'm not much of a human being, I know. But I'm really good with a gun, good with my hands."

"You don't look like a bank robber. You look like... maybe a stuntman for Westerns... the old kind of Western, Roy Rogers or Audie Murphy. I could see you falling backwards over a bar and into a mirror."

"You could, huh? I've been in enough brawls back in the day. Now I just take my risks one day a year, get my cash, and relax for three hundred and sixty-four days in a sunny place. I work a lot on my tan."

"You don't look very tan to me."

"Maybe I'm just feeding you a bunch of lies," he said with a grin. "Maybe I know you're grilling me so you can help the police find me. It isn't gonna be that easy, Chesya."

She rolled her eyes, ran a hand through her afro, disappointed he'd discovered her ruse. "Must be some kinda life," she said. "Always running from the law, the government. I'll take my nice, steady income over that any day."

"You don't see the romance in it, the life of a bank robber?"

"Hey, I see things in practical terms. You ever catch that movie about Bonnie and Clyde? They sure were romantic, especially when they were being gunned down at the end... all bullet holes and blood flying. Sorry, but not for me. I'll take my safe life, my 401(k), and my little apartment."

"You really don't see it, do you? Why it's worth all the problems?"

"No. Seems pretty ridiculous to me," she said, trying to hit him in his pride so he'd let some detail about his life slip. "But, hey, you want to rob a bunch of banks and risk your life, more power to you. I grew up in Over the Rhine, the worst part of the city. There were guns all over the place, and I watched my older brother die by a gun. He was shot six times by some punk in a rival gang after he killed one of their homies. My other brother overdosed in a back alley, so excuse me if I don't get excited over the gangster lifestyle you've chosen. I've seen the results firsthand."

"Hey, I'm not that bad," he said. "I just rob banks. I've never killed anyone during one of the robberies."

"You've never killed anyone? That tough guy persona is just an act?"

He nodded. "Yeah, I couldn't ever really hurt anyone."

"Tell that to Bob Gunner."

"Who?"

"The man you pistol-whipped and left to die on the floor."

"Aw, Christ, I didn't think of that," he said, and he winced. "I just wanted to knock him out and get him out of the way. You're right, though. He didn't start to change, did he?"

She shook her head slowly back and forth. "No. We forgot about him, left him out there for those things to get."

"Aw, shit."

"Yeah... shit. He was a good man. A good boss. He had three kids and a wife. He's just meat now."

Her voice was rising with emotion, and Rick thought he'd finally distracted her from gathering incriminating facts about him. He did regret leaving that guy to be killed.

"We were running for our lives," he explained, trying to sound more disturbed than he was, not an easy task. "I just forgot about him."

She said, "I forgot, too, so I'll take some of the blame. Still, you didn't need to hit him with the gun. He wouldn't have caused any trouble. He would've just stayed on the floor, thinking about his kids. They were good kids, too."

"Okay, so maybe through neglect I accidentally killed a man," he said. "One man in six robberies—and that wouldn't have happened if those... those things hadn't shown up." Quickly, he added, "Of course, I could be lying again. I could've killed dozens of men over the years. Bodies could've been left all over the place."

Chesya sighed. "I don't think any of it matters much, anyway. We're talking about all this morality and philosophy, and I think that when we open that door in the morning, we're going to have a lot more to worry about than who got hurt in a robbery. I think it's going to be terrible. Like the Apocalypse."

"You think it's happening all over?"

"Yeah. You saw how fast Gloria and all of your friends changed. It only took a couple of minutes."

"And all those sirens."

"Huh?"

"I heard car alarms and sirens going off all over the place outside the bank, and I mean a lot of them."

"Yeah. It doesn't look very good, does it?"

"If that's going on all over the place, I don't know if there'll be anyone left alive in the morning."

"Some people had to have gotten away, hidden themselves some-place safe, just like we did. I mean, we were lucky to be where we were with an open vault only a few dozen feet away. Maybe people hid out in their houses or their basements."

They were quiet for a while, and Rick glanced at his watch. It was just after 10 p.m.. They had at least ten more hours until the automated lock would slide open and allow them to exit.

Suddenly, he wasn't sure he wanted the doors to open. What would be left of the world on the other side?

"Yeah," he said. "Maybe some of them hid. Maybe…"

They listened to the hum of the lights, wondering what the morning would bring.

CHAPTER 4

September 17, 6:30 a.m.

Cathy Wright was trying to get to sleep with Karl, spooning him, her arm wrapped around his thickening middle. They had slept in the same position for over eighteen years. If they altered their arms or faced a different direction, they would both remain awake until they settled back into the old, familiar stance. Nineteen years of marriage brought many such traditions, and it was easier to settle into them than to fight them. When things were difficult, even impossible to handle, she scurried back to the nuclear model her mother had taught her. She chose to embrace the comfortable, mellowing into her middle age, ignoring the tough questions.

And there had certainly been tough questions lately.

Cathy felt the roll of Karl's stomach beneath her fingers as he breathed softly. She'd chastised him to get to the gym more often, to watch his diet. He agreed that these were good ideas, but so far he had not acted upon them. Acting on advice was something Karl saved for the law offices of Wright, Steptoe, and Stevenson. Within his walls, he was the king, and there was little room for advice.

Little room for opposition and debate.

Listening to her husband's snoring, she wondered if she had time to have another child, or if Karl would agree to an adoption. After Christian's disappearance, she had been feeling the emptiness of her house during the daytime when Karl was at work. She missed the sound of her boy's voice and his bragging tenor ringing from the dining room where he always seemed to be eating.

After what had happened, after all the accusations and sleepless nights of brutal refutations, Cathy doubted Karl would allow another child into their lives. Even a baby can eventually be corrupted, can turn against his parents.

The parenting books she had devoured while she was pregnant had not addressed this. It was something that happened to other families, poor families. Rich children didn't just disappear in the night after accusing their parents of abuse and neglect. It was as though someone had switched scripts on her, and she had to admit, if only in the deepest part of the night with her arm around her husband, that she was floundering.

She thought she had known her own child, then he simply changed overnight into a creature she no longer recognized. Where did that little boy go? And could he ever return to her?

Cathy felt something moving in the depths of Karl's flabby stomach. At first, it was a tickling sensation beneath her fingers, then hair began to sprout from his skin. He awoke, clutching at his abdomen and screeching in pain, shoving her away.

In the moonlight that streamed through the opened window, she watched her husband's transformation in awe and alarm. She reached out to him, and he tried to grasp her hand, his eyes somehow reflecting the moonlight in an odd, golden manner. His hand lashed out, then the wrist changed, snapped into a slanted, dog-like position, the fingers elongating as she watched, his fingernails growing long and black and sharp.

An animal—that's what Christian had called him. Karl seemed to be changing in affirmation to this charge.

When he dropped to all fours, he turned his massive head towards her, and she saw the hunger in his eyes, the desire... the frightening lack of recognition. She turned and rushed for the bathroom before he was accustomed to his four legs. Stumbling over the nightgown, she nearly fell, but she caught herself with her hands and hurled forward. She slammed the door, locking it behind her, thanking God that the contractor had insisted upon the heavy oak.

He smashed his body into the door several times, until something else eventually caught his attention. He sniffled, gave a low growl, then started tearing the bedroom apart. After several minutes of ripping and crashing noises, he howled and bounded off somewhere.

She didn't hear another sound through most of the night, except for some noises from the street, separated from the house by a good two acres of manicured lawns and swimming pools. There were a few distant screams, some loud cars zooming past, and once she thought she heard something mechanical smash into pieces. There were a few minutes of crashing sounds from downstairs, muffled by the walls. Then, it grew eerily quiet.

Taking a deep breath, she opened the door to the dawn and looked upon the bedroom. One hand remained on the door to slam it shut if anything suddenly moved towards her. The other hand held a pair of scissors that she'd discovered in the vanity drawer. They weren't very sharp, but they'd inflict damage in a pinch.

Her stomach growled, demanding sustenance.

"Karl?" she called into the brightening room. Orange and yellow hues sparkled off the crown molding.

The bedroom had been torn to pieces. The bedclothes were shredded, and long strips had been clawed out of the mattress, matching sets of five talon marks each. The dresser had been overturned, the drawers torn from it and tossed across the room, and the curtains were canted, hanging by a single side of the window treatment. The window itself was smashed, glass scattered across the floor. The closet doors were crumpled in the middle. The bottom half of one of the doors had been flung near the bed, but the top halves hung like batwing doors in a Western saloon. Her clothes, torn and shredded into ribbons, were dispersed all over the room. She could smell stale piss, and she discovered the puddle near the bookshelves, which were, oddly, untouched.

"Oh God, Karl."

Dawn had arrived in a cloudless, autumn sky in Cincinnati, edging the bridges that spanned the Ohio River in tones of gold and crisp yellow. The sky was blue, almost aqua, and the birds began to call out to each other, gossiping in singsong. The temperature rose to a warm seventy degrees, a vestige of the Indian Summer.

Cathy couldn't bring herself to become enthusiastic about the weather.

She searched the house, discovering some new brand of destruction in nearly every room. She tried the phone, dialing 9-1-1, but was greeted by a dead line. She attempted the same call on her cell phone, but she only received a busy signal. She wondered how many other people were trying to call for help.

Setting down her phone, she moved to the foyer. The front door had been torn from its hinges, and she ran her hand over the splintered wood.

Then, like so many others in the city, Cathy Wright put on a pair of shoes and, after peeking through the doorway and ascertaining there was no immediate danger, stepped out into a new world.

CHAPTER 5

September 17, 6:05 a.m.

Chesya eyed Rick as he paced the length of the vault. She'd always been a people-watcher, and she could usually define behaviors of customers and co-workers. In turn, this helped her business sense. She could always tell when someone was nervous about a loan, no matter how well the applicant struggled to maintain a smile. Now, as Rick paced and attempted to contain his hysteria, she noticed little things about him, telltale signals that she alone would heed.

Rick's hair was graying at the temples, and she thought he was self-conscious of it because he ran his fingers through it just above his ears, where the new gray mixed with the sandy-brown. His arms were muscular beneath his shirt, stretching the fabric across his chest, but his legs appeared thin through his tight jeans. This told Chesya that he worked out, but he didn't discipline himself to complete the training, probably skipping his legs altogether. His desire for a cigarette belied a dependency upon smoking, and the frustration he exhibited showed that he rarely went without one of the cancer sticks. His nails were chewed down to the quick, a nervous habit.

All of these things showed a different man than he had wanted to personify during the robbery, a different image than the tough guy he'd been trying to display during the night. This was a man who was worried, afraid, a man who had trouble coping when things didn't go his way. It showed someone who could be careless and haphazard.

Despite the way he tried to affect a devil-may-care attitude, the way he was pacing showed a different side to him, a hidden facet that only she could notice.

And Chesya was determined to use it.

He would screw up eventually. When the door to the vault opened in the morning, he would probably dash for the nearest exit, but if he didn't, she would prepare herself for an escape.

"How long have we got left?" he asked, slumping down on the floor. His leg began bobbing nervously up and down.

"About three hours."

"Jesus Christ! I'd sell my soul for a cigarette right now, for half a cigarette," he said. "There's a pack in the car, just outside the damn bank. For all the good that does me."

"Those things'll kill you," she said, grinning at him.

"Very funny. I think those monsters out there will probably get to me first. We can't stay in here forever."

"At the rate you're going," Chesya said, "You're not gonna last the night. Get a grip, man."

"You ever smoke?"

"No. It's a nasty habit." She wrinkled her nose.

He laughed. "Well, nasty or not, it's harder than hell to stop. I've tried a couple times, but I couldn't stick with it. Even tried the patches, but I ended up smoking anyway and getting really sick."

Hmmm, she thought. *Also unable to finish projects that he starts.*

She said, "Well, if you want to get your mind off things, we can always talk."

Throughout the night, there had been long stretches of silence bookended by staccato bursts of whining and ranting. It didn't do much to endear Rick to her, but at least she was beginning to realize he was human, that he was as scared as she was.

Chesya just kept her emotions buried deep within herself, a personal cemetery of stifled anger and fear and disgust. One of her ex-boyfriends had often commented upon her inability to show her feelings. He had told her he knew she had the feelings, but it would be nice if she shared them with him occasionally. He left her soon after that conversation, and she'd placed him within her cemetery, burying him among the other failed relationships. Not that there were all that many.

"Talk?" he asked. "What else can we talk about? I'm about talked out."

"Who are you?"

"Oh, I think you know enough about me already. You're a sly one, you are. What else is there? I'm Rick. I rob banks. Sometimes, for shits and giggles, I tell terrible fibs to bank tellers."

She ignored his remark, intuiting that he was telling more truths than lies, just something she felt in her gut. She asked, "Do you have a wife? Kids?"

"No wife. Definitely no kids." He wiggled his eyebrows Groucho-style. "At least, none I know about."

"You ever wish for that kind of life?"

"What? White picket fence, two point four children, and a dog named Scamp? Naw, I don't see it. I think it's fine for other jerks, but I don't think I could stand it for more than a couple of days." He paused for a moment. "Yeah, it might be nice to have a woman waiting for me at home, but I can go to any bar in town and pick up a woman for the night."

She believed he probably could do it, too. He was certainly handsome, in a rugged, Marlboro Man style. He projected bravado when he wasn't in the process of losing control, and many women would find that self-confidence attractive. She didn't include herself among their ranks.

"What about you?" he asked. "You said you had no family, brothers killed. You got a man stashed away behind a white picket fence?"

"No, and I don't have a dog, either. I did have a cat, but she ran away one night. No fences, just a nice little apartment about a mile to the north. With my income, I can't afford a house."

He grinned at her. When he smiled, he was much more attractive. "I could float you a loan. Hell, you won't even have to repay me. Just tell the cops I took it all. That is why you're leaning against that door, isn't it? You've been stretched out against that thing since we got locked in here."

"What?" Her wide eyes implied innocence. "This door?"

"That's where the cash is kept, isn't it? How's about we open that sucker up and take a look."

"You're still thinking about money? With those things loose out there? We could die when that door opens."

"Then, baby, I wanna die a rich man. Open her up. Let's take a look at what's inside."

She stood, wiping dust off her black cotton slacks. Two more locks were on this door, and she used one key from her own key chain and one from the bank manager Rick had knocked cold. The door opened slowly, another five inches of steel.

As she exposed its interior, Chesya said, "You're worried about cops and money. The whole world looked like it was ending last night. It looked like something out of a Left Behind novel... the Apocalypse."

"You read that crap?"

"Yes, and last night looked like the beasts were inheriting the earth."

"You don't know that. We don't know much of anything locked in here like this. When those doors open, I want to be ready for whatever is waiting. If things are quiet and back to normal, then I'll be off to Florida again, and you can return to your apartment and keep living your boring life."

"I'd really like to believe that," she said. "But what makes you think anything will ever be normal again? We saw shit last night that I still don't understand. I mean, werewolves!"

"Come on, come on," he whispered. "Swing that baby wide open for me."

Rolling her eyes, she finished opening the door, revealing the shelves inside the metal closet. They were lined with neatly wrapped stacks of cash, rows separated by the type of currency. The air seemed a bit colder than that in the vault, and Rick searched for a vent for the air conditioning.

With a whoop of delight, he swooped down on the money, stuffing hundreds into his pockets. He started moving to the twenties, humming "We're in the Money." His facial expression had altered from glum and nervous to a child-like wonder. Chesya had noticed this awe in nearly everyone she had ever trained to work the vault. When they first saw the money, they entered a fantasyland, wondering what they would do with such riches, what they could buy.

Rick's new enthusiasm frightened Chesya. The sight of all that money had turned some switch in him, and he was acting foolishly, as though he had become oblivious to their real problems. People with that much confidence made mistakes, and mistakes, even small ones, could get them killed now. She preferred the frightened man, the coward. It brought out the mother and sister in her. She could comfort him, help him, and she knew exactly where she stood with him.

"I take it you're feeling a little better now?" she asked.

"Oh, yes."

"The money make you happy?"

"You know, it doesn't take much to get me to forget my problems. A couple hundred thousand dollars does it pretty fucking quick."

"That's not really your money."

"It is now."

"It's the bank's money. The people who've invested here, who trust us..."

"Sing it to the choir, sister. It's insured. If I had to go through the shit I've gone through in the last twelve hours, I expect to come out ahead."

"Where do you live?" she asked, sneaking in the question.

He gave her a knowing wink and said, "Wherever I feel like. This much money, in cash, can get you a lease damn near anywhere."

"It doesn't seem right."

"You handle cash like this every day, right? I don't mean fondling it, just that a lot of money passes through here all the time. What stops you from just taking it?"

"Are you crazy?"

"Maybe just a little."

She sighed. "I don't take it because it isn't mine to take. There's a moral line, but you wouldn't know about that."

"Here," he said, tossing her a bundle of wrapped hundred dollar bills. She caught it, and he continued, "Tell me that doesn't feel good. You have five thousand dollars in your hands. How many months of rent would that pay on that little apartment of yours? Here." He threw another bundle, and she caught it. "Take two. That should pay the rent for the rest of the year. Or put a down payment on that house you wanted. Make sure there's a picket fence. That ought to make this long night worthwhile."

She stepped over to the money closet and replaced the bills. "It's wrong," she said.

"In the eye of the beholder."

"No, any way you look at it. It's wrong."

"Chesya, da-a-arling," he drew out the word like a seduction. "If that door opens in the morning and the whole world is overrun with werewolf monsters, are you going to tell me that all the rules still apply? You telling me you won't grab what you can to survive? I'm taking the cash. You can do what you want."

He was frightening her more with every passing minute, with every calculated remark he made. She knew he was going to do something crazy, and she knew she couldn't rely on him now. She could control the blithering coward. This new persona was a different matter entirely.

She hesitated. "I don't know."

"I would think that we're going to have to make some new rules if the world's changed as much as last night. And the first rule I create is—every man for himself."

"I don't know..."

"Hey," he said, stuffing a plastic bag full of currency. "How about a little help here. And how long have we got now until the door opens?"

With a shudder, she walked over to him, praying he would lose some of his newfound confidence before they were released from this prison.

CHAPTER 6

September 17, 6:09 a.m.

Christian had fallen asleep in the freight elevator, his legs tucked underneath his body, cuddling the transistor radio. He had kept it on during the night, listening to static instead of the horrible noises from outside. Every once in a while, another (or was it the same?) beast would scrabble at the elevator doors in an attempt to force them open. The sound was terrifying, growling and scratching and what once almost sounded like an animal's vain attempt at speech, the words mumbled through ragged lips and extended teeth. At these times, he would turn up the volume of the little radio, but the white noise couldn't entirely dispel the vocalizations of the monsters.

He had concluded that these most definitely were monsters, possibly even aliens from another world. The invasion had come, the ships spewing forth these beast-men into the world's cities. It made sense to him, more sense than his other theory...

There were werewolves loose in Cincinnati. And there were a hell of a lot of them out there.

Eventually, when the adrenaline had dissipated, he had fallen asleep, cradling the radio in the crook of his arm, intent upon its static. The soothing noise had helped him sleep. He didn't know how long he had slumbered, but his dreams were packed with full moons and howling.

"Hello... hello... is anyone out there?"

The voice was soft, yet urgent. It was a man, and his cries startled Christian from his sleeping state. Looking around, he took note that he was still locked in the elevator, and he was still safe, still alone.

"Hello…"

Except for the radio.

The static had finally ceased, replaced by a voice, broadcasting its immense loneliness and horror with every word.

"I'm here at WKPX in Milford. There's nobody else in the radio studio. If anyone can hear me out there, I think it's safe to come out now. They're gone. The creatures seemed to have changed back. I haven't seen one in nearly an hour."

Sitting up, Christian listened intently.

"I… I think it's safe to come out now. This is not a trick. If you're locked up somewhere, you can unlock your doors. Everyone seems to have… changed back into themselves. I don't understand it, but it's true. I should warn you, it looks pretty bad out there. A couple of times, I thought I heard gunshots. Rifles. I suggest we all get back to our families, and we start burying the dead. My name is Juan Cabrone, and if you're out there, Laurie, I'll be home soon."

The static resumed. As though the man had never been broadcasting at all.

Christian took a few deep breaths and pulled opened the elevator doors.

The sunlight from the dawn was stunning.

***

Jean Cowell looked around at the chaos that had once been his laboratory at Bio-Gen headquarters. Bottles and beakers were smashed into glittering jewels around him, ground beneath padded feet during the night. A foul stench emerged from some of the spilled chemicals, and his notes blew lazily in the breeze venting from a busted window. He picked up one of the pages and read through it, smiling at the work it had taken to prove his hypothesis.

He had tried to prove so many things in his life. Sighing, placing the page on the counter near the back of the lab, he realized the time for tendering proof was almost over. In fact, much of what he considered reality had been shattered like the glass that clinked beneath his shoes. When the very fabric of reality, of belief, was broken, no theoretical proof would ever put the Humpty Dumpty god of the real world back together again. Waking life had warped into mythology. Nothing would ever be the same.

And this thought kept clanging in the brilliant man's mind, a wake-up call for what was to come.

He had once been a wise man, his mind adroit and quick. And he had attempted to be a good man, albeit without much success. The bugaboos of his true self haunted him throughout his life—his taste for rich foods and wine, his dependence upon marijuana to lull him to sleep, and his taste for young men. The younger, the better.

His mind turned to Christian, the latest of his purchased boys. Christian was so appreciative of every small kindness, every shower, any small bite of food, that Jean found himself trying to go further with this gamin. He wanted Christian off the streets, someplace safe and warm, and he had invited the boy into his life, only to be refused. One more disappointment in a long series of disappointments.

There were no longer any safe places, he had to chide himself. There was no place to hide. If you ran away, where could you run? How do you escape from yourself?

The night had been terrifying, a flurry of teeth and claws and blood. But he had survived it. Many had not. The urges that had compelled him during the night were primitive, animalistic, and, to Jean, completely terrifying. His basest needs had taken physical form during the nocturnal hours, the need for food, for sex, for sheer physical ecstasy. With these guarded secrets unleashed, he had felt true power, unlimited excitement. He had tasted blood and semen, licked at wounds and inflicted new ones upon others who had challenged him. His true inner self was on full display for the world to see.

It had demolished all those carefully built walls that had protected the world from his real conceits.

And it hadn't been a pretty sight.

Moving to his desk, he took a seat near the broken window, relishing the cool breeze that trickled across his sweat-soaked, naked skin. He sighed, opening the drawer.

In his mind, he thought of the ways he had survived over the years. He remembered the death camp of Auschwitz, remembered his friends and relatives fed to the ovens while he had assisted the Nazis in their repellent experiments. Had he been so different from them? He thought back to the men in his life, and the boys who had eventually replaced them, their faces growing ever younger, always more innocent. He saw the day that the US government approached him, the day he had signed the contract that had certainly damned his soul for all eternity.

And he saw Christian's face, his lean body, the way the boy looked when Jean handed him the measly twenty-five dollars. The boy was probably ruined now, his purity discarded like a shucked skin.

Picking up his journal, he wrote a few lines on the final pages, a last gasp of humanity before he ended everything.

"I am only a man, with a man's weaknesses," he scribbled. "The world is a terrible place, and I have made it more so. How many have died so far because of what I've done? There is a serum, one which can counteract this evil, can possibly cure the world. I no longer wish to be cured. I've witnessed the baser side of humankind, tasted the darkness, and I see only one way out. I need to send my soul to Hell. Maybe I could stay and be of service to someone, but I cannot live with the knowledge of my own evils, the ones twisting and gnawing at my brains. I cannot live with myself. Nor can I accept what I've loosed on the world. It's too horrible to consider, and I cannot bear to see the visage of accusation again. I've seen that scowling face before, and I would rather die than look upon its disappointment and disapproval once again. I'm too old and too weak to handle it. When blame is assigned... and it will be... blame me for it all. I deserve nothing less. Goodbye, my sweet Christian. Goodbye, my fellow scientists. I pray to God my untested serum works."

His mind raced through the pages of his time on Earth, powerful recollections resurfacing like Proustian whales. Some were good memories, but many of them reflected the more sordid side of his life. It made it easier to take the gun from the drawer and insert it into his mouth. The barrel tasted of nothing. The cold taste of guilt against his lips, phallic metal, hard, unyielding.

All the king's horses and all the king's men, and all the king's scientists and brilliant researchers...

Forgive me, he thought. He knew there would be no absolution for his crimes, not for the misdemeanors of his cravings, nor for the greatest crime ever wrought on humanity.

Too much to bear.

A breeze blew his papers across the room, and he was struck by an urge to pick them up and organize them again. He laughed at the ridiculousness of the idea.

Closing his eyes, he pulled softly on the trigger. In the moment that he died, he heard someone calling from a distant room, calling his name, and he knew that he had made a mistake.

What if the serum had worked?

My God, what have I done?

The bullet tore through his tortured mind, and his brains and bits of skull spattered on the white wall behind him.

All over the country, the killing shot echoed, as others faced what they had done during the night.

As others were overcome with the guilt of their actions.

As others lost control.

CHAPTER 7

September 17, 8:20 a.m.

Rick had started his therapeutic pacing in the bank vault again, moving faster as the timed opening approached. *Just need to get through a few more minutes. Just a few more minutes,* he thought.

Chesya listened to his footfalls, trying not to watch him. If she met his eyes, he only grew more agitated, and she wanted to keep him cool and calm until they could safely evacuate the vault. Plus, he was beginning to really aggravate her.

The man simply had no morals. She listened with growing incredulity to the way he described his "exciting" life of danger, his tales of robberies that he had executed while never hurting anyone. He had repeated throughout the night, that nobody had been seriously injured during one of his hold-ups, a self-deluding mantra.

Chesya knew differently. She could still see the eyes of her fellow employees, people who weren't as strong as she was, simply because they hadn't experienced the streets as she had. Witnessing the terror in their subdued movements, she knew they had been injured, even if they had never been struck. Rick wasn't accounting for the torture he inflicted upon his hostages, what that did to them. She had no doubt that somewhere, therapists were raking in the dough alleviating the mental agony Rick and his comrades had caused other people to endure.

"When can we get out of here?" he asked.

"About fifteen minutes," she said. "Ten minutes less than the last time you asked me. And why don't you have a watch? Big, successful man like you?"

"Don't like them," he said. "They get in the way sometimes."

"Sit down. You're making me nervous."

"I don't think I can sit now. It's so close. We're almost free of this damn thing. What do you think's going to be on the other side of that door when it opens? You think we'll get out, just go on with our lives?"

"You can head back to Florida, and I'll go back home, just like you suggested. I'm not gonna stand in your way."

"What if it's bad outside? It could be really bad."

She answered, "I imagine it'll be pretty ugly, but that doesn't mean I'm sticking around with you. If those things are everywhere, we're screwed no matter what we do. I think I'd rather be alone, take my chances by depending on just me, myself, and I."

"You would, huh?"

"Rick, you're a criminal. You have the scruples of an ambulance-chasing lawyer, and even that may be giving you too much credit. You rob banks, and you don't care about little people like me. You're egotistical."

"I'm what?"

That stopped him from pacing. She continued, "You are. Everything is about you. Is it safe for you outside? How will you get to Florida? How long will you be locked up in here? You're a conceited, selfish punk who doesn't have any qualms about pistol-whipping an old security guard and leaving him for those things to eat."

He turned away from her, crossing his arms in a childish pout. He knew she was right, but he felt some inscrutable need to defend himself. "Hey, I said I was sorry for that. I wasn't thinking like I usually do. But you're forgetting something."

"What's that?"

He smiled. "I may be a selfish, conceited punk, just like you say, but I'm also a human being. Not like those monsters out there. I think any humans left should be sticking together. We're probably gonna need each other, especially if those things are still running around the city. And what if they've changed back? How are you gonna know which ones you can be around when they decide to turn into monsters again? I may be a pain in the ass sometimes, but at least you know what you're getting. No surprises."

She hadn't accepted that the world had spun so far out of control, even though the idea had been poking at her persistently through the night like a renegade bedspring. Rick had a point. It might be better to band together, but the state of the world would have to be pretty insane for her to remain by his side. She had to draw the line somewhere.

"You think about what I'm suggesting," he said. "You and I know we aren't infected with whatever caused this shit in the first place. We can trust each other, trust each other as humans."

He prayed she would stick with him. Although he hated to admit it, Rick was afraid of what he'd seen. He was even more frightened of what might be waiting for them on the other side of the vault door.

Despite herself, Chesya knew he was right. It would be hard to stay near anyone after she had witnessed the other bank employees changing into animals and tearing each other apart. From what she had seen, anybody could turn into one of those creatures. Anyone, that is, except for this morally reprehensible thief and herself.

"I still think you'll toss me to the wolves if I get in the way," she said. She paused a moment, almost grinned. "No pun intended."

"Well, I think I'd rather have you by my side if worse comes to worse."

She shrugged. The silence inside the metal walls made the air heavier, pressed itself down upon her shoulders. The longer the quietude lasted, the heavier it all seemed. She felt as though she would break beneath its burden.

Trailing his fingers along the side of the vault, Rick began to pace again. He stopped for a moment to look inside the plastic bags crammed full to bursting with cash, and he smiled. The sight of all that money just waiting to be spent relieved him a bit.

"This is a damned good haul," he said.

"For all the good it's going to do you."

With a *sss* of air and a clicking of pins dropping into place, the vault door popped open an inch, startling the two prisoners. They had grown so accustomed to the silence that even the soft wheeze of the time locks being released seemed deafening. They listened for other noises through the crack, and, hearing nothing, crept close to the breach. Rick motioned for Chesya to stand behind him, which surprised her, and he put a protective arm out to shield her. It was an unconscious impulse, a gentlemanly relic, and it gave her another glimpse into the man obscured behind the bank robber.

"Do you see anything?" she asked.

"No. Don't hear anything either."

"You think it's safe?"

He shook his head and turned towards her. "No, but what the hell. Is anything gonna be safe anymore?"

"Probably not."

He motioned with his head towards the loot stashed in the corner. "Grab a bag and help me carry it to the car. Then you can head home if you want. Take that bubble bath. I won't stop you."

Nodding, she picked up one of the Hefty bags, surprised by the weight of the bills. She would help him get the money to his car, since he still had the gun. Then she hoped he would drive away, leaving her with only a memory of this awful night. She clutched the bag with both hands as Rick grabbed two more. He cradled them in one bulging arm and nudged the door open with the barrel of his gun. The steel portal opened easily, swinging wide, exposing the rest of the bank.

"Oh, my sweet Lord…" Chesya muttered.

The wrecked car that had slammed through the glass front of the building had been turned over onto its back. The gas tank had blown. There were no flames left, only the charred chassis and the twisted, blackened bodies inside. Two naked men had been ripped in half by the blast, their body parts scattered around the lobby in twisted Picasso angles. There was no sign of Jones' bisected body near the front of the automobile. It had probably been blown to hell with the explosion. The marble counter the car had hit had cracked down the middle, collapsing into rubble on one side, charred down the left. Smoke still wafted up from it, although the fire had been extinguished.

Money and papers were strewn all over the room, drifting with a gentle wind that blew through what remained of the front of the bank. All the windows were smashed, the desks were overturned, and the drawers were pulled out and thrown across the area. One drawer was lodged in the chandelier that had stubbornly remained intact twenty feet above them, swaying in the wind.

Ten to twelve ravaged bodies lay on the floor, naked and bloody, so torn apart it was difficult to assign an actual number to the corpses.

"Rick," Chesya said; she had dropped her bag of money on the floor and was pointing at the vault. "Look at the doors."

He set his bags down too. Something had scratched the burnished steel. He put one finger on each of the claw marks, feeling the roughness of the edges, following their path downwards with his hand.

"They were trying to get in," he said. "And we couldn't even hear them. We didn't even know."

"What kind of a demon can scratch steel? I mean, that would break anyone's fingernails, right?"

"Those things are a hell of a lot stronger than we thought."

"I don't recall werewolves doing that in movies, but I guess this isn't the movies, huh?"

"No, I don't think so."

"I'm not sure if I want to go out there," she said, and he saw real fear in her eyes for the first time. Through the night, Chesya had remained the strong one, the glue that had held him together during his bout of claustrophobia, and now she was being confronted with a world turned on its head and she wasn't coping as well. Back on the outside, where he could see what he was dealing with, even if he didn't understand it, Rick became even more energized and emboldened.

And after seeing the state of the bank lobby, he really, really didn't want to lose his connection to what could turn out to be the only other human being left on Earth.

"I think we have to," he said, touching her shoulder. "Where else do we go? Back in the vault?"

She seemed to grow more solid beneath his fingers, sapping strength from him as if through osmosis. "I know you're right. We need to see what else is happening, but it's safe in there. We're certain of that after last night. I'll hold on to the keys, in case we need a fortress again."

Rick nodded. He looked around the bank again, took a step forward. "Hello?" he called, the word echoing slightly in the burnt-out chamber. The chandelier creaked above them. "Anyone out there?"

In the distance, a car alarm blared, its notes flat, distorting along with the death of the car's battery. Other than that, the city was appallingly silent.

"Listen," Rick said. "Do you hear anything? Any cars or buses? Any people talking?"

"No. Just that alarm, and it sounds exhausted."

They took another few steps forward, then Rick exclaimed, "The money! Shit, we almost forgot the money."

"Forget it, Rick. It isn't going to help us now."

"It sure as hell won't hurt us, either."

"But it will weigh us down. I don't think I want to go out there lugging around all that heavy cash."

"Well, at least take a few rolls of hundreds. I don't know how much this'll be worth out there..." he motioned towards the streets "...but we should be prepared."

After some debate, she stuffed six rolls of money in her pockets; Rick managed to fill his with nine rolls, all one hundred dollar bills.

Chesya held more than she made in six months, and the thought awed her. She knew she should leave the money, that it wasn't hers to take. She knew she was becoming an accomplice to Rick's crime, and she loathed herself for it, but she looked around what remained of her old workplace, and she could see the reason in stealing. The world and its laws no longer applied, and they might need the money to get out of town. Besides, he still had the gun, even if it wasn't pointing at her now.

A pistol gleamed on the floor, and Rick picked it up, checked the chamber and found four bullets left. He handed it to Chesya. She abhorred guns, blamed them for much of the violence in her old neighborhood, the violence that had claimed her brothers.

Times had changed, though. She wanted to be ready in case she saw those things again. She took the gun.

"Thanks," she said.

"You know how to use that?"

"Yeah. I've seen my brothers use them."

"Okay," he said. "Come on. Let's see what's out there."

They weaved through the smoldering corpses and wound around the wreckage until they reached the hole where the police cruiser had crashed through. Looking out at the streets of Cincinnati, they found themselves dealing with more emotions than either thought the other possessed. Tears streamed down Chesya's face, and Rick's gun hand shook uncontrollably.

It was far worse than they had imagined.

CHAPTER 8

September 17, 9:00 a.m.

Cathy Wright didn't spend more than a few minutes outside. Her Indian Hills neighborhood seemed to be burning around her. She'd walked all the way to the front gates, and she'd watched through the meager security that the wrought iron bars offered. Two houses that she could see were on fire—one of them belonged to a halfback for the Cincinnati Bengals—and a third house had been hit by a semi-truck, collapsing upon itself, trapping the vehicle.

None of the local hired security patrolled the streets.

Naked bodies, bloody and torn, dotted the manicured lawns. Cathy couldn't make out their faces, which were either turned away or torn to shreds. One hung upside down from a topiary, its guts spilling out of its chest, and another floated facedown in a swimming pool. She spotted a Lexis overturned into a fountain on another neighbor's lawn, blood smearing the windshield. More corpses lined the otherwise clean ditches.

Those could be my neighbors, she thought. *People I've known for years. All dead.*

Bloody paw prints, huge and disturbing in their sheer number, tracked along the road and up private drives, meandering to and from the various corpses. Kneeling, she examined one of the prints in more detail. It contained one large pad, triangular in shape, with four smaller rectangular shapes above it. Four pinpricks of blood swathed out from these rectangles, and she knew these were the crimson-covered tips of claws. They appeared vaguely bear-ish to her, not at all like the wolf prints she had seen in books and magazines. For some reason, this alarmed her more than the dead people did, even though she was beginning to recognize some of her neighbors. Standing, she backed away from the gates. After seven steps, she turned and ran back to the relative security of her house.

Cathy slammed the doors behind her, leaning her back against them. The heavy wood was comforting, even cool to the touch. But her living room, decorated by one of the city's most fashionable designers, was a war zone of devastation. Beirut by way of Debbie Travis.

Cathy hadn't worked since she married Karl. While he made a good living as a defense attorney, she preferred the life of leisure, spending time with her favorite charities and making sure the house was run as best she could. She supervised the two maids and four gardeners, chaired various committees such as Cincinnati's AIDS Awareness Foundation and a halfway house for mentally challenged adults. Her life had been as neatly arranged as her furniture. Everything was in its place, and she didn't cope as well when disorganization interfered.

And it had interfered. After the terrible arguments and accusations that had been flung around by Christian and her husband, she'd marveled that the walls weren't stained with bile and vitriol.

Now this.

The maids probably wouldn't work today—she could hardly blame them—so she began to straighten the living room, keeping her mind focused on the project at hand. It had worked before, the way her numerous charities and activities masking the hurt that festered within her. It was working again. After shoving the sofa back towards the picture window, she searched for the pillows. One of them had been clawed. She simply turned it over, hiding the places where the stuffing escaped from the material. The illusion of normalcy satisfied her. For the moment, all seemed balanced and sane.

If I can concentrate on cleaning this house, she thought. *I can forget about the rest for a while... about Karl and Christian and... and all the rest of it...*

One room at a time, she cleaned, replacing the furniture to the original locations, sweeping glass into a dustpan, throwing anything that was unsalvageable into the garage for disposal later. She placed boards over broken windows, duct-taping them in place, and she straightened art on the walls. She would have vacuumed if there had been any electricity.

Before long, Cathy had completed the living room, dining room, and kitchen, which had been the messiest. Silverware had been tossed around the room, and the light fixture had been yanked from its moorings. The floor was covered with bits of plaster and dust.

Looking around at her cleansing efforts, she felt a reassuring sense of accomplishment. She had twelve more rooms to clean, but her success with these three gave her a bit of hope. Maybe the world wasn't ending. Maybe people could find a way to restore order and return to normal lives.

It had been a while since her life had been normal. If she could return to that happy time, before her boy became a teenager, before he became wild, before all the horrible lies, she knew she could be happy again. It had been such a long time since she had been happy.

She was leaning on her broom, looking out at the dining room, when she heard a sound behind her in the kitchen. It wasn't much, and she sensed it more than she heard it.

Naked and barefoot, her husband Karl walked into the kitchen from the back yard. He closed the slashed screen door behind him, raising his eyes to hers. He appeared tired and wary of her, and she realized she was wielding the broomstick like a lance.

"Cathy..." he said, and he took a few steps into the kitchen, placing his hands on the back of a chair and inclining himself against it.

"Karl, are you okay?"

He shook his head. "No, I don't think I'll ever be okay again."

As he sat down in the chair, she observed the specks of blood around his mouth and hands. A zigzag of crimson had dried across his chest during the night, a bizarre super-hero emblem. She stepped to the sink and ran some cold water over a towel, thanking heaven that there was still running water, even if it wouldn't get hot.

"Here," she said, handing him the towel. "You've got blood on your face and chest. Please, wipe it off before we start talking." Her formality, her manners-before-all-else attitude was downright Noel Coward-ish.

He clutched the towel in his hand as though he were uncomfortable with it, unaccustomed to the very notion of cleaning with a cloth. Slowly, he patted his face, looked down at his chest. Wiping with small, clumsy, circular motions, he eventually removed most of the blood, leaving red blotches where he had rubbed too hard. She took the filthy rag from him and tossed it into the garbage can.

"Oh Christ, Cathy..."

"What happened?" she asked.

"It was horrible. I... I did things... terrible things..."

Taking a seat across from him, still holding the broom in case he made any sudden moves, Cathy looked at him and tried to see her husband. She kept imagining animalistic traits in his motions, his little tics. It was hard to regard him as the man who had shared her bed for nineteen years.

"What happened, Karl? Start from the beginning, and tell me everything you remember."

"You'll hate me for it. I hate myself. I'm... sick from what I did."

From what you did this time? she thought, then chased away the seditious notions. She needed to concentrate on what had happened last night, not months ago.

"Do you remember changing?" she asked.

He shook his head. "No. There was some itching. We were in bed together, and I started to feel this itch. Then there was pain and the smell of blood, all copper and sweet. That's all I remember. Pain and blood... I think it was your blood, Cathy. But I was in a place where you didn't matter, where nothing mattered but the smell, and the hunger, and the sheer sexuality of it."

"The sexuality? What are you talking about?"

"Oh, Cathy, that's what drove me. I wanted to insert my mouth into a body, to drink the blood, lap it up like a dog. It... compelled me to do it. I believe it was you I went after, but it could have been anyone. I wanted my face inside of you... can you understand that? Inside of you? I wanted the blood in my mouth, in my eyes, my face inside your ribcage, my hands elbow-deep in the gore. I wanted to cover my body in it, then have it licked off by someone else... anyone else."

He was getting aroused just speaking about it. Embarrassed, Cathy hurried upstairs, telling him to wait a minute. She returned with his robe, which had miraculously survived the night in one piece. Karl had started a pot of coffee. He smiled at her and slipped on the thick cotton robe, tying it at his waist with a sash.

"Thanks," he said. "And I'm sorry."

"Do you know you tried to kill me last night?"

"Yes. I suspected as much."

"You turned into… some sort of monster. Right in front of my eyes, you became some… I don't know, werewolf or something."

"Apparently, there were a lot of us that changed. You should see the city. I woke up in a gutter near the Milford movie theater. Everything's so fucked up."

"A lot of others were the same? Changed?"

"Yeah. There are tons of dead, naked people out there, and a lot of live ones, all waking up at dawn. I think we all changed. I think people who didn't, people like you, are really in the minority."

"Are you going to change again?" she asked. "I need to know, Karl. When and where… I can't just wait around for you to grow fangs and kill me."

"I don't know. I can still feel something… bristling inside me. Like hair that's grown on the inside of my skin. So, yeah, I'll probably do it again, because I can feel it just itching to release itself. I can't tell you when or where. But I think it's coming."

They sat across from each other, the man in his bathrobe, the woman in jeans and a white shirt, her legs tucked beneath herself. They sipped their coffee as golden sunlight streamed through the kitchen windows. It all seemed so normal and prosaic.

Just what she had always longed for.

But his words disturbed the peaceful scene, his suggestion that he was hairy on the inside of his skin, his violent actions hidden from her.

How much had he hidden in the previous months, when her world was imploding?

Had he been a monster before this transformation?

CHAPTER 9

September 17, 9:16 a.m.

Rick placed his arm around Chesya's shoulder, feeling the necessity to steady himself against someone. Mistaking his gesture for one of solace, she leaned into the muscular arm, his bicep solid against her face. They stood at the entrance of the bank, framed by jagged pieces of glass in the doorway, staring out at the destruction that had overwhelmed them into silence.

It was too much.

"How do people go on?" Chesya asked, her eyes adjusting to the bright sunlight. "Something like this happens… how do people just go on with their lives?"

Rick shook his head. "I don't know. But they do. Somehow."

"Like the people in New York City after 9/11?"

"Chesya, I think this is gonna be a lot worse than that."

Sixth Street of downtown Cincinnati lay in ruins. A gas main had burst, blowing a wide hole in the street and blasting chunks of blacktop everywhere, through the glass of various buildings, into cars. The explosion had shattered windows for a block in every direction, and the roads sparkled with bits of glass. Several automobiles had been driven into the gaping disaster, taillights still blinking. The road had cracked in several directions, occasionally dropping into darkness, like sinkholes. One of these holes had opened in a parking lot near Race Street, nipping at the corner of a rather large hotel, causing the thirty-six-story building to lean, wavering dangerously in the breeze. The explosion must have ruptured a water main, as most of the street was covered in a wet sheen, and water spumed from the cracked sidewalk like oil from deep inside the Earth.

Near the end of the street, a city Metro bus had overturned, smashing over the tops of several cars, creating a blockade. Blood caked the inside of the bus, blocking the view. In the distance, someone had piled the hot dog carts into a huge pile and set them on fire. The flames had spread, burning several storefronts. Far away, sirens wailed, but Rick couldn't discern if they belonged to the fire or police departments.

Not that it mattered. The streets were completely blocked by cars bumper to bumper, some crashed into each other, locked in a fatal embrace, and the overturned bus effectively closed off the end of the road. A Brink's truck, probably headed towards the bank for a pick-up, lay tumbled on its passenger side, smashed between two SUVs. Nothing was going to be going in or out of the city for quite some time. Not on these blocked streets. Not in this mess.

Then there were the bodies. They were scattered, dotting the landscape like punctuation, commas of ruined flesh. Burnt bodies, still smoking, charred to little but blackened skin and bones. Bodies with their throats torn out, the blood pooled halo-like around their heads. Crushed bodies, smashed between vehicles or trapped within a car that had been battered by traffic or squashed beneath a rolling, burning bus. Some bodies consisted of little more than a few pieces, limbs scattered, torn from sockets and tossed to the wind. Bodies bitten and chewed, half-eaten. Women and men ravaged by some new bestial creature, most of them with their clothes ripped from their bodies. Hands reached up in futile gestures from beneath rubble, an ear rested on a bus stop bench, a woman on her stomach, her back ripped to shreds while she had attempted to crawl away from something, her dress pulled up to her waist, exposing bloody, rounded buttocks.

The smell was overwhelming—burnt flesh, coppery blood, a faint stench of over-cooked hot dogs. Chesya could smell gasoline and oil and grease, fire and sweat and something else, something raw and pungent.

Like wet dog?

Rick thought he heard a gunshot in the distance.

"Jesus Christ…" he said, stepping outside, hearing the crunch of glass beneath his heels.

"Please, don't swear like that."

"I just said Jesus…"

"I know what you said." Chesya stepped away from him, and he could see the strength building in her eyes. He thought this was probably a good thing. "But please refrain from using the name of my Lord like that. It sickens me. You've been doing it all night, and I won't stand for it anymore. My God's important to me. He's almost all I have right now."

"That's not quite true."

She turned to him, and he tried to smile, witnessing the way her indignation rose. "Oh no?"

"No. You got me."

She laughed once, putting her hands on her hips. "Huh. Hell of a lot of good that'll do me."

"Well, I'm just saying it could be worse. Look out there. Look at those poor bastards."

Here and there, along the sidewalks, people were walking, stumbling like zombies in one of those cheap Italian movies Rick used to like so much. They looked dazed, insane, and they didn't seem to move with any purpose. Rick expected them to head towards each other, to band together as survivors, but they stayed in the shadows as much as possible, avoiding contact with other people. Something about the way they moved reminded him of crabs or spiders.

"I wonder what they saw last night," Chesya said, squinting at them. "They sure don't trust each other, do they?"

"Doesn't look like it. You think they had friends change in front of them? You think they saw the whole metamorphosis, or just what came after?"

"Maybe they changed, themselves. You think they'll remember anything that happened in the night? Anything they did while they were… animals? If they can remember it all, it would easily drive them crazy. I don't know if I could handle it."

A gunshot rang out, followed by two more. This time, there was no mistaking the noise. Rick grabbed Chesya and shoved her to the rough sidewalk, covering her with his own body. She looked up at him as he scanned the streets, his five-o-clock shadow sandy brown, like his hair.

"You see anything?" she asked.

He shook his head. "No. It wasn't very far away, though. Just a couple of blocks. I didn't even think about all the wack jobs with guns that'll be shooting at everything that moves. Probably forming posses right now."

"Maybe it was something that deserved being shot at."

He got off of her and sat down beside her. With his weight suddenly gone, she felt cool air rush between them. She missed his weight over her, holding her. It was comforting somehow, a soft edge to a tough guy, the brush of human flesh against her skin. Moving back, she leaned against the brick wall of the bank, crossing her long legs in front of herself.

Rick said, "I don't know. You see any of those things out here?"

"No. Looks like just a few people, lotta dead folks."

"Right. It looks like they're sleeping in the daylight, hiding out somewhere."

"Rick, you're creeping me out."

"Or maybe, holy shit, maybe they're really like werewolves, and they only turn under the full moon. There was a full moon last night. I remember seeing it through the blinds just as we started robbing the bank. What if they really work that way?"

"Werewolves? For real?"

"You saw those things. They were all over the goddamn bank."

"What I tell you about taking the name of the Lord in vain?"

"You're that religious? Damn, Chesya, I think that sometimes situations call for a little harsh fucking language, and this is one of those mother-fucking, sonofabitching, goddamn times."

She shook her head, and when she spoke, her voice was suffused with a growing sadness. "Yeah, Rick. I am that religious, and I've heard bad language before. Used it myself sometimes, but I firmly believe in my God. You want me by your side, and I don't think we should separate right now, so you better put a halt to the profanity. I look around, and I see people hiding, afraid of their shadows. I don't think you want to ally yourself with any of them. I'm a strong black woman who's still got all her senses. I'd think you'd want someone like me around."

"I do." He sounded chastened, but she didn't believe it yet.

"Then lose the profane use of my Lord's name. I'll stick by you if you do."

"You're kidding me, right? You'd actually leave me if I use the name…"

He could tell by her somber expression she wasn't joking, so he sighed and stood up. Holding out his hand, he grasped her forearm and raised her to her feet. Her palms were sweating, and that delectable anger burned in her eyes again.

"Out of all the women I could end up locked in a vault with… I had to find myself a righteous church lady."

"Damn skippy," she said, brushing off her slacks.

He sighed. "All right. I'll try, but if something scares me or surprises me, something might just slip out. I don't know if I can always control it. Never had to before now."

"I think in extreme situations, even God can forgive such a trespass."

"Well then," he said. "Let's get moving. A couple of those weird people have been eyeballing us for a few minutes. I suggest we see if we can find anyone else that survived the night with their sanity intact."

"Which way do we go?"

"Looks pretty bad in either direction, but that bus crash has nearly cut off the sidewalks on the east side, so… let's head west." He pointed towards the Marriott Hotel, which seemed to teeter towards them. "I don't like the looks of that building, either. The sooner we can get past it, the better, in my opinion. That thing looks like it could fall at any minute."

Chesya nodded, and they began walking up Sixth Street, heading west. The journey was slow going, as the obstacles seemed to accumulate the farther they traveled. Cars had been smashed into street lamps or driven onto sidewalks and parked there, the doors left open, as though someone were fleeing from them. A few of the buildings were on fire, and they crossed the streets to avoid getting too close to them. Sometimes, this entailed crawling over the hoods of abandoned cars.

Lifting themselves over the turtled Brinks truck, Chesya peered inside, but saw no bodies. Only a few specks of dried blood. She saw Rick unconsciously look for scattered cash in the back of the truck. When he realized he was caught, he shrugged and gave her one of his endearing grins.

At one point, they heard a loud explosion from the river, followed by a loud splash. Immediately, a second blast echoed through the buildings, and Rick thought he could feel the ground trembling beneath his feet.

Most of the wild-eyed people who wandered the streets avoided them, scuttling like beetles into dark places, but one man approached. Rick pushed Chesya behind him as the pitiful creature rushed forward. His eyes were red-rimmed, his motions bird-like and excited. He wore filthy rags and he smelled of BO.

"Did you see them?" he asked. "Did you see them? They were beautiful... so very beautiful."

Rick didn't want to encourage the man, but he was curious, so he asked, "What did you see? We didn't see anything."

"The beasts... they were all over the streets. Big and sleek and powerful. They ran the streets, biting and snapping at the ones who didn't turn, people like me. There weren't a lot of us, people who didn't turn. They tried to take us all."

"How'd you get away?"

"Jesus saved me," the man said, and he reached out for Rick, clutching at his shirt. "Jesus is God, and He saved me. He saved me. He's inside me now."

Chesya rolled her eyes, and she unhooked the vagrant's butterfly hands from Rick. "Come on," she said. "He's crazy."

As they walked away from the man, he began shouting after them. "Jesus could save you, too. You need to accept Him into your heart and pray you never suffer the mark of the Beast. That's why they all turned. Because they had the mark on them. Just like Cain. Just like Judas. Just like Larry Talbot."

"I don't think he was sane before last night," Rick said. "Looked and smelled like a homeless person to me. Like he'd been on the streets a long time." He glanced over at her. "I'm surprised, in a way, that you don't agree with him."

"What? 'Cause I'm religious? That doesn't make me a nutcase. I think something bad happened, but I'm not about to blame it on the Bible, so you can relax. This whole mess reeks of biological warfare, and that's no part of my God."

"I was thinking about that, too. Seems kinda weird that this disease, if it is a disease, just sprung up outta nowhere. I think it's government..."

"Oh my sweet Lord," Chesya whispered, stopping near the Interstate. She pointed, and Rick followed her finger.

The road was covered in car wrecks and bodies, worse than the city streets because of the speed the vehicles had been traveling. A blackened swath of earth stretched back to the Greater Cincinnati Airport, the same airport that had greeted Rick when he had flown in from Florida a week earlier. The landscape around the airport was dotted with large dark forms, the wreckage of what appeared to be several planes that had crashed into the fields surrounding the runways. The bridge across the river was jammed with cars packed together so tightly nobody could walk between them.

"All those people," she muttered.

"Nobody could still be alive in there," he said, staring slack-jawed into the eye of the inferno, overwhelmed by the magnitude of the blaze.

"Hey, do you hear that?"

"What?" Rick asked, still stunned.

"I hear voices, from over there."

She pointed north.

Rick strained his ears, listening. He could, indeed, hear voices, dim and far away.

"Come on," he said, pulling Chesya forward by the hand. They raced up the hill, dodging sinkholes, corpses, and the spidery people in the shadows. The sound grew louder, until they had sprinted five blocks.

In the silence, they could also hear a loud mechanical sound, and they headed east for another block. The noise issued from the Lone Wolf Cafe, a small diner and corner bar. This area didn't seem to be as thoroughly ravaged as Sixth Street. The automobiles had been parked in the street, instead of crashed into each other. None had hopped the curb and been totaled along the sidewalk. No buildings seemed ready to fall on them, and the fire damage was minimal.

Pressing the door open, Rick heard the sounds grow louder, and he recognized the mechanical puttering. "It's a generator," he shouted, stepping into the cafe. Chesya followed cautiously. A bell announced their entry, tinkling softly over the sound of a man's voice. She locked the door behind her.

"A television," she said, taking a seat at the lunch counter.

Above the cooking area was a thirty-two-inch TV, and an announcer sat at the news desk of Channel Five. Rick scanned the room, saw nobody, so he cautiously moved down the aisle. The counter and stools were on his right-hand side, and booths lined the opposite flank near large, unbroken windows. The tinny voice of the news anchor followed him.

"The generator must be back this way," he said, pushing aside a curtain at the end of the cafe. "Yeah, there's a room back here. Looks like the owner has an apartment…"

He stopped suddenly, the sound of the generator very loud in his ears and the stench of burning gasoline filling his nostrils. On the floor before him lay a dead man, a gun in his hand, his legs twisted over each other, his brains decorating the white sofa behind him. A few feet away, slumped in a chair, was a middle-aged woman, the left side of her face missing where the man had shot her.

Fighting the urge to vomit, Rick backed out of the little apartment. He could almost taste the stifling death in the room.

Chesya had found her way around the counter and had opened a walk-in freezer.

"Hey," she said. "You find the owners?"

"They're dead." He took a seat at the counter, turning his face towards the TV set. "Killed themselves rather than face each other in the daylight."

"Oh Rick, I'm sorry. You saw them?"

He nodded.

"… until further details arrive, we are trying to piece together what occurred last night…" the talking head on the television said.

Chesya pulled food from the freezer, slices of ham and a carton of eggs and milk. Setting them on the counter, she turned on the grill. "I can make us some food as soon as this heats up. Are you hungry?"

He hadn't thought about it, but he hadn't eaten in nearly a day. As if on cue, his stomach rumbled. He nodded at her, still thinking about the owners, who had wanted to die before they saw anything else.

"Eggs and ham all right?"

"Yeah." His voice seemed hollow, smaller, lacking all of the bravado he'd been managing to fake.

"You'll feel a little better when you get something in your stomach," she said, holding her hand over the warming grill. "That was always my Mamma's philosophy. Then we can sit and think this out, watch the news and see what's actually going on out there."

He nodded, hungry and salivating over the faint smell of food. Taking a stool at the counter, he placed his Glock next to the salt and pepper shakers, comforted a bit by its proximity. There were still, what, eight shots remaining in the clip?

Their eyes moved to the anchorman, who sat behind a desk, in a white shirt, circles of perspiration around his armpits and across his chest. He had not waited to have his hair or makeup completed, and he seemed waxy and pale under the studio lights.

CHAPTER 10

September 17, 10:45 a.m.

Newscast—
GRAPHIC IN-Emergency Bulletin... Channel 5 news... - GRAPHIC OUT
MUSIC CUE-
RUNNING BANNER-alternating emergency shelters as added by authorities
CUE ANCHOR-
Fred Mikelson-Good morning. Fred Mikelson, Channel Five news. Channel Five will continue its emergency coverage of what has been christened the Lycanthrope Syndrome by authorities everywhere. News is still sparse, but we will strive to keep you informed of any new discoveries and relate any safety precautions you should take. On the banner below, you'll find the names of hospitals or shelters where you can find medical attention, food, and clean water. You'll have to excuse us. We're working with a skeleton crew here at the station, but we will do everything we can to keep you informed.

To recap, as night fell yesterday, most of the human beings in the tri-county area mutated into werewolf-like creatures, leaving only a few people unchanged. There was no indication of what caused this sudden transformation in over ninety-five percent of the population, but it has resulted in terrible chaos and loss of life.

It's difficult to believe that this has happened, but we have exclusive Channel Five footage from a surveillance camera outside Fountain Square.

CUE FOOTAGE-ROLL TAPE-

In black and white, shaky, silent footage, heavy traffic in the streets stops, several cars bumping into each other. One car veers wildly to the left, running over a couple holding hands and slamming into a wall. There is movement within the cars, shadowy and indistinct. A few doors open, and people stumble out of their automobiles, tearing at their clothes as more traffic piles up around them.

Fred Mikelson-As a warning to our viewers, some of this footage is shocking and graphic, and if small children are watching, we advise that you send them to another room. As you can plainly see, the transformation seems to have occurred in everyone at roughly the same time.

TAPE ROLLING-A man falls on the hood of a car, ripping off his shirt, exposing his naked back. Odd shifts in his skeletal structure are clearly seen, as is the sprouting of thick fur along his bare skin. He seems to be struggling with the transformation, shuddering as though caught in an epileptic fit.

Fred Mikelson-From what we can tell, the metamorphosis begins between the shoulder blades. You can see the way the back changes, the bones relocating beneath the skin as he starts to grow hair over his body. As he turns, you can see the way his face elongates into a snout. Witnesses have stated that the sounds of crunching bone can be heard during this process. Observe the way the ears seem to stretch, fold themselves forward into concave shapes, similar to a dog or a bear. Can we slow this bit down, Alan? Thanks.

TAPE ROLLING-The man's mouth opens, and the tape crawls in slow motion, a frame at a time. His teeth seem to push outward from bleeding gums, making room for longer, sharper fangs that shove their way past the normal teeth. The old teeth remain, crowded into a growing maw that makes room for the additional dental work. The hair distends a frame at a time.

Fred Mikelson-The entire process seems to take about two to three minutes. The resulting hybrid appears to be similar to a wolf, but with bear-like aspects, especially in the way they rear up on their hind legs. The claws appear to be a little more than an inch long, and the teeth about three to four inches at their largest. The animal, once completely transformed from the human, is aggressive and carnal.

TAPE ROLLING-The creature flips itself to its four legs on the hood of the car, smashing the metal beneath heavy feet. Whipping its head from side to side, it pounces upon a woman who was in the process of transforming. It rips out her throat in a single, massive bite. She claws for a moment, then dies as the beast feeds on her. Blood shoots across the street in an arterial spray. Behind them, others have changed and are racing through the stalled cars, attacking other animals. Several of them begin copulating, the male thrusting from behind, the females raising their heads to the night sky and howling silently. Some of the females fight back, clawing and biting, but the males continue their incessant pounding.

TAPE STOP-

Fred Mikelson-We have in the studio Dr. Ralph Graver, a specialist in the behavior of mammals, especially wolves. Doctor Graver, let me start by being blunt. Are these actually werewolves?

Ralph Graver-No, Fred, I don't believe they are, although they display some of the distinctive physical traits of wolves, the pointed ears, the elongated canine snout. This is something else altogether.

Fred Mikelson-Like what?

Ralph Graver-In East European mythology, the werewolf is an offshoot of the Lycanthrope, a mystical human who can shapeshift into a large animal, like a wolf or bear or lion. Although the European Lycanthrope can only be killed using silver, whether pummeled to death by something silver or the infamous silver bullet, these creatures last night could be killed in any manner that a human could. Many were torn apart or shot by regular bullets or run over with cars. Still, there could be a grain of truth in these myths, and it would be easier if we simply refer to them as Lycanthropes. It's as good a name as any.

Fred Mikelson-It does appear as though all of them changed back this morning in the daylight. What can you tell us about these creatures' behaviors?

Ralph Graver-Very little, as of yet. We need to study the people who have changed, as well as the ones who didn't. From the tapes I've watched, it seems that they become extremely animalistic, lacking anything resembling human social amenities. They exist simply to kill, eat, and reproduce. The basest needs of ourselves and of the animals these creatures seem to emulate.

Fred Mikelson-Food and sex?

Ralph Graver-Yes. I believe that's right, but we should know more in a few days. I do want to warn people that tonight there will be another full moon, just like last night. Taking precautions wouldn't be such a bad idea, especially if they have family members who did not transform yesterday.

Fred Mikelson-Dr. Graver, just what effect does the full moon have on the transformation?

Ralph Graver-Once again, we aren't sure. It could have something to do with the wavelength of the moonlight during a full moon, a physical catalyst to the change. Then again, several werewolf myths maintain it's related to the effect of the moon on tides. The blood is affected in a similar manner, you see? In any case, there's a full moon tonight, and there will be a full moon for a few hours on the following night. It's best not to take chances. If you didn't change, it's very important that you relocate to one of the shelters that we'll soon announce. We are in the process of setting up these shelters for such people, safe houses where they can sleep tonight. We need to interview them, to find out why they are immune to the metamorphosis. We also need to be sure they remain safe, even if that means hiding them someplace.

Fred Mikelson-We'll know more about that later, as the mayor, the vice mayor, the chief of police, and even this station's manager are still missing.

Ralph Graver-Well, if they haven't shown up yet, they're probably dead.

Fred Mikelson-Um… Thank you, Doctor Graver. More later. As a reminder, the rolling banner below shows places where you can receive medical attention as well as eat breakfast. They can tell you where to go in case the moon actually does bring about this metamorphosis tonight.

So far, we aren't sure about the extent of this epidemic. Phone lines are down, as is the electricity in most areas. We have managed to email a fellow television station in London, and they report that there've been no occurrences of the Lycanthrope Syndrome in Great Britain. This is also the case with affliates in Mexico and Australia. Our stations in New

York and Los Angeles report that there have been no sightings. In the meantime, we have sent a reporter with a camera to the Ohio River, where several people have reported sustained gunfire and explosions. When he returns, we hope to have more data, but it seems as though, so far, the phenomena is limited to the immediate Cincinnati area. Stay tuned...

CHAPTER 11

September 17, 11:55 a.m.

When Christian saw the damage the beast-men had inflicted upon his city, he could think of only one man who might have answers. Since living on the streets, he knew only one smart person: the old Frenchman who paid him for sexual favors… Jean. He was a scientist. He would know what was causing this insanity.

Christian knew where the old man lived, having eaten there, showered there, and sometimes transacted business there. Tracking down the old man was going to be difficult for him, as it added a lot of baggage. Still, if he was going to survive, unlike the mutilated corpses he was stepping over in the streets, he would need someone who could guide him. He would need an adult, even if it was some old dude who liked young guys.

He could, of course, return home, but the monsters that dwelled there were far more daunting than the ones that had run wild in the streets. The werewolf-things seemed to have gone away in the daylight, but his father's face always seemed more sinister in the morning, hiding his true visage behind a smile. He'd promised himself that he would never go back home, never have to withstand that life again. He would rather die.

Christian had learned to trust the old man, sensing something out of the ordinary about the way Jean treated him. Trust was a scarce commodity on the streets of the city. Once earned, it wasn't easy to dispatch. He'd misplaced his trust before... in his father, who had raped him and handed him over to other pedophiles. Once, he'd trusted his mother, but she'd been so busy looking the other way and attending social functions that she never noticed the bruises or the bleeding.

Christian had been on his own for long enough that he felt he couldn't trust anyone. Unscrupulous johns had beaten him and stolen his money. Bashers had chased him into dark alleys and kicked and clobbered him to a bloody pulp, their cries of "faggot" ringing in the night. Policemen often ignored him, or worse, demanded favors for their discretion.

But Jean Cowell, this old guy with a boy-toy fixation, had given Christian access to his apartment, his showers, and his food, bundling meals for him to take back to the warehouse. He had even offered to move Christian into his place, to take care of him, like a father, but Christian had already escaped the clutches of one father-rapist, and he didn't think he could live with another. He'd always believed that if worse came to worse, he could crash in the old man's extra room, but he hadn't arrived at that desperate point yet.

Until today.

He scrambled over puddles of blood to reach the classy apartment on Fourth Street, trying not to trip over any bodies, not to step in the remains of some poor soul. The farther he walked into the downtown area, the harder it became to avoid the corpses.

Jean's home was on the corner of Fourth and Plum, only five blocks away from the warehouse where Christian lived in his elevator. Still, it took almost an hour to reach the building. Cincinnati, it appeared, had erupted into a bubbling volcano of chaos.

He climbed over cars that were stalled in the streets, their batteries run down, doors gaping open. Once, when leaping back onto the ground, he put his foot through somebody's ribcage. The crunching sound made him sick, and the ribs seemed to clutch at his foot. He shook his leg violently to extract himself from the corpse's terrible grip.

At several points he encountered other people, lost souls who muttered to themselves, their eyes wide with shock and suspicion. One old lady, the left side of her face covered in blood, said a rosary while she fondled herself. A young couple threw a brick through the front window of a camera store.

Christian tried to steer a wide berth around them, preferring to trust only in himself. He'd had altercations with crazy street people before, and they were always stronger than they looked. Many of them were drug addicts, or they were mentally deranged in ways he'd never understood. Better to stick to the opposite side of the sidewalk and avoid dark alleys.

He didn't see any of the beast-men on the streets. The sun was shining, and if he looked into the sky, at the buildings towering around him, he could almost pretend nothing strange had occurred. Only a few shattered, smoking windows near the top of some skyscrapers spoiled the effect. He wondered how those windows had broken. Had people leapt from them?

Every few minutes he heard gunshots, usually from the Kentucky side of the river. A loud boom drowned out the rifle cracks. He wondered what wars were being waged beyond his vision.

When he reached the apartment complex, he noticed the door was ajar, barely hanging from one hinge. The awning over the entrance had been torn down, and the bit of fabric that remained flapped lazily in the breeze, a tattered, clawed mess. The doorman wasn't on duty, and there didn't seem to be anyone manning the desk in the lobby, so he tiptoed across the marble floor, amazed at the wreckage that had once been furniture, chairs and end tables. Now, it had been reduced to rubble, the pieces flung about the corners of the room.

The electricity was still out, so he couldn't take the elevator. Sighing, he thought, *Twenty-six fuckin' floors. Jean, you couldn't live near the bottom, could you? Oh well, may as well get started. This could take a while.*

His steps echoed in the stairwell, which was surprisingly devoid of dead bodies and garbage. The silence was creepier than the gibbering of the crazy people in the street.

Taking the stairs two at a time, he ascended to the sixteenth floor; he stopped, his hand clutching the guardrail, his breath coming in fast pants. The air was stifling and hot.

In the middle of the landing, near a small window, someone had dropped a Raggedy Anne doll. It lay face up, its empty eyes staring at the ceiling, its mouth stitched into a moonstruck grin, arms and legs akimbo. As Christian leaned over the doll, he saw a single drop of blood on the floor beside the doll's head, about an inch in diameter. It was a shocking reminder that things were seriously amiss with the world, that families, including small children, had recently dashed down these stairs, possibly running for their lives.

Children weren't exempt from the horrors of the night. Christian knew this better than most people.

Moving around it so he wouldn't put his foot in the stain, he continued his ascent.

A few floors higher, he heard someone open and shut one of the fire doors that led to the stairwell. The sound clanged off the cement walls, vibrant and alarming. He couldn't be sure that the person was an ally or an enemy, but he knew he had little recourse except to climb higher, to reach the twenty-sixth floor where he hoped to find Jean. He just prayed he wouldn't meet someone on the stairs

He wondered if the old man was even home. He could have been infected, too, could have roamed the streets, his fur a silver-tinged shade of brown, his muzzle grayed. Christian wasn't sure what he would find in the apartment.

But it was all he had to work with. A single lifeline to grab hold of, a final straw before he took to the streets in search of other survivors. If Jean were alive, and if he wasn't one of the beast-men, then he was company Christian could trust. He needed a friend, any sort of human companionship, more and more as the hours ticked by.

He stopped for a moment, listening to the echoes that haunted the stairway, lingering like memories almost lost to time. A shuffling overhead, a few soft footfalls, then the opening of yet another door, this one farther away from him.

That clinched it; there was another person in the building, and it sounded as though they were roaming the hallways one by one, attempting to find someone, a family member, or perhaps just anyone who had managed to survive. From the staggering number of bodies in the streets, Christian was certain that at least half the human population had died last night.

While he continued to climb the stairs, he kept himself wary of his surroundings. If someone attacked him, he would have to be fast, because he was thin and tired, inexperienced as a fighter. He had fled from danger many times in his brief life. Running had become his customary manner of dealing with adversity.

He arrived on the twenty-sixth-floor landing without incident. He was out of breath, and sweat drenched his hair and soaked through his shirt, sliding down his armpits and sides. Sitting on the top stair, he used his shirt to wipe the moisture from his face and chest. Once he caught his breath, he stood and opened the door to the hallway.

When he first stepped into the corridor, nothing seemed askew, but as he began to walk down the quiet passage, little things caught his eye. A picture on the wall in the hallway was tilted. Another had been clawed, five neat, parallel rips. Here and there on the thick white carpet, bloodstains blossomed, poppies of past savagery.

All the doors had been closed except Jean's. It was gaping wide, as though someone had deserted the place in a hurry. Christian stuck his head into the doorway.

"Hello?" he called. "Jean? You there?"

No one answered.

Taking a few steps into the apartment, he glanced around. The sofa had been overturned and shoved into a far corner near the kitchen, long tears in its fabric. The open kitchen was a jumble of broken glass and spoiling food that seeped from the open refrigerator. Very little meat remained. Lamps were on the floor, a dining room chair was smashed to splinters, and the windows had all been broken from the inside.

"Jean? Hey, old man, are you there?" Deep down, he knew the old Frenchman was gone. The apartment displayed the demeanor of a long-abandoned murder scene.

Closing the door behind himself, he decided to take a bath and wash the night off his skin. Then, maybe, a bit of dinner if the food wasn't all ruined, followed by a nap. His throbbing legs were tired from the climb, and he hadn't slept for more than a few hours the previous night.

The shower refreshed him, despite the chilliness of the water, and he put on a white, fluffy robe that had been wadded into a ball in a corner of the bathroom. It smelled of Jean's Old Spice cologne.

In the kitchen, he ate soup cold from the can. It would have been better warm, but without electricity, he wasn't sure how to heat it up without starting a fire and possibly burning the whole place down.

Christian remained discomfited by his concern for Jean. He knew he shouldn't feel anything for the old john, but he kept remembering little conversations they'd had when he had slept over in the big, feather bed.

"I can tell you are a smart boy," Jean had once told him as they lay beside each other, drifting toward sleep. The man's accent was thick. "I think you understand more about my research than you pretend. Did you like science in school?"

"Yeah. It was probably my favorite subject."

"Do you know Bio-Gen? The company I work for?"

"No. Don't know a whole lot about the real stuff out there, just the theoretical."

Jean had attempted to explain his research to Christian before, but the old man sprinkled his monologues with incomprehensible scientific jargon, and Christian no longer had time to ruminate over scientific advancement. He barely had time to figure out where his next dinner was coming from.

"Well," Jean said, "I should take you there one day, show you what I do, the vast importance of my work. I have been mapping out various aspects of the human genome, especially those that may be linked to violence in an early age. I believe I can put a stop to certain genetic psychoses, perhaps put a stop to certain kinds of violent crime. Think of it, Christian—a world without violence! I am very close to a solution. Then, we shall see whether my solution is viable."

"I don't think your boss would appreciate you bringing your teen-age boyfriend to work. Somehow, I think the company would frown on it."

"But Bio-Gen is a mere four blocks away. If I keep you hidden behind me…. No… no, you are correct. It would be distracting, possibly calamitous for me. Now that the work is almost finished. When I retire next year, you might consider being by my side? Huh?"

"Uh… yeah, sure. Hey, what's on TV tonight?"

It was simple, uncensored pillow talk, but it got Christian thinking. Maybe the old man was at work. If he had been worried about anything, it would have been his laboratory, his experiments; he was probably shacked up in the Bio-Gen building, cleaning up what was left of his notes and beakers of mysterious chemicals.

Only four blocks away.

Christian tossed his robe into a corner and stepped into his jeans.

The stairs were easier on the way down than they'd been during his ascent. Christian almost felt as if he were flying.

CHAPTER 12

Cathy Wright looked in her back yard at the white stone garden path that ran between hydrangea bushes. Past the white and yellow gazebo, she spied the shed where the gardener kept all of his mysterious tools and the lawn mower. The shed was made of pine wood, about twelve feet long and eight feet wide, braced by ornate wrought iron across the front of its doors. They'd purchased it because the gardener kept complaining that his rakes and hoes were going missing, the most recent victims of over-privileged kids who were bored out of their skulls and had nothing better to do. The two locks on the doors were probably overkill, but they hadn't had an incident of theft since they'd installed it.

"Karl," she called. He was somewhere in the house. She didn't care as long as he wasn't right next to her. She was still feeling the heebie-jeebies from his confession in the morning. "Karl, come out here."

Opening the screen door, she stepped into the back yard, feeling a momentary and, given her circumstances, rather silly burst of pride over the flower gardens. She walked toward the shed, past the tiger lilies, listening for the steps of her husband behind her. She'd nearly reached it when she heard the door from the kitchen open.

"Yeah," Karl said, stepping outside. "What is it?"

"I just thought of something."

She placed her hands on the side of the shed and shoved as hard as she could. There was a slight rocking motion, but the window-less structure appeared to be as stalwart as she had hoped. Trying again, she barely felt the wood jostle.

"The shed," she said.

"I can see that." Karl's voice conveyed a certain impatience. "What of it?"

She turned back to him. "You and I both think you're going to change again, right?"

"Well… we don't really know that…"

"We need to have you in a safe place, some place where you can't hurt me. Or anyone else, for that matter. After last night, I'm scared of being too close to you. I'm sorry, Karl, but there it is. You scare me."

"You want to lock me in the fucking garden shed?" His voice deepened like it always did when he was pissed off.

"Just for the night. You didn't change until the night, after we'd gone to bed at 7:30, and you reversed back to yourself in the morning, when the sun came out. Am I right about this so far?"

"Yeah." He rubbed his jaw, his other hand tracing small circles on the side of his thigh through his jeans.

"Then you'll change again tonight, when it gets dark."

"Probably."

"You're going to come after me again, Karl. We both know it."

He ran his fingers through his graying, thinning hair, and deep furrows lined his forehead. "You think that little shed will hold me? I don't remember a lot, but I do remember the power I felt, the new muscles. I was pretty damn strong."

She nodded. "You were. It was scary, and I don't want to go through it again. Tell you what… we have a nice dinner, about five o'clock. Then, when dusk starts falling, I lock you in the shed."

"I don't like it." He crossed his arms, pouting like an insolent child.

"Well, Karl, if you have a better idea, this is a good time to present it. I'm starting to get sick of all this whining and moping. You're a hardcore litigator, a real man of business; I always thought you were tougher than this."

"Oh, I'm weak? Is that what you're saying? Are you starting to take the boy's side after all this time? 'Poor Karl, he just can't control himself...'"

Not this again, Cathy thought. *I can't get into this bullshit now.*

"No," she answered. "I'm just telling you that you're being a baby about it. 'Poor me, I turned into a monster.' In case you didn't notice, I was the one you tried to kill. I was the one who was almost a victim here. You're going to try to eat me again. Don't deny it, Karl. I don't want it to happen, so I'm being pro-active."

He looked at her a moment, and the creases in his forehead lessened, then vanished. His hand stopped its incessant circling motion against his leg.

"I'm an ass," he mumbled.

She moved to his side, took his hand in hers. Softening her voice, she said, "No, you're just messed up. I'd be just as confused had I been the one affected. Still, it wasn't me, and I don't fancy turning into werewolf chow. We need to keep me protected, and you need to be restrained from harming anyone. Maybe the shed can do that for us." Karl glanced at the structure. He didn't think it was sturdy enough to contain him, but at least it was an option.

Options were getting harder to come by in this freakish new world.

Nodding, he said, "Okay. We'll try it, but I want you locked in the house as well. Lock every door and window..."

"Some of them are smashed," she reminded him.

"Well, then. We'd best be getting to work boarding them up. Come on, Cathy. We'll pretend it's a new home improvement project we're working on."

Leading her into the house, he resisted the itching beneath his skin. Cathy, in turn, pretended not to notice his twitching fingers.

They began to board up the windows, the hammer falls echoing throughout Indian Hills. They almost sounded like gunshots.

CHAPTER 13

September 17, 3:45 p.m.

Chesya peered over the counter to the window; the name of the diner, printed backwards from her angle, partially obscured her view of the street.

The place still reeked of grease from their last meal, and a slice of half-eaten apple pie lay before her.

Sitting on the other side of the counter, Rick shoveled the last of his own extra-large slice into his mouth. He dropped the fork and looked up at her, noticing her stillness.

"What?" he asked, mouth still half-full.

"There are people out there. And I don't mean the crazy people, but couples and families. They're just… walking around. Like zombies or shell-shocked soldiers. I just noticed them."

"Probably just now daring to come outside." He brushed his face with his napkin, feeling the rough stubble of his beard beneath the paper.

The television played in the background, a constant buzz. Occasionally, they heard some new tidbit of information from the news anchor, who had remained in his chair all day. There were no commercials. Even the money-grubbing networks seemed to acknowledge this was a state of emergency.

They had hung up the useless phone in the corner of the place, and they nervously awaited any kind of ring. From time to time, one of them checked it for a dial tone, to no avail.

"The doors are locked, right?" Rick asked.

Chesya nodded. "Checked them a few minutes ago."

"You think there'll be problems?"

"People are bound to act according to their worst natures. They want to get food for their families, someplace safe for the night. Some fools'll try to make some money out of this situation… looting, stealing. Who knows?"

As they watched, a young man with a beard pulled a blond woman alongside. They looked around, as though dazed. The woman was pregnant.

"I hate ignoring them like this," Chesya said, sitting opposite Rick. "Especially when we have food to spare."

"Well, we have it now. It isn't going to last. Much as we want, we can't just let anyone walk in off the street for a free lunch."

"It would be the Christian thing to do."

"It'd be the stupid thing to do," Rick said. "You let people in here, we'll have dozens of them, and who's to say which ones are all right and which ones will try to hurt us, try to take away what we found? This is our restaurant. We found it, cleared out the bodies. I lay claim to it."

"That woman was pregnant."

"There's plenty of food for them out there," Rick said. "I'm more worried about who's going to change into those monsters. We don't even know when they'll do it."

"The news said it happens at night, when the moon is shining. Something about a reaction to moonlight."

"You believe everything you hear on TV? Especially now?"

"No," she replied.

"Good. As far as anyone knows right now, that's the truth, but I don't wanna risk it. Do you?"

She shook her head, staring down into the remains of her pie. "No." Her voice cracked.

"That's right. You wanna bring in a dozen people, hell, five people, and have them change on us in here? We got a padlocked back door and one way out the front. Options are pretty limited."

"I still don't like it. It feels... mean, somehow."

He moved around the counter, put a hand on her shoulder. He was surprised to find it shaking. "I know," he said. "I don't like it much, either. But we need to be sure. Neither of us became creatures last night. We're certain that we're each safe to be around. Anyone else, I want to watch them first, watch them sit in the moonlight and not change. Then, and only then, will I trust them."

Chesya had to admit it made sense, but as she watched the numbed survivors marching blindly down the street, she felt a deep pang of guilt. A family strode by, two little girls holding hands. One of the girls, her eyes glazed with shock, turned her head and looked into the dimness of the diner. She raised her hand in a halfhearted wave. Chesya started to wave back, but the child had passed from sight.

"So what do we do, Rick? You planning on staying here all day, boarding up the windows? I saw that in an old black-and-white zombie flick, and it didn't work for the people then. I don't think it'll work now. Those things were so strong. They got themselves killed doing just what we're doing... watching television."

"I thought we'd head for the bank again. Lock ourselves in the vault. You said there were a couple of days left on the battery's power."

"It was safe there," she agreed.

"Nothing's going to get through all that steel, not even those damn werewolves... bears... whatever the hell they are."

A chill ran through her. "I don't like it, getting locked in like that. Don't get me wrong, I'll do it to save my life. But it gives me the willies."

"How do you think I feel?" he asked. "I went bat shit in there last night. But I don't see a lot of other options."

The news anchor droned on. "I've just been handed an update. Police officials have contracted several tow-truck companies to clear the streets. If you have an automobile parked or trapped in traffic, please find the car and remain near it. If an owner is with his or her car, they will not tow it to storage. If your car is towed, it will be safely stored in a nearby field or yard. Your local police station will have details as to which cars went to which holding place. It may take several days, but the roads will soon be clear of debris. Authorities also wish to warn that if you have family, keep them near at all times. The police highly recommend that you do not wait with your car through the day. If you have an automobile trapped in traffic, it will be towed to a safe area, and you can reclaim it when officials decide it is safe. This should take no more than a day or two, and we suggest everyone go home and wait until the tow trucks have cleared all streets. Do not separate from your family. More details will follow.

"In other news, the vice mayor was discovered in her home, the victim of an apparent suicide, a single shot from a pistol registered in her name. The mayor of Cincinnati has yet to be found; he is presumed dead.

"This is just one of many suicides blamed upon recent events. In the few notes that have been discovered, the deceased all state that guilt drove them to suicide. Many people seem to have been psychologically damaged by the violence they committed while under the influence of the Lycanthrope Syndrome. We have local psychiatrist Dr. Ford Bradley in the studio to tell us…"

Chesya reached up, placing her dark hand over Rick's pale one, pressing it farther into the meat of her shoulder. She knew she shouldn't feel comforted by this evil man, this bank robber, but the contact reassured her more than any words could.

Human contact.

Skin on skin.

Outside the diner, more people shambled past.

"I think you're right," she said. "We'll head for the bank before it gets dark, seal ourselves in the vault. We can figure out more in the morning."

"I believe it's the smart thing to do," he said. "We might even get some sleep."

Watching the people walk past the diner, the empty faces, the questioning looks, she knew he was right.

Suspicion lingered in the air like a foul odor. Nobody knew whom to trust. Many didn't even trust themselves.

Chesya said, "Let's stock up on supplies to take with us, all right?"

"Sounds like a good idea," Rick answered.

They moved towards the back room, carefully stepping over the bodies of the owner and his wife. Chesya tried not to look, but she found herself compelled to glance at the dead people. Shivering, she followed Rick into the rear of the diner.

CHAPTER 14

September 17, 5:25 p.m.

When Christian started his trek to Bio-Gen, the streets were teeming with people. It was as though all of the survivors that had disappeared into their homes that morning had all decided to walk around the city at the same time. Families wandered through the parking lots that had once been busy city streets, some sitting on their cars, waiting for the tow trucks to free them. Others were searching for loved ones. They called out names into the boisterous, urban symphony.

One family rested against a Ford Taurus, obviously laying claim to the car. The man had his arm around the woman's shoulders, and the children played between the stranded automobiles. The wife had laid out a picnic supper on the hood of the car, and the husband calmly ate a chicken leg, as if refuting the state of the world, ignoring all of the events of the previous night, a lovely family picnic held in the middle of catastrophe, even as, thirty feet away, two men were arguing, swearing at each other, and pointing at crumpled fenders.

Christian concluded that they were fighting over whose insurance would pay for the accident. As though insurance still existed. As though any of it really mattered anymore.

He could still see the street-crazies, wide, watery eyes staring out from the darkness of alleyways, from behind the protection of Dumpsters. Preferring not to get involved, they scurried like cockroaches away from the light. Christian supposed they chose the relative safety of the shadows over the glaring, noisy, highly-populated light of the streets. Shadows couldn't change into ferocious beasts. Shadows couldn't harm you. Shadows didn't argue or lie or fail you. They only hid you, cloaked your sins so that others couldn't see them.

Hadn't he been hiding in an elevator in a warehouse until this very morning? Hadn't he escaped from this very same smiling family bull-shit, happy faces that hid deep secrets and even deeper wounds? His father had smiled just like the man with the chicken leg.

One tall African-American man, his shirt shredded in several places, his cheeks stippled with garbage and blood, glared at the boy as he stepped past him. Then, silently, he backed away, his face obscured by the shadows.

Glancing nervously at the sky, Christian saw that the sun was set-ting. He didn't want to be caught on the street in the dark. If the monsters didn't get him, the street people would. He picked up the pace, clambering over the stalled cars. He eased his way around a pile of hot dog carts, tipped on their sides. He could smell the rotting meat.

The city bristled with more and more life. A young man held a girl's hand, his eyes scanning the horizon. Another man led a ten-year-old boy through the maze of trapped machinery, never pausing to look down at the child. Other people spoke with their new friends, rationally discussing the strange things that were happening.

He didn't see any of the tow trucks that were supposed to be clear-ing the streets, but he heard from several people that the problem was extensive. Highways were blocked, side streets were full of wreckage. Power lines and phone lines were down, lying like inert snakes along roadsides. It would be a long time before the tow trucks made a passage through the mess.

Christian saw the doors, but for a moment he didn't register the words painted upon them. Exhaustion was eating its way through his bones, acidic and debilitating. When he finally focused enough to read the sign that said "Bio-Gen," he grew more determined.

He had to find Jean.

He had to ask the old man what was happening.

He wanted to feel safe again.

Christian opened the door and went inside.

While he had been playing house in Jean's apartment that morning, he had scribbled down the old man's office number, which he had discovered on a piece of junk mail that Jean had brought home from the lab. Office number 316. It was on the third floor.

Sighing, Christian began to search for the stairwell, amazed at the cleanliness of the lobby. Other than a capsized desk, it didn't seem to have been traumatized by the beasts.

A phone lay on the floor, still attached to the wall, and he dashed towards it. Listening to the receiver, he let out a frustrated sigh. He should have expected it, but the lack of a dial tone confirmed his worst fears about the damage sustained by the city overnight.

Christian was unnerved by the sterility of the hallway, the lack of any signs or art on the white walls, the floors shining and scrubbed and buffed clean. His sneakers squeaked as he walked down the long corridor that led from the lobby. He passed the doors, labeled 101, 103, 105, and so on. These were the rooms where Jean had toiled.

Again, Christian wondered why he was here looking for the old man, despite his need for answers and companionship. No matter how kind the Frenchman had been to him, he had still used him for his own needs, had still taken away some small part of Christian. The boy could almost taste the old man in his mouth, and perspiration broke out across his forehead. He wiped away the cool, wet sweat.

The walls in his home in Indian Hills had always seemed wet to him, as if sweating from the effort of hiding secrets from the neighbors. The rough hands that shook him awake late at night, the same callused hands that held his head down, shoved his face into the pillows... sometimes they belonged to his father, and sometimes they ended in the hairy, muscular arms of his father's buddies. Their breath always reeked of alcohol and cloves, cigarettes and sin.

107, 109, 111...

His mother had watched him carefully during the day, terrified that he might leak the clandestine proclivities of his father. In turn, Christian had observed her hesitant motions, her tired, half-lidded eyes. Christian believed she knew all about what her husband was doing, and she did nothing to change him. She didn't grab her boy and run. She embraced the monster, slept with him after he'd washed the sperm from his belly, kissed him on the same lips he'd used to ravage her son. She must have known about it. She had to. How could anyone be so naïve?

To all appearances, they were a perfect family.

113, 115, 117...

After he ran away from that house, he could still smell the sweat from the rapists. He could still feel their taint on his skin. It was two weeks before he managed to stink enough from his lack of bathing to cover up the stench of defilement.

When he had met another runaway, a boy younger than himself, he had thought the friendship would last. He'd been tired and hungry and thin as a rail. The boy, whose name Christian had forgotten, had told him how to make money for food. He'd shown him where to find older men, safer men, men with wives and kids at home. These were men with secrets, and men with secrets would give money away in order to keep those secrets buried.

119, 121, 123...

He'd been repulsed by the thought of another man touching him that way, horrified that the abuse would start again. He'd resisted for as long as he could, passing the parking garages and vacant lots where such men gathered. These weren't typical gay men, men who accepted who they were and built good, solid lives despite adversity. They weren't the type of homosexuals Christian respected. These men were liars, telling themselves they were straight, respectable citizens, who had wives and families and mortgages, living lives half-shadowed, darkened by the subterfuge. Soon, Christian found it difficult to think of them as men at all. They were something else. Something dead.

It made giving in to them easier.

125, 127, 129...

At first, he vomited after having sex with these nocturnal creatures, vampires with fetishes for young flesh. It was a reflex, regurgitated memories of his father and his buddies. Eventually, though, he'd been able to act charming to the men. That's all it had been: acting. Once upon a time, as a student, he'd been a member of the drama club. He had even scored a role in a school production of *Carousel.* But that was before...

Christian found a fire door and a red sign that showed a Keith Har-ing-type figure descending a flight of stairs with flames roaring behind him. Shoving the door open, he began to ascend the stairs. The heavy door clanged shut behind him, the sound ringing off the concrete walls.

Entering the third story, he found himself in a hallway identical to the one on the first floor. No art adorned the glossy white walls. He took in his surroundings and headed toward room 316. His footfalls echoed in the halls.

When he found Jean's office, he skidded to a stop. The door was missing, torn from its hinges and tossed someplace. On the wall, beside the nameplate that read "Doctor Jean Cowell," someone had left a single, bloody handprint. A few dribbles had trickled from the print, etching crimson trails to the floor. Christian peered around the corner and into the old man's office.

"Jean?" he whispered, the sound alarming in the quiet. "Jean, are you there? It's Christian."

There was no answer; he took a few steps into the room.

"Aw, shit," he said.

He turned away for a few moments, swallowing bile. This was a man he'd known, and the familiarity made it a hundred times worse than any of the anonymous dead people in the streets. He felt sweat on his forehead, and he knew he had to enter the office, had to know for certain Jean was dead. Turning, he moved towards the body.

Amidst a flurry of papers, Jean lay facedown on his desk, his wrinkled head in a pool of blood. It was tacky-looking, so Christian thought he had died much earlier in the day. The pistol he had used to shoot himself lay three inches from his right hand. A spattering of gore soaked the wall behind him, a small bullet hole exposed in the center of the blood and brain. A book lay on the floor by Jean's right elbow, spattered by the spray from the old man's temple.

Moving into the office, Christian stepped on shards of broken glass. The entire room was torn apart. If a cyclone had swept through the place, it wouldn't have looked more chaotic.

He took the pistol from the desk and checked for bullets: five in the chamber. He flicked it shut again like the police on television. Even though it seemed like he was robbing a grave, he knew the gun would prove useful. He knew it was important that he arm himself.

Could a bullet stop one of those things from last night? It seemed a feeble defense. But it was better than nothing.

"Jean," he said, addressing the corpse. "Why? You couldn't wait? You couldn't help me out? You were always there to help me out. What the hell did you do? What was so awful that you had to go and kill yourself?"

As if in answer, he heard a voice, heavily accented, crying out down the hall. "Help me! Is somebody there? For God's sake, help me!"

CHAPTER 15

September 17, 5:15 p.m.

Chesya eyed the darkening sky with a sinking feeling of dread, then she looked over at Rick, who was smoking a cigarette. He'd smashed into the machine and nabbed several packs, two of which he had tossed into their "survival bag." They had found a large shopping bag in the back of the diner and had packed it with cans of peaches and potted meat, along with a can opener and a loaf of bread. A six-pack of bottled water was the heaviest item, but they also scrounged several large knives, some tuna, toilet paper, matches, toothpaste and razors from the dead couple's medicine cabinet, a pack of aspirin, bandages, and the keys to the diner. Rick had checked the gun the couple had used to commit suicide, but the chamber was empty, so he left it behind. They each already had a gun, so one more wouldn't help, especially if it was out of bullets. The bag was heavy, but not drastically so. It wouldn't get in their way.

"It's starting to get dark out there," Chesya warned.

Looking up at the front door, Rick said, "We'd better get moving."

"I keep thinking we've forgotten something."

"Well, if we did, it can't be too important. Let's go."

They stepped out into the evening, and the cool air hit Chesya in the face, a breeze blowing on a balmy September day. She inhaled deeply, tired of the stale air of the diner, which smelled depressingly of eggs and bacon and grease. The fresh air invigorated her.

When Rick was finished locking the door, he said, "We found this place. I don't want to lose it if we don't have to."

Chesya nodded. "It's not too far from the bank, but I'll feel a lot safer when we get there."

"I know what you mean."

All around them, hundreds of people milled through the stalled cars, leaning against buildings, lying supine on the hoods of vehicles. Some of them conversed intently with others, but most of them watched Rick and Chesya as they passed, their eyes asking unanswerable questions, curiosity piqued. Shadow-hiders skirted around the periphery of the scene.

Through the maze of stalled cars, a heavyset man in a crewneck sweater chased a screaming woman. They disappeared into an alley, and a low, gurgling scream issued from the darkness. As Rick and Chesya passed, the young woman emerged, her mouth and throat streaked with fresh blood. She giggled, moving towards them.

"Rick," Chesya warned, and he flashed his gun.

The woman, apparently not too regressed to understand how the pistol worked, laughed as she retreated into the alleyway.

"You think all these people changed last night?" Chesya asked, breathing a sigh of relief.

"I dunno. Probably most of them. Outta the whole bank staff and my crew, only you and I didn't become creatures. Oh, and the dude I knocked out. I don't like the odds with this many out in the open. Didn't anyone listen to the news? They should be at home."

"Well, you know how people are. Most of them don't have a lick of sense. Probably blame a liberal media bias," she said. "What do you think will happen when it gets dark? When the moon rises again?"

"I don't even want to think about it," he said. "I just wanna hole up in that vault where it's nice and safe and wait for morning."

They passed a car that contained a family of four, windows rolled up, doors locked, radio blaring. Rick caught some of the broadcast.

"... stay in your homes. If the metamorphosis happens again, you must take cover immediately. It's not known if the process will occur again this evening, but authorities say that if you... became altered last night, if you became a... beast, then you should try to lock yourself in a room in your house. If you did not change last night, it's suggested that you find a safe place to hide, somewhere secure. Forget about your cars until morning…"

Chesya heard it, too, and she looked back at Rick. "I don't think anyone's paying attention to any authority," she said.

Some of the families, especially those with small children, began to disperse. They weaved their way between cars. Most of the people on the street avoided eye contact with each other. Rick wondered if they were ashamed of the animal state they had embodied. Or were they simply embarrassed because of what they had done while they were in animal form?

Does a beast feel shame?

"How many more blocks?" Rick asked.

"Two. We better step it up," Chesya said. "It's getting darker."

"It's just the tall buildings. They block the sun. Maybe they'll block the moonlight, too."

"You are really starting to think that these are werewolves, aren't you?"

He nodded, climbing over the hood of a car. A man shouted, "Hey! You can't do that!" Rick ignored him, helping Chesya over the hood. The man shook his fist at them, swearing, but he did nothing to stop their progress.

"Well, if it looks like a werewolf and acts like a werewolf…"

"I know," she said. "It just seems weird saying it. It's like we suddenly found out that all those terrible things we thought were lurking under the bed were real all along. Mom lied to us. There really is a boogeyman."

"Yeah," Rick said. "And the boogeyman's been inside of us all along."

"I wonder how long it's been there, waiting to be released?"

He shrugged, shoving his way through a crowd of teenagers who were drinking beers. They looked to be about fifteen or sixteen. A few of them shouted at Rick and Chesya, but most just laughed, drunk, happy to be together. One fell on his ass, and the group roared its approval. One of the teens leapt off the car and started kicking his fallen comrade as the others cheered.

Lighting a cigarette, Rick said, "These people…"

"Just about a block left to go," Chesya said.

"... don't they see the danger? Don't they wonder if it's all gonna start again when it gets dark?"

"Maybe they don't care. There's bound to be a percentage of the population that actually likes reverting to their animal instincts. A lot of them would probably embrace it. There are all kinds of wackos out there, serial killers and such. They're gonna love the change."

"That's so fuckin'... I mean, that's so sick."

She grinned at him. "Thanks for censoring yourself. Even if it was too late."

"Yeah, well..." Taking a last drag, he flicked the cigarette into an alley.

"Hey, look. There's the bank."

As they approached the building, edging around the Brink's truck that lay on its side like some saurian turtle, Rick saw that looters had infiltrated the broken windows of the building. Even more glass had been busted out from the window frames, and the bags of money they had left behind were missing. The vault door was gaping wide, and all the safety deposit boxes had been ripped open, probably with a crowbar. Documents and inferior jewelry littered the floor of the vault.

"All the money's gone," Chesya said. She looked at Rick, waiting for a reaction—disappointment, anger, anything.

He sighed. "Doesn't seem so important all of a sudden."

She nodded. "It's getting pretty dark out there. What time is it?"

Glancing at the watch he'd stripped from the dead diner-owner's hand, he answered, "Almost seven o'clock."

"Then we'd better set up house for the night."

He dropped the bag of necessities from his shoulder, letting it fall to the floor of the bank vault. He thought, *It's kind of dark in here.*

"Oh, no," Chesya moaned.

"What?"

"No lights," she said, flipping the switch several times, willing it to turn on the fluorescent bulbs. "The electricity's out. The battery must have died. Maybe from having the vault door open all day. I don't get it. The manager always said..."

"Does this mean what I think it means?" Rick asked.

Something outside the bank howled, low and mournful. The hairs on the back of his head stood up, one by one.

"It means we can't stay in the vault. The air won't circulate, the lights won't come on. The timer on the lock is out for some reason. Maybe sabotage."

A second howl, this one lower, growling, joined the first.

"It means," she said. "We don't have any safe place to stay tonight."

CHAPTER 16

September 17, 6:50 p.m.

Cathy Wright placed a bag of groceries on the floor of the shed in her back yard, just a few things she had thrown together from the kitchen. She caught sight of her bicycle, neglected in a corner of the structure. Years ago, she had made a point to ride it every day, even entering in some races, but as years of marriage and luxury sped by, she had forgotten the bike. Her muscles, once so hard and strong, had become flabby. She thought she might start riding again, after everything had settled back to normal.

If anything were ever normal again.

Looking down at the bags of food, she sighed. She hadn't trusted the freshness of the meat in her refrigerator. The electricity had remained disconnected. The bread was still good, and she had made Karl peanut butter sandwiches with juice to drink. There were also some oranges, a pear, and a couple of granola bars.

It didn't seem right, somehow, providing her husband with such a pathetic meal. Over the years, as their lifestyle had become more grandiose, they had eaten out more than they had cooked, and there was a woman who came in to make their dinner and clean the kitchen every evening. Cathy had grown accustomed to this little bustling woman. She wondered if the woman—what was her name again?—was still alive.

Running a hand through her hair and heading back towards the house, she realized she had grown accustomed to a great many things. Karl was so successful they rarely did without. If she saw a dress or a hat that she desired, she simply charged it. When she asked for a new car because the last one was two years old, Karl bought her a lovely BMW. A gardener took care of the lawn and landscaping, a maid cleaned the house, and the cook worked her magic in the kitchen, a room that pretty much stupefied Cathy.

Trying to remember a time when she had been forced to take care of everything herself, Cathy discovered she really couldn't recall such a period. Her parents had been well-to-do. They had paid for her college and her room and board so that she did not have to work while studying French literature at an Ivy League school. She had met Karl at a dance thrown by her sorority, and they married six weeks after graduation.

A weed poked through the stone sidewalk, and she leaned down, pinched it off, and tossed it into the yard. Now the sidewalk was perfect, beautiful in its sloping curve of white stone. Smiling, she brushed her hands on her jeans.

Opening the back door into the kitchen, she realized things would never be quite the same. Even if this bizarre metamorphosis had been a one-night event, people were going to be different. She wondered again why she was immune to the symptoms that had claimed her husband and neighbors and, according to the battery-operated radio in the kitchen, most everyone in the tri-state area. It seemed odd that, out of so many people, she had been the one graced with an exemption.

Washing her hands in the sink (which sparkled from her cleaning earlier), she called out to her husband. "Karl, I have the shed ready for you. I put a six-pack of bottled water out there for you, too."

He stepped into the room. He had showered and shaved and had put on khaki slacks and an Arrow button-down shirt. He looked almost normal, except for the bruises on his arms and the cut below his right eye.

He had claimed he still felt hairy on the inside, she reminded herself.

"Is that what you're wearing?" she asked, joking.

"If you have any suggestions, I'd be willing to hear them." He leaned against the center island in the kitchen. "Seriously, I'm comfortable in these clothes."

"I'd think jeans or sweats would be more comfortable."

He shrugged. "You work enough hours in a certain kind of outfit, you get used to it. Also, and I know this sounds stupid, but I feel more… well, human in these clothes. More respectable. Less savage."

"Are you ready?"

"I don't know. It's going to be cramped and wet and…"

"You can take a bit of discomfort, Karl. This is to protect you from doing something you'll regret tomorrow, and to protect me from having to defend myself against you."

"I know, honey," he said, whining. "I know. It's just… degrading."

"You want to know what's degrading? Having to sit across a table from you, listening to you talk about drinking blood and chasing prey through the streets, and acting as though it were the normal thing to do nowadays. I had to be a good wife. I couldn't turn away from you in revulsion, because a good wife doesn't do that. She supports her husband. I've supported you before, if you remember. But this good wife wants to be here in the morning."

"I'm a jackass." He looked sheepish, younger than his years.

"Yes, you are," she said, kissing him on the forehead. "Now, let's get you locked up safe and sound."

They held hands as they walked down the garden path. The shed seemed rather small to Cathy now. Cramped and frail. The wood didn't appear nearly as sturdy as it had in the noontime sun. The shadows of dusk seemed to eat away the soundness of the little structure, like some fungus that deteriorated the boards.

Karl gave her a peck on the cheek, fleeting and insubstantial. She had been ready to kiss him on the lips, but he turned his head, saying, "I love you, Cathy. Know that. After everything…"

She touched her cheek, the residue of the kiss still evaporating. "I do know that, Karl. And I love you, too." Her words seemed hollow.

From within the darkness of the shed, his face glowed. It reminded her of Marlon Brando in that Vietnam movie she hated so much and that Karl adored. He nodded to her once.

"Do it," he said.

And then his face melted back into the shadows.

Fumbling a bit, Cathy closed the shed's door and used a key to clinch it. She latched it with two padlocks, one which Karl had installed earlier that day. As her husband had instructed, she also overturned the wheelbarrow in front of the door, digging it into the ground, just one more safety precaution.

Moving toward the house, she raised a hand to her face, touching the spot where he had kissed her. She wondered if this was the last kiss she would ever receive from him. She wanted to rush back to the shed, hold his head in her hands and kiss him passionately, feel his hand roaming over her body... at least one more time.

As they had kissed... so long before...

Passion had been absent from their marriage since the second year. Instead of a wild sex life, they had settled into something different, but just as nice in its own way. They had grown familiar with each other, their friendship deepening. They still loved each other. She had witnessed it in his eyes just a moment earlier, or at least it was deceptively close. Still, she felt this would have been a time for passion. This would have been the occasion for a real kiss. It could have compensated for so much that had gone wrong.

After securing all three locks on the kitchen door, she moved into the dining room. She shoved the heavy table against the kitchen door. If Karl was going to come after her, she decided to make it as difficult as possible.

In the hall, she struggled to shift a bureau so that it blocked the doorway. It took a few minutes, and she could hear the China tinkling inside. She also blocked the top of the stairway with two small end tables.

Finally, she locked herself in the second-story bathroom, using three locks, two of which Karl had installed. Pulling the final dead bolt into position, she exhaled.

The little window provided a view of the back yard, the stone pathway, and part of the shed. She put the toilet seat down and sat on it, watching the shadows of the trees elongate, hand-like apparitions that reached for her. Grabbing a bag of potato chips, she started to eat them, compulsively tossing one after another into her mouth.

Somehow, even with all the precautions they had taken, she didn't feel safe.

She tried to remember the last time she had truly felt safe and secure in her marriage. It must have been before the troubles, before the terrible accusations.

The first animalistic growling that she heard came from the street in front of her house. She waited for it to begin in the shed.

PART 2

CHAPTER 17

September 17, 5:58 p.m.

Christian rushed towards the sound of the crying man. The shouts were tricky to pinpoint, because the empty hallways of Bio-Gen amplified and bounced them back and forth. He stopped to get a better fix on the direction.

"Help me, please! I hear you out there. Please, help me." The cries sounded raspy, indicating that the screamer had been calling out for some time. There also seemed to be an accent to the words. Russian, Serbo-Croatian? Christian wasn't sure, but the man's hard consonants, like his C's and K's, contained a harsh vibrato; his vowels seemed to be drawn out, spoken in broader tones.

Christian prayed the shouter wasn't laying down some sort of trap, luring him into a darkened room only to pounce upon him. Confidence in human nature didn't come easy to him. And the mayhem last night hadn't helped. For all he knew, the voice calling him belonged to one of the beast-men, alone and hungry in this maze of an office building.

But, the cries had seemed to be genuine. They seemed to be coming from a person in need of help.

"Oh, God, are you still out there?" the voice came again, low and guttural. The accent was even more pronounced. "Is anybody out there? I am starving in here. I am dying. " In his native language, the shouter added, "Ya ne mogu bolshe terpet'. Esus Hristos, Ya molius, shto-bi ti poslal mne kovo-nibud na pomosh. Pozhaluista…."

Christian closed his eyes, decided the voice was coming from his left, maybe only a few doors down the corridor. Turning, he raced down the hallway, his feet smacking the floor, pounding like his heartbeat. He burst into one of the rooms where the voice seemed to originate. It was another office, vacated or abandoned, very much like Jean's, only in pristine condition. Even the garbage cans had been emptied.

Immediately, the cries resumed. "Please, you are so close. I hear you. Please, to not let an unhappy man suffer."

As Christian opened the next door, the shadows in the hallway began to stretch. Night was approaching. He needed a safe place to hide, and he didn't have time to return to his elevator.

The entry opened onto a huge room, a laboratory from the look of it. The door was heavy as it swung open. Locks and bars covered the back of it—protection taken to extremes. Three long tables were arranged into a cross formation, metal folding chairs scattered around it. At the far right side of the room sat three oak desks, each covered and surrounded by papers. One of the desks still sported a nameplate—"Jean Cowell." Bits of glass had sprayed in every direction, covering the floor with a gleaming layer of sharp edges. A single painting of boats on a river hung on the far wall. Above the third desk, someone had printed the words "I'm sorry" in ragged letters of blood, the writing child-like, the sentiment murky and smeared.

As he entered the room, Christian saw the body, a man, lying behind one of the three desks, his corpse surrounded by shards of ruined beakers. Blood had pooled around the body, congealing throughout the day. Shoddy, amateurish, ragged wounds disfigured the skin from the man's wrists to his elbows. The suicide disturbed Christian, as had Jean's, yet he felt himself moving towards the dead man.

He had to be sure.

When he had almost reached the body, noting that the man's chest wasn't moving, Christian heard something move behind him.

"Thank God," came that heavily accented voice, crackling at the edges, exhausted.

Spinning, Christian saw what the door had obscured from him as he had walked into the lab. The entire left side of the room appeared to be a prison. A Plexiglas barrier separated the cell from the rest of the room, ascending all the way to the ceiling and stretching from wall to wall. A door had been cut into the shielding, replete with six heavy-duty locks, and a circle of small holes, barely large enough for a housefly to fit through the Plexiglas, were placed at face level. The holes reminded Christian of the pattern cut into a telephone receiver, and he knew this was used to communicate with the man inside the cell.

The naked man.

Pressed against the Plexiglas, his hands pushing against the barrier, the man appeared to be in his late forties. His bearded face was a mask of terror, his blue eyes opened wide, his mouth a slice of grimace. His body was muscular with broad shoulders and a thick waist, but the man was not very tall. He had the sort of stocky shape usually associated with Rugby players. His body was rather hirsute, with curly, wiry hair that covered even his shoulders.

His cell took up about twelve-by-twenty feet of the room, a good fourth of the laboratory's square footage. In the corner were a stained toilet, a couple of rolls of toilet paper, and a cheap air freshener. The bed was situated against the opposing wall, tiny, but it looked comfortable... softer than the stained, burnt, discarded mattresses Christian had been using in the warehouse. A night table and bureau were placed on either side of the bed, the night table supporting a lamp and a few books. By the lamp, there was an overstuffed chair, a television, and a small stereo unit. Several DVDs and CDs were placed on various surfaces. All in all, if you had to be imprisoned somewhere, this was the way to do it.

"Please, to help me?" the naked man asked, and Christian could see the worry lines in his face deepen. "I... I have not eaten in two days."

"Who locked you in there?" Christian asked.

"I am... so very hungry."

The boy moved towards the Plexiglas barrier of the cell. It reminded him of the bug jars in which he'd imprisoned praying mantises when he was a child. Something about the way you could view what had been captured from every possible angle. Even the tiny holes cut in the Plexiglas... air holes?

"First, tell me who you are," Christian demanded.

"So hungry… they feed me by now usually, but Dr. Hodder over there, he kill himself today. I have to stay here and watch him die. I could do nothing. Nothing."

"Why are you in there? What did you do?"

The man's eyes darted across the floor, as preoccupied as his mind. "He cut himself. Bleed all day. It took him so long to die."

Okay, Christian thought. *If he wants to talk about the dead guy, we'll talk about the dead guy.*

"Who was he? Doctor Hodder?"

"A good man. It took him so long… so long to bleed. He could not… what is the word… cope. He could not cope with the things he did when he was animal. I believe he kill his grandson."

"What was his job here?"

"To take care of me. To watch me. Observe. I am so very hungry. Please to give me some food."

"Why did he watch you?"

"Please… food?"

Christian looked around the room. "Okay, I'll get you something."

"Behind the cabinet. There is a small refrigerator with some meat in it. Please to get me the meat."

Walking across the room, Christian crunched refuse beneath his feet. He located the little fridge, opened it, and recoiled at the smell.

"Dude," he said. "I don't think this stuff's any good. It smells rotten."

"It smells… delicious. Please… through the little door."

Pulling the rancid lunch meat from the refrigerator, the boy wrinkled his nose. He stepped back to the barrier, finding a handle attached to the Plexiglas. When he pulled it, the mechanism rolled inside of it, exposing a gap in its metal machinations.

"Huh," Christian said. "Just like the drive-in teller at the bank."

He placed the meat within the hole and closed the little door. The naked man hurried over to the other side of the tray. After several beeps and hydraulic whirs, the other side of the machine opened up for the inmate, who greedily reached into the hole and grabbed the meat. He sniffed it, smiled at Christian, and began to tear into it with the ferocity of a wild dog.

"Oh," he said, his mouth full of the rancid stuff. "That is so good."

Christian turned away, revolted that the man was chewing the nasty-smelling meat with his mouth open, his eyes wide and crazed. He kept his back to the man as he ate. Not only did the scene gross him out, but the eating of this bologna seemed to be a private matter, like sex or defecation. Although with the toilet in plain view, it didn't seem as though this guy was worried about his privacy… let alone shitting where he ate.

"What's your name?" Christian asked, trying to glean information through the simplest of methods… asking direct questions.

"Andrei Sokosovich," the man said with his mouth full.

"You aren't from around here, are you?"

"No. I am from Siberia, a small village called Kirskania."

"Then why are you here? In America? In Cincinnati, for Chrissake?"

"I was hunted."

Christian spun around, facing the naked man, who was licking his fingers and looking at the dissipating light from the window. The meat was gone.

"What?" Christian asked.

The man seemed worried, his gaze fastened upon the window. "It is almost time again."

"Time for what?"

The man smiled at him, a wide, wolfish grin. "Time to change."

"You were hunted down and brought here?" Christian asked, trying to circle back to a subject he could comprehend. "From your village in Siberia, right?"

"Yes. It was a nice place to live. The cold was welcoming to me. This American heat seems ridiculous."

"Tell me about the people who hunted you."

"There is not much time." He resorted to that same love-struck, mooning appearance as he looked back at the window.

"Then tell me fast."

"My family was cursed for many generations. It has taken one of us from each… litter. I was the one who was cursed this time. We had many safeties at the house, but I was smart. I sometimes got loose. I loved the taste of sheep."

"What are you talking about?"

"I am a shapeshifter. The doctors here, when they were alive, called me a Lycanthrope."

Christian remembered black-and-white movies from his childhood, flickering across televisions in the basement where his father took him. "You mean, like, a werewolf?"

The naked man smiled. "Yes… and no. Bigger than a wolf. More like a bear and a lion all mixed up."

"Like those things last night."

Andrei Sokosovich sighed. "A mistake. Something happened here. Something… that will happen again. Bigger. Worse this time."

Christian was becoming confused. Waving his hands in the air, he said, "So, you inherited the curse, just like in the werewolf movies, only a bigger monster."

"I do not like this word… *monster.*"

"But you changed. Shapeshifted."

"Yes. It was glorious. When I could roam the land freely, I was the master of all. The villagers would lock themselves away. They would bar their doors. I would wander in the moonlight, eating and drinking and fucking…"

"Whoa there! You said you had safety precautions."

"Yes. My family was wise to our ways. We had a little prison in the basement, with chains for the feet and hands. It was uncomfortable. I did not like it."

"But sometimes…" Christian coaxed.

"Sometimes… oh, sometimes they would tell the villagers and allow me to run free. That is probably how the men found out about me."

"Which men?"

"The authorities. The secret police."

"I thought they didn't have any more secret police? I thought they did away with them during glasnost."

The man smiled again, and his teeth glinted. They looked slightly larger to Christian, but he couldn't be sure of it.

"Oh, you are young. So young and so naïve. Mother Russia may have hidden her watchdogs well, but hidden watchdogs are still dogs. They still need to sniff around. They still need to bite sometimes."

"But they didn't bite like you could, did they Andrei?"

"No," the man said. "They merely chased me. Reported me. I think they called other men. The men who are now dead in this building. They paid me money to come here. The old Frenchman." He took a deep breath. "I can smell their blood. Even the old... how you say it... ah, the old homosexual. He is four or five rooms away, yes?"

Christian nodded, "Yes."

The man laughed, and his voice was growing deeper, more guttural. "I should not make fun. They were good to me. They send money to my family. But now look at them..."

Something was happening to the man as Christian watched from the other side of the protective barricade. His speech was becoming garbled, and his jaw line seemed to sink lower into his face.

"It... ish... time..." Andrei said, his mouth filling with sharpened, stiletto teeth.

He began to laugh, and Christian ran for the door.

Then, the boy stopped. The Plexiglas had kept the beast-man secure in his cell last night, and, presumably, for many nights before that one. His scientific curiosity was aroused, and he realized he would never get a chance like this one again.

He walked to the door, listening to the sounds of bones rearranging beneath the Russian's skin. Closing the heavy door, he turned all the locks and shoved the safety bars until they clicked into their locked and stable positions.

Then, placing the gun he had taken off of Jean's body on the desk beside himself, he took a seat to watch the show.

CHAPTER 18

September 17, 7:14 p.m.

"This is bad," Rick moaned, looking outside of the bank's lobby into the streets. Sounds of various animals—jaguars, bears, even a rapid-fire laugh that sounded like a hyena—seeped into the confines of the building. The sun had set enough that shadows had eaten most of the light, and things were happening in those shadows... things Rick didn't want to see.

"Well, we can't stay in the vault," Chesya said. "If we shut the doors, we'd never get back out, unless they manage to get the electricity running again tonight. You willing to take that kind of chance?"

"No," he said. "But we better think of something quick. We've only got a few minutes before all those poor bastards out there finish changing. Then we're really up shit creek." He snapped his fingers. "Hey, I got it. Why don't we make for the restaurant, hide out in the walk-in freezer."

"It took us more than a half hour to get here through that mess out there. No way those things are gonna wait that long."

Something darted past the front of the bank. In the darkness, Rick could see it flailing its arms in the air, howling as if in pain. Every time its feet hit the pavement, bones cracked and snapped, reforming themselves.

"Christ," he said. "How many bullets you have left in that pistol I gave you?"

Clumsily opening the chamber, she said, "Four."

"I've got eight left in my Glock. You a good shot?"

"A gun like this killed my brother. I have no use for the damned things. Well, until now."

"Maybe you should give the gun to me."

Something crashed outside, glass and metal protesting, a machine giving up its ghost.

She shook her head, clutching the gun to her chest. "Uh-uh. I may not like the things, but this is making me feel a lot safer than I'd feel without it."

He chuckled. "Everyone hates guns until they need one."

She seemed to be looking off into the distance, staring at nothing. "Safer…" she whispered. "Not necessarily any better."

Snapping his fingers in front of her eyes, Rick said, "We got ourselves a situation here, Chesya. We gonna wait for those things to get inside before we do anything?"

"No," she said, smiling. "We're going out there."

"Out there? Are you fuckin' nuts?"

"Language! Yeah, the Brink's truck. Didn't you see it? Maybe a block and a half away from here?"

"It was on its side," he said.

"Yeah, but the back doors were open. You know how strong those trucks are? They're practically bank vaults on wheels."

"You're sure the back door is open?" he asked. "I'd hate to think what would happen if we get out there and it's locked up tight."

"You have any other suggestions?"

"Nope. Sounds good to me. Here…" He took her pistol and cocked it. "Keep the safety off. You point it. You pull the trigger. Any of those things get in your way, you send them to Hell."

"You sound like a Clint Eastwood movie," she said, moving to the doorway.

He followed her. "What's wrong with Clint Eastwood? I like his movies."

"It figures."

Looking at the street, they could see the semi-obscured motions in the shadows, fervent jerking and spasming. The death throes of humanity. The painful birth of something else, something base and primitive.

There were gunshots in the distance, growing louder, more fervent.

"If we're gonna make a go for it, we don't have a lot of time," he said. "Leave the bags. We don't need to be weighed down. Most important thing is getting somewhere safe."

Nodding, she began to run, pistol held awkwardly in front of herself. He chased after her, praying that she was right, that the Brink's truck was unlocked.

He thought, *What if someone else out here found it, secured the door behind themselves.* If such a thing happened, they may as well be wearing dinner bells around their necks, a free range human buffet. Come and get it while it's hot!

It was nearly dark, but the orange vestiges of daylight exposed the terrible metamorphosis transpiring all around them. One man lay on his back on the hood of a car, his body shaking as if in the grip of an epileptic seizure, his mouth and nose fusing into a snout. On their right, a woman crawled on all fours, the bones in her arms and legs snapping and reinventing themselves. She raised her head, howling at the sky in shattering defiance.

Chesya stuck to the sidewalk for the first twenty feet, keeping the brick building to her back. They were walking through ankle-deep water, still flowing from a fire hydrant that had been run over by a car. The wreck blocked their path on the sidewalk, the automobile's front end crumpled accordion-style into the side of the bank.

Two small children who couldn't be more than three years old traipsed through the water towards them. They were naked, and Chesya stopped moving, watching them approach. They laughed, splashing through the pool of water.

Rick saw the golden eyeshine that reflected from the meager moonlight. Their faces were a feral combination of the cherubic and the bestial. Their sharp teeth gleamed in their open maws. Falling to his hands and knees, the first child shook his head like a dog with a rat in its mouth.

"Come on!" Rick shouted, pulling Chesya forward by her elbow.

"The kids…" she said. "I hadn't really realized."

The second child fell to the sidewalk, writhing on its back as its wrist cracked, bent in the opposite direction. The first was sprouting hair all over its torso, crying as its muzzle extended in short, quick punches.

They had reached the wrecked car that barred the sidewalk. Rick hoisted Chesya onto the hood, giving her a shove to encourage her to hurry. She scooted across it, careful to avoid the crumpled, sharp edges. The last thing they needed was to start bleeding. She was certain that the smell of a wound would bring packs of the creatures running.

As soon as she landed safely on the sidewalk, Rick tucked himself into a tight ball and rolled across the hood of the car, alighting deftly on his feet. He saw the children sniffing the air, and they rushed the car.

They suddenly disappeared. Peering over the hood, Rick couldn't see them anywhere on the sidewalk.

If they weren't visible, then…

"Rick, come on!" Chesya whispered.

… then they were probably…

Two pairs of hands grasped Rick around the ankles, jerking him off balance. Waving his arms, he felt the gun fly off through the air, probably lost to him forever. He landed on his ass, and the pain made his eyes water. He cried out, cursed, certain he had broken his coccyx.

The hands began to haul Rick under the car. He could see only darkness there, and the occasional glimmer of golden eyeshine. Talons dug into his legs. He kicked at the children, but they refused to let go, emitting short yelps every time he made contact with one of them.

"Hold on!" Chesya said.

She grabbed him underneath his arms in a rough half nelson and turned, tugging as hard as she could. The beast-children pulled harder. Chesya yanked again, her sneakers skidding on the sidewalk.

Thirty feet away, atop a Ford pickup, one of the fully formed monsters raised itself onto its back legs, lifted its massive head, and growled at the sky. It was a huge beast, some terrible coalition of wolf, cat, and bear silhouetted by the moon. Chesya pulled on Rick, and it snapped its head around, its eyes glowing softly. It furrowed its brow and peeled back its black lips to expose rows of saurian teeth.

"Lord, help me out here," she groaned, pulling harder on Rick.

He was still kicking at the little beasts beneath the car, pummeling them as hard as he could. They would not release him. If anything, they tightened their grip, and one of them began shredding his pant leg with its tiny claws.

"Chesya!"

The huge creature atop the pickup dropped to all fours and lowered its head. It growled, took a step forward.

Chesya dropped Rick, and he landed hard on the sidewalk, bumping his head. He swore at her. Kneeling next to the crashed automobile, she pointed her gun into the darkness beneath the car and blasted two blind shots.

"Shit! Watch my fuckin' feet!" Rick screeched.

The big monster leaped from the pickup truck and loped towards her, slinking between the stalled cars.

One of the small monsters beneath the car shrieked, let go of Rick's leg; he pulled himself from the second one's clutches. He was lucky they were just kids, not as strong as a fully-grown werewolf. His right leg was bloody, his jeans torn and ragged where the little beasts had attacked him. He stood, trembling, his eyes darting around for his lost gun.

The huge, fully transformed creature leapt onto the hood of the wrecked car, which shuddered beneath its massive weight. On all fours, it stood nearly five feet tall, and it towered over Rick and Chesya. Opening its mouth, it let out a triumphant howl.

Rick fell backwards, landing directly on his ass, and he winced at the intensified pain in his tailbone. The agony careened through his vertebrae and scrotum, and he heard himself screaming.

Behind them, another shape arose from the darkness of a nearby alley, alerted to the cries of easy prey.

Chesya raised her gun to the head of the huge beast perched on top of the automobile. Pulling the trigger, she jerked, and the shot went wide, winging the nearby hotel that seemed ready to crumble. The monster paused a moment, a startled look on its face.

Rick saw something from the corner of his eye, a glint of steel. Turning, he saw his gun lying near the alley entrance.

He also saw the lumbering creature standing two feet away from it, and it was looking in his direction. With a snarl, it dropped to all fours and hurdled towards him.

He had to get that gun!

Rick rolled to the side, and the beast landed where he had been lying. The pain in his coccyx throbbed, and he moaned.

He crawled towards the alley, reaching for his gun. The beast next to him slapped a gargantuan paw on his back, and the claws raked across his shirt, peeling away the material and exposing the delicate skin.

The gun was four feet away from him. He could see it just out of reach, but he couldn't move. The monster held him down like a cat playing with a mouse.

"Chesya!"

"Not now," she said, aiming again at the beast on top of the car. No longer distracted, it hunched its shoulders and launched itself at her.

The thing's brains exploded from the back of its skull, and it squealed once. Then it dropped to the ground with a resounding thud.

The creature holding Rick down was startled by the gunshot, and it turned to face its new nemesis, momentarily releasing its hold on the man. Rick scrabbled for the gun. He reached it, turned around, pulled the pistol high to aim.

In sync with the gunshot, the monster's brains exploded, the top of its canine skull dropping between Rick's legs. He stumbled backwards, watching the beast crumple to its knees, sway for a moment, then fall face-first to the sidewalk. Turning, he saw Chesya pointing the now-empty revolver at the dead beast, only a couple of feet away.

"I have to get close to hit them," she said. "Guess I counted the bullets wrong; there were five."

"Well, fuck me," he said. "I'll just call you Annie Oakley from now on."

"Come on, get up," she said. "We got another block to go. And what'd I tell you about the cussing?"

They sprinted down the sidewalk, watching the shadows for any movement. Every step caused a painful throb in Rick's lower back. They saw hundreds of beasts and people changing into beasts. Many of them looked terrified caught in the thrall of the metamorphosis. Some smiled, greeted it like old friends. Others screamed in agony, fighting the change.

"You realize you're out of bullets," Rick said.

"Yeah, but I'm holding on to the gun. We may need it."

He grunted, stepping over a young man who was snapping his sprouting teeth at shadows on the brick wall. He didn't seem to notice them.

Throughout the streets, the monsters were getting their bearings after their transformations. They shook their massive heads, scratched themselves like dogs.

"There's the truck," Chesya said, pointing to the middle of the street. All four lanes were crammed with vehicles. Two cars away from them, the Brink's truck lay dolefully on its side, half-crushing a SUV. One of the back doors was tantalizingly open.

"Oh, thank God," Rick said.

He helped Chesya onto the hood of the first car, and she managed to stand. From the hood of the automobile, she could see much farther down the street.

"Oh... fucking shit..." she said.

As he pulled himself up to her level, Rick said, "I thought you were against swearing, and you just blurted out a real lulu."

"I think I have an excuse," she replied.

The streets teemed with life, barely hidden beneath the new night's cloak. Rick and Chesya could see hundreds, maybe more than a thousand beasts running through the streets, savaging each other with claws and teeth, grappling with each other, screwing each other. Males lined up impatiently to take turns with the females. Others battled over partners, tearing at fur, biting into muscular flesh. It was an orgy of animalistic sex and violence...

... and Rick and Chesya were standing on top of a car, practically wearing neon signs that read, "Eat Me. I'm delicious."

Hundreds of pairs of golden eyes squinted at them.

"Let's get in the truck right now," Chesya suggested.

"I'm down with that."

They turned and ran across the second car. Rick slipped, falling into the space between the automobile and the security truck; the open door beat him in the chest. Wincing, crying out, he opened it. Chesya was right behind him.

"Oh, that's gonna bruise," he said, gritting his teeth.

The monsters kept approaching, attacking, hundreds of eyes and open, slavering jaws; Rick kept firing his gun, losing track of how many shots he had left.

Chesya stopped suddenly. Her expression went from relief to shock to fear to anger in a second.

"What?" he asked.

She pointed towards the back of the truck.

It was already occupied.

The creature stood on its back two legs. It lowered its head and roared at them, exposing blackened gums and needle-teeth. It was smaller than the one that had pinned Rick to the sidewalk, and its muzzle was flecked with gray hair. Its ears flicked angrily. Taking a step towards them, it lashed out with razor-sharp claws.

Rick slammed the door, hitting the beast's face. It bellowed.

Putting his back against the door, Rick tried to hold the creature within the back of the truck, but it pounded so hard that it pushed him forward with every blow.

"I hate to tell you this," Chesya said, "but we have company."

"I know, I know!" Rick shouted. "I'm going to pull the door wide on its next—*umph*." The beast hammered on the door, nearly knocking him over. "You gotta get up here so you can—*umph*—hop in when it falls."

She adjusted her position so she was directly beside the door. Rick timed the beast's poundings, which seemed to be fairly rhythmic, a metronome of violence.

"Okay," he said. "On the count of three."

The other beasts were getting closer, smelling the scent of their prey. One of them raised its head and howled mournfully.

"One…"

A huge Lycanthrope leaped onto a Kia, crumpling the metal roof. It stared at the two humans, eyes glowing yellow.

"Two…"

Chesya saw movement near the bottom of the truck, something slinking between the cars.

"Three!"

Rick opened the door, and the beast plummeted from the back of the truck, landing on the ground. Chesya jumped, felt her grip on the gun loosen, felt it fall from her grasp. She pulled Rick into the Brink's truck behind her. The door slammed. Chesya reached for the locks, and Rick shoved the metal bars into place.

One of the creatures slammed its heavy body into the back doors, and the truck slid off the mangled SUV. The front end dropped first. Rick tripped, tumbled to the fore of the vehicle. Chesya followed, crushing him as the back end of the Brink's van slipped to the ground. Rick heard her head hit something, clanging like a bell. When he reached for her, she was unconscious, and he tried to slap her face to wake her up.

"Chesya, Chesya…"

The pounding began on the truck's exterior.

And Rick realized it was going to be a very long night.

CHAPTER 19

September 17, 7:05 p.m.

Cathy Wright watched from her station in the bathroom. The window offered a perfect view of the back yard and the shed where she had incarcerated her husband. From this vantage point, it didn't seem nearly as sturdy as she had imagined, and the long shadows of the elm trees that separated her yard from the neighbors crept slowly eastward until the lawn was cloaked in darkness.

Sighing, she wondered how long it would take him to change… if he even changed at all. She was running on caffeine and supposition, unsure of how this metamorphosis worked.

In the movies, when people altered in front of the full moon, gypsies were sure to be hiding in the forest, and you could only kill the monsters with silver bullets. Cathy didn't have any silver bullets, and she wasn't even sure how to get some. Do you traipse over to the next-door neighbors and ask for a cup of silver-plated bullets? Hell, they didn't even own a gun, so the question was moot anyway.

Even a man who is pure of heart, and says his prayers by night…

Was Karl pure of heart? She doubted it. The more time that elapsed, the more she thought about the things her son had said, the things she couldn't bring herself to believe.

Shaking her head, she wondered why this was happening to her. Her world, the aristocracy of Cincinnati, her fellow residents of Indian Hills, didn't operate under these rules. Plans were made, men were married, children were born, and the wealthy grew wealthier through wise investments and well-established connections. Weekends were spent traveling or swimming in the Olympic-sized pool in the back yard, boating, sailing, networking over Barbecue. There were cocktail parties and dinners at the Country Club, libraries of unread books and two-hundred-dollar-a-plate luncheons for some cause or another. Children were sent to boarding school...

... children. The one thing she had wanted more than anything. Karl had claimed that he wasn't ready to raise a child, but Cathy had argued her point until he had finally given in to her demands. She felt she had been a competent mother, even with all the problems during the teen years. Now their child was grown, flown from the nest she'd attempted to feather with insulation against the world. Still, you could shield your kids from harsh reality, but things always festered in the house. Accusations she couldn't bring herself to believe, problems she couldn't understand. She wondered how much those problems really mattered anymore... with the way the world had turned upside down. With what Karl had become.

There was a loud thump from inside the shed, loud enough for her to hear it within the thick, brick walls of the house. She placed a hand to her chest, feeling her heartbeat... a hummingbird fluttering beneath her skin.

... with what Karl had become.

She realized, when the second loud noise came from the back yard, she was terrified of her husband. She'd spent the day comforting him, soothing his ego, trying to help him understand what was happening, even if she wasn't sure herself. They had set right back into the cozy groove of their marriage. He worked, and she helped him. Helped him with dinners with the boss.

Thump!

Helped him by providing a comfortable home and supervising the house staff.

Thump!

Even helped him with his legal briefs when he needed advice on one of them.

THUMP!

Helped him by supporting him, even against the indignation of their child.

THUMP!

She wondered if she had been protecting the wrong person.

Cathy stood, gasping; that last noise had seemed louder than the rest.

Outside the window, the entire shed was shaking, rocking with the violence of the beast trapped within. She could hear the growling, biting sounds, the clawing and scraping. Holes appeared in the sides of the wood as Karl punched them out.

No, the shed didn't appear so durable now. In fact, it seemed to be almost paper thin. Like a Chinese house.

She would need something more than all the feeble fortresses she had constructed between the shed and her bathroom. Even if it only meant holding something solid in her hands… a weapon.

They had no guns, but she remembered Karl's softball bat was in their bedroom closet, just down the hallway. That would feel solid. Taking another look out the window, she saw the shed splinter near its door, finally giving in to the incessant pummeling.

If he could get out of that strong shed, it wouldn't take much more to pound his way through the barricades and into this bathroom. Not long at all…

Running to the bathroom door, she unlocked all three locks and pulled back the deadbolt that Karl had installed. As she moved into the hallway, the noises from the shed seemed to dissipate the farther she moved into the house.

In their bedroom, she opened the French doors to her closet. She rifled through the clothes and found his old aluminum bat, the baseball glove hanging from its neck. She tossed the glove on the shelf above the clothes and closed the doors. Then she hurried back to the bathroom, the heavy bat gripped tightly in her hands. Not willing to set it down, she continued held it in her right hand while she relocked the door with her left.

Despite her heavy breathing, the night had grown quiet. No loud noises came from the back yard, so she stepped over to the window to investigate.

"Oh, no," she said, covering her mouth with her hands.

The doors had been torn from their hinges and tossed across the lawn into the koi pond. The shed appeared empty.

Karl, or the thing that had once been Karl, moved close to the house, loping to the back doors. It was huge, with an oversized head that swung back and forth on a massive, muscular neck. It was on all fours, and she barely saw its hairy back before it was out of sight. She caught the motion of a back leg, the ankle twisted all wrong.

She heard nothing for a moment, only the soft chirping of crickets. Then glass was breaking, and something heavy was tossed aside, landing with a horrendous noise. Karl had breached the back door, had thrown that heavy table like it was a toy. She could hear a soft growling from downstairs, a cracking of glass, and she knew it was in the house.

Somewhere closer, something skidded against the hardwood floor. He was in the living room, knocking the furniture aside in his attempts to find his wife. Another loud skid, followed by something heavy creaking and falling over. The sound of smashing China told her that Karl had knocked the heavy bureau aside, that he was in the hallway, probably on the stairs.

Placing an ear against the fragile door of the bathroom, she heard his toenails click-click-clicking on the hard wood of the stairs, followed by the sound of the tables she had placed there crashing to the floor below.

Briefly, she wondered how this animal knew where she was hiding. Did it retain Karl's memories? Could it remember all the ways they had tried to bar its path to her? It was certainly making a beeline for the bathroom, trashing everything in its way.

Stepping back, Cathy was struck by the insanity of the situation. Husbands didn't turn into monsters and attack their wives, especially husbands who were litigators living on the right side of town. Wives in Indian Hills didn't wait for their monster-husbands to break down doors so they could bash their brains out. These sorts of things just didn't happen. They just couldn't happen. Not here. Not now.

But Karl had claimed he was itching on the inside, as if hair were growing deep within his guts. Human on the outside, animal within. And it suddenly hit Cathy like a fist to the jaw.

Her husband had always been hairy on the inside. Under that handsome, respectable exterior, he had hidden his true bestial self. Only this past night had exposed his true emotional state.

Her son hadn't lied about what her husband had done to him.

And she'd supported the wrong family member all along, even to the extent that her boy ran away from his affluent neighborhood and Catholic school, ending up... God knows where.

Gripping the baseball bat in both hands, as though she were stepping up to home plate, she listened to Karl's toenails click until the beast had reached the door. It sniffed the cracks, and she realized it was operating on an acute sense of smell. It had trailed her through the house like a hunting dog sniffing out pheasants in a field. It took big, snuffling breaths, and she moved her grip a bit higher on her weapon.

This was not her husband.

This was not a man she knew, not a man she could love.

He roared.

She wanted to weep, but her fear overrode her grief and anger; the tears would not come.

The beast scraped its claws along the bathroom door, teasing her, trying to scare her. She could imagine the wood curling beneath its claws.

"Karl," she warned. "Don't come in here. I'm armed."

Whatever restraint the creature was showing dissolved in an instant. It clamored at the door, and cracks began to form. Screaming, she backed away from it, the bat held high.

"Karl, no!"

The beast began to throw its heavy shoulders into the door... once, twice... The wood split in the center on the third blow, spilling the monster onto the Italian tile.

It raised its golden eyes, strings of thick saliva dripping from its jaws. Pulling back its lips, it growled, exposed giant teeth, too many teeth to fit in one mouth. It blinked its eyes.

And Cathy realized there was no humanity in them. There was only an animal, and the needs of an animal... blood, food, meat.

"Oh... Karl," she said.

The beast prepared to pounce, lowering its head, gaining a good hold on the floor with its back legs. Cathy swung the bat with all of her strength, grunting as it hit the beast along its jaw line. Sharp teeth flew across the room, and the monster turned to her, surprised, dripping blood from its injured mouth. She raised the bat again.

This time, Cathy clubbed the beast on the top of its skull, and she was rewarded with a loud crack. She knew she had been incredibly lucky, and she raised the baseball bat over her head again. The monster dropped to the floor. Its legs quivered in a terrible parody of a dance.

And she hit it again and again and again… until the tiled floor was awash with blood and brains. She smashed it until the beast's legs stopped their awful twitching ballet. Then she dropped to the floor, hitting her knees on the expensive Italian tile she had insisted Karl buy last year.

As she watched, the monster she had destroyed slowly changed back into her husband. A single sob escaped her lips as she reached for his hand. The trauma to his face seemed so much worse than it had when he had inhabited the bestial form.

"Oh, Karl," she said. "I'm so sorry. I'm so, so terribly sorry."

She stood, moved slightly away from him, as his blood pooled around her feet, the dented baseball bat forgotten by the bathtub.

CHAPTER 20

Christian leaned back in the office chair, watching as Andrei Sokoso-vich transformed into one of the beast-men. The process seemed painful, and there was no shortage of screaming mixed in with the growls and the snapping of his bones as they converted. While the boy watched, the Russian sprouted hair all over his body, the tendrils twisting out of his pores like some bizarre Karillion photography. The beast-man scratched himself, as though the growing hair made him itch. When the cracking of his joints grew more insistent, Andrei fell on his back, writhing on the floor of the cell in what could only be agony.

While he observed the transformation, Christian noted with some surprise that he was detached from the cries of the Russian. It was almost like he was watching a movie through a Plexiglas viewscreen. Somehow, he didn't think this was a commendable attribute, this indifference. He knew he should feel pity for this man, this human being going through such a painful and tumultuous metamorphosis, but he found himself fascinated by the intricacies of the change, the raw physicality of it.

He stood, walked right next to the Plexiglas barrier so he could wit-ness the event as closely as possible. It was probably what the scientists of Bio-Gen had done, taking notes and watching Andrei. Christian's eyes grew wide with astonishment.

When Andrei's hands mutated, the fingers fused together, stretching out longer and developing an extra joint near the wrist. Three pads seemed to pop out of the skin of his palm, as heat would raise blisters, and his fingernails were shoved from their moorings by long black talons. His ears elongated, extending towards the ceiling, then folding in upon themselves as though the cartilage were alive beneath the skin. The folding created a triangular point at the top of the ear, and delicate fur tufted from it.

The entire transmutation took less than three minutes. When it was over, Christian was face to muzzle with one of the beast-men, and he got his first good look at one of them.

It wasn't pretty.

The thing in the cell began to rage, throwing itself against the walls, pushing at the Plexiglas with its shoulder until the boy was certain the shield would give beneath the pressure. It clamored at the barrier, attempting to scratch its way out of the see-through jail, spittle flooding from its hideous face. It tried to bite the Plexiglas, its jaws opening wider than seemed possible, dragging its black tongue across the barrier, its teeth making a squeaking noise. No matter how hard it pounded and ripped and tore at the barrier, it made no progress towards escape. The beast-man began to pace back and forth in its cell, its short tail tucked between its legs. It cast a wicked glance at Christian every once in a while, but it seemed intent in its pacing. Eventually, it grew tired of this, and it lay on the floor, curled into a ball like an exhausted, monstrous dog. When it fell asleep, it almost seemed benign.

Christian moved away from the barrier to search the room.

In the three desks at the other end, he found more computer print-outs than he thought could ever be necessary. Some of them involved charts and diagrams, but the words were written in a scientific jargon that may as well have been Greek.

Then he remembered the book he had seen near Jean's corpse. It had to be some sort of journal. He couldn't recall any writing on the cover. He had been too preoccupied with the body laying over it.

Checking that he still had Jean's pistol, he took a final look at the beast-man in the cell. He was still sleeping, giving nary a thought to the boy. Cautiously, Christian walked to the door, unlocked the numerous locks and bolts, and stepped into the hallway. He moved back to Jean's office, where he had seen the Frenchman's dead body, practically tiptoeing into the room. He attempted to shut the door behind himself, feeling around in the darkness, but he remembered the door had been ripped from its hinges.

In the bright moonlight that flooded the office, Jean still leaned into his desk, his face ignominiously resting in a puddle of gore. The blood appeared darker in the blue light, and it had become tackier, resulting in a sticky, jelly-like halo around his skull. On the table, there was a white, empty spot in the shape of the gun he had removed from Jean's grip, a photoflash image of the weapon in reverse.

The book remained on the floor, its corner stuck in a pool of gummy blood. It was leather-bound, approximately two hundred pages in length. There was no writing on the covers.

Christian picked it up and moved out into the hallway, away from Jean's body. The smell of urine and blood, of meat left outside too long, overwhelmed him. This was someone he had known, and it physically hurt him to see Jean reduced to a corpse.

Walking down the hallway, he ruffled through the pages. Only the first half of the journal had been filled with writing. The second half remained blank. He leaned against a wall for a better look at the journal.

Was the answer in these bloodstained pages? Christian wondered if he would even be able to comprehend Jean's words. His scientific research had to be connected to the insanity that had overrun the world.

Flipping through the journal, he saw several words and phrases that he could identify, so he thought he might be smart enough to read the book. It was worth a shot.

Christian also knew he was growing very tired. Even though it was still early in the evening, he had not slept long enough the previous night. He decided to try to read some of the journal and then attempt to sleep afterwards.

From three floors below him came the angry, hateful growls of the people who had changed in the streets. He could hear some of them engaged in terrible battles, full of the sound of biting, tearing, howling. As he walked back to the room where the Andrei-creature was incarcerated, he heard the sound of metal scraping against metal, and he wondered what the beasts on the street were doing.

The beast-man in the cell narrowed its eyes as the boy entered the laboratory. Christian looked down at the corpse at his feet. Wrinkling his nose, he set the book on a desk and grasped the body by its ankles. He pulled it out of sight, so that it now rested in the hallway. The room still smelled of copper and bile, but he found some Lysol and sprayed large circles of the aerosol around his body. The smell dissipated under the disinfectant. After locking and barring the door, Christian took a seat in front of Andrei's cell.

The beast knew if it was patient enough, if it waited long enough, someone was going to open the door and set him free.

And the young boy reading the leather-bound book smelled so succulent that it had to use its dark tongue to lick up its increasing saliva.

CHAPTER 21

September 17, 9:00 p.m.

Rick had removed his jacket, fluffing it into the semblance of a pillow, and he'd rested Chesya's head on it. When the Brink's truck had shifted, she'd slammed her skull into one of the shelves in the back, landing on Rick with a thud. Once the vehicle had settled on the ground, he had tried not to move her, fearful of hidden injuries. Now that almost an hour had passed, he thought she would be all right. Her breathing was regular, but the only outward sign of trauma was a large, purple bruise that had formed on the right side of her forehead. A knot was solidifying beneath the discoloration.

And she still slept. He had tried calling out her name and gently shaking her arm, but she didn't respond. Rick wasn't sure what this meant, but it couldn't be good. He needed to get her to a doctor or an emergency room.

From the sounds that reached him from outside the truck, he knew he wasn't going anywhere with her for a while, no matter how serious her injuries. Those monsters were everywhere, running through the streets, hurling themselves at anything that moved. They'd clawed fruitlessly at the truck for a good fifteen minutes, but had finally given up to hunt elsewhere. He could hear them now, growling and screeching, their voices rising as high as a hyena's maniacal giggling, then dropping into low, bear-like huffs. Sometimes he heard fights breaking out among them, the growls and snarls just outside his shelter.

He stroked Chesya's hair. It was soft now that her hairspray had worn off.

Checking his Glock, he saw he had used every bullet in the clip. He cursed himself for his carelessness. He knew of several gun shops in the vicinity, places where he could reload the weapon, but they were all far out in the suburbs. With the way the roads were clogged, he didn't have a chance in hell of reaching one of them. The gun was essentially useless now. He tossed it across the back of the Brink's truck.

Sometimes, one or more of the beasts discovered the back windows of the vehicle and peered in, eyes shining in the moonlight. Rick kept still, and he thought the shadows in the truck must have hid them from the animals' curious eyes. The doors must have sealed off their scent. The beasts sniffed around the handle, probably smelling where Rick had pulled on the back doors to open the truck. Following the scent, they moved their muzzles around the cracks of the door, grunting with dissatisfaction.

Rick could swear he heard more gunfire in the distance.

It seemed as though they were safe for the moment, and Rick allowed himself to breathe easier every time one of their furry, massive heads swung away from the back of the truck.

It was quite dark inside the armored vehicle, but Rick's eyes had become accustomed to the gloom. Bags of cash and coins had spilled across the side of the van that now served as the floor. It was more money than he had ever hoped to grab during a bank heist, more money than he'd ever seen in one place in his entire life. Just twenty-four hours ago, he would have been on his hands and knees, stuffing his pockets with as much cash as possible. Now it seemed like mere paper. Useless fossils of another age.

That didn't mean he wouldn't snatch up some of it while Chesya slept. He was no dummy. He'd make sure he got enough in his pockets to provide for himself when things started rolling again. He was confident the world would eventually adapt to this new horror, just as it had always adapted and evolved. When the world was back on its feet, he would be sure to have enough money stashed away to take care of himself.

And, perhaps, to take care of Chesya.

Looking down at her face, he could make out the slope of her rounded jaw line in the darkness. He traced the curve with his thumb, feeling the flesh soft and pillow-like. Her nose turned up slightly, small in the middle of her broad face, and her eyes seemed to have been swallowed up by shadows, although he knew they were brown under the lids. If he had passed her on the street, he wouldn't sneak a second look.

Rick's type of woman usually consisted of large breasts, small waist, surgically spherical ass. He tended to like the strippers he saw at Harry's Gentleman's Club (Gentlemen... Ha!). Chesya's body was nothing like a stripper's.

Still, she moved him somehow, especially now, when she was lying quietly beneath his stroking fingers. She was a few pounds overweight, but the extra bulk wasn't unattractive. It rounded her figure and face into the effigy of an Earth mother. There was a fire within her, an energy that was the result of a tough childhood in a tougher part of the city. Most women he knew, especially the strippers, would have lost it entirely when their friends started turning into creatures, would have freaked out, done something stupid, and would have probably died. Not Chesya. She seemed to grow ever stronger, adapting to the problems, trying to puzzle out the best ways to stay alive.

It was her innate strength. He was becoming attracted to this part of her, and it scared him. This was not the time to be falling in love with someone, not a good time to begin any kind of relationship.

But as he watched her breathing, unconscious in his big, clumsy hands, he knew a part of him was taking a spill over this woman, that he was head over heels, so to speak. He couldn't help it. Whether it was real emotion or he was reaching out for something sturdy while the world tilted, he just couldn't say.

He just knew he cared for her, that the feeling was growing as time slowly ticked by. Forcing himself to accept the fact, he bent his head a little, giving her the softest of kisses. When his lips brushed hers, something stirred within him.

He realized he would protect her no matter what came their way.

And for the first time in years, he prayed. It was easy to accept that there was a higher power when the world was going crazy all around you, when you discovered that you actually did possess a soft side. God seemed to be a simpler concept when you loved someone.

"If you're there, God," he whispered, still stroking Chesya's soft hair, "don't let her die. I think I need her, and… maybe she needs me. Don't take her away just yet."

Something scratched along the side of the Brink's van, long nails on metal, and Rick continued his prayer in silence. The thing had heard him whisper. They must have incredible powers of hearing. It reached the back of the truck, grazing its claws along the vehicle, and raised its face to the glass. Its eyes gleamed golden as it squinted into the darkness, trying to make out what had made the noise inside the van.

Rick didn't move, and he held his breath for a full minute as the thing glared at him. When he had to exhale, he did it slowly, easily, so the beast couldn't hear the sound. As long as he remained still and quiet in the dark, things would be all right. They wouldn't know he was there.

He felt a flutter beneath his fingertips and looked down. Chesya's eyelids were blinking. She was waking up.

Oh, shit, no! he thought.

She adjusted her leg, raising it to be more comfortable. With her right hand, she brushed away Rick's caressing fingers, slapping at him as though at a bothersome insect.

The beast-man at the back of the truck immediately sensed the motion, and its lips pulled back into a toothy snarl.

"What the… what are you doing? What happened?" she asked, her words seeming thunderous in the quiet.

Rick shushed her.

"Why am I … oh…"

She got it. Too late.

The creature pummeled the doors with its fists, scratched at the bulletproof glass. Opening its mouth wider than Rick thought was possible, it began biting at the chicken wire that covered the panes, leaving saliva trails on the windows.

Its struggles with the van attracted two more of the monsters, which promptly began gnawing at the chicken wire on the other window, pounding against the side of the truck with their fists, pulling and plucking at the wire.

Meanwhile, the first monster pulled the protective wire free with its teeth, tossing it away with a shake of its head. It landed several yards off, alerting three more passing creatures. These newcomers loped towards the van, began scratching at the sides, tearing at the metal in an attempt to get at the tender morsels inside.

Chesya said, "I'm sorry. It was me, wasn't it?"

Rick nodded. "You were unconscious. You couldn't help it."

The noise was growing to a terrifying, incomprehensible level. The truck began to shake as more of the beasts tried to get inside.

"Damn."

"Does your head hurt?"

"Yeah, I've got a goose egg here." She touched the spot beneath the bruise and winced.

Rick looked out the back windows. The outside was completely covered with monsters. They shoved their faces forward, snapped at the glass. The chicken wire on the second window came loose and clattered to the ground.

He moaned. There were so many of them. Dozens, maybe up to a hundred of them circling the van, taking turns scratching or biting at the windows.

Two of the things started fighting, and Rick saw one of the beasts bite another just over the eyes. The flesh and hair peeled away from its forehead like the rind on a nectarine. Blood spattered the windows, and the creature turned and ran away.

"How many are there?" she asked, sitting up.

She closed her eyes, saw shooting stars because of the pain in her head.

"I don't know. A lot. A hell of a lot," he said.

"Can they get in?"

"I don't think so." His voice conveyed his assurance.

Chesya pushed herself back, farther from the windows that were teeming with seething faces, teeth gnashing and spit flying in ropes. She counted nine pairs of eyes, but the monsters kept shoving each other aside. One would replace another, then snap at a third, then one would be trampled as two more leapt at the glass, battering it with their hard skulls.

It sounded like there were many more around the van, some even on top of it.

"Stay still," Rick said, allowing Chesya to lean back against his chest. He put an arm around her. "They'll grow bored or tired soon, maybe go after easier game."

He could smell her sweat. Her head rested against his throat, and he had to swallow.

"They'll go away eventually," he said.

Outside the van, something inhuman, something mechanical groaned.

"You promise?" she asked.

He couldn't answer her.

The only reply she got was the incessant noise of the monsters clawing and biting and scratching and growling... determination made visceral.

CHAPTER 22

September 17, 10:40 p.m.

Blood covered Cathy's legs from the knees to the ankles, a solid sheen of dark rust. Her blouse was spattered with Karl's bodily fluids, and her hands were beginning to grow cold and sticky. Her kneecap was sore where she had fallen on the tiles, and she knew a bruise was forming beneath her jeans. The baseball bat, forgotten, had rolled over to the bathtub, leaving streaks of crimson across the tiled floor.

Cathy grasped the bat in both hands and lifted herself to her feet. She nearly dropped to the floor again. Her legs had fallen asleep while she had sat cross-legged across from Karl, and her skin was suddenly punctured by thousands of pinpricks. Walking it off, she left bloody footprints on the floor.

Karl was dead. Her partnered, lawyer husband, her provider, was gone. He lay naked on his back, his smashed face turned to the side, oozing brain tissue and blood. One of his eyes stared at Cathy from across the room.

"Oh, Karl," she said, looking down at his demolished head. "You bastard, you did everything for me. You made all the decisions. Even the bad ones. Now what do I do? What on earth do I do?"

Karl didn't reply.

So Cathy began performing the role she'd perfected over the years of comfort and security. She made things right. She made things pretty. She accomplished.

Her time leading committees and planning for parties would come in useful after all. Her wasted life was suddenly not so worthless. She knew how to do some things—planning, maintaining, making sure everything was just right.

… as long as everything didn't include her own family relations…

"I'm sorry, Karl," she said, bending down and lifting his broken body in her arms. He seemed very light, as though something was missing from within him. She pulled the corpse by its feet from the bathroom to their bed. She nearly laid him on the ruffled bedspread, but changed her mind at the last minute. At the far end of the bedroom was a loveseat situated next to her morning table, where she applied her face every day. Grunting, she wrestled him down on the loveseat.

"See," she said. "You'll be comfortable here. You always loved the cushions on the loveseat. Besides, I'll have to sleep somewhere, and I can't do that if the bed is covered in your blood. I loved you, Karl, but I'm not sleeping next to your body. Sorry. Not after this. Not after what you did…"

Shaking her head, she flushed the thoughts from her mind. She couldn't think of that now. Not now. Not yet. She wasn't ready.

Hurrying back to the bathroom, she pulled on a pair of rubber gloves and retrieved two rolls of paper towels and cleanser from the closet. The cleanser was supposed to be gentle, so it shouldn't harm the expensive imported tiles; Cathy didn't know for sure because the maid had done all the cleaning. She scrubbed the blood from the floor, changing the water in her bucket five times so it wouldn't streak. She put her face just next to the tiling, squinting in the moonlight to be sure she got it all cleaned. As terrible as it appeared now, it would seem far worse in the daylight tomorrow.

She emptied another bucket of pink water into the toilet. Flushing it, she grimaced.

Cathy continued speaking to her husband, as though he could hear her. "You always told me how to handle things, Karl. You took control, and I always took your advice. Now look where that got us. Our son has run away… God knows where he is now. Turns out, you were telling me lies, weren't you, Karl? You made me believe you, just as you always did."

Outside, something howled in the night. Now and then, a scream pierced the darkness. She wondered who was being killed... or what.

"I guess I should have listened to Christian, should have believed him, but you were so sincere. You'd never lied to me before... or had you? Karl, was everything a lie? My entire life, your lawyer friends who came over? Was this all some kind of play I've been living, and was this beautiful house the stage? I... I don't understand."

Looking out the window across the hallway, she saw nothing unusual about the street. The magnificent homes rested belligerently within their manicured lawns, the landscaping diverse and beautifully maintained by an army of gardeners. Each house on the street cost more than 1.5 million dollars, each one a work of architectural genius. The iron gates that surrounded each property matched, maintaining the illusion of continuity. She wondered if the security guards were still watching over the outside gates, or if they, too, had changed into monsters and prowled the bushes.

The gated community had been created to keep out the riffraff, the undesirables. It hadn't stopped the devil from invading Indian Hills. It hadn't even given him pause.

Folding her arms across her chest, she nodded approvingly at the clean floor across the room. It sparkled.

"You could eat off that floor," she said. "Karl, you could eat off of it. And if our son was here..."

The thought of Christian stopped her, and she placed her hands over her mouth. *I will not cry*, she thought, clenching her eyes shut. *I will not. I will not. I will not cry. He's gone—they both are. And I have to learn to go on without them.*

She removed her clothes and stepped into the shower. The water was cold, and she had to fumble a bit in the dark for soap and the washrag. The blood on her legs was sticky, but she scrubbed until she could no longer feel its tackiness.

Shivering with the chill, she stepped out of the shower and toweled herself dry.

Planning... doing... accomplishing...

She cleaned the bathroom, paying special care to the baseball bat that had saved her. By the time she wrapped the extension cord around the handle of the vacuum, she decided to make a small fire downstairs. She was cold for some reason.

Plan... do... accomplish... move on to the next task...

Walking back up the stairs, she tried to plan what should be done next. What needed cleaning? What detail had she forgotten in the moonlight?

Her eyes kept returning to Karl. His head was leaking onto the armrest of the loveseat. She would have to eventually take care of it. After she moved Karl's body.

But move it where?

Were funeral homes still operating amidst the chaos? Surely, if she offered enough money, someone would bury him. Funerals, however, were huge events, and they required a lot of planning. She began to draft her blueprints for Karl's wake and funeral ceremony. Only a few friends. Flowers were perfectly fine, as there were probably not many charities left to which mourners could donate.

She wondered if funerals were even necessary in this new world. Could she just bury him beneath the rose bushes? Wasn't there a law against that? What did it matter now? She could certainly save herself a lot of trouble by burying him in the back yard. It had nothing to do with expense and everything to do with convenience.

Something howled.

Loudly.

Close.

Scurrying to a window, she looked at the back yard. Three of the creatures were snuffling around the shed. A fourth stepped from the shadows and looked right up at her. It seemed to grin, then it dashed for the door.

The door that Karl had destroyed when he had come for her.

What to do? Plan... execute... accomplish...

The bedroom and bathroom were wide open with nothing to barricade her from the creatures. Karl had seen to that.

Something growled inside the house. Toenails clicked on the hardwood floors below her.

The attic! It came to her suddenly that there was only one way into it and one way out: a ladder that she could pull up after herself. They wouldn't be able to reach her; she was certain of it.

Rushing into the hallway, she grabbed the iron bar hidden behind a display case for Hummel figures. It fit into the panel in the ceiling, and she twisted it. The panel slid back, and a ladder dropped from the hole. She flung the iron rod across the hallway, then turned back to grab it, just in case those things were smart enough to figure out that it was the key to the attic.

One of the monsters howled, a low, sad sound. They were close, on the stairs.

She wriggled into the hole that led to the attic and turned, pulled the ladder up. She slammed the panel back into place and dropped the iron pole on the floor.

As the hatch closed, the beasts leapt after it, stretching on their hind legs to reach the panel. Cathy shoved some heavy boxes over the entrance.

Below her, the beasts gnashed their teeth and howled their rage.

CHAPTER 23

September 17, 10:30 p.m.

Christian closed the journal, rubbing at his weary eyes. Despite the furious sounds of the beast-men outside the building, he had been able to get through a good thirty pages of Jean's scientific diary. The book was enlightening, but reading it sapped his energy. He hadn't slept in so long; he was growing very tired. He yawned, stood and stretched.

Andrei was still in the shape of a monster, pacing in his Plexiglas prison. After his initial bout of rage and violence, he had calmed a bit, walking back and forth in the little room as though anxious or bored. Christian couldn't tell. He watched the beast-man for a while, marveling at the musculature beneath the skin, how broad the chest had grown, how strong the arms and legs. Its neck was a template of muscle, thick intertwining ropes to hold its massive head high. The jaws never seemed to stop dripping saliva from between the enlarged fangs.

"The better to eat you with, my dear," Christian muttered, remembering the line from a half-forgotten fairy tale. It seemed appropriate again.

Sitting back in his chair, facing the creature in his plastic cage, Christian picked up the book again and resumed reading.

What he had perused so far was fascinating, even if he couldn't understand all of it. Most of the writing was accessible, and the boy had always been a good reader, above average for his age. Still, some of the scientific terminology went beyond anything he'd assimilated during his classes in high school. Plus the journal was evidently for Jean's private use, and he employed abbreviations that would be familiar only to him. It made reading slow and tedious, even if the subject matter was engrossing.

The writing in the journal explained how Jean had been obsessed with the werewolf mythology of Eastern Europe since he was a teenager. He had been taken to Auschwitz by train and forced to work with the other Jews in the death camp, watching in horror as Nazis fed the weakest prisoners to the gas chambers. Jean adapted his behaviors, showing his captors respectfulness, acquiescence, submissiveness. As humiliated as he had been, spurned by his own people for his alleged bootlicking, Jean had survived the camp, which was more than most of the prisoners could say.

Once, while serving the officers drinks on a silver platter, he'd overheard them talking about "the werewolves," a covert group of dissidents, anarchists, spreading bombs and sabotage like some vengeful Johnny Appleseed. Witnesses claimed that animals were the only things near train stations just before explosions ripped trains from their tracks, and spies had reported the saboteurs could actually turn into wolves to better undermine the Third Reich.

Although he had not completely believed the story, his imagination had been sparked, and a lifetime of research had begun. He spent his nights wishing he could turn into an animal, burrow under the fences and run away from that horrible place. He wanted to be a creature that could run fast enough to elude the searchlights and the tracking dogs, fast enough to dodge the bullets. Perhaps such a drastic metamorphosis could cure him of his growing love for young men, something he found distasteful but irresistible. If only he could change… While no such transformation ever occurred, the fanciful notion had been planted in his head.

When he had finally been freed by Americans arriving in tanks (a strange hybrid he saw as half man, half machine, not quite as interesting as his own hybrid, animal and man), he'd returned to college, graduating with honors. He'd worked in various laboratories for different corporations around the world, solving chemical problems and seizing upon this new scientific field: genetics. While he'd toiled in the labs in the daytime, he bought and read every book on Lycanthropy and shapeshifting he could find.

In his research, he found that nearly every civilization had its own shapeshifter myth. In Eastern Europe, the wolf was the preferred animal that Lycanthropes could become. In Russia, they turned into huge bears. In China, men became jaguars. In India, they became tigers. The common denominator was that they were all predators, all well endowed with teeth and claws for hunting. Jean had wondered if the myths were some vestige of an ancient past, when man needed to be stronger in order to hunt and kill food for his family, a buried memory from the Stone Age.

Surely, he reasoned, if so many different civilizations possessed superstitions about a very similar beast, there had to be something genuine about it.

Jean believed that man was endowed with two alter egos: one human, with all the attributes of the selfish, destructive race of man; the other animal, manifesting the characteristics of the predatory animal kingdom. He saw the animalistic side of man as the true identity, a pure soul untouched by greed and hatred, existing only to exist... feeding, copulating, and nurturing its family. The human side contained all that he had witnessed at Auschwitz.

Jean had been reading about sightings of a huge animal in East Siberia, north of Noril'sk. The beast seemed to appear every full moon cycle, and the sightings had been taking place for several generations. Only a few incidents of humans being killed and half-devoured had occurred during the past forty years, but several dozen animal mutilations, usually cattle, were reported. Jean had researched the area more, placing pins on a map for every verified sighting, using different colored pushpins for every animal mutilation. They seemed centralized around a small village on the plains, Chakl'sa.

This could be the proof he had sought for so long, a true shapeshifter. If he could find the one person in the village who had been there during the entire time the attacks had taken place, if he could isolate which one of them was the Lycanthrope, he was certain it would lead to more and more discoveries about the animalistic side of mankind. Perhaps he could isolate the cause of the disease and cure it.

Maybe he could make sure that there would never again be a Third Reich.

He traveled to Siberia, where he—

Christian was startled out of his reading by a noise from outside the laboratory. Flicking off the flashlight he was using, he glanced up at Andrei, who had stopped his frenetic pacing and stared at the doors, growling. The beast-man had heard something as well.

Christian grabbed the pistol Jean had used to shoot himself. There were still five bullets in the chamber. He wondered if it would be enough.

Slowly opening the door, he stuck his head into the hallway. It was very quiet. Christian crept into the hall, looking each way, waiting for a repeat of the sound.

It didn't take long.

Something scratched at the stairs in the stairwell, claws scrabbling for a better hold on each step. Something muffled, then a growl followed by a high-pitched yipe. Growls interrupted the clicking sound for a few seconds as the creatures broke into a fight.

Christian slowly backed up to the room he had left. He raised the pistol to point at the door leading to the stairs. A twelve-by-six-inch window displayed only darkness on the other side of the door.

Can they work doorknobs? he wondered. *Can they get their filthy paws around them without opposable thumbs?*

His breathing was the only sound once the fight had run its course. It seemed terribly loud in the hallway, and he attempted to slow it down, exhaling through his mouth, breathing in through his nostrils.

The silence dragged on for what seemed like hours, but Christian knew it couldn't be more than thirty seconds.

A few clicks from the stairwell. Something's talons scraped on the stairs.

Christian held his breath. His hands were shaking.

The pistol wavered.

Darkness filled the window, then suddenly a huge head and snout appeared at the glass. A long black tongue licked the pane.

Even in the darkness of the stairwell, Christian could see the monster's golden eyeshine, scanning the hallway. As he stepped backwards into the laboratory, the eyes latched on to him, and the beast, reinvigorated by the sight of tender, juicy flesh, pounded on the door.

Christian pushed a heavy desk in front of the entrance to the lab.

Andrei began howling in short, powerful bursts, as if to signal the beast-men in the stairwell.

Something smashed in the hall—the glass window in the door to the stairs.

Christian looked around the room—there had to be something here to save him, a weapon, a point of escape—but he could see very little. The only light fell from the full moon, slipping through the window and draping the sill.

Andrei's howls grew higher in pitch, then he huffed like a grizzly bear. He tore at the Plexiglas again in a futile effort to escape.

In the hall, something clanked, loud, like a bullet being fired.

The growling grew excited, stertorous.

They had managed to open the stairwell door. Now all that stood between Christian and who knew how many sets of claws and teeth was a single door, mostly made of glass, and a heavy desk.

There had to be someplace to hide…

Through the frosted glass with the names painted on it, he could see two silhouettes rise up from the ground. The creatures were gigantic, at least seven feet tall when standing on their hind legs. One turned its head sideways, and Christian got a good glimpse of its crooked fangs.

"Shit. Shit, shit, shit!"

Both of the heads snapped back so they were facing the door.

Christian slapped a hand over his mouth. He had just given away his position. He began to rush around the room, looking for any escape route, anything other than the pistol, which now seemed ridiculously inadequate. He wanted an ax, something solid and sharp.

There was nothing.

His eyes were drawn to Jean's journal, which he'd left on the chair, open to maintain his place in the narrative. He couldn't lose this book, he realized. It offered too many clues as to what was happening, why people were changing. He snatched it up and stuffed it in the front of his pants.

There was only one way out of the room. He unlatched the window and yanked it open. The air was surprisingly cool on his skin, and it smelled much better than the stale laboratory. The edge of a metal ladder, covered in flaking paint, gleamed in the pale moonlight.

Yes! he thought, his heart rushing with triumph and adrenaline, so hard it threatened to burst from his ribcage.

The glass on the door shattered, and the low animal noises gave way to victorious roars.

Don't look back, don't look back, Christian told himself as he hopped through the window and hooked his leg over the end of the metal ladder, which was six inches higher than would be comfortable. *Don't you fucking look back!*

Of course, as soon as he turned to slam down the window, he looked back.

"Oh, shit, shit, shit, shit!"

There were more of them than he'd thought, at least five or six. The door splintered beneath the heavy shoulders of the first creature in line. The wood cracked and fell to the floor, and the creature stepped over the broken barrier, sniffing at the room.

It had deep brown fur, and its body was muscular, especially around the neck and shoulders. Its barrel chest heaved as it stood awkwardly on its hind legs, exposing withered dugs. Raising its head, it howled at the ceiling.

As the second monster loped into the room, the first spotted Christian outside the window.

The ladder, rusted metal with brown spots on the grips from years of use, was mounted perpendicular to the side of the Bio-Gen building, sticking out a few inches from the brick. It rose to the fire escape leading to the roof. If Christian could get up there, he might be safe. At least for a while.

He grabbed the ladder, shifting his balance to the rungs under his feet. To his surprise and horror, the ladder was on a pulley, and it dropped eight feet, well below the fragile protection of the window he'd just closed. The ladder dropped toward the alley, where vague, ominous shapes moved in the shadows. Luckily, it stopped with a jolt, six feet from the pavement, and Christian climbed, hand over hand, the rungs cool to his touch.

When the boy reached the window of the lab, the first beast-man began pounding tentatively on the glass. Christian knew the window wouldn't last long, and he moved faster, climbing the rungs as quickly as his hands could manage. The book began to work its way out of his jeans, and he could feel it escaping. No way was he losing this precious volume!

His feet were a mere six inches above the window when the glass shattered into the alley beneath him.

The monster shoved its upper body through the jagged space, yelping when it cut its torso on the broken glass. Its clumsy hands reached for the ladder, not adapted for such tasks, fingers resembling talons, pads replacing most of the palm. It fumbled with one of the rungs two feet beneath Christian's sneakers.

He ascended faster, each rung taking him four more inches away from the horror below.

Just as the journal almost liberated itself from his pants, Christian grabbed it and put it in his mouth, clenching his teeth around the soft leather. The scent of it infiltrated his nostrils.

The creature below him was being shoved aside by another inside the laboratory. It grasped at the ladder for half a second, then it fell three stories into the alley, landing with a crash on its head. Brains and blood shot from the shattered skull.

Christian reached the uppermost segment of the ladder, and the pulleys, not restricted by a Lycanthrope's fumbling paws, retracted, raising the ladder to its original position, six inches above the window. The boy laughed, the sound stunted by the book he clenched in his jaws.

Two more feet, and the ladder led to a hole in a fire escape landing. Pulling himself onto the platform, Christian allowed himself a glance down at the window of the lab. The creatures glared up at him, the moonlight reflected in their eyes, saliva bubbling over their blackened gums. One of them would reach for the ladder, but then it would be knocked aside by another of the monsters. Then they would slash and tear at each other, fighting like curs in the street. At this point, another monster would shoulder its way through the broken window and scowl up at him, bellowing with rage and hunger.

Christian allowed himself a few minutes to get his breathing back to normal and let his heart stop pounding so furiously. He took the journal from his mouth started climbing the stairs to the roof.

Below, one of the werewolves grabbed the ladder and shook it. Christian clutched the handrail, dropping the leather journal.

It bounced off a few rusty rungs before landing in the alley amidst a congregation of beast-men.

"Oh, damn it," Christian muttered.

At least fifteen creatures waited in the alley for him to fall. Any hope the journal may have offered, any wisdom it could have imparted would now have to wait until morning. If it was still there. Saying a silent prayer to whatever god might be listening, Christian ascended the fire escape to the roof. By the time he got there, he could hear the beast-men in the lab, but they had left the window. They seemed to have lost interest.

Unless they were trying a new and different way to get at him.

Looking around the rooftop, he saw only one other entrance, a door that was padlocked. He figured it led to the stairwell. Although it was locked, he wasn't sure how long it would hold up to the beast-men's attacks. He would do well to keep an eye on it.

All around him, he saw other empty rooftops, some a few stories higher, most at the same level or lower. Some of the buildings were separated by alleys, and some by wide city streets. Some had signs or smokeless chimneys. The city looked dead from this angle, quiet and almost peaceful. As though everything was still normal.

But in the streets, Lycanthropes ran through the maze of stalled cars and trucks, several fighting minor wars, biting and lashing out. Pairs of them fornicated, the male mounting the female from behind, sinking its teeth into the nape of her neck. The creatures were fucking each other, plain and simple. This was no lovemaking, this was down and dirty instinct.

Christian focused on a particular cluster of monsters. Three or four dozen fought and gnashed their teeth, attempting to get into a big truck turned on its side.

"Oh wow," he whispered, almost admiring the way so many of them went after the truck, scratching at its metal walls, knocking each other aside to have a chance at it.

Christian hoped that whoever was in the truck—and he harbored no doubts that somebody was locked inside of it—remained safe until morning, when the things would revert back to their harmless, human form.

Looking around at the city, he feared that cleaning up this mess could take months, maybe even years. Small fires burned in various spots, and in the distance towards the Western Hills area, he could see a huge blaze, so big he wondered if it was a forest fire. It lit up the west like the dawn making a morning mistake.

The cars in the streets below him had been overturned, shuffled during the night. One fire hydrant had been demolished, and water spurted, dark and oily, through the streets. Two of the creatures lapped at it, an urban watering hole. In the middle of the destruction, he saw one hotel, at least thirty stories high, that seemed to wave in the wind. An explosion had removed a good portion of its cornerstone, and it looked as though it could topple at any minute.

It all became too much for him.

Keeping his face to the padlocked door, he waited for the dawn, scanning the rooftops for various exits in case the creatures discovered his hiding place. His hands shook with the rush of adrenaline, and the tears fell from his eyes, a mixture of terror and relief.

CHAPTER 24

September 17, 11:45 p.m.

The Brink's truck rocked under the attack of dozens of the creatures, but it seemed to be holding up against the assailment. No matter how much the beast-men tore and slashed at it, they couldn't create any access to the interior, where Rick held Chesya in his arms. Claws snapped off from the beasts' fingers as they ripped at the metal flanks of the truck; teeth shattered when they tried to bite their way in. The noise was deafening, full of snarling, growling, and scratching. In their frustration, many of them pounded relentlessly against the sides of the truck. Some of them tried to gain entrance through the bottom, tearing off the pipes and carburetor from the exposed belly of the vehicle.

Tucked in a corner, Rick could feel Chesya shaking as he held her in his arms. She had held up so valiantly for such a long time, it was difficult to see her so terrified. He moved aside a strand of hair that covered her eye, and he tried to calm her, drawing her closer and whispering things he hoped would console her.

They both kept their eyes on the two windows, which she assured him were made of bulletproof glass. Neither of them could see much, as the windows seemed to be full of rotating variations on a theme… one monster after another peering into the back of the truck, sizing them up, rubbing their snouts on the glass and licking it. They gnashed their teeth, tried to bite their way through the windows.

After what seemed like an eternity, the beasts went in search of new, less-restricted prey. Still, they were around the truck, going about their business. Rick and Chesya kept their voices in low, quiet whispers.

"'We have seen the enemy, and it is us.' I remember reading that in a comic strip when I was a kid. You ever read *Pogo?*" she asked.

"I was more of a *Hagar the Horrible* type of guy."

"The most horrible monstrosity we could think up, and it was dormant inside of us all this time. It's like looking at the world's soul," she whispered. He felt her breath on his shoulder when she continued. "And it ain't a pretty sight."

"You think that's what the world's soul looks like?" He motioned towards the unseen monsters outside the truck.

"Pretty much. Watch them. They're all looking out for number one, which is probably a good thing. If they started cooperating, learning to work together, we'd be screwed. But that's pretty much the way I see the world... everyone looking out for themselves, stepping on as many people as they can. You get in my way, I'm going to knock you aside."

"It's a pretty bleak outlook, if you ask me."

"Well, it's a pretty bleak world. People fly airplanes into skyscrapers to prove absurd religious points. Politicians lie and cheat, helping all their fat cat friends in order to get money for re-election time. 'You scratch my back, and I'll scratch yours.' You always hear that. You never hear someone say they'll just scratch your back. No reciprocation required. Everybody needs something in return. I think these monsters are a lot like that. They have their needs, and their instincts are all about filling those needs. They get hungry, they eat someone. They feel sexy, they screw someone. All about taking care of themselves."

He glanced down at the top of her head. "Does this have something to do with your family? Your brothers?"

"Maybe. I watched them both die, watched the way people looked at their deaths. Just another couple of dead niggers from the 'hood. Most of them didn't say it, but you could see it in their eyes. Broke my mamma's heart. That woman worked her fingers to the bone to provide for us, to help us find a way out of the ghetto-trap. And for what? It tore her apart, and she died that way, thinking that it all amounted to nothing in the end."

"Not everyone's like that."

"Maybe not, but enough *are* that it starts making its way into your brain. I fought it and fought it and fought it, till I was tired of fighting."

"You told me yourself that you were a strong, black woman."

She looked at him, tried to read his face in the darkness, but it was cast in shadows. "Why didn't I just call myself a strong woman? Because it's ingrained in me. It shouldn't be important, but somehow it is."

"It's a part of who you are. Me, I'm a mutt from all over Europe. Got some Irish, some Italian, some Spanish blood in there."

"You got Spanish in you?"

"Yeah, I—"

He was interrupted by a grinding noise as several of the Lycanthropes pushed the front of the truck. It careened on its side, sparks igniting off the pavement beneath it. The sudden movement knocked Chesya from his arms. She fell back against the ceiling of the van, and Rick fell off balance. It took him a moment to regain it, to find his way back to her side.

"Rick!"

"I know, I'm here," he said, holding her close to his chest. She could hear the pounding of his heart, loud and swift against her ear.

The truck rocked. He figured one or more of them were shaking the van, jumping on the top of it.

"God," Chesya moaned. "I'm going to be seasick."

From a distance, they heard a long, groaning sound. It was intense, all-pervasive, covering the terrible noise of the creatures outside. It didn't sound organic.

"What is that?" Chesya asked.

"I don't know. Sounds like metal."

The noise came again, a deep rumbling of steel grinding against steel, the sound of iron twisting against its will.

"You ever see that movie *Titanic*?" Chesya asked.

"Yeah," he answered. "Who the hell didn't?"

"That's the noise that ship made just before it broke in two... metal tearing or stretching."

"It sounds like it's groaning."

When the noise stopped, they noticed that the monsters had ceased attacking the vehicle. In fact, the beast-men had grown eerily quiet, and this sent a chill through Rick.

He edged toward the windows, moving slowly so as not to incite the monsters into another round of "let's bash the truck." When he reached the glass, he peered out into the night. The streets were dark without the normal illumination of streetlamps, the tall buildings of downtown Cincinnati casting long shadows that hid so much from his view.

"What is it? What do you see?" Chesya asked.

"They've stopped moving," he said. "They're all looking around, and their ears are all pricked up. They don't know what that sound is any more than we do. I don't think they like it, either."

Some of the beasts whined softly, keening to themselves, the sound of dozens of terrified dogs. When the metallic noise came again, the grinding sounded deeper than before, more insistent. Many of the beast-men scattered.

"What is it, Rick?"

"They're running away."

"What?"

"They're scared of something."

"I don't like it," she said. "What's so frightening that it scares them?"

When the moaning metal sound erupted again, it was ear-splitting. Chesya put her head in her lap and covered her ears.

"Make it stop!"

Rick shouted over the din, "I don't know what the hell it is!"

"Make it stop! Make it stop!"

He looked from side to side out the windows at the rapidly vacating streets. The creatures slinked between cars or leapt over the hoods, pounding paw prints into the metal. He wondered if the sound hurt their ears, their super-sensitive hearing.

"Oh, please Rick, make it stop!"

He raised his eyes, listening carefully to the terrible babble, the sound of iron and steel twisting and screaming.

And he knew what was making the sound.

"Oh shit," he said.

"What? What is it?"

He rushed to her side, grabbing her. "Chesya, stay away from the windows!"

"Why? What's happening?" She was so frightened that tears were streaming down her plump face.

The noise grew louder, calling out for supplication.

"Stay away from the windows!"

"Why?"

"You remember that hotel, the one that had one of its corners blasted away by that car wreck?" he asked.

"Yeah," she said, sensing where this was going.

"That huge building, that hotel..."

"Yeah, yeah."

He swallowed, took a breath, and shouted over the increasing reverberation. The air was practically vibrating with the grinding, creaking, moaning, shifting...

"That huge building is about to fall over."

"Oh my God," she gasped. "How far away are we from it?"

"You said this bastard was made of reinforced steel?" he asked, knocking on the side of the Brink's truck.

"It's that close, huh?"

"Maybe a half a block away."

The sound became so loud they could no longer hear each other. They could feel vibrations from the collapse of the hotel, the street trembling beneath the armored car.

"Hold on," he screamed, bracing himself for the impact.

CHAPTER 25

September 17, 11:55 p.m.

Christian felt the sound before he heard it, low and metallic, steel twisting in the breeze. It set his teeth on edge, and he could feel his fillings rattling within his mouth. In the street below, the creatures rushed into nearby alleys, fleeing the open spaces on all fours. They abandoned the Brink's truck, leaving the steel gouged and scarred, the lettering scratched, a terrible testimony to their perseverance. He shivered in the cool breeze, wrapped his arms around himself. They were stronger than he had suspected.

The strange sound came again, creaking and grating. Christian located the direction from which the terrible screeching originated, and he drew in his breath.

The air reeked with animal piss and danger. He could taste it in his mouth, detect it deep in his nasal passages.

The rumbling came from the thirty-six-story hotel half a block down the street, the Marriott. An explosion had taken out the cornerstone of the building, leaving a wide, fire-blackened hole at least fifteen feet high and thirty feet wide.

Christian watched in horror as the building leaned towards the street, towards the Brink's truck, towards where he was standing at this very moment. The sound of metal stretching and tearing seemed even louder as he watched the hotel. Like it or not, the thing was going to fall over.

Quickly, he tried to do the math… thirty-six stories, twelve feet or so a level… how far away was he from the top of the hotel if it tumbled in his direction, as it seemed destined to do? He'd always detested fucking word problems! It was going to be close… too close for him to remain where he stood.

Earlier, he had determined the distance between this building and the next one down the block; it was about twelve feet away. Now, moving to the side, he looked down the six stories at the alley below him. Several of the creatures blinked up at him, their eyes suddenly filled with hunger and desire. At least ten of them were in the darkness of the alley, screwing against the garbage dumpsters, reaching towards him with their long talons. If he leapt and fell, those things would feast on his wrecked body.

The hotel groaned again. It seemed to loom over him, a tidal wave of glass and steel that could be hurtling towards him at any moment. Suddenly, he felt extremely vulnerable and small.

Those twelve feet of air between the buildings suddenly didn't seem so impossible. The next building was even a little shorter than the Bio-Gen offices. If he could get a good running start…

… he could drop into the alley, into the rendering claws of the beast-men below, torn limb from limb, eaten, his bones gnawed…

The listing hotel gave a deep sigh and resigned itself to inertia.

Looking down at the Brink's truck, he saw movement in the back windows, and he realized he had been right. There were people trapped inside, protected from the monsters by the truck's steel exterior. But could the vehicle withstand an entire building falling on it? Would it crumple beneath the weight of all that pressure?

From the rooftop, he shouted into the street, "Hey! Hey, you in the truck! You need to get out and run. The Marriott's falling."

He waited a moment, until the hotel moaned louder, and he knew it was starting to tear loose from its mooring. They were probably safer inside the truck now than running unprotected down the street. Christian wished them luck, then turned to the space between this building and the next.

He tried to convince himself that twelve feet wasn't that much. He could jump it, if he could get enough speed.

"I can do this," he said aloud, over the horribly escalating noise of the hotel crumbling behind him. "I can do it. I can do it."

Behind him, the middle floors of the hotel buckled beneath the pressure, and the behemoth plummeted towards the street, towards the Bio-Gen building. Plaster and furniture tumbled from holes that were rupturing in the concrete. Steel beams had snapped, bursting from inside of the hotel like broken bones erupting through someone's skin.

Christian still wasn't sure if the thing was going to reach the roof he stood upon. It might not be tall enough.

Then again, it might be.

He only had a few seconds. It was now or never.

Pumping his arms, he started to run with all the strength his skinny legs could muster. The wind was cool, roaring in his ears beneath the horrible, overwhelming sound of the disaster behind him. With each step he took, each time his sneakers slammed against the roof, the area between the two buildings grew closer...

... and grew larger. It seemed too big to jump over, even with the burst of speed he put on at the end.

"Fuck!" he screamed, looking at the gaping hole in front of him, hearing the whines of the Lycanthropes beneath him. "No way!"

Spinning at the last minute, he turned where the rooftop ended, running alongside the edge of the Bio-Gen offices. He slowed himself down, turned towards the Marriott.

It toppled, taking large chunks of another hotel and an office building down with it, landing no more than ten feet from the Bio-Gen headquarters. Towards the end of its fall, it disintegrated, the bricks separating from its mortar, steel beams spinning wildly through the air. He heard the *whumph* of an explosion, and fireballs erupted from several windows, spewing glass and metal over the city. Dust mushroomed from where it dropped, rising in the air and clouding Christian's sight.

He pulled his shirt over his mouth, choking on the dust. Holding his breath, he covered his head with his arms. He could hear the heavy thunks of bricks and small pieces of the Marriott plummeting all around him, like miniature meteors. Luckily, none of them hit him.

He moved to the border of the rooftop and stared down at the wreckage. He had to squint to see through the soot and plaster powder, but what he could see was an awe-inspiring sight, Armageddon in miniature. His eyes began to tear up, although he wasn't sure why. The devastation just seemed so… final.

After its descent, the Marriott barely even resembled the hotel it had once been. It had smashed into the earth, crushing everything in its path. The two buildings it had struck on its passage to the street now appeared to be wavering in the breeze. Fires burned in various places in the wreckage, and pipes had snapped, spewing water and gas like blood bubbling from the wounds of one of the Titans.

Searching for the Brink's truck, he realized he couldn't find it anywhere. Maybe it was trapped beneath the hotel debris, smashed beyond recognition, the poor people inside mangled and broken.

Suddenly, a huge wall of flame spewed from a damaged gas pipe, blasting forty feet into the air, singeing Christian's eyebrows. He cursed and stepped back as the flame died down, slowly eating away at other parts of the rubble. Bits of the plaster dust caught fire, miniature fireflies floating through the air. He hoped the rest of the dust would put out the fires.

Where was that truck? He couldn't find it anywhere on the street.

Something clattered behind him, and Christian turned to see the rooftop door with the padlock shaking. The things had found their way up the stairwell, and they were rattling the door, pounding on it with their paws. Their efforts gained in determination, and he realized they probably smelled him on the roof, through the cracks of the door. One of them gave a long, decisive howl.

"Oh come on," Christian muttered, looking towards the heavens.

The padlock appeared as though it could give way at any moment, and Christian looked back at the twelve feet that separated him from the rooftop of the next building over.

If he could reach that roof and hide inside the building, do something to eliminate his scent…

The padlock gave way, and the door burst from its hinges, falling to the roof with a loud clang. The first creature stuck its shaggy head out from the stairwell, and its gaze immediately focused upon the boy. With a roar, it ran towards him.

Christian sprinted across the rooftop, heading for the space, praying he would make it to the other roof.

Feeling the air suddenly beneath his feet, he knew he was going to fall short, was going to plummet into the alley, into the waiting mouths of the Lycanthropes beneath him. Swinging his arms, he closed his eyes and resigned himself to destiny.

CHAPTER 26

Cathy fumbled in the near-darkness of the attic, listening to the frustrated sounds of the creatures one floor below her. She doubted they could get through the trapdoor without a ladder, but their incessant howling and jumping unnerved her. The shadows created by the moonlight streaming through the lone window didn't help either. It seemed as though something lurked behind every mildewed stack of boxes, every trunk or garbage bag full of old clothes.

She found a broken leg from a kitchen chair, a remnant from a dining room set she'd thought was disposed of years ago. Picking it up, she enjoyed the heft of the cherry wood in her hands. She swung it a few times, practiced a few defensive moves. It made her feel better.

Starting in the farthest corner from the window, she searched the attic. She knew she wouldn't consider herself safe for the night until she was certain there wasn't anyone lurking in the shadows, waiting to spring out at her. She lifted drop cloths with the table leg, peering in the dim light at more old furniture, rolled-up carpets, and boxes and boxes of stuff. Sometimes, she disturbed insects, which scuttled away.

The beast-men were still protesting her getaway, howling and roaring their displeasure under her feet. Her sense of security was diminished by these monsters, only a few meager yards away from her.

She eventually wound her way to the window, finally assured that she was alone in the attic. There was a window seat, and she sat on it, peering out at the full moon. It hung bright and ominous in the sky. She wasn't sure if she had ever seen a moon so large, as though it were heading on a collision course for the Earth. Clouds had started to border it, surrounding the moon like frames.

Wanting some fresh air, she yanked at the window latch. When it opened, she took deep gulps, smelling dew and grass. It was a wonderful smell, refreshing after the mustiness of the room and its contents. She continued to breathe deeply… inhale and exhale, relaxing, calming herself.

She spotted something white in the farthest corner, and she headed towards it. Using the table leg to uncover it, she discovered her wedding gown. Part of the veil had been exposed when it had been packed away into the attic. She pulled it from its box, almost smiling.

The dress was beautiful, with sparkling hand-sewn beadwork across the bodice. The lace was ornate and expensive. The elbow-length gloves had also been stashed in the same box, but they had become discolored over the years, brown and dirty-looking. Leaving them alone, she stroked the delicate fabric of the dress. She held it in front of herself and saw that it was now a good two sizes too small.

Her wedding day had been a beautiful affair, catered and designed by the very best the city had to offer. Karl had looked so handsome, and they had suffered through the formal ceremony for their parents' sake. Then at the reception, they'd had too much to drink, danced through the evening to a live band that was surprisingly good, and snuck away twice during the festivities to make love, once in a closet, once in their car. The honeymoon had been in Nice and Florence. It had been a perfect beginning to their lives together.

A perfect beginning…

It struck her like a blow to her gut. That life was over. Karl lay dead on the floor below her, probably half-eaten by those creatures.

When did everything change? she wondered.

She knew it hadn't happened overnight. Things had been rocky for years in their marriage, especially in bed. Something had gone wrong in their relationship, and she was at a loss to remember when it had happened.

They'd been so happy on the day she had worn this strapless, white gown that she now held in her hands….a gown that had been rotting away in the house for years, forgotten, boxed away. Rotting in the same manner that their marriage had decayed.

If she'd only chosen to trust her boy.

Now Karl was dead. The world was falling apart, and she was locked in the attic, staring at the oversized moon.

Nothing would ever be the same, she realized. She would never return to those halcyon days of their early marriage. Perhaps they were only delusions of her youthful enthusiasm. Perhaps those wonderful times had never existed, the rot setting in early in their relationship. She would never go back to before.

Dropping her wedding gown to the floor, she covered her face with her hands and wept through her fingers.

CHAPTER 27

September 18, 12:02 a.m.

When Christian leaped over the void, arms and legs pedaling as if that could gain him a few inches, he knew he was going to fall a bit short of Bio-Gen's neighboring building. His chest hit the edge of the rooftop, and he reached for something to grasp hold of. The roof was cement, and there was a slight lip around the top. He sank a bit, hitting his chin, but his outstretched arms stopped his fall. He was holding on by his armpits.

He tried wriggling his bottom half, hiking his leg higher and higher until he caught his sneaker on the edge of the building. Swinging his other leg after it, he rolled himself onto the rooftop.

Breathing heavily, he faced the night sky, astounded at the size of the moon. It seemed to be devouring the entire night, star by star.

Then, he remembered that he had company, and he glanced back at the Bio-Gen rooftop. Six beast-men paced the length of the building, similar to the anxious way Andrei had walked back and forth in his cell. They displayed the same eagerness, the same jittery agitation as the Siberian. The largest one stood on top of the roof, baying at him.

It took a few steps backwards, and Christian cursed under his breath as he realized what the creature was doing.

The thing was going to jump after him.

Scanning the area, he saw another building, this one a bit closer, maybe ten or eleven feet away, but a good foot taller than where he stood. Its corners had been carved into sinister-looking gargoyles.

Across the alley, the huge leader of the pack began to run towards the edge of the building. Its muscles moved beautifully beneath its heavy brown fur, every muscle a part of a powerful machine, each working separately and together.

Christian knew it would make the jump. If he had made it, a mere human, this mighty animal would clear the edge with no problem.

He started running as the beast-man leapt from Bio-Gen, soaring mightily through the air. Strings of thick saliva fell from its jaws. Christian counted the steps… three, four, five… then he was pushing himself off of the roof. While he was in the air, he heard the huge creature land behind him with a grunt.

Stretching, Christian snagged the wing of a gargoyle with his fingers. One leg straddled the stone monster, and he pulled himself onto the next roof.

With a hiss of pain, he realized he had pulled a muscle in his leg. He took a few steps, wincing. The leg hurt a lot, and he had trouble walking on it. There was no way he could run across the roof and jump over alleys any longer.

Looking back, he saw the Lycanthrope roar at him, scratching at the roof's tarpaper with its sharp claws. A second creature had joined it while he had been testing his leg.

"Come on, Christian," he said aloud. "Walk it off. It could just be a cramp. Walk it off."

It did feel a little better after a few steps. As he watched, a third creature jumped from the Bio-Gen building to join its pack. It missed the lip of the roof and fell, yowling. He could hear the monsters in the alley as they attacked their fallen comrade. Bones snapped, flesh tore. Fights broke out, and in the streets more Lycanthropes rushed towards the smell of blood… a feeding frenzy.

Watching out for the vents and pipes that stuck out on the roof, Christian half ran, half hobbled to the other side. The next building was much farther away, at least thirteen feet. He moved backwards a bit, finding the trapdoor that led into the top floors. It was locked from the inside; he pulled and yanked as hard as he could, but it would not open.

Beneath his feet, the roof shook as something large landed on it.

"Aw, no," Christian said, turning to see the leader of the pack raising itself onto its forearms. It lowered its head, glaring at him with starving, golden eyes. Its lips pulled back in a snarl...

And Christian took off running. Every other step sent stabs of agony up his leg, like someone was sticking him with butcher knives. He cried out each time, and he made damn sure he jumped using his other leg for support.

Suddenly, there was nothing beneath him but air. The wind blew in his ears, angry and growing in its intensity. His arms windmilled, and he found himself slapping his palms against the side of a brick wall.

He'd missed the rooftop.

And he was falling.

He wanted to cry, to shout out and curse God and the heavens for everything that had happened to him. He wanted to yell at himself for not returning to the warehouse and the safety of the elevator.

His palms shredded as he tried to grab hold of the brick wall, scraping off a layer of skin, slippery with blood.

Then he landed with a clanging sound on a fire escape landing. It took him by surprise. He hadn't seen it there when he was jumping; he'd been too focused on the rooftop. He crumpled to his knees on the metal slats, the pain in his right leg throbbing now in time with his heart.

On the rooftop he'd just escaped, the leader peeked down at him between two gargoyles. Its eyes held a curiosity that Christian hadn't seen in the beasts before now. There was something intelligent lurking behind the compulsion to eat and kill.

Struggling to his feet, ignoring the pain, Christian began to descend the iron stairs of the fire escape. His footfalls echoed loudly in the alley, and he wondered what lay below him in the darkness.

Looking back up, he saw the leader soar over his head and land on the roof he had just missed. He stopped a moment. A second monster, then a third gracefully bridged the gap between the buildings. As the fourth jumped, the leader showed its face, staring down at the fire escape a story below it. It reached out a paw and swung at the metal, but it didn't have the reach. It whined deep in its throat, a disappointed sound.

A fifth beast tried to jump over the alley. It missed, striking its head on the brick wall. Knocked unconscious, it dropped, landing on the fire escape a foot away from Christian. Its weight was too much for the old, rusted metal, and it shook the structure so hard Christian was knocked down a flight, saving himself from falling by grabbing a stair. Part of the supports that were screwed into the side of the building gave in to the pressure. Bolts popped out of the wall, and the entire structure wavered, barely supported by the bolts at the bottom of the contraption. The fallen beast-man slid off and dropped to the ground below. It landed with a wet splat, knocking over garbage cans.

The entire fire escape began to swing across the alley. A few more bolts popped from their moorings, and the stairs creaked as they swung across the open space. The top half was no longer attached, and the bolts that had secured the fire escape to the wall were being tugged out one by one with loud *chunk*ing sounds, shooting down past Christian, who clung to the stairs, his arms looped around a single step.

"Give me a fucking break!" he said, almost laughing. "Just one!"

With a high-pitched screech, the entire fire escape pulled from the building. It leaned over the alley, hovering in the middle for a moment. Holding on tightly, Christian screamed as the structure buckled and leaned. Below him, two of the monsters entered the alley, called by the blood of the creature that had fallen.

The whole stairway dropped ten feet as the last bolts pulled out of the wall. Christian shouted, felt the sudden jolt as the bottom of the stairs struck pavement. Then the whole world went sideways for the boy.

The top of the fire escape struck the neighboring building and stopped its falling motion, although the metal still creaked loudly. Christian clung to the stairs. He was afraid to move, lest he disturb the delicate balance and fall where more creatures were now gathering to feast on the monster that had dropped to the ground.

The dead beast-man turned human again as the others chowed down on the corpse. They pulled intestines from the lower abdomen, ripped the arms from their sockets. Their eating noises were loud with the crunching of bones.

Somehow, watching them eat a man was far worse than watching them eat one of their own. The man's eyes stared accusingly at Christian, his face spattered with blood. The boy had to turn his head.

As he did, the fire escape began to slide, sparks shooting from where metal scratched against brick. He stopped moving, and the balance was restored. Christian saw he was right next to a window. He could see office furniture inside the room.

If he could get to that window, which was a good six feet away, he could get out of this mess.

When he reached for the window, the top of the fire escape slid towards the ground. Christian lost his grip on the stair step. His upper torso fell off the fire escape and hung over the dark alley.

The creatures looked up, startled by the noise.

Christian's right foot was snagged beneath one of the stairs, which was the only reason he didn't drop to the pavement three stories below. The top of the metal landing caught on a window-box filled with orange and yellow flowers, forcing it to a sudden stop. It almost dislodged Christian's foot, but he grabbed the railing.

This caused his feet to swing out beneath him, and he found himself hanging by his hands, halfway down the rusty fire escape. He felt like a trapeze artist. His grip began slipping, his scratched palms slick with blood.

Below him, the creatures jumped, stretched, and reached for his legs. There had to be ten of them now, and more joined their ranks every second.

Christian tried to swing his leg back onto the fire escape. The frame of it shook, shuddered, but it no longer slid downwards. The top remained lodged on that window-box. *Thank God for urban renewal,* he thought. He raised his leg again, wincing as the pulled muscle protested the motion.

Something creaked above him, that grating, groaning, twisting-metal sound the collapsing hotel had made.

Below him, a creature found the bottom of the fire escape and tested it with one of its claws. It jumped backwards when the noise grew louder. Cautiously, it approached the stairs again, looking at the steps that led up to the boy.

Christian couldn't raise his leg enough to hike it around the railing, and his hands kept slipping.

The beast took a step up the collapsed fire escape, then a second, then a third.

The sound of metal tearing increased, echoing off the brick walls of the alley. Several of the creatures looked around, frightened of it.

The bravest of the beast-men had ascended to the fifth stair.

Beneath his hands, Christian felt the entire fire escape, stretched out between the two buildings, buckle in the middle.

The monster set its weight down on the sixth step.

And the window-box that held the yellow and orange flowers snapped from the wall. The fire escape plummeted.

Christian found his balance and hopped on top of the falling structure. He rode it like a horse, like Slim Pickens had ridden that bomb in *Dr. Strangelove.*

Alarmed, the Lycanthropes beneath him scattered, yelping beneath their breath.

The one that had reached the sixth step was crushed between the metal railings as they folded. It formed a rusted cage, trapping the beast inside. Part of it bent as it dropped, snapping the creature's spine and its back legs. It howled, but didn't die. It scrabbled against the iron with its front paws, its back legs paralyzed and useless.

Christian rode the fire escape the final fifteen feet to the blacktop, falling away from it at the moment of impact. He curled himself into a ball and rolled away from it, towards the base of the structure, towards the broken, trapped monster that was struggling to free itself.

It bled badly from a wound in its right haunch, and Christian knew the scent of blood would bring more of them.

Limping slightly, he ran, trying to ignore the distress his right leg was causing. He was still alive. At least, for now. He needed to find shelter. He needed to find someplace safe until morning.

From the alley, he emerged onto the street and stopped in his tracks. The hotel had collapsed right down this road. Cars were crushed beneath it. Huge chunks of ravaged concrete and wires and plumbing stuck up from all angles. It reminded him of pictures he'd seen of the London Blitz, and he was awed by the destruction.

He remembered that there was a Brink's truck somewhere amidst the rubble, and he began searching for it through the ever-settling, ever-present dust, the beast-men running after him.

CHAPTER 28

September 18, 12:06 a.m.

"Hold on!" Rick shouted over the cacophony of the hotel toppling towards them. Wrapping his arms around Chesya, he felt hers curl around his waist, pressing her face hard into his abdomen. He braced himself, shoving his back against one wall and thrusting his legs out so they met solidly with a steel support beam. The back of the truck, which had seemed so sturdy and impervious, now appeared to be little more than a tin coffin.

As the noise grew louder outside, Rick noticed he could no longer see the moonlight through the back windows. The falling structure had blocked out the sky.

Glancing down at Chesya, he wanted to say something to reassure her. She'd closed her eyes tightly, and he could feel her heart beating beneath his arms. He knew she was afraid. Hell, he was too, but it seemed wrong to remain silent when they both might die in a moment.

Chesya was wondering how she had come to this. She was clutching wildly to a certified bank robber, a man who'd held a gun to her face thirty hours ago, a man who'd tried to protect her from the monsters that lurked in the night, a man who professed to being a "bad guy." She almost laughed at the thought, as fleeting as it was. Her brothers had brought "bad guys" home with them, men who beat women, prostituted their wives and children, men who sold dope on street corners and in playgrounds, men who had killed, ruined lives, lashed out at the world as though their very souls depended upon it. In the hierarchy of so-called bad guys, Rick was probably on the lowest rung of the ladder. How many of her brothers' friends would have remained at her side during the last day? Not a single one, she realized.

This man, Rick, had stayed with her, had tried to comfort her. He had even started censoring his filthy language for her. Had any other man done more? She wasn't falling in love with him. That would be ridiculous; there was much more to be worried about than romance. There just wasn't time for it.

Still, if there had been time… she wondered what might have happened.

The darkness outside the windows seemed to increase. The noise was thunderous, and she felt the vibrations of the earth beneath the tires of the truck. She closed her eyes tighter, afraid that they'd be jarred right out of her head.

When the impact came, it shook her so hard her fingers unclasped, and she was tossed to the opposite side of the truck, striking her head against the doors. The momentum of the hotel's collapse sent the truck skidding on its side, sparks flying from the sudden friction against the blacktop. Chesya fell onto her back, her eyes rising to the windows.

Bricks bumped against the bulletproof glass, and swirls of dust blocked most of her view. A large piece of concrete, metal support rods jutting from its sides, dropped and settled on the ground in front of the doors, effectively blocking her view of the outside.

Rick shouted, "Chesya, are you all right?"

Raising a hand to her head, she felt a wetness there. The back of the truck was dark, all moonlight eclipsed by the concrete slab. She didn't need to see the sticky substance on her hand to know it was blood. Although her head rang from the impact against the doors, she yelled back at Rick. "I bumped my head. Again. But I think I'm okay. You?"

"I'm all right," he answered over the din.

Pieces of bricks and mortar and steel came down like a vicious rain. The truck was taking a beating, but it was still in one piece, still protecting them from the destructive forces outside. Chesya wished she could see how deep the dents were, if there were any holes appearing in the Brink's van, but she could see nothing.

"Don't try to move yet," Rick warned.

"I would have to go and slam my fool head against something, wouldn't I?"

"Is it bad?" he asked.

"I don't think so. My ears are ringing."

"Mine are, too. I think it was the explosion."

"What explosion?"

"You didn't hear that? Sounded like a gas explosion. I'm going to move towards you. Keep talking, and I'll find you."

"I must have blacked out for a while," she said. "I don't remember an explosion, just the hotel dropping on us, the bricks falling. I don't know if we'll be able to open the doors, because there's chunks of concrete blocking the way. I don't know how big they are."

He reached her, held her, and she felt the reassuring touch of his hands. They fluttered like hummingbirds around her head.

"Yeah, there's a lot of blood. Head injuries bleed a lot, though."

"You're always so full of interesting facts," she said.

He sighed, leaned away from her, and she immediately missed the close contact with him. "You're all right if you can make jokes…"

"I told you I was fine. Don't believe me."

"I won't."

"Good."

"Fine."

They were silent for a few seconds, then each of them burst into laughter. "You asshole," she said between giggles.

"Oh my God," he said. "I can't believe we just survived that. I mean, a fucking… um, sorry. A really big building just fell on us. We should be dead."

"Luck of the Irish," she said.

"But you're not Irish."

"No, but you are… at least in part."

"So you have been listening to what I've been saying."

"Of course. What else do I have to do?"

She felt him move away from her a bit, heard him testing the doors. Cursing, he moved back to her side.

"I don't think we're going anywhere," he said. "There's a lot of rubble blocking the door. It doesn't feel very heavy, but someone'll have to clear it away in the morning to let us out."

"I hate being trapped like this."

"Yeah, well, it's better than allowing any of those things to get in here. I doubt they'll bother us again tonight."

"Even the windows are intact? They aren't broken?"

"I didn't feel any sharp edges."

"It's a miracle."

"Yeah," he said. "Yeah, maybe it is."

"Why don't you try to get some sleep? I don't think we need to worry about anything until morning. Then we'll need to find someone to get us out of here."

"I don't know if I can sleep. My pulse is racing like crazy."

"Close your eyes. You'll be surprised how quick it'll happen."

Shutting her eyelids, she marveled at the lack of difference in the darkness. It was how a blind person must feel.

She snuggled back into Rick's arm. He jerked for a second, alarmed by her movement, and then he melted down into her, forming a protective barrier around her body.

"I think some sleep will do both of us a lot of good," he said.

They rested for a moment, and Chesya was shocked to find herself on the verge of nodding off, when she heard something muffled and definitely human.

"Did you hear that?" she asked Rick. She placed one of her ears against the doors of the truck, the better to listen.

"Hear what?"

"That, that," she said. "It sounded like... a voice. A kid's voice."

He listened along with her, and he heard it too. It was muted, but it was definitely a young person shouting.

"Are you still in there?" came the voice. Then, the sound of debris being moved. "Tell me you're still in there."

"It's human," Chesya said. "Do we answer?"

"Please tell me I can get in there. Anyone still there?" The voice was growing louder.

"I don't know," Rick answered her.

"Oh, Jesus," the young man screamed. "They're almost here. Let me in!"

CHAPTER 29

September 18, 12:20 a.m.

Chesya and Rick dashed for the back doors of the Brink's truck, practically knocking each other aside in their haste to reach the handles. The boy outside continued to shout.

"Jesus, I'm human like you. Let me in!"

They could see his face through the windows as he pushed away the rubble blocking the door. His eyes pleaded for help, and his clothes were dirty and torn. Several bruises and bleeding cuts ran along his arms and throat, testimonials to what he had endured.

Rick said, "You get the handles, I'll get the bars."

He pulled back on the sliding bars that acted as locks, and she popped the ones in the door. She gave them a shove, and the doors opened, slamming into the boy's chest.

He stumbled back, stunned by the impact. Behind him, hordes of creatures rushed the truck. There were dozens of them.

Christian, regaining his balance, leapt inside the Brink's van, and Chesya slammed the door behind him.

Rick shoved the bars back into place while she locked the doors. Then she turned to the boy as Rick finished with the last of the locks.

"Are you all right?" she asked.

Christian had pushed himself to the back of the van, and he was nearly hidden in the darkness. "I think so—"

The first of the beasts slammed into the truck. Then another, and another. They leaped up on the side, growling and sniffing for an entrance. Some of them shoved at the sides of the vehicle, but as before, they couldn't get in.

While the creatures pounded on the walls in frustration, Chesya crawled over to where the boy sat. Rick moved behind her, placing an assured hand on her shoulder.

"You're... normal. Like us," Chesya said.

"Yeah. I think so. I haven't changed into one of them. Not yet, at least."

"I'm Chesya, and this here's Rick. We thought we were the only humans left. What's your name?"

"Christian," he said. "Christian Wright. And it's good to see you too. Nice to know there's... someone else left out there. And thanks for opening those doors. You could've left me outside. It would have been the smart thing to do."

"No." Rick grinned at the kid. "I don't think we could have done that. What about your family, Christian? They change too?"

"I don't know. I... I left them a while back... sorta ran away. It's a long story."

"Well," Chesya laughed over the angry howling outside the truck. "We have a long night ahead of us. Those things aren't going away until morning... well, I'm not really sure how they work yet, but it seems like they only change at night."

"I think it's the moon," Rick said. "Like werewolves."

"You're part right," Christian said. "It is like a werewolf."

He gave them an edited account of his life as a runaway, telling them he'd met an old Frenchman who'd helped him through some rough times, who'd given him meals and a warm place to stay.

Chesya raised her eyebrows. She could read between the lines. The boy had sold himself; he possessed as little self-esteem as any prostitute.

She could tell by the sad, knowing look in Rick's eyes that he wasn't buying the "kindly old gentleman" bit, either. It confirmed her idea that Rick's "bad boy" status was mostly just an act, covering up hidden layers. In fact, he displayed a rather surprising amount of empathy.

Christian wrapped up his PG-13 account of his NC-17 story, and he told them about the leather-bound journal he had dropped. "I think all the answers are in that book. Jean kept a detailed record about what he called Lycanthropy, and he had hunted one down in Siberia."

"Hunted down a werewolf?" Rick asked.

"Yeah, I think so. I'll need to get the journal in the morning so I can finish it, but there's a naked man in a cell up there on the third floor of the Bio-Gen building, and he changed into one of those monsters while I watched. He started to tell me a story, but then he began mutating, so I only got the beginning."

"He's still there?" Chesya asked.

"As far as I know. I think Jean captured him and brought him here for experiments. Jean believed that Lycanthropy was a genetic disease. I kinda deciphered that much. They were probably testing him, observing him, trying to cure him. I think something backfired. They created something in the lab, and I think it started all of this. Maybe released it into the air somehow, like an airborne virus."

"See," Rick said. "I told you it was some kind of virus."

"Yes, you did," she said.

"So what happened to you guys?" Christian asked. "You look like you've been through hell."

Rick and Chesya related their own story, and Christian listened attentively as they interrupted each other, sparring with their words while making the whole thing sound like some wonderful adventure. Rick realized he was cleaning it up for the boy, but turnabout was fair play. Chesya watched the kid, saw him yawn in a huge, theatrical manner, and something stirred within her, something protective and (she hated to even think the word) maternal. The boy had been through so much, ever since he had entered adolescence. The release of the Lycanthropy disease was merely the icing on a spoiled and rotten cake.

By the time Rick and Chesya had completed their tale, all but a few beasts had deserted the Brink's van, loping off in search of some other form of dinner. The truck had stopped rocking, and the sounds from outside had dulled down to a few yips and growls here and there.

With a yawn, Chesya resigned to the fact that they were safe for the night. She hadn't realized she was so sleepy, but now that her adrenaline had stopped pumping, she could feel her muscles aching and her eyelids drooping.

"I think we should all get some rest," she suggested.

"Sounds like a damned good idea," Rick said.

The boy nodded, although he could still feel his heart racing in his chest. He knew he was secure inside the impenetrable Brink's truck with these people. The chase that evening had taken almost everything out of him. He rested his back against the side of the truck, wondering if he could ever sleep again.

He was snoring within two minutes

CHAPTER 30

September 18, 2:40 a.m.

Cathy had assembled a makeshift bed (more of a nest, really) out of several old blankets and curtains she'd discovered in the attic. She still occasionally overheard the beasts outside her house, but she was so exhausted that she couldn't pay attention to them. They were reminders on the fringe of her tired mind, grace notes to the evening's debacle.

Lying down in her pile of blankets, she mashed a few into the semblance of a pillow and dropped her head upon them. She pulled a dusty velvet curtain over herself to keep out the chill, luxuriating in the softness of the fabric. She couldn't remember when she had banished these curtains to the faraway kingdom of the attic, but she was glad she had. The material was warm against her skin.

She closed her eyes for a moment, and the bizarre concerto of animal sounds that surrounded her began to fade, a decrescendo of the horrors that lurked outside.

And she felt the familiar breath of Karl against the back of her neck.

Karl, the betrayer, the pervert, the husband.

"Hello, Cathy," he whispered. The puffs of air disturbed the downy hairs that trailed down her neck to her spine. A chill swept through her.

Turning over, she snapped her eyes open. Karl's eyes were white, occluded by mysterious cataracts. He was nude, but he was tucked beneath her covers with her, his cold body pressed against hers.

Backing away from him, she said, "You're dead." Her voice was quiet, overwhelmed by a fatigue that pressed down on her like a heavy weight. She knew she should leap from her nest and run for the nearest exit, but she was too tired to even consider such a move.

This was her dead husband next to her.

She had killed him hours earlier. She'd smeared the entire bathroom with his blood.

She refused to believe he was here, cozying up to her.

Then again, the world was full of such conundrums now. What was one more?

He smiled at her, the familiar, self-effacing, charming grin he reserved for his happiest moments. "Come on, Cathy. You have to concede that I'm here. Look…" He shook his hands free of the covers, exposing pale-white skin. "Nothing up my sleeve. No wires. No tricks. Just me and you."

"I killed you," she hissed.

"And a damn fine job you did of it, too." He shrugged. "Something less messy would have been preferable, but you work with what you're given. I've always loved that about you."

"Have you, really?" The sarcasm dripped from her lips like poison.

"You're a good woman, Cathy. I know I never appreciated you very much during our marriage, but I always respected you."

"By screwing our son?" Saying the words aloud gave them flesh, realized them from the mists of rumor. She realized she sounded shrill, like her mother, the shrewish wife she had never wanted to become. Lowering her volume a bit, she said, "You really did it, didn't you?"

"I had needs." He shrugged.

"Needs? Jesus Christ, you raped your own child."

"Oh, Cathy… it was sometimes worse than that."

"You bastard."

"Hey, I admit it… I was a fucker. You must know that."

"I want you to go away." She closed her eyes and turned her back to him.

Karl touched her shoulder, and his fingers burned her skin, frostbite from his caress infecting her. "Like you want all problems to go away, Cathy? Like you wanted my problem to go away?"

"Shut up," she said. It was a feeble, impotent protestation.

"You ignored it, and it didn't vanish. At least, not until Christian ran away. Not until we lost our boy forever. You know you had your chance to confront me. You didn't take advantage at the time, and he's gone now, isn't he? Out there someplace. Do you ever wonder if he's even alive?"

"Please... please shut up." The first tear fell from her eye.

"Has he survived through this cataclysm? Did he find refuge somewhere? Tell me, Cathy, do you ever think about him?"

She focused on the moonlight that spilled into the room from the window, immersing herself in its blue security.

"I always think about Christian. He was a good boy." Her voice was little more than a whisper.

"You're tellin' me."

"Please," she begged, and he was silent. "I didn't want to believe that you could do such a thing. Even when all the evidence pointed in that direction... I couldn't allow myself to think that you were abusing our son, that you preferred our boy to me. It was the wrong thing to do, but I closed my eyes to it. If I didn't take notice of it, if I never actually acknowledged the sin, then it didn't exist. Did it? Did it?"

"Oh, my dear, it existed. I was there."

"Now... Christian... out there... someplace..."

She buried her face in the makeshift pillow as sobs wracked her body. No longer concerned with appearances, of what the neighbors might think, she wept for the loss of her son, for her inability to confront her husband and stop the abuse.

"I've... I've lost him," she admitted, saying the words aloud for the first time. "I've lost my son."

The cold hand that was stroking her back evaporated into a cool mist. "You can still find him," Karl said, wispy and far away. "It isn't too late, because Christian's still alive."

The condensation on her back dried, and she turned over. Karl had disappeared. He left a cold space where he had lain. Through the window, she could see the first orange reconnaissance of the sun as it began to rise.

Was it a dream? she wondered. *Or did he really visit me?*

Standing and stretching, she moved to the window. Bodies dotted the perfectly gardened and trimmed landscaping of the nearby houses.

Several floated facedown in the man-made lake, which reflected the sunrise in all of its Van Gogh glory.

Cathy decided it didn't matter whether he was a ghost, or just some figment of her subconscious. The words he had spoken were true.

Her son was alive. She knew it with that unswerving, maternal certainty that came to her sometimes… that materialized within all mothers in times of strife.

Christian was alive. Out there.

And she was going to have to find him.

Somehow.

CHAPTER 31

September 18, 5:30 a.m.

Christian awoke with a start, and it took him several moments of panic before he realized where he'd been sleeping. The world seemed topsy-turvy, on its side, and there were others here, snoring away their own bad dreams. Dawn was breaking outside the Brink's truck, and tepid sunlight streamed in through the gunports in the sides of the truck where men had once-upon-a-time held shotguns... modern-day turrets.

He shifted, trying to lean against the back of the vehicle (or was it the bottom?). He moved slowly, quietly, so as not to wake the others. Peering through the murkiness, he could see they were spooning, as though they were lovers. The man had his arm draped casually over the woman, and she had the faintest of smiles on her lips.

He wondered if these people, who had also resisted the change into monsters, were to become his companions. He'd tried not to warm to them last night, but there was something about being with your own kind. He felt safe with them, almost comfortable, in a way he hadn't felt since his father had taken those first dreadful steps into his room at night.

Thinking of his father again, he sensed the tears building in his eyes. Long ago, he'd taught himself that crying displayed a weakness, and any show of vulnerability on the street was a flashing sign, evidence for the stronger to pounce and prove their dominance. It was a form of street Darwinism. The strong certainly did prevail over the weak. But if they didn't realize you were fragile, they tended to leave you alone until they could be certain. Therefore, tears, like any exhibition of a troubled mind, were forbidden.

They were flowing pretty freely now, though. He cried silently, using his sleeve to wipe his nose.

In the safety of the Brink's truck, he could let himself go, could think about all the things he hadn't allowed himself to consider since he had run away.

Like, if his mother were still alive… or his father.

Christian found himself hoping his mother had survived. Even though she had ignored his accusations against Karl, she hadn't willingly contributed to the abuse.

They had been so close as he had grown up, especially during his early teen years. He had been able to speak with her about subjects that he'd never dare to broach with his father. Often, he'd share a bowl of popcorn with her, lean up against her warm side, and watch an old movie on the late show. She'd seemed to welcome the intimacy, sometimes kissing the top of his head, often mussing his hair with a laugh. She had always enjoyed the classic romantic comedies, co-starring Hepburn and Tracey or Doris Day and Rock Hudson. Christian had also taken pleasure in the frivolous films, laughing at the jokes and feeling as though he was peering through a keyhole at a lost time.

As he rested in the Brink's truck, he thought that perhaps his mother had enjoyed the films for a different reason, that she was searching for some proof of happily ever after. He had noticed the chasm that was opening between his parents, had always sensed its cold wind blowing in their chilly conversations. It had remained on the periphery of his adolescent attention, always just out of sight.

But she had allowed the abuse to continue. She had ignored the signs.

She was his mother, and there was a special bond between a boy and his mother, no matter what form her inactions took. She was a human being, and, as such, was fallible. People made mistakes.

And they often paid dearly for them.

He wondered if Cathy had paid for her neglect, or if she had continued to play the part of the loving wife, social butterfly, and charity-event organizer.

"Morning."

Startled, Christian glanced over at the couple across the truck. Chesya was peering at him, squinting in the feeble morning light. As she spoke, Rick swiftly removed his arm from her side, acting like a boy caught with a girlfriend on the family sofa. He tried to cover up his move by yawning and stretching his arms as far as he could. Then he scratched his head and leaned away from the woman. Chesya, seeming more relaxed than Rick, lay on her side, cupping the plump curve of her face in her open palm. She watched Christian with wide, slightly yellow eyes.

"Hey," Christian said, his eyes flicking back to the window.

"Any action out there?" Rick asked, edging closer to the glass.

"No, seems pretty quiet. I can just about see the dawn starting."

"You have an important meeting to go to?" Rick asked. "You've been watching for the sunlight for a long time now. I saw you."

"I want to get that journal and get back to the Bio-Gen building. I'm positive there are more answers in Jean's writings."

"You know where it is, right?" Chesya asked.

He shrugged. "Pretty much. I just hope it's still there. I was just getting to the part where he was studying werewolves in Siberia."

"See, Chesya," Rick said with a grin. "Told you they were werewolves. The old Rickster comes through again."

"Look!" Christian shouted, pointing towards a small group of beast-men.

They fell to the ground, writhing in pain, transforming back into humans. Their bodies convulsed, jerked as if in a movie that had been sped up. The hair covering their bodies pulled back into their skin, and they scratched at themselves.

"No better time to go get that book," Rick said. "They're powerless, can't attack us. Let's go see if it's still where you lost it."

Chesya nodded, and Rick unlocked the truck door, pushed his way out of the vehicle.

"I hope we're doing the right thing," she said, stepping into the dim light of the dawn.

"This way," Christian declared. They rushed through the street, stepping around the prone, quivering bodies of the beasts, whose mouths opened and closed, exposing various versions of teeth, human and werewolf momentarily coexisting. They didn't bother the three humans hurrying through their midst. They were far too busy becoming people again.

The monsters shook like a woman Chesya had often seen in church, as if they were possessed by the Holy Spirit. But these poor sufferers weren't infused with anything holy. Their minds were probably a thick mélange of human despair and confusion and beastly blood lust.

It was Chesya and Rick's first good look at the streets since the Marriott had collapsed, and it made her want to stand in awe and take in the utter destruction. She grasped Rick's hand in hers, and he squeezed it once. She felt the calluses on his fingers.

"I turned here," Christian said.

As they progressed through the rubble, the monsters, nearly human, began to stand on awkward legs, balancing themselves against cars or piles of concrete. A fang would sometimes emerge from a lip, or a set of eyes would shine, flecked with gold. Many of them sniffed the air, as though still graced with a wolf's superior sense of smell.

"This is the alley where I dropped it," Christian said, identifying the dark passageway between buildings. "I'm ninety-nine percent sure."

"It's pretty dark in there still," Chesya noted. "Maybe we should wait for the sun to get higher."

"Hell with that," Christian said. "I'm not waiting to see just how crazy these bastards get today. You see them yesterday? Some of them actually looked like they could attack me."

"I think it's hard for a lot of people to stay sane after what they've done," Chesya explained. "They chose the path of least resistance."

"The path of crazy," Christian said, entering the mouth of the alley. Chesya and Rick, still holding hands, followed him. Rick turned every few steps to check their backs.

Even though the surrounding establishments were still intact, the alley was a mess. Shadows obscured half of everything. Huge trash dumpsters had been overturned and rooted through, and garbage was strewn all over the place. Dead men and women lay on the ground, naked, their newly-human bodies torn and twisted. Blood pooled around the corpses.

"You sure this is the right place?" Rick asked. "I don't see a journal anywhere."

"I'm sure. God, I hope it's still here," he said, wandering a little farther into the gloom.

Something moved from a pile of garbage, and the three of them turned; a rat wriggled from a hole in a plastic bag. They sighed, glad it wasn't something bigger, something dangerous.

In the brief silence, they heard other sounds, little, soft noises like something—or some things—trying not to be overheard. Chesya edged closer to Rick. The three of them stopped breathing as one, scanning the murky alley.

"There's the book!" Christian cried, rushing forward.

The corner of the leather binding peeked out from beneath the leg of a woman in her mid-fifties. She was naked and her throat had been torn out, exposing glistening cartilage and severed tubes. Other bites had been taken from various places on her body, but the blood had seeped in the opposite direction of the journal.

"Be careful, Christian," Chesya warned. "Those sounds…"

He grasped the leather and pulled it from beneath the corpse. Thankfully, the book hadn't been ripped to shreds or stained by the woman's bodily fluids. Christian held it up so Rick and Chesya could see it, could verify it was real.

A hand lashed out from a pile of black garbage bags, grabbing Christian's ankle and yanking him off balance. He fell forward, scratching his palms on the blacktop as he hit. Jean's journal fell to his left.

"What have we here?" came a rasping voice from the piles of rotten food and paper. "Breakfast for Mommy?"

As the detritus fell away, a pale, obese woman stood nude from her hiding place. Her dimpled body was covered in old grease and coffee grounds, and her lips were stained with blood. From her eyes, still dappled with the golden eyeshine, insanity leaked out like tears.

She pulled Christian closer to her, and he struggled, kicking up at her face; she was stronger than he suspected. In a moment, she had the screaming boy in her arms, enveloping him in her folds.

Rick raised his gun, but Chesya pushed it away, glaring at him.

"Save the bullets for the creatures," she said, stepping forward and picking up a brick. Realizing she was right, Rick grabbed a long metal pipe.

The woman licked Christian's cheek and smeared him with the filth on her skin. He got an arm free and struck her in the face.

"Breakfast needs to be still," she said, and she squeezed him in her surprisingly muscular arms. The breath left his lungs in a whoosh.

Chesya threw the brick, and it glanced off the woman's temple, opening a small gash that erupted in blood. The crazy howled, but she maintained her grip on Christian, perhaps squeezing even tighter, constricting his chest like a python.

She bit his shoulder and shook her head like a dog, trying to tear through the jacket and the shirt to get at the soft skin.

Christian attempted to shriek, but it came out as little more than a whistle.

Rick struck the woman across the back of the head with his pipe. There was a loud crunching noise, and the woman finally let go of Christian. The boy fell to the ground, breathing heavily. Chesya retrieved her brick.

Farther back in the alley, something groaned and hissed, shuffling through the trash.

The fat woman fell to her knees, and Rick hit her again in the same spot. Her skull caved in, spilling brains and gore across her shoulders and her lanky, brown hair. She collapsed in a heap close to Christian, who shuffled backwards, crab-style, to the other end of the alley.

"They're getting crazier," Chesya said. "Two nights of changing has made them even worse."

"Worse?" Rick asked.

"They saw a lot more last night," Chesya said. "More than people should see. I think a lot of people would go crazy if they didn't have anyone to talk to, anyone to lean on in the night. They just... attack and kill."

"I bet a lot of them murdered their own families... their friends," Christian whispered.

The silence was broken by a maniacal giggle that was too close for comfort.

Something in the dark end of the alley grabbed one of the corpses and dragged it into the shadows.

"What the hell was that?" Rick asked.

Moist tearing sounds emerged from the darkness where the body had disappeared.

"There's more of them," Chesya answered. "I thought I heard something back there, but…"

"Let's get someplace safe," Rick said. "Now."

Christian nodded and scooped up the journal. He clutched it to his chest and motioned with his head. "This is the Bio-Gen building," he said. "The Siberian guy… the one I told you about… he's upstairs."

"Is it safe in there?"

"Safe as anyplace, probably."

"Then what are we waiting for?"

They exited the alley and Christian led them to the front door; on the wall next to the entrance hung a little brass plaque engraved with the company's name.

"This is it?" Rick asked, looking up at the building. "Somehow, I thought it'd be bigger."

Chesya nodded. "Yeah. Something that causes this much heart-ache, hurts this many people… you'd think it would come from some huge corporation, some international conglomerate."

Inside, the front foyer was in even worse shape than when Christian had entered it yesterday. Claw marks gouged the walls, and several pieces of furniture and vases were scattered across the parquet floor. Decorative plants had been pulled up by their roots and tossed around the room.

They spent some time blocking the front door before taking seats in the lobby.

"I want to finish reading this thing," Christian said, holding up the journal. "I'm sure there are clues in it, and I don't want to face Andrei again before I actually know what's happening. I think he knows, but I don't trust him."

"Read it aloud," Chesya said.

"You sure?"

"Yeah. I think we should all know."

Christian turned to the words on the page, the neat scrawl of the old man, and he began to read.

CHAPTER 32

September 18, 6:30 a.m.

Jean Cowell had traveled to Kirskania, a remote village in Siberia, from which the multi-generational rumors of a shapeshifter had emerged. His initial goal had been to interview the inhabitants of the village. If he could find a person who had lived in the vicinity for the right amount of years, he would have his Lycanthrope.

While he traveled across the destitute farms and dirt roads, the swirling snow seemed to cloud his thoughts. He debated if he was actually on the right track, if he could truly segregate the two halves of man… the bestial and the human. His mission, his *obsession*, was to repress the animalistic side, to prevent another Holocaust. But hadn't similar experiments caused the noble Dr. Jekyll to morph into the evil Mr. Hyde? Could you immunize against evil?

Every time he grew doubtful, he glanced at the numbers tattooed upon his right hand, and his resolution grew stauncher.

At the outskirts of Kirskania, Jean's sledge driver abruptly stopped. He would go no farther, and as soon as Jean stepped out, the driver turned his team of horses away from the small thatched buildings and lashed out at them. The horses galloped away in a burst of fear and pain.

Kirskania had no inn, but Jean found a bar with an extra room upstairs. After agreeing on a fair sum with the owner, he began his research by haunting the pub, eating all his meals there, warming himself by the fire.

To his great surprise, the villagers had no qualms about discussing what they called the area's "beastie." It had been in the village for so long, they had become accustomed to its presence. One old woman, straight out of a Gogol short story, had advised him to remain inside when the moon was full, that if he kept himself hidden during those three nights, he would be safe. Allegedly, the beastie rarely harmed human beings, preferring to devour a stray goat or dog. There had been incidents when a man or child had been attacked, but accounts of deaths were infrequent.

Jean had asked the old woman, "These people who were injured… did they also become shapeshifters during the next full moon, as described in the fairy stories?"

The woman had laughed, exposing black, rotten teeth and mottled gums. She drew her black veil around her head, so that only her wise, brown eyes showed, and she said, "Of course not, sir. Those are tales for children. What we have in the village is a beastie. A shapeshifter. Nothing more to it than that."

Eventually, Jean found a man who had seemed afraid of the questions. Sidestepping many of the most important inquiries, he had uttered, "I dare not say more."

With this as encouragement, Jean asked, "What more is there to tell?"

The man left the pub, and Jean followed him, continuing his barrage of questions.

In frustration, the villager spun to face Jean, and the scientist could see the man's naked terror. "If you need to know so much," the man shouted, "then stay outside tomorrow. It's a full moon, you know. Then you'll see. Oh yes, then you'll see."

The next evening, as the moon rose, it covered the snowy plains in pale, indigo light, glistening off the ends of icicles and along snowdrifts. Jean bundled himself up in his heaviest coat and gloves, covering his head with a furred cap that had earflaps. Through his interviews, he'd discerned that the monster preferred to prowl the outskirts of the village. He bought a lamb from one of the local farmers, paying far too much, and he pulled the wailing animal to the end of the main road, where the plains began. After he'd slit the poor creature's throat, he placed the bleeding lamb on top of a small mound of dirt. He took his position behind a tree a few yards away, video camera in one hand, notebook in the other.

Then he waited. Eventually, he grew tired, and he leaned back against the tree, sighing. The blood of the lamb seemed to have frozen to the ground, an ice slick of deep crimson.

At last, he heard the howl of the beastie from the east. A dark shape, outlined against the blanched landscape, raised itself on its hind legs like a man, sniffing the air as an animal would. With several powerful bounds, it rushed to the lamb's corpse, and in six or seven bites it devoured the meal, licking its black lips with delight.

As Jean videotaped the creature, he got his first good look at the Lycanthrope. He was astonished by its size and musculature. Everything about the animal disclosed its power... the firm, gigantic stature, the length of its teeth, the gargantuan paws tipped with black talons. It was terrifying, yet somehow exhilarating to watch.

The beastie turned its head, sniffing the air, and it stared directly into Jean's camera. It snarled, revealing its blackened gums, and its chest swelled with indignation.

Jean dropped the camera and began to climb the tree. His adversary snorted with each leap that it made towards him. The old man climbed, as he hadn't done since he was a child, grasping each tree limb, hand over hand. He hadn't realized that he could still be so agile.

Surprised to find himself at the top of the tree, twenty feet above ground, he looked down at the monster.

The beastie leaned against the trunk, glaring up at him with golden-yellow eyes. It snorted once, the air steaming from its nostrils. For a moment, Jean thought it would leave him alone, continue with its business.

Instead, the creature tore at the bark of the tree, shook it beneath its paws. Jostled, Jean clutched at a nearby limb with all of his strength. Luckily, the tree was sturdy and very old.

Finally, the creature relented, choosing to wait Jean out. It paced and glared up at him every few minutes, its breath huffing in little clouds of condensation.

Jean grew tired, but he maintained his hold on the branches. His joints grew stiff, and his arthritis flared into staccato bursts of agony.

The old man wasn't sure how much time had passed, but his inflamed joints made it feel like an eternity. The creature grew tired of the game, and as the sun was about to rise, it loped off towards the east. When the sun crept over the horizon, filtering the plains with a subdued yellow light, the beast fell to its knees.

Cautiously, Jean crawled down from his perch, hugging the trunk of the tree as he descended. He snatched his video camera from the ground and turned it back on. The battery light still working, and he approached the changing monstrosity, filming its transformation.

The metamorphosis from beast to human was difficult and painful, but when it was over, Jean found himself standing before a muscular, thick-necked man. He was naked and mumbling in Russian. Without an interpreter, Jean couldn't understand a word the man said, but he removed his long jacket, wrapped it around his naked shoulders, and walked him to his home on the outskirts of town.

That evening, speaking through the carefully chosen translations of a teen-aged boy, Jean learned the man's name: Andrei. He had lived in the village for his entire life. His wife Betta sat beside him, holding their infant daughter. An older child, a boy, clung to his father's cotton shirt. They were a poor family of farmers, eking out a meager living from potatoes and beets.

Since he had turned sixteen years old, Andrei had been changing, morphing into his bestial form for three nights with every full moon. He had a root cellar in the small house where Betta and the children spent the nights when he changed. His father had built it in order to protect his own wife and child.

"This curse goes back in his family as long as anyone can remember," the boy said, translating Andrei's words into rough English. "He say that his father don't remember when it start. It always happen to the Sokosovich family. They turn to these beasties."

Jean promised Andrei that he would find a cure for his genetic disorder—for he was certain that's what it was—and he would pay Betta well if he would come to America to be studied. Crops had been especially poor that year, and Jean recognized the concern when the huge man looked down at his eight-year-old son.

"It would mean a better life for them," he said. "They could live off this stipend alone, if they needed to. And maybe we could cure you, stop this plague before it touches your boy. You'd like him to lead a full, normal life, wouldn't you?"

As he'd expected, Andrei traveled back to America with Jean, back to Bio-Gen headquarters in Cincinnati. Within a few months of study, the scientist had isolated the cause of the Lycanthropy.

The pattern of transformation was always the same, beginning on the first night of the full moon and ending three moons later at some point that lay unpredictably before dawn. It never varied, never altered in any way, except the precise moment when the final reversal to human form took place.

Rick laughed, breaking Christian's concentration. "We only have one more day of this shit to get through! Three nights and it's over, and we've made it through two already."

"Until next month," Chesya said with a sigh. "Until the next full moon. You want to go through this every month? I don't think so."

"There's a bit more..." Christian said.

Jean determined that the metamorphosis was caused by strange bacteria in Andrei's blood. None of Bio-Gen's experts had ever seen such a thing before, and they suspected it existed only in specific genetic bloodlines. That was why there had been so few accounts of the Lycanthropy. Jean had suspected it existed in several places around the globe, but only within a few tainted families. That was why so many various cultures had shapeshifters within their mythologies.

The scientists isolated the bacteria and attempted to destroy it. The prokaryotic nature of the cells didn't give them a distinct shape. It also made them hard to destroy.

In various cultures, the Bio-Gen scientists tried to kill the microscopic bugs, but nothing seemed to work except waiting for three days. In a manner similar to the moon cycles, the bacteria always perished after three days outside of its host. It couldn't survive any longer, and the outer shell, the capsule, liquefied. Within the host, the bacteria thrived.

While the other scientists studied the way the disease worked within Andrei's body, Jean developed a serum that could destroy the bacteria within a Petri dish; he designated it Serum A, as it was his first attempt, but he wasn't sure if it could work on a human host. He needed to test it. Fortunately, Andrei agreed to be his subject. The Siberian understood the dangers, but the hope of liberating himself and his family overruled his fears.

They never got a chance to test it.

In the day before Andrei was to be inoculated, the day of the first full moon, the cells Jean had been experimenting with took on a new shape, appearing more like spirals. They had mutated, and this new strain did not die like its predecessor. It was distressing, and Jean had been studying the new bacteria when…

… the journal abruptly stopped.

"That's all there is?" Chesya asked.

Christian shrugged.

"Goddamned scientists," Rick shouted, kicking an uprooted plant across the lobby floor. "They leave the fucking bacteria out in the open to study, probably got it in the air, and it spread from there. Who knows how many people were infected before they started changing."

"It's gotta be pretty widespread," Chesya said. "We haven't seen anything but local news. No radio. Cell phones weren't even working."

Outside, visible through the windows, naked people milled about in the streets, confused. A few of them covered their nudity and hurried out of sight. Others wandered aimlessly, unaware of their nakedness, while some attacked each other, emitting a stream of hysterical laughter. One couple writhed in the throes of passion on the hood of a SUV.

Chesya asked, "And this guy… Andrei… he's being held prisoner? Upstairs?"

Christian nodded.

"Then we need to go up there. If only to talk to the poor man."

Rick added. "And to get away from all the crazies. They can see in that window just as easily as we can see out."

"This way," Christian said, nodding to the stairs. "The elevator's not working."

"What the hell is?" Rick asked, and Chesya giggled, despite herself. The man beamed.

As they walked toward the stairs, several red-rimmed eyes observed them through the glass, watching them as they left the foyer. Then the eyes looked elsewhere as someone else started screaming from the streets.

CHAPTER 33

September 18, 8:30 a.m.

From the attic window, Cathy Wright hadn't seen any creatures since dawn. During the night's last gasps, they had run across the neighbors' lawns, tearing at the partially eaten bodies that punctuated the emerald-green grass. Now only the corpses remained... at least the parts that hadn't been consumed by the beasts.

Cathy peeked through the trapdoor and saw no threats, so she threw down the ladder and descended, clutching the rungs tightly in case she had to retreat to the attic.

In the hallway, she stood still and listened. The silence wrapped around her, until she had to shout a few times to make sure she hadn't gone deaf.

"Hello? *Hello?*"

She blushed, feeling foolish.

All around her, her house lay in ruins. There wasn't a picture left on a wall. Every knickknack or lamp had been swept from its shelf, knocked to the floor and trampled. Windows were broken, and she noticed that not one piece of furniture had remained unscathed. Strips of wallpaper hung wearily in shreds.

This house had been her life, nearly her entire world. The consistently well-run atmosphere had been her doing, her one major accomplishment in life, other than the birth of her son. But this wasn't her house any longer. It had been invaded, and everything that had made it hers—the cleanliness, the perfect decor, the style—had been stolen. Her country club was probably burned to the ground, if any members were still alive, and her social standing seemed rather silly at this point. Her husband, what was left of him, was dead, and her son was missing, under the impression that she was a willing accessory to his father's filthy habits. She felt empty, raped.

Sinking to her knees amidst the ruins of her life, the tattered remnants of her home, Cathy began to cry. The tears came fast, unbidden, and they surprised her in their potency. The sobs tore at the inside of her breasts, heaving and gasping in their efforts to get out of her. Covering her face with her hands, she let every angry, sad, terrified emotion bubble out of her.

After a few moments, she realized if anyone should enter her house, or even peer into the hole where the front door hung from its crippled bottom hinge, they would see her in an inexcusably vulnerable position. They would witness the tears and frustrations, and she knew they would judge her by them.

She couldn't allow this to happen… wouldn't allow it!

Wiping her face with the back of her hand, she shakily stood up. The carpet squished beneath her sneakers, and she wondered if it was water or something else.

This was what was left of her life… this broken cage she had once called home.

Blinking, she decided it was time to begin a different life. She needed to start fresh, and there was only one way that she could effectively separate herself from Karl and the lifestyle to which she had become accustomed.

It all had to go away.

Go away where she could never find it again, where it couldn't call out to her, where it couldn't remind her of what she had once been.

With a startling burst of energy, she pulled the overturned sofa into the center of what had once been the living room, and she piled table legs and lampshades and everything else she could find on top of it, including her wedding photograph, in which she seemed so young and naive. She swept up stray glass and bits of garbage, and she dumped this on top of the pile. Looking around, she saw the spotless floor, the bare walls, and she nodded to herself. It was nearly finished.

In the kitchen, she searched through her pantry, which had been dumped on the floor, the doors torn from their hinges and tossed through the back windows. She picked up an assortment of bills that had been waiting to be paid. The paper and cellophane crackled beneath her fingers. Finally, she found her candle lighter, and she marched back to the living room, a look of triumph on her face.

She scattered the bills over the pile of furniture and debris, then set them on fire with the lighter.

Leaning her back against the fireplace, Cathy admired the way the blaze caught, spread from one area to the next. Smoke billowed from the sofa cushions, and Cathy had to open a window, her eyes never leaving the fire. She half-wondered if the smoke was toxic.

She watched as her previous life went up in flames, a conflagration consisting of everything she'd once deemed so damned important.

And she smiled. A weight seemed to have lifted from her shoulders. She felt light, as though she could fly.

Soon, she noticed the floorboards had also caught fire, trails of flames emerging where the varnish was thickest. She was coughing, the smoke growing too thick to disburse through a single window.

Cathy took a final look over her shoulder. The room seemed alien to her, empty, devoid of any relevance to her life. It was an exhilarating notion, as though with this one crazy, defiant act, she had severed all links to Karl and her past role as one of Cincinnati's most important hostesses.

As she left the house, she saw Karl's cell phone and wallet on the table by the front door, where he always left them. This seemed to be the only part of the house that had been undisturbed by the monsters' rampage. Taking it as a sign, she put the wallet in her back pocket and shoved the cell phone deep into her jacket pocket. She left his keys on the table.

Then she stepped outside and admired the huge, dark clouds that dotted the sky. It looked like rain. She was only guessing; there was no weatherman to confirm her forecast.

For some reason, she wanted to see the back garden one more time before she started this new life. Stepping around the lawn, she walked through the rose bushes, stopped and smelled a few of them. When she reached the garden shed, she saw the doors that had been ripped from their moorings, tossed across a bed of perennials. A dark, musky odor emerged from the shed, the scent of what had once been her husband.

It appeared as if he had gone straight for the doors. The interior of the shed remained orderly. A small table of tools, coffee cans filled with various nails and screws. A small pile of firewood, stacked neatly. Her bike, leaning against the wall. Touching the seat, she couldn't recall the last time she had taken a ride.

Something in the house cracked. Leaning against the shed, Cathy watched as the flames approached the windows. Some of them began licking at the outside of the house, and she knew it would only be a matter of hours before the entire structure collapsed.

A hand touched her shoulder, dripping blood, and she turned to see her next-door neighbor, Marla Atcheson, of the New York Atchesons. The woman was still in her nightgown, one breast revealed through a gaping hole that had been ripped in the silk. Her eyes were rimmed in red, and her wrists had been sliced crudely open. The amount of blood was staggering.

"Oh God, Marla... what did you do?"

She held her hands toward Cathy, shredded wrists pointed upwards.

"I killed them... killed them all," the woman said, and when she smiled, Cathy thought she could see the madness that hovered behind her carefully assumed façade, the wolf hidden behind her skin. "I woke up today, and little Jackie and Frannie were dead... eaten... Mike is gone. I... I didn't know what to do... I know I killed them... or he did. They were... they were my fucking children, Cathy. I... I ate my fucking children!"

"We need to get those wrists bandaged," Cathy said, taking charge of the situation.

Marla shook her head, a sad smile crossing her face. "No... I want to die. I did it, don't you see? I murdered them. This is my absolution. I need to die. I want to die. I need to die."

"Come on," Cathy said, grabbing one of the woman's oozing wrists and leading her through the garden to the house next door. "I can't let you bleed to death."

"But it's what I want. You fool… you stupid woman! You think burning down your house will make it all better? Nothing… Christ. Nothing will be better again."

"I just know we need to get you fixed up."

Marla Atcheson pulled her hand out of Cathy's, rubbing the wrist, opening the wounds wider. She began to lick at the blood.

"You haven't seen what I've seen, Cathy," she said through crimson-smeared lips. "You haven't done what I've done. I've… killed… murdered… my own goddamn babies. I have to live with that."

"That's right," Cathy said. "You have to live with it."

Marla shook her head. "That's the problem, see? I can't live with it. That's why I took that soup can lid from the trash. I cut and I cut and I fucking cut. It… it only hurt a little bit. And once I bleed out, I can be with Jackie and Frannie again. I'll have paid my debt. I need to pay that debt."

"You're not yourself, Marla."

"Goddamn right, I'm not. I saw myself last night… in a mirror. I saw the teeth and the fur and the… the death buzzing all around me. I… I can't see that again. I suppose you can, um… you can deal with it. You've always been good at… you know… dealing with shit, Cathy. I've—oh God—I've admired you for that. God… damn… hurts.…"

"Ummm… thanks, but I don't think I'm all that strong.'"

"Hell… you're not—oh. Oh!"

With her soft exclamation, Marla fell to her knees. She tried to stop herself with her hands, but her bloody palms slid on the grass, and she fell face-first into the lawn. She remained that way, her bleeding wrists held above her head.

"Marla," Cathy cried. "Oh, no, Marla. Get up!"

As Cathy tried to pull her neighbor to her feet, Marla lashed out at her, snarling. "Don't you touch me! Don't… don't you fucking touch me! I'm… I'm almost gone."

"I know I can stop the bleeding."

"If you so much as try, I'll tear your… your… goddamn throat out." Marla was amazingly coherent. The beast hidden inside of her seemed to be speaking, all guttural snarls and whines. "Tear… your… throat…"

Marla slumped to the ground. Her eyes rolled back into her head, exposing the whites. She was dead.

Cathy moved away from her neighbor, away from her burning home, her torched life. She stepped out of her front gate.

Into a new, cruel world.

CHAPTER 34

September 18, 9:05 a.m.

"So, I've never claimed to be a very smart man…" Rick said, climbing the stairs of the Bio-Gen building.

Chesya snorted. "No kidding, Sherlock."

"… but let me try to get all this bacteria crap straight. It was inside this dude Andrei's blood, could only be passed to his children, then to their children, because their blood was, what—special?"

"I guess so," Christian said. "Like, that family… that bloodline… didn't have some defense mechanism. Apparently the rest of the world has one. Their white blood cells—"

"Phagocytes," Chesya said.

Rick giggled. "Ha! Fag-o-cytes!"

She shook her head. "Please tell me you don't find that funny."

"Hey, I'm just a twelve-year-old boy at heart."

"Thank you, Beavis," Christian said, although he, too, was grinning.

Rick laughed like Butthead's sidekick.

Chesya said, "For God's sake, don't encourage him. Go on about the white blood cells."

"Well, I think everyone else was immune to this, except for Andre's family. When the scientists started screwing around with the bacteria, it somehow mutated into a variant strain."

"You know," Rick said, "you don't talk like a teenager."

"Sleep with a scientist for two months and see if *you* don't pick up some of the lingo," Christian said. "So, anyway, they mess it up... how's that?"

"Even a poor, ignorant moron like myself can understand," Rick said.

"And it gets loose," Christian continued. "They take it home with them, spread it through the air... like it went airborne."

Rick nudged Chesya. "Didn't I suggest the same thing? And we're immune to it."

"Yeah," Christian said, "we're immune. But most people aren't. Just like any disease. Some people get it, other people don't. In this case, just about everyone got infected except a few lucky bastards. The virus will run its course through the three days of the full moon. Then, well... we'll have to see."

"It could start up again the next full moon, huh?" Chesya asked.

"That's what I think will happen. But that's almost a month away. In that month... who knows. Maybe this serum Jean made can actually immunize people against the new strain. In any case, it looks like we have another night to get through before we can even think about curing anybody."

As they reached the top of the stairs, Chesya added, "If there's anyone left to cure. Is there a television or radio up here anywhere?"

Christian shrugged. "Maybe you can look for one, find out what's happening out there... if anyone's left but the crazies in the streets."

She nodded. "Sounds good. What about you?"

"I need to go feed Andrei," Christian replied, "see what kind of shape he's in. Maybe I can find something else. You know, something like the journal."

"I'll go with you," Rick said. "Never met a Russian before. You'll stay close—right, Chesya?"

"I swear I'm not going any farther than a door or two down."

"Well, stay within yelling distance."

Christian led Rick into the laboratory. Naked, Andrei slept on his cot behind the Plexiglas, snoring loudly, his hairy arm thrown over his eyes. The furniture in his cell must have been expertly nailed to the floor, as the arrangement had not changed.

The laboratory, however, was another story.

Christian muttered, "Man, this is way worse than it was yesterday. Those creatures had a field day in here."

"Maybe I'm getting used to it," Rick said.

Every file cabinet had been dropped onto its side, the contents opened and torn. Christian couldn't see the tile through all the paper. Broken glass clinked beneath their heels as they entered the room.

"Christ, it's like they threw a wild bachelor party in here," Rick said. "If there ever really was a serum, there's no way it survived this shit storm."

"We have to try to find it," Christian said. He seemed to have aged twenty years, lines etched painfully in his face, his eyes encircled with dark ellipses. The kid looked older than Rick, but a determination shined behind his exhaustion. "If we can find the serum, we can see if it works on Andrei, and we can put a stop to this once and for all."

"Listen, kid, I—"

"Don't talk down to me. Don't you ever... fucking... talk down to me. I might be younger than you, but I survived two nights of bullshit you wouldn't believe to get here... to get to this point. Please, just help me look for the beaker. He called it serum A, so it's probably labeled that way."

"Jesus, sorry. I didn't mean to—"

"You can be a real pain in the ass, Rick. Anyone ever tell you that?"

"It has been said."

Christian got down on his hands and knees and started searching through the trash. After a moment, Rick joined him. He stuck his hand in a pile of excrement.

Andrei laughed.

Startled, Rick and Christian glanced over at him; they hadn't noticed the Siberian wake up.

Rick said, "I'm glad you find it so damn funny."

"Hehe... is funny. A good joke, no?"

"Are you hungry?" Christian asked.

"I am starving. I need food. You get some for me?"

As Andrei stood and stretched, Rick found himself face-to-face with the Siberian's shriveled penis, protected only by the layer of Plexiglas. Rolling his eyes, he said, "Get some clothes for the poor bastard, too."

"The clothes are not really needed," said Andrei, stretching and flexing. "I will be okay without. I need food, though. Very hungry."

"Well, I don't like him standing there waving his dick at me."

Christian started for the door. He said, "Feeling a little inadequate?"

"No, feeling a little embarrassed. Jeez... whatever. Just get him his fuckin' food. Maybe get something for me while you're at it."

Christian walked into the hallway, searching for a candy machine, a cafeteria, *anything*; he was hungry too. In a small alcove near the end of the hallway, he discovered a little kitchen with a sink, a built-in refrigerator, and a coffee machine that had somehow survived the night. The refrigerator contained a few cans of coffee, bread, lunchmeat, and assorted yogurts and bag lunches. The food smelled rotten after two days without power. Christian pulled out the bread. He also found a bag of potato chips, half-eaten, and a box of cheese crackers. He shoved a handful of the crackers into his mouth. The taste was heavenly. He snatched a tomato from the crisper and began to make his way back to the lab.

Near the sink, he spotted a cell phone. Someone had plugged it in to recharge. It seemed too much to hope that, out of all the phones he'd tested, this one would function. Still, he had to try.

Setting down his refrigerator booty, he picked up the phone.

He couldn't think of anyone else to contact, could remember no number except that of his parents. They had hurt him so much, but... could they still be alive? Could they start over?

Placing the phone to his ear, he held his breath, said a silent prayer, and pressed the TALK button. Behind a shimmer of static, he heard a dial tone, and he exhaled. Immediately, his fingers flew over the numbers. He only received a busy signal. The phones must still be out.

He redialed, entering the seven digits of his father's cell phone. This time, it rang.

"Oh my God," he said.

Chesya walked around the corner. "I found a TV," she said. "It's just inside—"

Christian shushed her and waved his hands. "I got a ring. I can hear it ringing."

After an eternity, he heard a click, and the ringing suddenly ceased. Through the mist of the heavy static, he recognized his mother's familiar greeting.

"Yes, hello?"

"Mom?" he shouted, and the tears started to flow from his eyes. He hadn't thought he would be so moved by her voice.

CHAPTER 35

September 18... 10:25 a.m.

Cathy nearly dropped the phone when it rang. She did scream, and she looked around her neighborhood to make sure nobody heard her. She had walked only a few blocks away from her burning house. The beautiful neighborhood had been corrupted during the night. Fires burned, valuables were left out in the open, and there wasn't a soul to be seen walking. She wondered if they were all dead or, perhaps, hiding.

Placing her hand to her pounding heart, she exhaled in relief. Either nobody had heard her, or nobody cared anymore. The streets had been so very full of shrieks during the night.

Reaching down for the cell phone in her jacket pocket, she opened the lid. The battery was low, and she could barely see the caller's number, even though gathering rain clouds blocked the glare of the sun. She pressed the TALK button and spoke into the dainty receiver.

"Yes, hello?" The words seemed ineffectual, clueless. They seemed hollow.

"Mom?"

The single word brought such an onrush of emotions... shame, elation, terror... that Cathy had to balance herself against a streetlamp. Her knees shivered, and her pulse immediately jumped.

"Oh, God, Chris? Is that you sweetheart?"

His voice was instantly recognizable, even through the static. Despite the chaos around her, Cathy found herself smiling, hugging the phone to her ear.

"Mom," he said. "I don't think I have much time. The battery's gonna die soon."

"I'm just so happy you're alive. I knew you were, somehow. I just... I knew you were."

"Mom, shut up a minute. This is important." The static escalated, and she lost some of what he was saying. "... in the Bio-Gen building. Do you know where that is?"

"No. I don't think so. But you're there now, is that right?"

"Yeah, go downtown. Sixth and Broadway."

"Downtown? I don't know... I'm not sure how I can get there."

"Mom, listen to me. Don't take a car. The highways are bumper to bumper with hundreds of car wrecks. You'd never get through...."

"Oh Chris, you're breaking up again. You're at Sixth and Broadway. What was the building called?"

Through the static, she could barely hear him. She repeated the corporate name again, and she realized that he was gone. She had lost him.

Again.

No, she decided. *I'll find him. He isn't gone, he's just downtown. If he stays where he is, I can get to him.*

How to get there was the question. She was at least twelve miles from Sixth Street, and Chris had told her not to use her car.

She had to get there. She needed to feel her son in her arms, to kiss his sturdy face, to never let him go again.

To apologize and make amends for her negligence and condescension.

Shoving the phone back into her pocket, she started back down the block towards what remained of her house. She didn't want to lose the phone. It felt like a connection to Chris, a lifeline, tenuous as it was.

The second story of the house had collapsed into the conflagration below, and flames were licking their way across the lawn, towards the neighbors' place. Cathy had done a complete job of it, and she wondered if the rest of the neighborhood was going to catch fire as well. Surprised, she found she didn't care if the whole damn place went up in smoke. It would cleanse this rich, hypocritical place of all its affectations and Tartuffery.

When she saw the fire hadn't reached the garden shed, she sighed and said, "Thank God for small favors."

She pulled out her bicycle, a five-year-old Schwinn racer she hadn't used in a long time. She had been quite an athlete during her college years, had worked off her pregnancy fat after Chris was born, had exercised in a gym that had cost a small fortune every month.

Hopping up on the seat, she concluded that her jeans wouldn't be as conducive to pedaling as something more elastic, but she had nothing else to wear. She'd burned her wardrobe right along with all of her worldly possessions.

Shaking her head, she thought, *This is no time for regret. Comfortable or not, I need to get to Chris before nightfall or before he moves on to some new hiding place.*

She wouldn't get this chance again, so she bit her lip and began to pedal down the street. It was downhill, and it seemed easy to her. Her rustiness only took a few moments to dissipate. As she began to shift gears for the hill, she discovered she'd already shifted, that she'd done so without even thinking about it.

The clouds overhead darkened, and a humid depression settled over the city. Cathy hoped it wouldn't rain. She had nearly fifteen miles to go.

As she turned onto the ramp to the outer belt, speeding past empty, abandoned cars, she felt the first warm aches in her calves. This was going to hurt by the time she arrived downtown. She wasn't used to this kind of relentless exercise anymore.

But Chris was there, and the thought of seeing him again spurred her on. With a burst of speed, she whooshed by the automobiles that blocked the freeway. She stayed by the side of the road, only swerving or slowing when a car had wrecked outside the lines or something blocked her path.

Hang on, Chris, she thought, feeling a steady throbbing in her thighs. *Mom will be there soon.*

CHAPTER 36

September 18, 10:40 a.m.

Christian shook the phone, as if to bring his mother's voice back on the line. "Mom? Goddamnit!"

She'd stirred up a hornet's nest of feelings, and he had to stop himself from calling out "Mommy" to her. The little boy behind his rough exterior wanted to break loose, but he refused to show any weakness.

Chesya asked, "Is she coming? She's really alive?"

He nodded, thankful for the way she pulled him out of his self-indulgent pity. "She said she was."

"Then it's settled. We stay here till she gets here. If it gets dark, we'll... well, we'll just have to see."

"I still can't believe it."

"Your father?"

"I don't know. She didn't say." He sat down at the Formica break table, resting his head in his hands. "You have family out there, Chesya? You don't seem very worried."

"I don't have anyone, not anymore. Except that fool in the other room. Funny, we only met a couple days ago, but... yeah, he feels like family to me."

"You like him?"

"Well, that's a strong word. I can put up with him. You realize when we met he had a gun pointed at me. Not the best first impression.

Still, there's something about him. He's smart, holds together pretty well. Know what I mean?"

"Yeah," the boy said with a sheepish grin. "It means you like him."

"Oh, go to hell." She laughed despite herself, covering her mouth. "How'd a kid like you get to be so smart?"

"Living on the street. It does that to you. You get smart, or you get dead."

In a humbler tone, she said, "It must've been terrible for you."

He shrugged. "Hey, didn't you say you found a TV?"

"Just a couple doors down. I can't get anything, though. Electric's still out. I didn't see a radio."

"Then let's look for one," Christian said. "There's bound to be one in this place somewhere, and it'll... it'll get my mind off my mom."

"Sounds like a plan," she said, and they moved down the hallway.

In the laboratory, Andrei watched Rick through the Plexiglas barrier. He pouted, his lower lip jutting out, his eyebrows lowered.

"You let me out now?" he asked.

Rick, who had been searching through the papers that blanketed the floor, turned to the voice. He was still a little embarrassed by the Siberian's nudity, but he tried to pretend it didn't matter.

"You gonna change into one of those things?" he asked.

"Yes. Tonight. I will be changing to beast again. At least, for some of night."

"Yeah, that's what the scientist guy said in the book. Three full moons, then you're right as rain for another month."

Rick found several broken beakers, but none of them were labeled. Their interiors were encrusted with something yellow and crumbling. They smelled terrible too. He wondered if these had contained the mysterious cure.

Turning to the naked man, but averting his eyes a bit, he asked, "You ever see the French scientist make something called Serum A?"

"Yes... yes!" The man moved towards the barrier. "You have found it? It is there?"

"What do you know about it?"

"I have seen it. He, what is word, bragged about it."

"Well, shit!" Rick said, standing from the mess; pieces of glass and paper stuck to his knees. "What's it look like? We need to find it and get it to somebody who can distribute it. It could save… I don't know how many people."

"I could help you," the Siberian said. "If you are willing to help with me."

Rick sighed. "Knew there was a fuckin' catch in there somewhere."

"I don't understand you. Catch?"

"Let me rephrase: What do you want?"

Andrei leaned against the back wall of his cell and crossed his arms over his hairy chest. "I want to get out of here. I want to go back to my home and see my family."

"I'm sure that can be arranged."

"I want out now."

"Well, sport, that's where we have a problem. You're going to change again, and we have enough on our hands without setting loose the original monster that started this clusterfuck."

"It was not me who started this. It was that Frenchman. He brought me here. He changed the disease and let it get loose on the city."

"In any case, we can let you out tomorrow morning, as long as we find the keys to that plastic cage. Just as soon as you go back to being human."

Andrei thought it over for a moment, then he asked, "How can I trust you to not run away?"

"You want outta there? We're your best chance. What's the serum look like?"

"It is clear, like water. The Frenchman keep it in a safe in the wall behind chart. Just over there."

Tacked up on the wall, the chart showed Andrei's metabolic rate as he changed into a Lycanthrope. Rick tore it away, let it fall to the floor. A digital safe was embedded in the plaster, the buttons arranged in rows of three, like a phone.

"Great. I don't suppose you know the combination?"

Andrei grinned, and Rick thought he could detect the animal in it. "I pay attention. I watch real close. The Frenchman opens it all the time."

"Well," Rick asked with a shrug, "what is it?"

"Ah, no. I think I don't give it to you. I think you let me out, and I will open safe. I want out of cage. I want for to be human all the time. Why would I lie to you?"

"I could think of a thousand reasons."

"It easiest thing in the world. You let me out. They keys are in the desk drawer on a… what you call it… a circle."

"A key ring?" Rick asked, opening the desk drawer.

"Yes. Ring for keys."

"So I let you out to open the safe—then what? You attack me? Overcome me? I do have a gun. I could just shoot you on the spot."

"But I have… oh, what is word, bargaining chit. I know where there is another weapon. A good weapon. If I let you have other weapon, you let me out so I open safe and get serum. I am human again. You watch me with weapon. Everyone happy as oysters."

"I still don't like it."

"You got other choice?"

"Yeah, I let you rot in there."

"That not a good choice."

"Looking pretty righteous to me."

"But if I am human again, then you get one more person to fight. Also, you get another bargaining chit. The serum. The army probably desires that, yes?"

"Yeah, they probably do. Where's this weapon you think's so great?"

"In filing cabinet, bottom part."

The cabinet rested on its side at the end of the room. Rick opened the bottom drawer and removed a dart gun, fully loaded with tranquilizing darts.

"Whoa," Rick said. "Like the big game hunters use?"

"They use it on me to make me sleep, and it always works."

"How many darts does this thing hold?"

"Six. That's six monsters we can force to go to sleep," Andrei said, pacing his cell restlessly. "Now you let me out? Now I get you serum, and I get somewhere safe."

"Looks pretty safe in that little cell of yours."

"You hear things in here. Like things going boom, blowing up. If it's bad in city…"

"Oh, it's worse than you think."

"… then, I no want to be blown up when a gas explosion comes."

Looking into the Siberian's eyes, Rick didn't think Andrei was lying. Then again, it could have been the beast within, using its wiles to get set free.

The heft of the dart gun in his hands made up his mind. He opened the desk drawer, pulling too hard and nearly dumping it. He caught it, but a large key ring spilled from inside, jangling to the floor. As Rick picked them up, he felt the reassuring weight of them in his hand. He walked over to the Plexiglas cage and began testing the keys in the locks. Within minutes, the door was opening with a pneumatic hiss. Andrei stepped out of his prison, stretching his arms.

"That feels wonderful," he said. "Thank you, my friend." He grabbed Rick, encircling him in a hairy bear hug. "I promise you I will be all better now. The shot… it will do the trick. No?"

"Hey, hey, buddy," Rick protested, trying to escape from the big man's clutches. "Watch it with the naked hugging, okay? How about opening that safe?"

Rick raised the dart gun and pointed it at Andrei's barrel chest. The Siberian shrugged, still grinning as though giddy with the fresh air.

"Yes. Is time."

Andrei punched several numbers into the safe, then turned the handle. Rick pushed him aside with the dart gun, and Andrei stepped away, hands in the air.

"Serum help me now, will it not?"

Rick pulled on the handle, keeping one eye on the Siberian and one on the opening safe. The door was heavy as he opened it, but he soon saw two shelves. One contained a stack of paperwork and a small stack of hundred dollar bills, which Rick swiftly pocketed, adding to the thousands he had stolen earlier.

The other shelf held three rows of beakers full of a clear fluid. Rick left them secure inside the safe.

Andrei leaned against the outside wall of his Plexiglas cell, arms crossed.

"Looks like you knew what you were talking about, Andrei. I'll get you out personally if this stuff works."

"Get me out?" he asked, confused. "But I am already—"

Rick shot him with a dart. The feathered shaft stuck out of Andrei's left hip. With fury burning in his eyes, the naked Siberian took one step towards Rick. He wavered, faltered on his second step, and fell to the floor.

"Sorry, buddy," Rick said. "I'm not taking any chances."

Setting the rifle aside, he grabbed Andrei's legs and dragged him into the cell. The man was heavy, solid with muscle, and Rick struggled to turn him through the entryway. He left Andrei in the middle of the cell and shut the door; the mechanism hissed and the bolt clicked into place.

Rick returned to the safe and pulled out the papers. Then he sat behind the desk and began to read, praying there was an answer to their problem within their pages. He whistled as he perused them.

CHAPTER 37

September 18, 11:30 a.m.

Cathy really began to feel the ache in her thighs and calves when she steered her bike through the stalled and wrecked cars that blocked the exit to State Route 71 South. It had started as a faint burning sensation, a comfortable, familiar glow from her past exercise regimes. Her blood was pumping hard, touching places that hadn't been stimulated in years. The lactic acid in her muscles pulsed. Her ass was also getting sore, unaccustomed to the shape and size of the bicycle seat.

Gritting her teeth, she fought the urge to stop, certain that she would cramp if she did. Chris was waiting for her downtown, and she raced with a passion she had never felt before in her life. The need to feel him in her arms again, if only for a moment, eased some of the agony. She'd never felt so maternal, so full of love for anyone... not even with Karl when they had first married.

As she biked south, she thought about her son, how she had held him on the day he was born, the sweet milky scent of him. He had her eyes, and he had her love of old films and the theater. Recalling the last time they had attended a musical at the Aranoff Center (how long ago had it been? what was the show?), tears welled up in her eyes. She shook her head, dispelling them when she felt the crick in her neck.

He had been her baby, her little boy, her awkward teenaged son, her little, quiet man. He'd been so much to her, and what had she been to him? A traitor.

Never again, she vowed. Never again would she turn a blind eye.

She wondered where this surge of feeling had originated. Had it been there all along, lying dormant within her? In any case, she could see what was important now. Funny, how that happened. Your world is turned upside down, shaken violently, and what was meaningful somehow floated to the top.

And she was going to grasp at those drifting emotions like the lifesavers they were.

The dark clouds she'd noticed earlier were now clustering closer together, giving the daytime a twilight feeling. A storm was definitely on the way, and she would probably get soaked, cold, and miserable. But it wouldn't stop her. Not from finding Chris. Not after she'd lived through so much.

As she passed a small quarry, she saw several nude people bobbing in the water, arms and legs outstretched in the classic Dead Man's Float. She remembered seeing several corpses in swimming pools back in Indian Hills, where every house had a pool. There'd been a few in the local lake as well. She hadn't taken much notice of it before, but the sight of those ten or eleven bodies in the quarry brought the memory back.

As she continued down the highway, never going as fast as she would have liked, she wondered whether the beasts could swim, or if their bodies were too heavy and broad for their smallish arms. Maybe they sank like stones.

Had they leapt to their deaths, knowing they wouldn't be able to swim in their monstrous states, or had they simply fallen in? Had they clawed at the sides of the quarry in a vain effort to escape?

She wondered if this would be the answer, if God would bring back the floodwaters and drown the evil world and all the cruel people in it. She wasn't a religious person, but the thought held a certain charm for her, a simplicity in a world that was no longer simple.

As she entered the shadow of a train overpass, her bike hit something—a dead woman's hand. The corpse was splayed on the pavement, just outside of a car door. Her back had been torn open between the shoulder blades, and most of her insides were pulled out, displayed neatly on the road.

The sight was so horrendous that Cathy turned the wheel too hard and found herself losing her balance. The bike spun from beneath her, and she landed next to the body. The skin peeled from her left hand when she tried to stop her tumble, and her right kneecap smacked against the pavement. Crying out, she tucked herself into a ball and rolled, watching as her bike skidded away from her.

When she stopped moving, she checked herself. Other than a sore knee and a skinned hand, she didn't detect any damage. She limped a bit as she walked back to her bicycle. It hadn't sustained any real damage either.

Leaning against a Mustang convertible, she caught her breath, legs throbbing from the unfamiliar exercise. Her hand didn't bleed much, but it stung like hell. She shook it, wiped it against the leg of her jeans.

Exhaling, she marveled at how good it felt to stop for a rest. The shade of the overpass felt more secure to her, as if she was hiding in plain sight. She stretched, pulling her limbs taut. Moaning softly, she sat on the hood of the Mustang.

Something moved on the overpass above her. A series of shadows scuttling back to their sanctuaries.

Cathy shivered, chastised herself for stopping.

She could see the Norwood lateral ahead of her, which marked the halfway point to her destination. If she'd been asked a year ago if she could bike that far, she would have denied it, laughing at the very concept. Now, despite her Jell-O-legs, her sore, blistering hands, and her mental exhaustion, she knew she would make it downtown.

But would she be in time?

Taking a few stretches in preparation, she jogged in place for a couple of minutes. She massaged her thighs. Her leg muscles quivered, but there were no actual spasms yet. A good sign.

She climbed back onto her bike.

"Hey, lady." A girl emerged from an ancient pick-up truck that had run off the road several yards away. She looked like she was coming out of a cave, blinking and holding a hand to the side of her face. Her hair was a dirty brown, loose around her shoulders, trembling in the breeze. She couldn't have been more than fifteen years old, and her floral-print cotton dress was torn and filthy.

Walking forward, the girl tilted her head, cocking it to the side, listening for something that Cathy couldn't hear. Her fingers scurried like spiders against her thighs, as though she were playing the strains of a long forgotten piano piece. Nervous tension emanated from her in almost-visible waves.

"Hey," she said, her voice low. "You seen anybody on the road?" She had a Southern twang.

Cathy shook her head, took a few tentative steps back as the girl stepped up to her. The stranger placed a thin arm on the handlebars of the bike. Cathy tightened her grip.

"No. I haven't seen anybody along the highway. I saw some people in Indian Hills."

"That where you're from? That rich place?"

"Yes. And I need to get moving."

"I got left here," the girl said. "Goddamn family ain't worth spit. They left me in the truck, said they was gonna look for someone else."

Cathy's eyes darted to the vehicle. Flies buzzed around the open bed of the truck, and on its dirty white paint job, a single crimson smear traversed from the passenger door to the bumper, a hideous racing stripe along the rusted-out side.

"How long have you been in there?"

"Couple days. We was going to the store for the groceries. I still got some left. You want some water? Or a pop?"

Cathy swallowed hard; her mouth and throat were parched. "A water might be nice."

The girl took her hand and grinned at her, but there was no humor behind her smile. There was something else.

Something old and primeval.

Suddenly, Cathy didn't want to go with the girl. She resisted, holding her bike tightly between her legs.

"Oh, come on," the girl said. "I ain't gonna hurt you none. What can I do? I'm just a kid."

It was true. When Christian was her age, he had been perfectly harmless.

Slowly, Cathy stepped off the bike and allowed herself to be pulled along. "Just one quick water," she said, her mouth feeling more and more like a desert. Even her voice sounded cracked and dry.

In the shadows of the overpass, something stirred. Then something else.

"My name's Beth Blue. My folks call me Bethie, but I like Beth better. Do you know what's happening? People were acting crazy, like they was animals. Did you see it?"

Cathy nodded. Each step brought them closer to the truck, and in the cloudy daylight, the stain along its side glowed almost a stop-sign red.

"Hell of a thing, wasn't it? My Daddy says it's God punishing us. Ain't no reason to lie. We're his kin, and all. He says people are getting what they deserve. Here we are."

They stopped at the edge of the truck. Someone was slumped forward over the steering wheel, and Cathy leaned forward to help him.

"Oh God, someone's hurt," she said.

Then the smell hit her, and she knew why the truck was swarmed with flies. She could see a man, his face battered and crushed, his guts trailing out the crack at the bottom of the driver's side door.

In the truck bed, there was another body, an older woman. Her head had been torn from her neck, and her corpse lay between paper bags and spilled groceries. Long strips of meat were missing from her nude, wrinkled body. A bright red apple had been placed in her mouth.

Wrapping her arms around Cathy's throat, the girl pulled backwards. Cathy couldn't breathe, and she spun, dragging the thin girl.

"We couldn't never afford no meat," Beth Blue cried gleefully as Cathy twisted beneath her. "Now, I got lots of meat. Hold still, why don't ya? It won't hurt."

Spots like solar flares passed across Cathy's vision. She needed to throw off her attacker, or she was going to pass out and end up another meal for this crazy child. But the girl was deceptively strong, and her arms were latched together and pulled back hard.

Turning, Cathy faced away from the old truck. She rushed backwards, slamming the girl into the side of the cab. Beth Blue's head flung back, and it shattered the window, forming a jagged halo around her face. The truck must have been so old it predated safety glass.

"Hey! Bitch, there ain't no cause for that! I was just hungry. You're only making it harder on yourself."

Her grip on Cathy strengthened. Cathy shoved backwards, harder this time. She was beginning to see tiny green flares of light. Most everything else was going black.

She didn't have much time left.

Several figures emerged from the shadows. Men and women with torn, stained clothing and the eagerness of hunters glowing gold in their eyes. They were still fifty feet away, but they seemed to move as a pack, with a young, muscular, shirtless man in the lead; the others followed him, skirting outwards to frame the highway.

Cathy rushed towards the truck, putting Beth Blue's head through the window. When Cathy moved back and forth a few times, the glass lodged in the skin and sinew of the girl's neck. Her hold on Cathy loosened, and her hands fluttered to the gash. Cathy could hear a gurgling sound behind her, loud even over her own coughing.

The shambling figures were thirty feet away, and the young man in the lead, obviously some kind of alpha dog, sniffed the air and motioned for the others to spread out farther.

"Goddamn you," Beth Blue cried out. "I was just... hungry. Goddamn you."

Cathy pulled loose, and the girl slumped to her knees, pressing her palms to the wounds, unable to contain the gushes of bright-red blood. When the girl's hands dropped to her sides, the arterial spray shot out of her like a mist, spattering the side of the white truck, creating odd pop art patterns. The girl fell gracefully onto her side, one hand beneath her cheek as though she were sleeping.

The pack of crazies was at least twenty strong, and they had bloodstains on their chins and cheeks. They'd been at someone recently.

Cathy hurried to her bike.

A teenage boy emerged from the shadows and ran to Beth Blue, sinking his teeth into her ruined throat and slurping at the blood. The others grew jittery, excited by the sight of so much gore spattered across the road. They shot nervous glances at their leader.

He was staring at Cathy. The skin on the back of her neck crawled beneath his empty gaze. His lips curled into a snarl. She threw a leg over her bike and took a seat, shifting one foot to the pedal.

Three more members of the ragged crew joined the teenager, surrounding Beth Blue's body like hyenas, snapping bones, sucking at the marrow.

Cathy pedaled south again, slowly, trying to stay on the edge of the highway. The pack leader tossed his curly-maned head at her and issued a growl to the others. He didn't speak, just grunted at them after he howled. They responded as if he'd given them orders.

The group of bloody crazies blocked the shadowed area under the overpass, and more emerged from the darkness. There was a hill on either side, and Cathy biked farther off the road.

The pack leader ran towards her, twelve of his followers behind him. They ran close to the ground, their backs hunched over, their noses guiding them.

Cathy ran into a fence just past the ditch and close to the hill. She leapt off her bike, tossed it over the chain link, and started climbing. She didn't dare turn to see how close the pack was.

When she dropped to the other side, Cathy barely noticed the pain in her legs as she landed. She grabbed her bike by the handlebars and scurried to the top of the hill, into the middle of the railroad tracks. Behind her, the chain link rattled as the crazy people scaled it. They dropped on the other side, crouching on all fours. The leader was already heading up the hill.

Ahead of Cathy, a few members of the shabby army stepped into the light from beneath the overpass. Behind her, one of the crazy people laughed and huffed like an animal.

She knew it was now or never. Cathy jumped on her bike and pedaled furiously down the other slope of the hill. Luckily there was no fence on this side. When she hit pavement, she lowered her head and steered between the wrecked cars.

The crazies leapt at her, but she'd gained enough speed that they soon fell far behind. Cathy didn't slow down.

She had been stupid and careless, and she couldn't afford to repeat that mistake. She wondered if the members of the pack had gone crazy because of something they had done in their primitive state, or if they had embraced their new, dark side.

Shuddering, Cathy nearly lost her balance, but she recovered, her determination overcoming her terror. She vowed to pedal until she reached the Bio-Gen building. Stopping again, even for only a brief respite, was too great of a risk.

Who knew what other dangerous things hovered just out of sight, hiding in the shadows, waiting for prey? How many other packs had formed, tenuous alliances forged to attain fresh meat?

She headed south again, steering between the cars until she was at the side of the highway. It was more difficult to bike through the grass, but there were fewer obstructions. And it kept her away from the things lurking amidst the vehicles.

CHAPTER 38

September 18, 12:30 p.m.

Chesya showed Christian to the breakroom, where she had discovered the television set. Even though she had checked it once, she turned it on again, but with the power failure no picture showed on the screen. Sighing, she dropped into one of the three overstuffed chairs in the room.

Christian immediately stepped over to the snack machine, which remained as untouched as the rest of the room. For some reason, the creatures hadn't destroyed this small area, and he realized just how lucky this had been for them. Using his elbow, he struck the glass front of the machine several times before it broke. He reached inside and retrieved several treats.

"Well, at least we won't go hungry," he said. "We'll have to take some of these to Andrei."

Chesya eyed the rest of the room. "You see a radio anywhere?"

He shook his head. "No."

"Me neither. There's got to be one in the building. I mean, even the banks have radios for the tellers to listen to while they work. I'd think it was pretty much standard everywhere."

Christian filled his pockets with candy bars, granola bars, and other snacks after eating a couple. Chesya plucked a couple of Snickers from the machine. She devoured them quickly, then grabbed a box of Junior Mints.

Munching on their candy, they checked out the other rooms. The last room in the hallway was a rat's maze of cubicles, each with their own computer and several with portable radios. They searched several stalls before they discovered a radio with batteries in it, an older model, well-used.

Christian hesitated before turning it on. "What if there's nobody out there?" he asked.

"It's worth a try."

He flipped the switch, and the air was filled with loud static, hissing and popping. Christian turned down the volume, then spun the dial to search the airwaves for a signal. He had no luck on the FM dial, but when he turned to the a.m. setting, he stumbled upon someone talking almost immediately.

"Let's take it back to the lab room," Chesya said. "That way we won't have to repeat everything to Rick."

Nodding, Christian followed her, carrying the radio on his shoulder and listening to the sturdy, male voice that emerged from the speakers. The voice sounded calm and paternal, a wizened, old anchorman sitting in a booth somewhere, relating the news as it came off of the AP wire.

"United States armed forces have surrounded the infected area, sealing it off along every road and placing armed guards every hundred feet or so. Bridges across the Ohio River have been partially destroyed to maintain the contaminated population. It still appears that only the immediate area of Cincinnati, Ohio and its surrounding suburbs are affected by the strange disease, and authorities say the contamination area has a radius of about forty square miles. As far as we can tell, nobody knows where the disease came from, but people are turning into beast-like creatures and wreaking havoc. No traffic is allowed in or out of the infected area, and any people attempting to escape from the guarded area are being shot and killed."

"Sweet Lord," Chesya whispered.

As they entered the laboratory, they noticed Andrei unconscious on the floor of his cell. "What happened to him?" Christian asked.

Looking up from his stack of papers, Rick said, "I'll tell you every-thing later. He's safe now, and so are we. Hey, you found a radio. Good work."

Nodding, Chesya put a finger to her lips. Christian placed the boom box on the desk next to Rick, who was still perusing the notes he had discovered in the wall safe. Then Christian dropped several candy bars and bags of chips into the slot in the cell. He shoved it forward into the confines of the Plexiglas prison.

Christian said, "Looks like you found something." He acknowledged the hidden safe, whose door still hung open. "That the serum in there?"

"I think so."

"Will you two hush a minute?" Chesya said. "Listen to what the man's saying. This is important."

The radio announcer droned on. "Authorities aren't sure how long the quarantine will last. Scientists are studying the virus, but we haven't heard whether any progress is being made. Our station news manager spoke with Captain Taylor Burns of the twenty-third brigade, who's stationed in Newport, Kentucky."

Chesya said, "That's just across the river! They're waiting right across the Ohio River."

A low-pitched, authoritative voice said, "We'll stand our ground until we find a way to eradicate this disease. Last night, we eliminated a couple... um, hundred of the things trying to cross the bridges from the Ohio side. They were monsters. That's all I can say. Monsters. But we secured this area when the disease first struck, blew the bridges, and got rid of anything that looked at us sideways. Everyone under my control's wearing biohazard suits, so none of us change like those things. I'm pretty certain we got the ones that were already over here on the Kentucky side, and the fire crews have gotten the blazes under control. We have effectively contained all of the other infected people... I use that term loosely... on the Ohio side within our established boundaries, but a lot of them want to cross what's left of the bridges. We got 'em last night."

"Captain Burns, what's happened to all the bodies?"

"Well, when we terminated 'em, they turned back into people, like they were before they turned into these creatures. The bodies are contaminated, so we're leaving them on the bridges, and we're taking care of them there."

"Setting them on fire?" the reporter asked.

"Yes, sir. We have flamethrowers, and their range is over twenty feet, so we can effectively extirpate the bodies and lower the risk of contamination to my men. We have the biohazard suits, but you never know. Better safe than sorry."

"Isn't it true that some of the troops have changed into monsters?"

"Where'd you hear that?"

"It's documented…. And how can you be so certain you've contained the disease? Surely, a few of the contaminated people got through your security someplace. What about people who were infected and got onto airplanes?"

"This interview's over. We're doing our job, keeping the rest of you people safe. I don't need to hear crap like that."

The fatherly anchor resumed speaking. "An interview with Captain Taylor Burns, one of the men in charge of guarding the containment area. Many of our questions remain unanswered. Once again, no one is being permitted to leave or enter the Greater Cincinnati area where this mysterious virus has been…"

Christian lowered the volume, so that the anchorman droned softly in the background. "They're right across the river," Christian whispered. "If we can just communicate with them, we can get to safety."

"Didn't you hear the man?" Rick asked, placing his finger in the journal to mark his place. "They're shooting anyone on what's left of the bridges. I don't think I wanna risk it. We only have one more night to get through."

"They don't know that. They probably think it'll just keep going on and on. We need to find a way to contact them."

Chesya asked, "How? Unless we find another cell phone…"

"Wait a minute," Rick interrupted. "You found a cell phone that actually worked?"

"Yeah. I used it to call my mom. She's on her way here now."

Rick raised his eyebrows. "You found a working cell phone, and you called your fucking mother?"

Christian nodded. "It's dead now, though."

"Jesus Christ…"

Chesya said, "Rick… watch it with the language."

"Bite my ass, Chesya. This little prick finds a cell phone that works, and he uses the battery up calling his mommy! We could've used it to, oh, I don't know, call the goddamned military."

"I've warned you about the blasphemy, Rick," Chesya said, her voice low. "I won't abide it."

"Fine! Fine! Then I'll just take the 'goddamn' serum and go across the 'goddamn' bridge and get 'goddamn' shot."

Chesya started to walk from the room. "Now you're just being unkind."

"We can talk about being kind when we're fucking safe. Jesus, you… you waste this invaluable opportunity, and you worry about my fucking language?"

Chesya looked at him, and he could feel the pain in her gaze. "You want to cuss and moan about what could have been, then fine. Just keep me out of it. It's just common courtesy."

"Courtesy?"

"Yeah, and that's what separates us from those creatures. We can be kind to each other. They don't know anything about being kind. They don't know anything about being considerate of other people. It's something we share because we're human beings. Rick, it's just plain, good old-fashioned respect."

Rick mulled this over for a moment. "Sorry. Guess what the kid did was irrational, but I can kinda understand it. I just thought… just thought about what we could have done with that cell phone."

Christian looked like he was about to cry. "I'm sorry, guys. I… I didn't think."

"Damn straight you didn't think," Rick said. "But I guess we need to work together. If you find another cell phone that works, would you mind sharing this information with me? If it isn't asking too much?" To Chesya, he said, "I'll try to restrain myself from cursing, but I want a little assurance that we can all work together to get out of this mess. We still have another night to get through, you know."

"I keep screwing up," Christian muttered, leaning against the wall and looking away from the others. "I had a gun we could use, the one Jean shot himself with. I lost it during the chase last night. That could've helped us a helluva lot."

"I lost a gun, too," Chesya said. "When you're running for your life, you just don't think about things like that. You're just trying to survive."

Christian shrugged. "I'd feel better with it."

"You know, when we found the radio," Chesya said, "It was inside a whole room full of stuff. It looked untouched, but there were dozens of cubicles."

"Looked like Dilbert used to work there," Christian said, rubbing his eyes. "There could be more stuff, maybe another cell phone."

Rick nodded. "Let's give it a look-see. Then maybe we can get hold of the military… or the media. Someone who can help us out."

Andrei moaned, stirring on the floor of his cell. He shook his head, then looked over at the three people watching him from the other side of the Plexiglas. For a moment, he seemed confused.

"You shoot me!" he shouted, propping himself up on his elbows. "I help you, and you shoot me… you son of a bitch!"

"I couldn't trust you not to turn," Rick said.

"I get serum for you, and you betray me."

"Listen," Chesya said. "Let's give him the shot. If it works, we have one more person on our side. If it doesn't, he's safe locked in there."

"That's what I was doing," Rick said.

"I no think I trust you."

Rick said, "Well, Andrei, I'll have to pass the syringe into the cage, and you'll have to administer the shot yourself. So it's not a matter of trusting me."

The Siberian grinned. "You a son of a bitch… but maybe all right after all."

Rick took one of the syringes from the safe and one of the sealed beakers marked with a big scarlet "A." He laughed, reminded of the Nathanial Hawthorne novel he'd been forced to read in high school. Pushing the needle past the seal, he filled it with 300 CCs of the serum, then, after withdrawing the syringe, he tapped the side of it a few times and squirted out about 50 CCs of the solution. Chesya and Christian looked at him in wonder and awe.

"Where'd you learn to do that?" she asked.

He shrugged. "I used to always watch *E.R.* What? You think I was a junkie or something?"

She blushed. He tried not to let it bother him, but he'd thought she'd known him well enough in the past few days to realize he would never mess with illegal drugs... the kind that destroyed her family.

Rick stepped up to the slot in the cell.

"Wait a second!" Christian yelled.

"What?"

"What if he breaks the needle? I mean, this is all the serum we have. If it gets destroyed, then we have nothing."

Chesya said, "For all we know, he likes being a monster."

"You seem like nice lady," the Siberian said. "You really think this of Andrei? I will do anything to get back to family. I miss my Betta. If you think I could do this, you not so nice of a lady."

"I don't think we have much choice," Rick said. "We're gonna have to trust him."

Christian shrugged. "I guess you're right."

"Yes," Andrei agreed heartily. "Man is right. The man is right."

Chesya said, "Okay. I just pray we're doing the right thing."

Rick put the hypo in the tray case in the slot and shoved it so that it reopened in the cell. The Siberian pounced upon it, eyeballing Rick suspiciously.

"What I do with it?" he asked. "I never give shot before."

Rolling his eyes, Rick said, "Tap your arm with your fingers. Really slap it, right there on the other side of your elbow. It'll bring the veins up to the skin."

Andrei hit himself until his skin reddened, and blue veins appeared on his bicep. "Now what?"

"Now aim for one of those suckers and stick in the needle. Push in the plunger. That's it. All the way now." Rick turned to Chesya. "If he misses the vein, it won't matter. The journal said that it could even be taken orally, but any reaction would be faster intravenously. Faster sounded good to me."

Andrei finished and withdrew the empty syringe. He massaged his arm a bit, where a small welt had formed.

"Now we wait," Rick said. "Hopefully, our friend in the plastic bubble there doesn't change tonight."

"In the meanwhile," Chesya suggested, "why don't we go to that workroom and find another cell phone. This many people working in one place, there's bound to be another one."

Eyeing Christian, Rick said, "There'd better be."

CHAPTER 39

September 18, 2:10 p.m.

Even though her pulse pounded in her legs, Cathy Wright pushed herself through the pain. Everything hurt... her back, her arms, her wrists, but especially her legs. With every revolution of the bike's pedals, icy knives split her calves, passed through her aching, swollen knees, and ripped through her thighs. The agony was nearly unbearable. Tears fell from her eyes, and she grunted, inching towards downtown Cincinnati.

She'd reached Clifton, straining to propel herself up the hill. She knew these highways, and she was certain that it was all downhill after the summit. She would be able to coast past Reading Road and into the streets between the skyscrapers.

There, she would find Chris again.

He was waiting for her.

She needed to be near him, to touch him again, to hear the way he laughed.

It had been a very, very long time since she'd heard him laugh. Since long before he had run away from home.

The thought drove her to push those pedals faster, to sweat through the cool afternoon air. The clouds that had threatened to erupt into showers all morning were even darker. She prayed she would reach the Bio-Gen building before the storms erupted.

She'd spotted bands of crazy people running in what could only be called packs. They had once tried to drop a large net over her from an overpass, but she'd steered the bike sideways and avoided the trap. Now that she was pedaling uphill, she prayed she wouldn't run into any of them. They would catch her for sure, as slow as she was going.

Gasping, she stopped, feeling an unfamiliar stabbing pain in her chest. If she was going to have a heart attack, she wasn't about to do it while riding a bike. The indignity of toppling over on to the macadam was too much to think about, even if there was no one to see her do it. She got off the bike and walked beside it. Her thighs protested this new form of exercise.

The highway on the hill remained eerily quiet. Empty cars clogged the lanes, and bodies had been tossed to the roadside; she didn't see a single living soul. Every once in a while, she'd hear a muffled giggle or a distant scream, but these people didn't let themselves be seen.

"One taco short of a combo platter," she said.

She walked beside her bike, pulling it along with her. The top of the hill was just in sight, barely a football field away. The distance seemed to loom ahead of her, taunting her with her inability to ride the bike up the entire ascent. Chugging, her breath coming in long gasps, she reached the top sooner than she'd thought she could.

Cathy looked down the hill, and she could see several of the tall buildings from downtown beckoning her. They stood majestic against the Stygian sky. In several areas, smoke rose from the city, and she prayed that downtown wasn't burning.

Straddling the bike, she gingerly placed her feet back on the pedals. A blister popped beneath her right big toe. She grimaced, yelped.

The descent from the hill looked daunting, and she knew she would have to take it in low gear. It wouldn't be smart to speed down the highway only to flatten herself against a stalled car or to wipe out against an open truck door. She needed to let herself go, let her feet spin with the rhythm of the bike, and move forward... always forward.

She released her death grip on the handlebars and brakes, and she began to drift. At first, the descent seemed fairly slow and easy. Soon, she picked up momentum, swerving and braking to avoid the pitfalls. Now that she wasn't pedaling, her legs throbbed with even more fervor, and she desperately wanted an aspirin... maybe a half a dozen.

Taking the hill at a relaxed pace, she let the wind twirl through her hair, felt the first raindrop smack against her forehead. It was a big one, and she knew it wouldn't be long before she was drenched.

A second raindrop reinforced her decision to ride faster. She pumped her legs, and they almost felt better when put to use. She knew it was probably psychosomatic, but what the hell.

She turned the corner of the hill near Reading Road, taking the nearby exit. The buildings now loomed over her, but they did little to stop the downpour. She heard thunder, rumbling low and menacing. It lasted almost thirty seconds. She could feel it within her ribcage, compressing her chest.

Then the deluge began.

It was no ordinary rainfall, but the kind that makes a sane man build arks in his back yard. It plastered her hair to her head, caused her clothes to grip her body in binding, uncomfortable ways. She could smell the lightning coming before it sizzled, striking a radio tower to her left.

Reading Road turned into Broadway, and she searched for a building labeled Bio-Gen, but the incessant rain stung her eyes and blurred her view. In fact, it was coming down so hard, it stung… no, it actually hurt!

Shrieking, she tossed the bike aside and took shelter under an awning attached to an empty warehouse. She could see Broadway just ahead of her, but she decided to wait out the storm.

When it began to hail, ice pinging like bullets on the aluminum awning, she leaned back against the building. She massaged her legs. She would have to get used to it. They were going to hurt for a while.

Looking out at the city, she once again found herself completely alone. Nobody wandered the streets. No families searched for loved ones. It seemed as though everyone was either locked up securely in their homes or dead. Even the crazies were keeping out of sight. The streets didn't seem to have many bodies littered across them. Perhaps something dragged them off the tarmac, back into darkened alleys, where their feasts were held.

Shivering, she watched the hail bounce off the sidewalk, the rain slicing down in broad sheets.

She observed a bloodstain on the sidewalk, and she watched until it was washed clean by the rain. All around her, the water cleansed the streets.

CHAPTER 40

September 18, 2:55 p.m.

In the room of cubicles, Rick didn't take long to discover more than ten cell phones, none of which worked for more than a few frustrating seconds. The dial tone would start, then dissipate to a tinny whine as Rick punched in the operator's number. Then nothing... the sound of empty space.

"Here's another one!" Christian shouted, pressing his ear to the phone. The dial tone began, then faded, replaced by a loud hissing. Checking the tiny monitor on the phone, he said, "It can't get a signal. I don't know why. Everything seems okay with it. There's plenty of charge left in the battery."

"The storm, you think?" Chesya asked.

Rick checked another cell phone he'd dug out of a coat pocket. All he could hear was a constant static, like waves.

"Damn it!" He threw it across a cubicle, and it shattered against a bulletin board filled with memos on colored paper. The sound it made, plastic and metal bits dropping to the floor, pleased him more than he wanted to admit.

"Well, that sure helps," Chesya said, instinctively placing her fists upon her hips. "All we need to do is find one that still has a dial tone. If we don't find it, we're no worse off than before."

"I wouldn't say that," he said. "We have another night of this crap. I don't know about you, but I'd like to have a safe place to sleep and a few weapons."

Christian placed a tiny phone to his ear, listened, then sighed and placed it back on the desk.

Chesya said, "Well, all your bitching and moaning don't help any."

"It's not hurting any, either," Rick said.

"That's a matter of opinion."

"Oh," he said. "I guess I should just shut up and sit quietly like a good little boy. Chesya, you knew going into this that I wasn't a saint."

She snorted. "You can say that again."

"One of these days, Alice...." he quoted Ralph Cramden, making a fist with his right hand and shaking it in the air.

"Will the two of you just shut the fuck up!" Christian shouted. "I'm sick of the whining and backbiting. This isn't a pissing contest."

Chesya and Rick turned towards the boy. He'd been so silent for so long, so quiet and polite, that this outburst seemed out of character. Christian himself seemed shocked by his words and their sudden reaction.

"Damn," Rick said, turning back to the desks. "Don't have to get all mad."

"Well, you two are acting like babies," he said. "I honestly don't think we're gonna find another phone in this place. That one in the snack room was probably a fluke. Why don't we just walk on down to the river and try to talk with the people in charge? It's got to be better than sitting with our thumbs up our asses here. It's not safe here."

Rick said, "I like the kid's idea."

Chesya was shaking her head. "Didn't you hear that radio? They said they had blown the bridges, that they were shooting anyone who tried to get across."

"We won't try to get across. We should just try to communicate with them."

"No," Chesya said. "I've seen what people in charge will do... police, Army, whatever. Shoot first, ask questions later. I've seen it too many times growing up in Over the Rhine. You wanna take the chance that they won't just kill you?"

"But we're normal. We didn't turn."

"How they gonna know about that? Everybody looks the same in the daylight. How many people do you think they've shot already?" She raised her voice, an awkward, unpleasant sound. "'Why, yes, officer. I'm just fine. The disease didn't affect me at all. What? You say I can't come over the river?' BLAM! Would you take chances if you were them? They gotta make sure this thing doesn't spread to the rest of the country."

Rick scratched his neck. "What if we go to the bridge during the nighttime?" Chesya shook her head again, but he kept going. "They'd know we weren't infected; they'd see it with their own eyes. Then they'd have to let us cross."

Christian thought about it for a moment. "I kinda like the idea. The only real problem I see is how are we gonna survive more than ten minutes out there. I don't know about you guys, but I'm tired as hell."

Chesya crossed her arms. "You really think someone in a position of power, someone with a damn gun, is gonna let us just row ourselves across that river? What if we're carriers of the virus? Ever think of that? We could spread it all over Kentucky just by crossing that bridge and breathing. Shooting us would be a way to easily contain the disease. If nobody gets out, neither does the virus."

Rick started grinning.

"You're always so damned amused. What now?" Chesya asked.

He giggled. "We'll have to cross that bridge when we come to it."

He laughed louder, clutching at his sides. The sound echoed, seemed to surround them, and Christian began to laugh too, sitting on the edge of a desk. He knew the joke wasn't that funny, but something about the way Rick giggled at his own infantile humor was hilarious. The laughter grew, became contagious, until even Chesya cracked a smile, then she joined in the hilarity. It sounded as though there were twenty people in the room instead of three, all of them broken up with joy over some terribly funny joke.

"Why are you all laughing?"

The voice stopped the laughter so suddenly that the newborn silence seemed ominous.

A woman stood in the doorway, soaking wet and dripping rainwater on the floor. Her blond hair was plastered to her scalp, and her blue eyes seemed large and full of curiosity. She was a bit hippy, but her figure was still good for her age, which Chesya placed at about forty-two or forty-three. Her tan was as artificial as the smile she wore. Something around her eyes bothered Chesya, a procession of emotions that flashed through her so fast that they barely had time to register.

The woman looked at them, still smiling, then she fell to her knees in a single, graceful, painful motion. When she hit the floor, she closed her eyes and grimaced. Her hands flew out in front of her in a familiar gesture, that of someone asking for a hug. Chesya felt Christian stir behind her.

"Christian," she said. "Is that woman your mother?"

"I made it," the woman said, opening those bright blue eyes to gaze at Christian. "I tried so hard to get here, and I actually made it."

"Mom?"

The boy moved forward, hesitating a bit. This woman looked older than the one he remembered, as though she had withered in the months he'd been gone. He saw that it was certainly her, but something in her had changed. She seemed tougher, wiser.

She nodded to him, stretching out her arms towards him.

"Yes, sweetie. It's me. I came for you."

And the gesture of the open arms was so familiar that Christian flew into their fold, resting his head on Cathy's shoulder. His arms encircled her waist, clutching as tightly as he could. She stroked his hair, his back, taking in the true solidity of him.

"Oh, God, Christian."

Her words broke him, and he began to sob into the crevice between her shoulder and her neck. She smelled of sweat, but there was also a half-forgotten scent that could only be his mother.

Stepping up behind Chesya, Rick placed a solid hand on her shoulder, watching the reunion with a big grin on his handsome, unshaven face. Chesya covered his hand with hers.

Beaming, Christian lifted his mother and spun her around in the air, just like she used to do to him when he was a child; Cathy's delighted laughter filled the room.

CHAPTER 41

September 18, 4:00 p.m.

After they had gathered four rolling chairs from the offices, everyone introduced themselves and told their respective stories, as though sitting around a campfire. Cathy could barely keep her hands off of Christian, patting him, picking some piece of lint from his shirt, and all the attention annoyed him. Still, he was having trouble not crying and shouting "Mommy!" at her.

"My God," she said, "you look so much bigger. Older, too."

"I am older," he said.

Chesya and Rick watched their interactions with a sort of perverse amusement. They could tell she was making Christian uncomfortable, but they also knew he was too polite to say anything about it. He just let her give him little hugs and pats, gritting his teeth all the while.

"What are we going to do now?" Cathy asked, brushing some dandruff from Christian's shoulder.

"That's pretty much where we were when you showed up," Rick said. "We need to get the attention of the men guarding the river, but we don't want to get shot."

Christian gently waved his mother's hand from his shoulder. "It all comes down to this... finding a safe place to be seen, so that the military, the police, whoever... can see that we don't change at night, that we're not one of them."

"One of us... one of us... one of us..." Rick intoned monotonously. When Chesya gave him a dark glare, he said, "What? You haven't seen that movie?"

Turning towards Cathy, Chesya said, "Ignore him. Don't encourage him. Sometimes it works."

"One of us... hehehe... I liked that movie."

"You have any ideas, Mom?" Christian asked. "We're stumped."

"Well," Cathy said, "I doubt they'll be moving over the river... the creatures, that is. The only way they have of getting across is the bridges. I don't think those things can swim. On my way here, I kept seeing them floating facedown in pools of water. I saw a bunch of them in a man-made lake. They're probably too heavy to swim."

"They were made for running, not for the breaststroke," Christian said, looking at his mother in amazement. "Their shoulders and chests are so massive, I think you might have something there, Mom."

Rick asked, "But how's that gonna help us? It's a nice thought and all, but..."

Christian jumped from his chair, sending it rolling backwards. "Oh God, I've got it! I really think I've got it! I've been living down here in a warehouse for some time now, and there isn't a lot to do when you don't have money or friends..."

Cathy's hands went to her chest. "Oh my god, you were living on the streets? Homeless?"

"Mom, not now. Anyway, you do what you can for entertainment, and I used to go down to the river, sit on the snake wall, and watch the boats go by... and the barges. They haul coal up and down the river to the various power plants."

"Am I dense?" Rick asked. "I still don't get it."

"Yes, you are dense," Chesya said, elbowing him. "Now let the boy talk."

"Thanks, Chesya. So, these barges float in the middle of the river. Get it? The middle of the river?"

Cathy was the first to grasp the idea. "Oh! So we get on a barge and float where the things can't reach us. They'll drown if they try."

Christian said, "And the officials in charge across the river will see us standing on the barge and they'll know that we're still human. They'll see we're immune."

"Jesus Christ," Rick said. "That is one fucking beautiful idea. Sorry, Chesya."

"I think even Jesus would understand getting caught up in the moment," Chesya said. "We only have a few hours until those things start changing again, so I propose we get going. Rick, find some flashlights and anything that we can use as a weapon. Also, you seem to have the best rapport with the Russian, so you better tell him where we're going."

"All right," he said, and he rushed from the room.

Clucking after him, Chesya said, "That boy's always running. Chris, I need you to get into those snack machines and fill some bags with the remaining food. I don't care what it is, we just need something to get us through the night."

Watching her son dash off to the breakroom, Cathy asked, "What do you want *me* to do?" Chesya could see in her eyes that she desperately wanted to follow Christian. He'd been out of her sight for long enough.

"I need you with me," Chesya replied. "Let's go through this office with a fine-tooth comb and grab anything you think we could use. I know you say those things can't swim, but we're working on sheer supposition here. We haven't actually seen any of them drown."

"Oh, Lord, you're right. What if I've—"

"Now, now, don't get upset. I think it's a good theory. Makes sense to me. Still, if we're out there and those creatures suddenly start making their way through the water towards us... well, I just want to be prepared. Also, try to stop fondling the boy."

Cathy blushed. "I'm just excited to see him. That's all."

"I understand that. But he's a man now, not your little kid."

"He'll always be my little kid."

"In your mind, woman. Look at him. He's been surviving on the streets, and he's more an adult now than that crazy bank robber in the next room. I think he's wearying of all your touches and pats, but he doesn't want to hurt your feelings. You've found him, and you've got him back. Now just be happy and let him prove himself to be the man he is."

Cathy frowned, but she knew Chesya had a point. She'd thought of him as her little boy for so long that the idea had overwhelmed the reality of his age and wisdom. Nodding, she said, "I'll try."

"That's all I can ask for."

They began searching through the desks, pulling out anything that might be useful outside. They talked a bit, and Chesya took advantage of Christian's absence.

"That son of yours has had a really hard time of it. He's been living on the streets, surviving any way he can. He's putting on a brave front for you, but I think it's gonna take a long time for his scars to heal."

"I know," Cathy sighed. "I hope you're not criticizing me."

"Oh, I was just—"

"What I mean to say is, I know I made a mistake. A really big one, and for once I'm not the one who paid for it. My son did. I'll do anything to make it up to him. Anything."

"Just be careful what you ask about what he did out there. Probably a lot of things a mother wouldn't want to know about her baby."

After depositing five pairs of scissors in a box, Cathy said, "I'm not naïve, Chesya. I've had a privileged life, and I realize that. I've lived most of my life in a gated community. Still, I know what happens in the world. I probably have a good idea what Chris has been through, and it makes me sick to my stomach. I could've prevented that from happening if I'd only acted sooner. But the sad fact is, I didn't do anything. And now… well, I hope Chris can get through the rest of his life without having nightmares. I pray that I can change his life, and maybe my own as well."

Chesya said, "Sounds like you're on the right—holy crap!" She reached into one of the drawers and held up a small pistol. A dainty Black Widow .22 Mag. She took aim across the room, marveled at how comfortable it felt in her small hands.

"Who you suppose kept this in their desk?" she asked.

"More important, why would they need such a thing at work? Is it loaded?"

After fumbling for a few seconds, Chesya popped out the magazine. "Yeah," she said, snapping it closed again. "Five itty-bitty bullets. Doesn't look like they'd do much harm. They're so small… but I suppose any bullet can do damage if it's aimed at the right place."

In the breakroom, Christian searched through the drawers. He discovered several plastic grocery bags in the trashcan. He filled the first bag with a set of knives he found in a drawer. The blades didn't look very sharp, but he figured if you stabbed hard enough, they'd puncture a Lycanthrope's skin. Walking over to the snack machine, he pulled out every remaining bag of chips, cookies, or candy, almost filling the second plastic bag.

Munching on a pilfered Snickers bar, he opened the refrigerator. The smell nearly knocked him down. There was definitely rancid meat in the warmth of the fridge. He couldn't find anything edible in there, but when he checked the freezer, he found it still slightly cool. Several people had left their frozen lunches in there, and he grabbed a Lean Cuisine and checked it. The surface of the lasagna had melted, but the center was still frozen. He looked around, saw no one, and quickly devoured the meal. It was disgusting, the center crunchy and the outside slick with sweat, but it filled his stomach, and he immediately felt better, stronger. The freezer held six more meals. He placed them in his third sack and took all his booty to the laboratory.

To Andrei, Rick was saying, "But we'll be back in the morning, probably with some kind of support from the Army."

"You leave me here? Alone? I take medicine. I will be all right now. You see. You see."

"I'm afraid we can't get you out of there just yet, dude," Rick said. "I don't want you turning on me. There's enough to fuckin' worry about already."

"You no worry about me," he replied. Andrei caught Christian's eye, and he pleaded with him. "Please, you tell him. I am all right. I am human now. The shot will stop me from the change. I feel good now. Not hairy."

"No dice, man," Rick said.

"Actually," Christian replied, "how are we gonna know if he becomes a creature tonight? How will we know when we come back in the morning? He'd be back to human anyway."

"I'll leave that to the goddamn scientists. They supposedly know what they're doing."

"Oh, yeah, right," Christian chuckled. "They really knew what they were doing when they unleashed this on the world."

"Don't be sarcastic."

Chesya entered the room, carrying the box of weapons they'd found in the desks of the workroom.

"We found a gun," Cathy said.

She handed it to Rick, who gave it a quick perusal after weighing the little gun in his hand. "Very nice. A Black Widow, .22 Mag, five-shot revolver. These babies have really nice fixed sights. You can get a good bead on your target. It's one of the best mini-revolvers out there."

"Two days ago, the fact that you knew that much about a specific gun would've scared me," Chesya said. "Now I can't help but be proud."

"So I'm impressing you with my thorough knowledge of weaponry?"

"I wouldn't go that far. Still, we can definitely use a gun. We have scissors and sharp envelope openers, too."

"I got a bunch of knives from the kitchen area. They aren't too sharp, though," Christian said.

Andrei approached the edge of the Plexiglas. "I know of weapon, too. I see them use it here. It would be very... how you say it, handy."

"Another weapon?" Rick asked. "Sounds like a con. What is it?"

The Siberian shook his head. "Oh no. For this I, how you say it, bargain. I come with you, then I will tell you about weapon."

Chesya shrugged. "I don't see the harm."

"Are you crazy, woman?" Rick shouted. "He'll turn on us the second the moon comes up."

"Not if the drug worked," Cathy reminded him.

"If... if... IF!"

"Is a good weapon."

Chesya aimed the barrel of the Black Widow special on the man in the cage, and she said, "If he starts to change, we'll take him out. One good shot to the head, and he's history. If he doesn't change, he'll be another person to help, another strong pair of arms. I say we vote on it. This is a democratic society. Or at least, it was."

"Fuck the democratic bullshit!" Rick said. "I say we leave him."

"I say we take him with us. We'll kill him if we have to," Chesya said.

Cathy added, "I don't think he'd be much of a problem. It's all of us against him. I say we take him."

"I have to say take him, too," Christian said, standing.

"I say I go also," Andrei shouted.

"You don't count, ya communist bastard," Rick said bitterly. "All right. I'm outvoted. But write this shit down and remember it: I don't like it. I'm against it. I wanted nothing to do with it."

"Noted," Chesya said. "Now how do we get him out of there?"

Rick said, "And get him some damn clothes. I'm not running beside this guy with his wang flopping around."

Cathy volunteered to find clothes, and Rick opened the cell with the key on the ring. The door hissed again, popping open a few inches. Immediately, Andrei stepped out of his prison, keeping his eyes on Rick in case he tried to shoot him with another dart.

"I still no trust you," Andrei said.

"The feeling's mutual, big guy."

"I feel human. No animal is left inside me. The hairy feeling, that is gone."

"For all of our sake, I hope so."

Cathy entered, holding a heavy one-piece coverall, the material stained with some kind of disinfectant. "I found these in the janitor's closet," she said. "They're a little dirty, but aren't we all?"

As Andrei stepped into the clothes and zipped up the front, Rick stepped towards the window. Looking outside, he said, "It's like a ghost town out there. The streets are completely empty as far as I can see."

Cathy asked, "Isn't that a good thing?"

"The freaks come out at night," Chesya sang. "And we don't have a lot of time left. We need to get ourselves down to the water and pray we can figure out how to get one of those barges into the middle of the Ohio River."

"While not getting shot in the process," Christian said.

"Hey, where's that weapon you promised?" Rick asked Andrei. He felt a little better now that the man was clothed.

The big Siberian smiled. "I am that weapon. It is me."

"You son of a bitch!"

"I can kill anyone with these hands... my, what, bare hands. I am strong, my friends."

"Better than spitting at them," Cathy replied.

"Is good weapon, no?"

"Hey, another set of eyes, another set of hands to hold those things off…" Chesya began.

"If he doesn't change into one himself," Rick said.

"Then we'll blow him away," Christian finished, looking at Andrei. "It won't be the time to get all emotional. You start changing, even a little, I'll kill you myself."

Cathy glanced at Chesya, not recognizing the low, serious tone of her son.

Chesya said, "I guess it's a good weapon, Andrei. Something tells me we'll need all the help we can get."

Rick patted the tall man on his back and said, "Yeah, well, I guess you're a part of the team now. Don't change tonight."

"No, I will not. Andrei makes promise."

"Come on. Let's get down to the river," Chesya suggested. "It's gonna be dark soon, and I don't want to be helpless and surrounded by those things when the sun sets."

The group moved for the hallway. Andrei, dart rifle slung over his shoulder, took a final look back at the open prison cell where he had been restrained for so long. He gave it a jaunty little salute before turning his back upon it, and leaving that part of his life behind him.

PART 3

CHAPTER 42

September 18, 5:45 p.m.

General Taylor Burns watched the banks of the Ohio River from his
perch in Covington, Kentucky. The binoculars wearied his nearsighted
eyes, and he handed them to his assistant, Chief Warrant Officer Tom
Granger. Blinking, the general let his pupils adjust to the dying light,
noted the position of the sinking sun. If he hadn't been wearing a bulky
biohazard suit, he would have run a hand through his salt and pep-
pered, close-shaved hair.

The muddy river ran slowly, churning as though troubled by the
bad weather. The Ohio River spanned the shores of Cincinnati and
Kentucky, about a thousand feet across and about forty-eight feet deep.
The undertow was treacherous, sucking several swimmers a year into its
murky embrace. Five bridges stretched across the river, the most
impressive being the Brent Spence Bridge, one of the largest suspension
bridges in the world. It had lost much of its previous grandeur when
the military had blown the middle out of it. The other five bridges had
also lost their centers to explosions, replaced with large, ragged, still
smoking holes that dropped into the dark river.

"It looks like the hydrogen bomb went off over there," Burns said,
motioning to the buildings of downtown Cincinnati. His voice was
tinny through the speaker on the outside of the orange suit. "Every
time I think I see someone moving, they disappear back into the
shadows. Can't trust these old eyes anymore."

Granger said, "Won't be long now, sir. We'll see plenty of those things, just like the other nights. Hundreds of 'em, sir, trying to get across, leaping from where we've blown up the bridges."

Burns sighed. Looking over to his left, he took in the parking lots the Army had commissioned as a temporary morgue. Torched, blackened skeletons of men, women, and even children were lined up in rows. The sheer number of them staggered the mind, and he felt a bead of sweat trickle down his brow. He wondered how he could be perspiring when the suit was air-conditioned and, truth be told, rather chilly.

Scanning the rest of the operation, he saw the regiments of Army mingling with the National Guardsmen, talking casually over coffee, only a few snipers and watchdogs to keep surveillance on the bridges. A few men and women were hauling the last of the previous night's burnt bodies off the Brent Spence Bridge, away from the still-smoking hole in the middle of the structure. The deserted city of Covington was dotted with combat engineer vehicles, 165mm demolition guns, and grounded helicopters. Searchlights rimmed the river, their massive bulbs switched off until darkness fell. The military men and vehicles stretched as far as he could see, encircling the parameter of the infected area. Every half-mile, there was a decontamination area with chemical showers for the soldiers who had infiltrated the infected area, returning with terrible stories of massacres and suicides, of mothers killing their children rather than letting them change again.

He leaned back on a Humvee, crossing his arms, and he squinted at the cityscape like John Wayne. With his southern drawl and broad face, he'd often been told he resembled The Duke. He took it as a compliment, as long as nobody referred to that piece of shit *The Conqueror.* Nobody liked Wayne in that one. What the hell had the casting director been thinking?

"The men ready to go?" Burns asked Tom.

"Troops are stationed at every bridge, sir. Nobody's getting through, just like last night."

"You wonder about all this?" Burns asked.

"Sir?"

"We're literally mowing them down while they're running towards us. You ever wonder if that's right? These are Americans, after all."

"Begging your pardon, sir, but they're monsters. They're gonna try to jump across that gap we blew in the bridge, maybe even try to swim across the river. We let them get through the parameter, there'd be panic everywhere. At least most of the country's kept safe this way."

"Sacrificing the few to save the many, huh Granger?"

"Well, yes, sir."

"You're right. As always. Still, I had trouble sleeping last night. Haven't had that since the first Gulf War, but this was different. When we took out the middle of that bridge, we blew the hell outta so many of them. The ones already across, the ones we had to burn… I kept seeing them." He motioned to the rows of corpses laid neatly side by side. "Their faces… before we set them on fire, before we fished them out of the river where they fell, burning, they looked like anyone from my old neighborhood. From any neighborhood. And what if anyone's still normal in there? We've been jamming the cell phones with satellite signals. I know it's so the media doesn't get hold of anyone inside, but, damn it, there are probably a lot of kids in there. The Pentagon seems more worried about media perception."

"Don't tell me you're getting sentimental?" Tom said. Realizing his mistake, he added, "Sir."

"I'm not going all soft, if that's what you mean. Don't worry. Just little conscience pangs."

From a few miles away, they heard automatic rifle fire, then silence descended again. "Someone else trying to get across," he said. "Damn it, why don't they listen?"

"Sounded like it came from Newport. We give them fair warning. Hey! Sir, what's that?"

Granger motioned towards the bottom of one of the bridges, and General Taylor Burns pulled the binoculars back to his eyes. Focusing, he saw several people approaching the water on the opposite side of the river, three men and two women. Each of them carried a pack. They looked back and forth, then the black woman pointed into the distance and they all trekked towards some determined destination.

"There's something… different about this bunch," Burns said. "Look at the way they move. It's organized. Like they have a goal or a set of plans."

"I imagine their goal is to get on to this side of the river, where it's safe, sir."

"Maybe. My point is, they're working together. You've seen the way people over there have been acting. They act alone, or in packs with a single leader barking orders, not in groups. Seems like even when they aren't beasts, they've become very independent and wary, like they can't trust anyone else. Most of these mugs that we've isolated act like they can't see more than ten seconds into the future. They just do what they want. They see something they like, they steal it. Look there, see how that guy just helped that woman up onto that rock? That's good manners. Common courtesy. I didn't even think that existed anymore."

"Looks like they're making for one of those coal barges, sir. We've been seeing this all day. People using boats and rafts and such. We can't let them get over here."

"I know my orders, Granger. You don't have to constantly remind me."

The group was, indeed, stepping onto the deck of one of the barges that was docked near the bridge. Burns told Granger to report to him if they did anything suspicious, and then he retired to his tent. He felt very tired.

He prayed the little group wouldn't try to cross the river. They'd seemed like good people in the few minutes he'd observed them, very unlike anyone else he'd encountered from the infected area. He would hate to have to kill them.

CHAPTER 43

September 18, 6:00 p.m.

The five-block trip from the Bio-Gen building to the riverfront was more harrowing than Rick had thought it would be. Not because there were so many dangers in their path, but because of the eerie stillness that had clouded the city streets. Nothing moved as they weaved through the parked cars, climbing over them when necessary. Their voices echoed off the empty buildings, so they refrained from conversation while they traveled to the Serpentine Wall that separated Cincinnati proper from the Ohio River. Inside, Rick roiled with the urge to shout something, to break this unnatural quiet. He kept it under control, though, walking briskly south, watching from the corners of his eyes for any movement.

Chesya repeatedly turned her head from side to side, aware that someone was watching her from the dark alleys between buildings. Occasionally, a noise emerged from the shadows, proof that there were still people out there. They just preferred the darkness of the side streets. This predilection for staying hidden frightened her worse than their existence.

With a knife in each hand, she gave herself a mental pat on the back. She had proven herself to be a stronger woman than she thought she could be, given the circumstances. She knew her brothers wouldn't have fared any better, and they had both been street thugs, wise to the ways of the world.

Andrei could barely control his delight at being set free after so long. He touched things as he walked: automobiles, street signs, fire hydrants that still trickled water. Raising his wet fingers to his mouth, he grinned as he sucked down the water from a cupped palm. His arms and legs would sometimes reach out and stretch without him being conscious of it, flexing muscles that had been imprisoned for too long. He had had plenty of room in the cell, but he'd never been able to feel that he'd actually flexed. The world was a huge empty space again, and it contained more than enough room for his big body. Even the slight wind on his face was deeply satisfying. He only wished that since the rainstorm had passed, the clouds would part for the sun. He yearned to feel sunshine on his pale skin, to strip down to the waist and enjoy the prickling as he tanned a dark, chestnut brown, as he'd been in the old country.

Behind him, Cathy walked alongside Christian. Her hands kept flitting at him, worrying a speck of lint from his coat, running fingers through his long hair. All the time, she ignored the creepiness of the deserted streets, focusing completely on her son, even as she wondered where the crazies had gone. She felt she knew for the first time in her pampered life what it was to be a mother. This was what it meant to care about another person more than you'd ever cared about anything before. To feel as if you'd protect your child no matter what danger came at you. These intense emotions had been buried within her for so long, covered and encumbered by responsibilities of the house and the role of a doting wife and mother. Losing nearly everything and burning the rest to the ground had seemed to disinter these feelings, and she embraced them. She didn't ever want to let go of Christian's hand. Grasping it tightly, she realized she wasn't surprised by these overwhelming sensations. They had been there all along.

For his part, Christian knew that the clutchy-grabby woman needed him far more than he needed her. He was certainly happy to see her, but he wanted to brush her hands away, tell her to stop. Sighing, he realized he could do no such thing. She had proven she loved him, had taken a ridiculous risk to hunt him down. She could have imprisoned herself in her cozy million dollar house and waited out this ordeal, but she didn't. And he loved her for it, knew that he had actually missed her since he'd run away from home. So he could endure a doting mother for a while longer, if it pleased her. At least it took her mind off the dangerous situation at hand.

When they reached the Serpentine Wall, they scanned the river for the barges. Pointing west, Rick said, "I see one over there, under that bridge."

It was probably a half mile away from where they stood, the empty eye of Sawyer Point's amphitheater glaring at them. In fact, it was a procession of three barges, each loaded with a mountain of coal, and they were attached to a feeble-looking tugboat in the lead.

As they jogged towards it, Cathy asked, "That little boat pulls all that weight? It doesn't seem possible."

"Let's pray that it is possible," Chesya said. "We need to get those flat barges out to the middle of the river... and fast. It's starting to get dark."

A little stone stairway was carved into the bank of the river, and they walked down it until they stood on the silt that lined the rushing water. The river was a bit swollen from the deluge earlier that day, and the water seemed to turn in upon itself, rolling with some hidden mentality, an undertow, as though it planned to pull them down into its brown, dirty, polluted grasp.

The little band of survivors stepped across the soggy plywood plank, from the shore to the tugboat. In a few moments, they were all crowding the boat's cabin.

Rick was amazed that everything had remained intact over the previous two nights. Apparently, the beasts hadn't attempted to sail away on the river. This only reinforced Cathy's claim that they were afraid of the water, that it posed a danger to them.

The bank of instruments in the tugboat seemed deceptively simple.

"That's the speedometer," Cathy said, "and that's the ignition. I don't see a key, though. That lever moves the boat forward or backward and determines your speed."

"You can really drive this thing?" Chesya asked.

Cathy nodded. "I think so. It's a lot like our little yacht we keep down in Florida." She continued pointing. "That's the GPS system, a lot like what you have in your car."

Chesya snorted. "Not in my car. I'm lucky to have a cassette player."

"The radio!" Christian said, lunging forward. "It's got a radio." He pulled the mic from its handle and clicked it twice, flipping on the metal switch with his other hand. "Is there anyone out there that can hear me?" he asked, speaking into the mic. "This is an emergency. Is there anyone listening?"

"My God," Chesya said. "If we can get the military on this thing… You think they're monitoring this frequency?"

"I wouldn't doubt if they were listening to every frequency," Christian answered, and he tried raising someone on the radio again.

They waited for a few moments as static crackled from the little speaker. Christian switched frequencies and tried again, only to be answered by the same pop of white noise.

Andrei said, "I do not think it works, no? Shouldn't we hear, what, talking talking talking?"

Rick shrugged. "I'm outta my element."

"What that mean?"

"It means I've never had enough cash to buy one of these babies, my Siberian friend. Probably never will."

Chesya glanced up at him as Christian continued to scan various frequencies. She said, "I thought you did well for yourself? Bank-robbing not pay as much as it used to?"

"I got one nerve left, Chesya. Don't get on it." He leaned back, sulking a bit. Listening to Christian's unanswered bellows, he chewed the inside of his lip, then waved at Chesya.

"Sorry," he said. "I've been having a chance to look back at my life, and I'm discovering it isn't so exciting or wonderful. Not where I planned to be by now, at least."

"You wanted a boat?"

"Oh, yeah, baby," he said with a Cheshire Cat grin. "I wanted the boat and the house and the cars and the women. All the things that make up the stereotypical good life. Never quite made it there, though. Still one of the suffering middle class."

"Just enough to get by?"

"I guess that's right."

"Maybe you shouldn't be looking back," she suggested. "Maybe it's time to start looking forward. To the future."

He laughed. "You think there's gonna be anything to look forward to?"

"If we get through this night, I am going to take the hottest, longest bubble bath of my life. Then I think I'll eat a huge meal... steak and a gigantic, heart-attack-inducing dessert. Something really sinful."

"Sounds good. Mind if I join you?"

"For the bubble bath or the dinner?" As soon as she said the words, she couldn't believe she'd done it.

"Well, well," he said, a wolfish look overtaking his rugged features. "Is that an invitation?"

"Um... to dinner. Yes."

"Tell you what," he said. "We get through this night without becoming werewolf chow, and I'll personally pay for everything and throw in a massage to boot."

Blushing, she said, "Okay. It's a deal."

Rick smiled. He didn't mention the money in his jacket. Chesya didn't need to know he would use money ripped off from her own bank to pay for their date. He had enough stashed in various pockets to live fairly well for at least a year.

"Is very touching," Andrei said. "Like Russian novel."

"Oh, go to hell," Rick said. He leaned out of the cabin of the little boat and looked towards the far shore. A small cluster of soldiers were pointing in their direction.

"They've spotted us," he said. "See how all those guns are pointing at us now? Guess since they're not shooting, they aren't too worried, yet."

Cathy eyed the darkening sky. "We'd better get out into the middle of the river. The clouds are making it get dark early."

"Those look like storm clouds, too," Rick said. "It's gonna pour down pretty soon."

"Figures," Chesya said. "Way our luck's going, it'll end up a hurricane."

As if in answer, the bottoms of several clouds lit up from within, then boomed with thunder.

Cathy said, "I can drive this thing out there, but there's no key."

"The captain probably took it with him."

"He's dead by now," Chesya predicted.

"Okay," Rick said, "stand back." With a screwdriver he found on the floor, he popped the ignition mechanism from the panel. "If it's anything like a car, we'll be business in another minute or two."

"And if it isn't like a car?" Christian asked, the radio microphone still in his hands.

"Well, maybe we won't have to worry about surviving the rest of the night."

Everyone except Andrei stepped outside the cabin. Christian even hopped over to the first barge of coal. It was only a few feet from the tugboat, but if Rick was going to cause an explosion, he wanted to be as far away as possible. "Come on," he said, motioning to his mother and Chesya. They followed him. Andrei stayed put, peering into the cabin at Rick's activities.

After an agonizing couple of minutes, they heard the sound of the engine catching. It putt-putted for a few seconds, then stopped. Rick's cursing soon followed, then the engine chugged into life and remained on. The little group standing next to the mounds of coal gave a cheer and hopped back to the cabin, where they were soon patting Rick on the back.

"Who says crime doesn't pay?" he asked, grinning widely.

The sky got darker, with little flashes of lightning every once in a while. The water became choppy, and Chesya felt her stomach give a small lurch.

Christian picked up the mic and began speaking into it again, trying different wavelengths. "Can anyone hear me? Mayday. Mayday."

Cathy pushed forward, looking down at the controls. "Okay... this looks like the anchor."

Flicking a switch, she nodded in satisfaction when a whirring sound began, followed by the clanking of a chain on the starboard side.

After a minute, they heard a thunk and the grinding noise stopped, the anchor raised. The river churned, probably flooding someplace to the west, and suddenly the little boat veered towards the center of the river, rocked and carried by the current. The plywood plank dropped into the river and was swiftly carried off to the east.

"Can you handle this thing?" Rick asked.

"Let me try," Cathy answered.

She pushed the lever forward, and the motor's sound grew louder. Chesya nearly fell when the boat jerked forward, then stopped suddenly because of the weight of the barges pulling against the forward momentum. Thankfully, the coal's weight slowed their movements on the river. Cathy pulled back a bit, and the boat inched forward.

"These things obviously weren't meant to go very fast," she said with an apologetic look. "Not like the yacht."

Soon, they were positioned in the center of the river, choppy waves rushing by them on either side. As Cathy pushed the button and lowered the anchor, stationing the boat and its two coal-laden barges almost exactly in the middle of the Ohio River, beneath the destroyed Brent Spence Bridge that had once connected Cincinnati to Covington, Kentucky.

Christian said, "You did it, Mom! Excellent!"

"I just hope she doesn't break loose from the anchor in this storm," Cathy said.

It was nearly dark now, and everyone turned to look at Andrei.

"What?" he asked, shrugging. Noticing the encroaching darkness, the big man said, "Oh. That."

CHAPTER 44

September 18, 6:40 p.m.

The wind blew so strongly, General Taylor Burns struggled to maintain balance in the biohazard suit. The storm was gathering strength, and he prayed that it wouldn't result in another deluge. His men found it hard enough to spot the creatures running across the destroyed bridges and leaping towards Kentucky in the daylight while it rained. If it happened during the night, who knew how many beasts could find their way into the safe zone?

A flash of lightning, still contained within the clouds, confirmed his darkest fears. He could feel the electricity in the air, could almost smell the ozone. This was going to be one humdinger of a T-storm, and there wasn't a thing he could do to pacify it.

He had tried to lie down in his tent, get a few minutes of shuteye, but his thoughts had returned to the small band of people with their mysterious purpose. Curiosity had gotten the better of him, and he was watching them again through his binoculars.

The little group boarded the tugboat and maneuvered it into the center of the river. The person piloting the vessel, a middle-aged woman, was doing rather well under the turbulent circumstances. He was astonished when they dropped anchor, stopping halfway across the water. He had already ordered a group of soldiers to gather at the shore-line in formation, their rifles pointed across the river at the barges. They were still awaiting orders to shoot.

Scratching his head, Burns turned to Tom Granger. "Why'd they stop like that? It doesn't make sense."

"Maybe their primary goal wasn't crossing the river, sir."

"Isn't that what you would do in their position, Granger? Try to get across the river?"

"Begging your pardon, sir, but we don't really know what their position might be. They're definitely acting according to some strategy. Watch how they move together. These people have been companions, at least for a while."

"That big guy, the one in the overalls, he seems a little stand-off-ish."

"Yeah, he's a problem," Granger chewed his lip. "Sir, what do we do? Should I instruct the men to open fire?"

General Burns thought about it for a moment. If he let his men slaughter these people, would he be protecting the rest of the nation from their infiltration? Containing the situation within the city and its outlying areas had taken a hell of a lot of work, and the powers that resided in the Pentagon hadn't minced words when they had ordered him to protect his side of the river. They had seemed eerily prepared for the situation, as though they'd suspected it would happen one day and had drawn specific plans of war. He wondered, not for the first time, how they had known werewolves would suddenly overtake an entire city, how they had been so certain that there'd be no one left uninfected.

He didn't want to admit it, but he suspected that the whole thing had been germ warfare gone horribly wrong. It explained the government's sudden preparedness. It also sent shivers down his spine. Germ warfare was something that other nations, crazy-militant countries, did to America. Not something America did to anyone else.

And the American government doesn't jam cell phone signals so people can't spew their stories to the media, either, Burns thought sardonically, frowning at the large satellite dishes on trailers behind him.

He raised a hand to wipe the sweat from his forehead—then realized he couldn't penetrate the sanctity of the suit.

"Don't shoot just yet," he told his second in command.

"Sir?"

"I said not to fire. They've anchored, so they aren't going any-where. Not yet. Keep one man posted on surveillance, and if they take up the anchor and approach this side of the river, or if they take off downstream, then we take them out."

Burns glanced over at the soldiers who were watching the little boat through the nightscopes of their rifles. They were mostly young men, and one woman, clean-cut National Guardsmen, weekend warri-ors with strong ideals and families that loved them. They would consent to any order he gave them, even if it went against their own personal values. They would kill their fellow citizens.

But it was different when your fellow citizens were covered in fur and rushing at you with sharp claws and teeth. Or when their sanity had fled, leaving crazed husks of sheer instinct. These people on the boat... they were still people, very much like those families back home. Some-times he hated being the decision maker, despised being in control.

Raising his binoculars again, he whispered, "What in the hell are they doing out there? What are they waiting for?"

Overhead, thunder rumbled, rolling from cloud to cloud.

CHAPTER 45

September 18, 6:48 p.m.

The sun had crept very low on the horizon, but the storm clouds distilled most of its light. The group on the tugboat could only see hazy shades of orange swirling through the cloud banks, vestiges of the sunset.

Rick turned to Andrei. He said, "We still don't know if that shot worked on you, buddy. I think you'd better move to the side of the boat, just in case you start to change."

"I feel no different, not at all," the Siberian man said, not moving.

Christian grabbed a long pole used to guide the tugboat towards shore. It had a pronged end, the better to catch itself upon piers or docks. Pointing it towards Andrei's chest, he said, "I think you'd better do what he says. Just stand close to the edge of the boat. If you don't change in the next half hour, we'll know you're okay, that the serum did its job. If you do change, I'm pushing you into the water myself."

"But I will drown."

"That's the general idea," Rick said. "Please, man, just do it. We aren't going to hurt you if you don't turn into one of those things."

Rick added, "And hand over the dart gun."

Shrugging, the Siberian handed the gun to Rick, who slung it by its strap over his back. Andrei trudged to the back of the boat, and when he reached the edge, he faced the other four people, turning his back on the coal barges behind them. The pointed end of the pole nearly grazed his chest.

"Like this?" he asked. "This good?"

"Yeah," Chesya said, and she moved towards him. "Thank you."

"I no think I will change tonight."

"I hope not," she said. "This is all… just in case."

He gave her a little bow. "Thank you. You are a nice lady."

"And you're a true gentleman. If this serum works, you know you'll be quite famous for taking the risk."

"If serum works," Andrei said, "then I go back to village and live with my family. They are more… how you say, important than being famous. They are most important of all."

One by one, the little group moved towards the big, burly man. Chesya hugged him, and Rick shook his hand. "Good luck," he said.

"And to yourself."

Cathy gave him a bear hug, her arms unable to reach all the way around him. "I hope this turns out just as you wish," she said. "I'd like to see you back with your family. It's…" She turned towards Christian, then she completed her thought. "It's the most meaningful thing in the world. Family."

As she moved back, standing next to Christian, who still held the pole in front of himself, the teenager said, "Yeah. Good luck. But if you change, you're goin' overboard. It's just to save the rest of us. No hard feelings?"

"No. Take care of your mother. She love you. Even I see it."

Rick pulled his Black Widow special and leveled it against the big man's head. When Andrei looked at him quizzically, he said, "Hey, I'm not taking any chances."

They waited.

The wind picked up, and the water grew more turbulent. The boat rocked beneath them.

And they waited.

The light grew dimmer. The orange streaks in the clouds faded to black. Rick eventually had to aim at Andrei with one hand, using his other to grab hold of the side of the boat for balance. The first raindrops fell.

And, still, they waited.

A howl emerged from the depths of the city, followed by growls and more animalistic sounds. The streets of Cincinnati echoed with the noises the creatures made as they changed... the sounds of humans becoming beasts.

Andrei stood still, watching them, not daring to move. He eyeballed the gun that Rick held to his head. Searching within himself, he tried to find the familiar tickle of the hairs struggling to burrow their way out of his skin. He felt nothing except the pleasant plop of heavy raindrops on his shoulders.

Cathy shouted, "Look!"

She pointed towards the shore, towards the city. A dozen monsters emerged from the buildings and paced alongside the river. They growled at the tugboat. One tested the water with a clawed and padded foot and determined it didn't want to attempt swimming to the boat.

"How do you feel, Andrei?" Chesya asked.

"A little scared. But I feel no change feelings. I think I am fine."

Ten more beasts joined the others, pacing back and forth along the shore, watching the boat with boiling red eyes.

Christian lowered his pole. "I don't think he's gonna do it. It must have worked."

"Sweet Jesus, thank you!" Chesya said, looking up at the sky and getting an eyeful of rain. "We have an antidote."

Lowering his gun, Rick extended his hand to the Siberian again. "Thanks for trying it," he said. "I don't think I would have had the balls to do it, not knowing how it would turn out. You could have died."

"I have been dead a long time now," Andrei said. Then he swept Rick up in a bear hug and twirled him around a few times. His laughter came out in deep bellowing guffaws, and soon everyone was grinning and patting him on the back. "I go home now!" Andrei cried. "I see my wife and children. I go home now."

Laughing, Rick handed the dart gun back to the Siberian, and Andrei hung it from his shoulder. He grinned and patted the rifle.

Meanwhile, on one side of the river, twenty more Lycanthropes joined the others, trying to figure out a way to get to the boat.

On the opposite bank, General Burns was ordering more soldiers to guard the shoreline, and the first creature started to lope across what was left of the Brent Spense Bridge, followed by a dozen others.

A gunshot rang out, echoing between the metal bridge and the windswept water, blasting the head off of the lead monster. Its body fell off the jagged edge where explosives had ripped the Kentucky end of the bridge into the water, leaving broken concrete and metal rods sticking out of the collapsed section. The creature smacked into one of the rods, hanging from the end like a flag in the wind. Eventually, the corpse twisted too much. It fell into the churning water of the Ohio River and disappeared from sight.

CHAPTER 46

September 18, 7:05 p.m.

General Burns knew the situation was about to get precarious on his side of the river. The creatures were already amassing on the other side, howling and leaping into the air, snapping their massive jaws. He wondered if they'd already devoured everyone on the Cincinnati side of the river, depleted their food source, if that was why they were so determined to cross to Kentucky.

The transformation seemed to take less time each evening. Tonight, it happened in the blink of an eye. If he had not prepared for this moment all day, he would have been flabbergasted at how quickly people dropped to all fours.

Looking at the line of soldiers, a sea of orange in their biohazard suits, their rifles aimed at a point halfway across the bridges, he swelled in admiration for the men and women defending this shoreline. They came from all walks of life: family men, husbands, wives, girlfriends, sons and daughters. They grew up in the city or on surrounding farms. The two common factors they shared were that they hadn't changed into beasts, and they had all rushed to stop the spread of the virus. With a few exceptions, the disease hadn't radiated beyond the boundaries of Cincinnati proper, thank God. Burns didn't want to contemplate what would have happened if the government hadn't moved so quickly.

There it was again, that nagging at the back of his skull when he thought about how swiftly the Pentagon had deployed troops. Shaking the doubt from his head, he faced the city just as the first wave of creatures began to run across the bridges. There were dozens, maybe hundreds of them, an onslaught of teeth and claws, madness made flesh.

Raising his arm, he shouted, "Ready, men? Steady with your shots. Make every bullet count. Steady… aim… FIRE!"

As hundreds of bullets whizzed past him, he watched as the first group of monsters were mowed down, red, wet holes appearing across their furry bodies. They toppled onto each other, forming the first of many small fortresses made up of Lycanthrope corpses. The next wave of creatures would need to crawl over the obstructions. When they did, the troops would be ready for them.

As several beasts retreated to the Cincinnati side, Taylor Burns looked through his binoculars at the tugboat anchored in the center of the river. What he saw amazed him.

"Good job men!" he shouted over the crack and pinging of ammunition being fired. Another creature fell as it retreated, the back of its skull opening like a ripe cantaloupe.

To his second in command, Burns shouted, "Hey, Granger. Come over here."

The smaller man scuttled over to his superior officer and saluted. "Yes, sir? Seems like a lot of them tonight, and it looks like they're pretty damned determined."

"Why don't you take a gander out at that boat and those barges?"

"Sir?"

"Said the night wind to the little lamb…"

Tom Granger cocked his head in confusion, peering through the pouring rain. Wiping the water from his faceplate, he raised his own binoculars and squinted through them, adjusting the focus.

"Do you see what I see?" Burns continued.

"They didn't change!"

"That's right. You think that's why they placed themselves securely within our sights? Someplace where we could observe that they were immune to this disease?"

"Sounds about right, sir. Should we let them float to this side?"

General Burns chewed the inside of his bottom lip, refusing to display any sign of nervousness. "I dunno. They could still be carriers. If they come over here, we could all be infected."

"Not with these suits, sir. We've been burning all those bodies over in the parking lots; they were as contaminated as they could be, and still..."

"Maybe we could have some kind of isolation tent made up. You think you could rig something like that?"

"I don't think it'll be a problem, sir."

Burns grunted, then looked up at the Brent Spence Bridge as the next deluge of monsters swarmed over their fallen brethren. Gunshots pierced the air, and thunder followed the fingers of lightning that reached towards the Earth. Like the hands of God, playing with His toys.

The General said, "Get to it, then. If we can keep them locked in a tent, something pretty damned airtight, I'll feel comfortable bringing them over. Until then, the poor bastards are on their own."

On the choppy water, the coal barges attached to the tugboat swung around like the second hand of a clock, gliding slowly in a semicircle, turning the whole boat to face the other direction. The people on it scurried to secure the tug.

Then something splashed into the water. Trying to escape the men's rifles, the beasts were leaping from the bridge. They were landing uncomfortably close to the coal barges.

"Poor sons of bitches," Burns said, then he turned his attention to his radio. The non-infected survivors were important enough to report to central command.

CHAPTER 47

September 18, 7:18 p.m.

As the rain came down in sheets, the river swelled with higher and higher waves, which tossed the tugboat enough to make Rick lean over the railing and vomit into the water. Lightning shot through the air, and thunder followed with alarming volume.

Everyone leaned against the side of the boat, holding onto the railing. The rain made the varnished wood slick, and they had a rough time keeping a good grip.

"Oh, Jesus," Rick said, raising his head and wiping his mouth.

Chesya scowled at him. "Rick…"

"I was praying, not cussing. We need this shit to stop."

Cathy asked, "Do you think they've spotted us yet? Realized we're different from the others?"

"I don't know," Chesya said. "They look pretty busy. They may not have noticed our little group with all the shooting they're doing."

"How many of those things you think they've killed?" Christian asked, his arm held protectively in front of his mother, securing her against the banister.

"Not enough," Rick gasped. "Never… enough." He had to turn suddenly, feeling the bile raise in the back of his throat.

"It isn't that bad," Cathy said. "I was in a hurricane once in a sailboat, when—"

"I'm not seasick," he replied between gagging sounds. "I just don't like the way the boat's moving."

"Speaking of moving…" Chesya said.

Andrei pointed to the barges, which had begun to swing around. "We are moving!" he shouted.

Chesya tightened her grip. "Hold on, everybody!"

The barges pulled the boat around in a semi-circle, then stopped with a jolt that dropped Cathy and Christian to the floor. They hurried to grab hold of something as the boat bobbed then steadied, facing the opposite direction of the river's current.

"I don't like this," Cathy said. "We should be pointed the other way."

"You have a suggestion?" Rick asked. "I'd be glad to hear it."

"We can't pull anchor," she said. "We'd float at the mercy of the river and the storm. The engines certainly wouldn't help us. They'd probably just burn out trying to pull us the wrong way."

A huge wave lifted them, then dropped them against the water. Andrei, losing his grip, slid across the deck. When his body smacked against the back edge, he flipped, and his legs dropped into the water between the barge and the tugboat. Screaming, he tried to haul himself back out of the river as the barge inched closer and closer to the boat, riding the crest of another wave.

"He'll be crushed!" Cathy shouted, and she dove forward, sliding on her stomach on the well-varnished deck. When she slammed into the opposite side of the boat, she placed her knees against the railing and grabbed Andrei's wrists.

The barge rose above his head and shoulders, and as if in slow motion, it tilted towards him at a forty-degree angle. It slid forward, threatening to cut him in half.

Cathy caught hold of the dart gun's strap, still wrapped around the Siberian's shoulder, and she pulled, unaware that Christian and Chesya had joined her.

Chesya grabbed Andrei's flailing hand, pulling him against the side of the boat, and Christian clutched the man's shirt collar, lifting the heavy man as he would a kitten by the scruff of its neck.

With a terrible groan and the crack of wood, the coal barge bumped the block and pulley that attached it to the tug, stopping about a foot away from the railing.

Chesya, Christian, and Cathy pulled Andrei onboard. Wood splintered as the pulley was forced against the back of the boat, and the two men and the two women crawled away on hands and knees.

The boat was taking on a lot of water from the storm. "Rick!" Cathy shouted. "Start the bilge pumps! They're under the cabin!"

He yelled back, "Fuck off! I'm not going anywhere."

The wood behind Cathy cracked loudly, and part of the ship's aft was pulled away by the strength of the now-retreating coal barge. It had slammed into the boat with enough force to pull a two-foot chunk out of the side, leaving behind long splinters.

"Rick, goddammit, we're gonna sink if you don't! And I mean now!" Cathy turned to Chesya, who was huddling next to her, and she apologized.

"No worries," Chesya said. "You know what you're doing a lot better than I do."

Reluctantly, Rick let loose of the side of the boat and threw himself down the small flight of stairs. He couldn't hear his footsteps over the roar of the storm and the incessant pounding of the rain. As he reached the bottom, he realized he was almost knee-deep in dirty water.

"Oh, here we go again," he said. "More problems."

After a brief search, he flicked a switch on the pumps, and he was rewarded with the sound of water draining back into the river. He leaned forward, catching himself with his arms and heaving a huge sigh of relief.

Outside, wood shattered and iron moaned as it rubbed against more wood and metal. Rick rushed above deck, blinking at the rain that suddenly blurred his vision.

The others had made their way to the front of the boat, but they were all staring at what was happening aft.

"I got the pumps on," he said.

"I don't know if that's enough," Cathy replied, and he followed their line of sight.

The back of the boat was attached to the first barge by a single cable, which was stuck in the pulley. As the next wave lifted the boat, then the barge, Rick desperately reached for anything that could steady him, finally clutching something metal. The others began to slide away from the cabin. Rick fumbled with the microphone of the radio. He kept hold of it as he slipped towards the hole carved in the side of the boat by the barge's incessant pummeling. By the time he stopped, the mic cord was stretched taut.

Then, with barely a clanking sound, the radio snapped from its moorings in the cabin. Rick raised his hands to his head just in time to deflect the flying radio box. It crushed two fingers and scraped the skin from the back of his wrist, then smacked into the railing and teetered into the river.

"Radio's gone!" he shouted.

Nobody listened to him. They were all watching as another gargantuan wave raised the barge high above the little boat. The cable that had kept the barge connected snapped loose with a loud twang and whipped wildly through the air.

"Get down!" Cathy screamed.

Andrei was the last to drop. The cable traveled harmlessly over the heads of Cathy, Christian, and Chesya. When it reached Andrei, he was on his knees, and the cable lashed the side of his face, severing the top of his left ear and slicing a bloody path across his cheek. He fell to the deck with a howl, pressing his hands against his ear.

Rick crawled over to him. "How bad is it?" he asked, and Andrei showed him the damage. Swallowing, Rick said, "I've seen worse. You'll be all right."

"But… so much blood!"

"Guys! The barge…"

Rick looked up. Lifted to its highest point by the big wave, the barge began to descend toward the back of the tugboat.

Beside them, something landed in the water, dropped as if from heaven.

Chesya shouted, "What now?"

One of the creatures broke the surface next to the tugboat. It grasped the railing with one clawed hand and launched itself onto the deck, two feet from Rick, halfway between him and the cabin.

The barge crashed against the side of the boat with a noise that seemed to overwhelm every sense at the same time. It reminded Rick of when the hotel had crumbled to the ground.

The Lycanthrope roared, bared its dripping fangs, took a step towards Rick.

The heavy coal barge caused the tugboat to tilt, the cabin rising to the sky.

"Come on!" Cathy shouted, and she and Christian jumped over to the coal barge.

Chesya also leapt from the tugboat, feeling a comforting weight beneath her feet when she landed. The barge seemed solid, stabilized by the heaviness of the coal, even if it was rocking and rolling with the waves.

When Rick started to run forward, the boat inclined to an angle nearly perpendicular to the water, and he tumbled, slammed against the side of the barge and rolled on to its ledge. Andrei dropped beside him, spattering blood from his wound all over Rick's face.

The creature that had lifted itself onto the deck careened towards them.

"Look out!" Andrei shouted.

The two men dove in the opposite direction, leaping aboard the barge. The beast smacked into the metal rail with its head, which promptly crunched open until its brains were scattered across the back of the sinking vessel.

The group, brushing themselves off, backed onto the barge, watching as the tugboat sank into the river, carried down by the weight of the water in its belly. The boat took less than a minute to disappear in a whirl of bubbles. When it was gone, Rick stood and cheered.

"Did you see that? Do you even fucking believe we're still alive!"

Another wave tossed the barge onto its shoulders, spilling coal down the sides of the piles. Rick dropped to all fours, nearly losing his balance.

"We aren't safe yet," Cathy said, holding her son. "We aren't anchored anymore. We're going to drift."

"We could end up back on shore in the city," Chesya wailed. "What then?"

Rick realized that he hadn't thrown up in quite a while. He didn't know whether to attribute this to his new sea legs or if he just didn't have any time to think about being sick.

Behind them, something landed on the coal pile with a soft thud. One of the monsters had flung itself from the Brent Spence Bridge to their barge, which was now positioned directly beneath the bridge and floating eastward.

As the creature stood up, its right arm hung broken and useless by its side. Still, it advanced, fury in its eyes, its tongue waving around its black mouth, running against its teeth.

Another fell behind it. When this one arose, it looked unscathed.

Chesya looked up at the bottom of the bridge, where dozens of creatures were retreating from the military's attack, the roar of automatic gunfire. More were leaping from the bridge into the water, sinking quickly beneath the waves. Some jumped for the safety of the barge.

A third beast landed safely, rolled down the coal pile. The rocks rattled beneath it, but it seemed to laugh as it stumbled towards Christian, who was the closest to it.

CHAPTER 48

September 18, 7:35 p.m.

Glancing over his shoulder, General Taylor Burns shouted for Granger, trying his best to be heard over the volley; the troops were firing nonstop at the creatures swarming the bridge, the hairy corpses piling higher, reverting to their human form.

"Sir?" Granger shouted. "Can't hear you, sir!"

Burns motioned his second in command closer and said, "I asked if that isolation tent was ready yet. Take a look out there."

Raising the binoculars to his face shield, Granger whistled. The tugboat was sinking under the weight of the first barge, its ass-end demolished; the group of refugees scrambled to get to a safe place near the piles of coal. Lycanthropes were leaping from the bridge, trying to escape the rain of bullets, inadvertently landing near the survivors. Licking their black lips, they approached the group.

"Get me a sniper," Burns demanded. "Someone really good."

"That'd be the Truitt woman, sir. Best eye in the unit."

"Get her here now, Granger. Before those things wipe out the only people we've seen who are probably immune to this virus."

Tom Granger ran to the rows of soldiers shooting the creatures as they attempted to cross the river. "Truitt!" he called. "Private Truitt! You're needed here."

A tall, lean woman with high cheekbones and dark eyes stepped forward. Her face looked tired behind the screen of her facemask, and her suit was smudged with dirt. A thin line of smoke trickled from the barrel of her M-16. Snapping a banana clip into the assault rifle, she asked, "Where?"

Granger led her back towards the side of the river. "You might want to grab the transfer device grapnel cannon," he told her. "That barge is caught in the current."

"Yes, sir," she said.

Burns was still watching the survivors through his binoculars, shaking his head. A single line of sweat dripped from beneath his hairline.

***

Christian glanced up at the top of the coal pile as the beast landed, its claws scrabbling for a hold on something solid. With a roar, it faced him, its eyes glowing yellow in the darkness. Its fur was matted and wet against its thick hide, and its paws sank deeper into the coal, dislodging several pieces. When the rocks shifted, it lost its footing and slid feet first towards the boy, snarling.

Christian reached into his jacket for a weapon, sliced himself on a knife. He had three blades. He pulled two out, one in each hand, just as the beast collided with him.

They rolled across the deck of the barge, away from the coal pile, the beast's jaws snapping as Christian tried to get into a better position. They stopped at the edge of the barge, and a wave crashed against Christian's face. It also soaked the creature, and the beast blinked several times, its triangular ears flapping to get the water out of them.

Taking advantage of the distraction, Christian rammed his knives into the creature's eyes. A dark, jelly-like substance squirted out of them, and blood trickled down its face like tears. The beast howled, lashing out at Christian as he tried to wriggle his legs out from beneath the monster. One of the beast's claws scraped long trails on the barge, generating blue sparks.

As it swung its head side to side, trying to shake loose the objects in its face, Christian dislodged the left knife and began stabbing it in the chest. It stood, relieving the pressure on his legs. Christian pushed himself backwards as the beast blindly lashed out at the wind and rain.

Cathy ran toward him, but the monster with the broken arm stood in her way. She brandished her only weapon, a pair of scissors.

"Get away from him!" she shouted.

The Lycanthrope cocked its head at her, then leaned forward and roared into her face. She could smell its breath, the scent of dead things eaten and partially digested. Falling backwards, she landed on her ass, wincing with the pain. The scissors fell from her grasp and slid away from her.

The beast lowered its head, preparing to take a bite out of her face, when something blue and feathery stuck into its neck. It screeched, clawing at the thing, and another appeared in its side, near its chest. The beast howled once, then wobbled in the wind. Its eyes began to droop.

"See... it's good weapon, no?" Andrei said, brandishing the dart gun, his face scratched and bloody.

Cathy kicked the monster's unsteady legs and cheered when it dropped into the water, sinking without a fight. "Yes, Andrei," she said with a smile. "A very good weapon, indeed."

The Siberian beamed, then was knocked aside as one of the monsters dropped just behind him. It turned, grabbed his head in each hand, and looked him in the eye.

Andrei saw the monster for what it was... another human under a curse. These Americans called it a virus or a disease, but those were just other words for "curse." This beast could have been him until that evening.

He swung the dart gun around to shoot the creature, but it slammed ineffectually against the thing's side. Annoyed, the beast struck out at the gun, tearing open Andrei's forearm and dislodging the weapon from his grip. It clattered across the deck.

Rick rushed at the thing that was squeezing Andrei's head tighter and tighter. He slipped on the rain-soaked deck, falling and taking Chesya with him as another monster landed atop the coal pile. It rolled down, somersaulting awkwardly. Chesya sidestepped it, but looked around and moaned softly. At least a dozen of the things were on the barge, with another ten on the second barge, making their way towards the humans.

"Too many," she cried. "Too many to fight."

Cathy ran for the dart gun, but another creature raised itself from where it had landed. Its legs seemed to be broken, but it pulled itself forward slowly with muscular arms.

Andrei screamed in agony, and Rick waited for his head to burst like some overripe fruit. The Siberian shouted something in his native language, swearing or praying, Rick couldn't tell.

Then the beast fell, a red blossom expanding between its eyes.

"They're shooting at us!" Cathy screamed, rolling the already changing corpse of a fallen creature into the water.

"No," Chesya said, ducking as a bullet winged overhead, smacking into the face of another werewolf. "They're trying to help us."

"Whoever's shooting is a hell of a crack shot," Christian said. "Can that just be one guy?"

All of the creatures that had leapt onto the first barge, at least a total of twelve, were either lying dead, reverting back to human form, or sinking to the bottom of the river. Traveling slowly eastward on the current, the barge was clear of the bridge. There were, however, eleven more creatures on the other barge, which was locked to this one by a pulley and cable system similar to the one that the tugboat had utilized. Barely four feet separated the two coal-laden barges.

"Guys," Christian said as the first creature jumped over to their barge. "I think we've got company."

Cathy rushed over to Andrei, who was holding his head in his hands. "Are you okay?" she asked.

He nodded, although she could see the lingering pain in his eyes. A trickle of blood seeped from his ear and down his neck. The creature had squeezed his skull so hard, she wondered if it was fractured.

But there wasn't time for that. She picked up the dart gun as a second beast leapt onto their barge from the other one. She wondered why the sniper had stopped firing at them, then she heard the bullet bounce off the metal. Sparks flew, and the pile of rags went up in flames.

Rick ran towards the fire, thinking he could quickly assemble a torch to ward off the beasts, but Chesya yelled, "Rick, damn it, you have a gun. You always seem to have a gun and you forget to use the stupid thing!"

He pulled the Black Widow from his waistband, amazed that he had forgotten the weapon, small as it was. He fired at the first monster that had invaded their barge. The bullet went wide, but the second one entered the creature's mouth and emerged from the back of its head. He didn't have to be a good shot when the beasts were this close.

Three bullets left, he thought.

Chesya ran towards the fire, but Cathy got there first. The older woman looked around, seeming confused. Chesya grabbed a bucket of what looked like water and threw it on the blaze.

"No!" Cathy screeched, but it was too late.

The bucket had held grease, leftover from a recent lube job on the tugboat. When it hit the small flames, they shot up six feet high, knocking Chesya backwards and singeing her eyebrows. The deck burned where the grease had spilled, and the coal ignited, turning red and orange.

"Um... oops," Chesya said. "Can we put it out with water?"

"It's a grease fire now," Cathy said. "And the coal's blazing. I don't think there's anything we can do."

Rick fired again, missed the creature running towards him. He shot again as it got closer, but the bullet only grazed its ear. When it was almost upon him, he held the gun between the beast's eyes and squeezed the trigger. Skull and pink brains spattered the coal pile behind it, sizzling on the embers like eggs on a griddle.

Shoving the body aside, he shouted, "Oh man, who started the goddamn fire? Like we didn't have enough problems?"

Chesya admitted, "I did it. Sorry."

"Sorry? You're fucking sorry? Oh, that helps a lot!"

Cathy shouted, "We can do without the sarcasm, Rick! Calm down."

"Calm down? We're being attacked by those creatures, we're on a runaway barge with no anchor, the fucking military's shooting at us, I'm out of bullets, and now we're on fire? Calm down? How in the fuck do you expect me to—"

Cathy slapped his face. Hard. He stared back at her with something that resembled awe.

Cathy said, "Another one's just jumped on board." She handed Rick the dart gun. "You're a better shot than me. You put a dart in that thing, and we'll drown it."

"Yes, ma'am," he said, turning towards the creature rushing towards them.

A blue dart appeared just above its right ear, and it cried out, fumbled with the dart, then slumped to the deck.

Another creature made the leap from their barge, landing behind the fallen monster.

"Where's Andrei?" Chesya asked.

"He's back... oh my God!" Cathy shouted.

Andrei sat on the deck, leaning against the pile of coal, his arms drooping at his sides. The fire was only a few feet from where he sat, and his eyes were closed.

Cathy began to run towards him when she heard a whistling sound and a huge, four-pronged, fishhook fell two feet in front of her.

She thought, *That looks like the Bat-hook, a whatchamacallit... grapnel hook.*

It snagged the cuff of Andrei's coveralls and dragged the unconscious Siberian toward the railing.

The group hurried after Andrei as he was dragged to the far end of the barge. He was slammed violently against the railing, then held there by the sharp points of the grapnel. He gave a single gasp of pain.

"What the hell are they thinking?" Cathy wondered, kneeling next to the Siberian.

"They're going to pull us in," Chesya said, smiling broadly. Behind her, another monster's skulls exploded, and it fell on its back, tongue lolling from its black mouth.

"Andrei, buddy," Rick said as he knelt next to him. He was troubled by the blood that still streamed from the Siberian's ear. "Wake up, man."

Christian tore at the coverall material with his remaining knife, dislodging the cuff from the flanges.

"Is he..." Chesya let the question hang in the air.

Rick shook his head, "No, he's still breathing, but... I dunno. He doesn't look very good."

"That thing had him by the head," Cathy said, a tear emerging from her eye.

Rick slapped the Siberian's stubbly cheek. "Hey, buddy, wake up. We've made it, man. I think we've made it."

The last creature on the second barge went down with a bullet to the head. It fell to its knees, wavered a moment, then collapsed.

"Look up!" Christian shouted.

They were being pulled backwards against the current by the grap-nel, which was tied to a pillar of the Brent Spence Bridge on the Ken-tucky side of the river. It stuck up several dozen yards away from the broken end of the bridge.

The barges quickly approached the point where the beasts could leap onto them again.

The fire was gaining strength, and they decided to make their way back to the second barge now that all the creatures on it were dead. They dragged Andrei, and the man groaned with every movement.

The flames spread across the deck like tributaries from some hell-ish lake. One small section of the deck had burned through, and the heavy coal above it slid through the hole, spilling into the river.

***

"I don't like the looks of that fire," General Burns said. "Can we speed up the winch?"

Private Truitt looked back at him and shook her head. "The barge they're on is too heavy."

"There isn't going to be much left to haul to shore if we wait too long."

Granger said, "It's only another two hundred yards or so, sir."

Truitt watched through her scope for any creatures that might try to get on the barge. Her fellow soldiers had killed hundreds, and the bodies piled up on the bridge as hundreds more of the Lycanthropes clawed and tore their way over the corpses.

They wouldn't stop. Not until every one of them was dead. The soldiers' flesh was too luring. Even with the end of the bridge blasted away, they leapt like fiends, their broken bodies landing in the water. A few dragged themselves to shore only to meet their doom. Yet they kept charging into the line of fire, and they kept falling, dead, torn apart by the barrage.

"Look," Burns said. "It's pulling them in faster."

"The coal, sir. It's falling through the bottom as it burns. It's mak-ing them lighter."

As the barge entered the shadow of the bridge, the rain stopped. Burns had not even noticed that the lightning and thunder finished minutes ago, that the storm clouds were trailing off in the distance. The moon began to emerge.

Its light revealed the barge moving beneath the bridge, and several of the creatures saw it at the same time. They leapt from the line of danger, into the water, several at a time.

"Shit," Truitt said, snapping another magazine into her rifle. "I'm gonna need some help with this!"

"We didn't see this coming?" Burns asked. "We're hauling them right back into the path of those things."

Granger said, "That pillar's the only thing sturdy enough to ground the grapnel winch, okay? Give me a break."

Burns fired his gun at the beasts as they landed on the barge. Granger, alongside the others, took careful aim, and killed one of the Lycanthropes as it fell to the barge.

"Hidden talents, Granger?" Burns smirked.

***

"Andrei, man, wake the hell up. You need to get back to your wife, right? Think of her." Rick was more upset by Andrei's condition than he thought he could be. He barely knew the man.

"I think he's gone," Cathy said. "We shouldn't have moved him."

Chesya said, "Not like we had a choice."

Andrei's eyes suddenly popped open, startling everyone. They were red instead of white, a sign of internal bleeding. He gasped, coughed a stream of blood and bile.

Rick grinned. "Good to have you back with us, buddy."

Christian noticed the first Lycanthropes dropping onto the barge from the bridge. He said, "Oh no..." Then the sound of gunfire broke through the air, and the creatures collapsed as soon as they hit the deck, some of them dead already. The soldiers on shore would take care of the beasts for them.

Andrei spoke through bubbles of blood. He said, "My family... you... you will tell them of me... of what I did."

Chesya was crying. She didn't want to, but she couldn't help it. "Tell us where they are, Andrei, and we'll find them."

He choked, and the blood poured from his mouth and streamed from the corners of his eyes.

The moon emerged completely from behind the dissipating clouds, and the river was flooded in pale, blue light.

"That look like a full moon to you?" Christian asked.

Rick glanced up along with the rest of them, and the moon did, indeed, look as though a sliver had been taken from one side.

"It's... it's..." Andrei said between gasps.

"What is it, Andrei?" Chesya gripped his hand as tightly as she could.

"It's... over," he said.

His hand went limp. It slipped from hers and hit the deck.

Cathy said, "Fifty feet from shore."

"Aw... aw shit," Rick said, looking down at Andrei. The Siberian's head slumped to one side. His blood-filled open eyes stared at them accusingly.

"For God's sake, close them," Christian said.

Rick pressed his fingers against Andrei's eyelids and pulled them closed. Chesya was praying softly next to them.

With a wet, shattered sound, a naked male body dropped to the barge. His neck snapped, but the bullet in his forehead had killed him. A female corpse dropped next, hitting the railing of the first barge and pinwheeling into the water.

They were thirty feet from the shore, where three figures in orange biohazard suits waited for them. They had stopped firing at the creatures, and they held their guns close to their chests. The roaring and crashing noises on the bridge ceased.

Chesya could see the piles of corpses above them, the blood dripping like rain from the supports of the bridge. There were no longer monsters to trample the bodies, only confused, terrified people.

The soldiers stopped firing, and the survivors turned away, ashamed in their nakedness, hurrying back home. Andrei had been right. He had sensed the cycle of the moon was over, and he'd told them so. He'd realized it just before he died.

Cathy ran into Christian's arms, sobbing into his shoulder with a mixture of relief and exaltation. The boy stroked his mother's hair, trying to comfort her, feeling much, much older than his seventeen years.

As the bottom of the barge scraped against gravel and land, Chesya turned to Rick. He looked small somehow, and he was still shaking, upset over Andrei's death. She took his filthy hand in hers and wondered if she looked as bad. Then she placed a hand against his cheek.

"We made it," she said.

"Didn't I tell you we would?" he replied, and he tried to grin. It came out wrong, a sad, disfiguring grimace. Then they were hugging each other.

The barge stopped a few feet from shore, and the big man waded out into the water until he was at the railing. "I'm General Taylor Burns," he said. "United States Army. You folks okay?"

"What do you say, Chesya?" Rick asked. "Are we okay?"

His grin seemed real this time… mitigation, exhaustion, and a calmness overtaking him. Chesya gave him another hug.

"Fuckin' A!" she said. "Yeah, we're just fine!"

EPILOGUE

October 3, 1:45 p.m.

As the bus bounced along the pockmarked excuse of a road, Cathy watched her son take photographs of the barren landscapes that flew by them. He was fascinated by this other world, so far from everything he'd ever seen, and she was glad that he still possessed something of a child-like wonder. She kneaded his shoulder through the flannel shirt. He was still too thin, in her opinion. The months he had spent on the street had taken a toll that wouldn't be refunded so quickly.

Sometimes at night, she could hear him crying out from his room. They were renting an apartment in Atlanta, Georgia, because she had wanted to move him far away from the horror of those three days, and far away from the more mundane, although still potent, terrors of her husband's abuse. Fleeing to another city had done some good, she was certain, but it couldn't wipe away the nightmares that woke him nearly every night. He was still running from demons.

Leaning back, watching the snowy trees out her window, she knew she was faring better than her son. When she'd burned down that house in Indian Hills, something steely had hardened within her, a resolve that life would be different now. She'd easily found a job with a publishing house, and though she wasn't living the life she'd been accustomed to, she was getting by just fine. She'd already made several friends in Atlanta, and she had discovered, almost by accident, how much Christian meant to her. She didn't want to let him leave her, but after he finished his last year in high school, he would go to college; he was a bright kid. She just hoped they could remain close, but there were no guarantees. There never were.

In the seat in front of his mother, Christian pondered the sheer amount of snow that lined the roads. Ohio received varying degrees of snowfall over the years, but this amazed him. It had to be four feet, higher in some of the drifts. It was a beautiful sight to him... pure, white, virginal, as though the countryside was erasing its mistakes, washing them away in a tide of purity. Eventually, the snow would melt, revealing what hid beneath the surface, but that was probably months away. Maybe, from the look of things, it could be years in the future.

School was proving difficult for him. He loved the classes he was taking, especially science and math, but his interest waned during the day. He found himself remembering so much... Jean, Andrei, and most of all his father, the things he had done to survive.... Still, he was in a secure place now, with his mother doting on him like a hen. The walls of their new home made him feel safe and cozy, as though nothing could ever hurt him again.

The nightmares, however, always refuted this sense of well being. They came and went, with decreasing regularity, but they were intense and all too real. There were things that could hurt you out there in the world. Monsters did exist, no matter what the adults told you. In fact, many of those adults were the beasts that haunted his dreams.

Across the aisle of the bus, Rick held his arm around Chesya. She felt good leaning into him, her cheek against his neck. He wasn't sure if this romance would last, but he'd give it a shot. After the government had disinfected, debriefed, and questioned them, after they had run genetic tests on their blood and released them, Rick and Chesya indulged in that bubble bath she'd invited him to share. Their lovemaking was slow and serious, but oddly lacking passion. For all they'd been through, there was no heat between them. Chesya said it meant they weren't supposed to be together. He said it meant he needed to try harder. The second time was better. Much, much better.

Deep inside, he doubted he could ever settle down forever with one woman, have kids, all that bull crap. Still, if anyone could drag him into the *Leave It to Beaver* lifestyle, it was this strong-willed woman beside him.

Although they'd discussed it, neither of them understood why they were immune to the disease. The Feds remained tight-lipped, so they'd chalked it up to sheer luck of the genetic draw.

The bus struck a pothole, and Chesya was jarred awake. Rick gave her a little peck on the cheek. Smiling sleepily, she asked, "Are we there yet?"

"Almost," he said.

She pulled herself away from him, from his familiar scent, and stretched her arms so that her back cracked. Behind the bus driver sat Mikael, the interpreter they had found. On the seat next to her was the urn.

With Rick's help, she had moved to Louisville, Kentucky. The bank found her another job in another branch, but they offered her a promotion to manager, probably because she'd informed the FBI that Rick had stashed money in his coat. She'd accepted, and she and Rick had set up house in a friendly suburban neighborhood. It still seemed vaguely wrong for her to live in that area, but she loved her job. And she thought she might love Rick. Their time together seemed enchanted somehow, but she wasn't letting the sudden conformity to bourgeois America fool her. Rick had been a thief, and she would never forget that. He'd done terrible things, even if he was atoning for those sins. He even went to church with her. Maybe they could make a go of it. Maybe not. She figured the Lord would steer them in the direction He wanted them to go, so she left it in His hands.

"This place really lives up to its reputation," Christian said. "I keep expecting to see a gulag out there."

"Look," Rick said, pointing to a sign. "What's that say?"

The interpreter answered, "Kirskania, three kilometers."

"Almost there," Chesya said, looking down at the urn, patting it gently. "Almost home, Andrei."

The bus stopped near a small house. The roof was thatched, but holes were visible, and the well outside the house obviously provided all the water. Two skinny cows were tied to the dilapidated fence in the back, and they lowed mournfully as the group exited the bus. Chesya carried the urn, wrapping her arms tightly around it.

"Doesn't look like Bio-Gen sent any money here," Christian said. "The bastards lied to him."

Rick replied, "Typical big corporation."

When the door opened, a woman looked out at them; light from a kerosene lantern faintly illuminated her face. She appeared to be about fifty, but Chesya was certain she was younger. A child in a long shirt peeked from behind the woman's patched skirts.

The woman asked, "Shto sluchilos'? Shto sluchilos' s moim Andre'em?"

The interpreter told her that these people had traveled all the way from America to see her, to tell her about her husband.

"What's happened? What's happened to my Andrei?" the translator repeated after the woman had spoken in Russian.

The woman looked as though she were about to cry, but she remained stiff-lipped and dignified.

Chesya said, "Tell her that her husband, Andrei, was a hero, a good man."

The interpreter translated her words as she spoke. The woman at the door had the saddest eyes Chesya had ever seen.

"Tell her that he died saving our lives, fighting against the monsters that were like him. Tell her how much we all appreciate and honor him, how many lives he saved. Tell her... he's dead."

When the interpreter told her these things, the woman dropped to her knees and wailed, pounding her fists into the snow. Chesya approached as the child scampered away. She placed the urn at the woman's side, watching as Andrei's wife removed the lid from it and sniffed at the ashes, hoping to find some familiar vestige of her husband.

Chesya had attempted this already; she'd detected nothing of Andrei's earthy scent in the remains.

"Tell her that what he did was so brave and so important, the people at the United States government gave him a lot of money, and that we came to give her this money."

She handed the stack of rubles to the woman, who began to count them. She looked up at Chesya, astonished at the staggering sum. Chesya just nodded; this cash would give the woman a whole new life, give Andrei's children a brand new start, a chance at a good education.

The government had not actually allotted funds for the Siberian's widow because, as Rick pointed out, the government didn't give a damn about a dead Russian. They *did* care about keeping the survivors quiet, and had paid them what Rick liked to call "hush money." Not that any of them refused it, but the whole transaction seemed underhanded.

Surprisingly, Rick was the one to propose that they give half of their money to Andrei's wife, along with the man's ashes and sentiments. And the serum, made especially for Andrei's children to break the bloodline of Lycanthropy. He had died while striving to find a cure, and the group was determined to protect Andrei's offspring, as they had not been able to protect the man himself.

"Please," Chesya said, "tell her that when he sacrificed his life, he was thinking only of her and the children. He wanted her to know that he loved them. He said…" She choked on her words, a tear streaming down her cheek. "He said that family was all that mattered."

Cathy grabbed hold of Christian, and he leaned into her, kissing her forehead.

The woman stood, motioning for the four Americans to come to her. They advanced until she wrapped them all in a robust bear hug that reminded them all too much of her husband. They laughed, and the woman invited them into her home to meet the children and to have a bowl of homemade *borsht*.

As the door closed behind them, it began to snow, the ghostly whiteness covering up any dirt that had settled on the ground until everything looked clean and uncomplicated and new.

Day by Day Armageddon

by J. L. Bourne

An ongoing journal depicting one man's personal struggle for survival, dealing with the trials of an undead world unfolding around him. An unknown plague sweeps the planet. The dead rise to claim the Earth as the new dominant species. Trapped in the midst of a global tragedy, he must make decisions... choices that that ultimately mean life, or the eternal curse to walk as one of them.

ISBN: 978-0-9789707-7-2

THUNDER AND ASHES
A ZOMBIE NOVEL BY Z.A. RECHT

A lot can change in three months: wars can be decided, nations can be forged... or entire species can be brought to the brink of annihilation. The Morningstar Virus, an incredibly virulent disease, has swept the face of the planet, infecting billions. Its hosts rampage, attacking anything that remains uninfected. Even death can't stop the virus—its victims return as cannibalistic shamblers.

Scattered across the world, embattled groups have persevered. For some, surviving is the pinnacle of achievement. Others hoard goods and weapons. And still others leverage power over the remnants of humanity in the form of a mysterious cure for Morningstar. Francis Sherman and Anna Demilio want only a vaccine, but to find it, they must cross a countryside in ruins, dodging not only the infected, but also the lawless living.

The bulk of the storm has passed over the world, leaving echoing thunder and softly drifting ashes. But for the survivors, the peril remains, and the search for a cure is just beginning...

ISBN: 978-1934861011

Permuted Press
The formula has been changed...
Shifted... Altered... Twisted.™
www.permutedpress.com

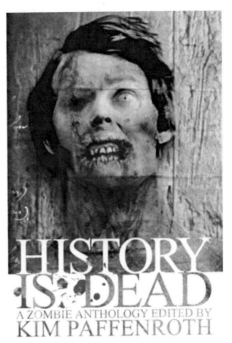

Printed in the United States
205232BV00002B/100-864/P

9 781934 861042